ALSO BY HOWARD V. HENDRIX

The Labyrinth Key

Better Angels

Empty Cities of the Full Moon

Möbius Highway

Lightpaths

Standing Wave

SPEARS OF GOD

BALLANTINE BOOKS / NEW YORK

SPEARS OF GOD

A NOVEL

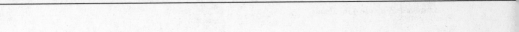

HOWARD V. HENDRIX

A Del Rey Books Trade Paperback Original

Published in the United States by Del Rey Books, an imprint of The Random House Publishing Group, a division of Random House, Inc., New York.

DEL REY is a registered trademark and the Del Rey colophon is a trademark of Random House, Inc.

Library of Congress Cataloging-in-Publication Data

Spears of God : a novel / Howard V. Hendrix.
   p.   cm.
"A Del Rey Books trade paperback original"—T.p. verso.
ISBN 0-345-45598-3
   1. Scientists—Fiction. 2. Meteorites—Fiction. 3. United States—Fiction. 4. South America—Fiction. 5. Middle East—Fiction. I. Title.
PS3558.E49526S64 2006
813'.54—dc22   2006042705

Printed in the United States of America

www.delreybooks.com

9 8 7 6 5 4 3 2 1

Book design by Lisa Sloane

To Laurel, again—

But the trew fayre, that is the gentle wit,
And vertuous mind, is much more praysd of me.

—Spenser, *Amoretti 79*
lines 3–4

NATIVE TO THE SKY

▶▶▶▶▶▶

"Don't worry about the rattlesnakes," Uncle Paul said as they stepped out of the August sun into the twilight of the shaft's entrance. "They won't hurt you so long as you stay outside striking range."

The boy nodded absently as the slithering, rattling chorus rose around them. Shining the feeble beam of his flashlight into the space before his feet, he still managed to notice that nearly all of the dozen or so snakes hereabouts seemed to be coiled up, poised to strike. Their triangular heads, dark bronze necks, and diamondback patterns might have seemed beautiful if he weren't so busy thinking of them as fatal.

His uncle, dressed in gray shirt and blue jeans, moved on ahead of him, casually flipping one rattler or another out of the way with his crooked walking stick.

"Your uncle Paul's not exactly OSHA-approved," the boy remembered his father saying, "but you can learn a lot from him if you pay attention."

Once past the gamut of snakes, the gangly fourteen-year-old warily followed the mine shaft as it angled downward into darkness. His parents had also talked about his uncle's "dangerous" obsession with caves. It had something to do with a trip to South America, and the death of his aunt Jacinta.

The boy had never quite been able to piece together the whole story on that. He wasn't exactly sure what he was supposed to be learning at the moment, either, but at least he felt a good deal cooler here than he had outside in the late summer sun.

The coolness of the mine shaft was probably why the snakes spent the day here. This late in the afternoon, at nearly four thousand feet above sea level, the temperature in the Diablo Mountains still hovered near the century mark. Yet even that was better than the 112-degree readings they'd endured down on the floor of the Great Central Valley.

"We're in an exploratory shaft that one of the mining companies abandoned," his uncle said suddenly, playing his flashlight over a lumpy wall. "My bet is there's still some good stuff hereabouts, in all this graywacke and blue schist. See where it sticks out like that, Michael? Those just might be nodules. Find a seam—a crack where it attaches to the wall. Hold your flashlight in your mouth and see if you can't cold-chisel open one of those cracks."

The old man followed his own advice and set to work. Watching him, the boy Michael did as he was told.

Even in the cool darkness of the mine shaft, the work made them sweat. Before long, however, they'd both broken lumps loose from the wall. Michael mouthed "Wow!" at what he saw in the sheared face of the stone—and the flashlight fell from his mouth. He had to scramble after it.

"Got something, eh?" Uncle Paul grunted, stifling a chuckle. "Let's have a look."

The boy cradled the chunk of rock in both hands. It was an unimpressive blue-gray on the outside, but the shear face revealed an interior that was quite another story: large bright crystals of sapphire blue and jet black, embedded in shining white.

"The white stuff is a natrolite matrix," his uncle said. "The black crystals are neptunite. The blue is what we're really after. Benitoite. Barium titanium silicate gemstone. Bluer than sapphire, more fiery than diamond, rarer and more valuable than either. The only place in the world where you find gem-quality benitoite is right here, in San Benito County, in the outcrop that runs through these hills."

As the boy set down the rock and returned to his work with renewed enthusiasm, his uncle continued his commentary.

"Back in 1907, a prospector named Couch discovered the benitoite," his uncle said, hammering away at the rock wall. "He was looking for cinnabar. He was clearing away brush, and found himself staring, all unexpected, at an exposed slump of benitoite and neptunite and natrolite—just like what you broke loose, only a lot bigger. He must've felt like he was standing inside an open-faced geode as big as a barn door."

The boy nodded. The seam he was working on cracked away into two wedges, each about the size of a generous slice of blueberry pie.

"Couch and everybody else thought the blue stuff was sapphire," his uncle said, cracking off a big hunk full of blue crystals. "Then a Professor Louderback from Berkeley examined it. Proved it was a new 'species' previously unknown to science. The first example in nature of a ditrigonal dipyramidal class of hexagonal crystal. Only hypothetical up to that point. Eventually—in the 1980s, I think it was—they named it the California state gem."

Soon they'd chiseled out several more good-size specimens. They were at last forced to stop working away at the rock when the boy's flashlight went dead, and his uncle's was fading fast.

Uncle Paul clicked his off, then pulled a battered Zippo lighter out of his shirt pocket and thumbed it into spark and flame. By its light they made their way back toward the entrance. As they approached the mouth of the tunnel, Michael wondered for a moment about the snakes, but all he heard were crickets and the crunch of rocks beneath their boots. He hoped that maybe the rattlers had moved on, or grown lethargic in the chill of evening.

Night had already fallen in the world outside. The light of the Zippo, held up ahead of Michael in his uncle's hand, was a closer star among stars. Uncle Paul flicked it shut and they made their way by starlight.

His uncle skidded down through rock and brush to where his pickup truck was parked. He returned with two medium-size duffel bags and some fresh batteries. Two more trips into the hillside and the bags were loaded with as much as Michael and his uncle could safely carry out.

Winded from toting the rock-laden duffels down the hillside, the boy and his uncle tossed the bags into the pickup bed, and then leaned against the truck. They paused, staring into the night sky. Shooting stars streaked by overhead, above the scattered pine trees and rounded peaks.

"Hey, Uncle Paul," the boy said, "if this benitoite is so special, if it's rarer and more valuable than diamonds, how come I've never heard of it?"

"Because it is so special," the older man said, pulling out his pipe, packing it with tobacco, and using the Zippo to light it. "Diamonds are precious enough, and kept just rare enough, to support a world market. There are enough of them to create broad demand. Some things are too rare to support that kind of market. Benitoite is like that. There's not enough for anyone to make a big business out of selling it, so there are only a few of us who pay much attention to it. I've been able to make my fortune because I've got a knack for picking customers with good taste who are willing to pay good money for this rock."

Michael thought about that, then nodded.

"Then it's the rarest gem on earth?"

"Nope," said the man wreathed in pipe smoke. A moment later, he pointed at a shooting star as it made a quick, fiery slash across the vault of heaven, then sheathed itself again in night. "That's the rarest."

"A shooting star? What do you mean?"

"It's a meteoroid when it's traveling through space, a meteor when it's burning in the atmosphere. It becomes a meteorite when it reaches the ground. The 'ite' part is added to indicate that a rock is native to a particular place."

"Like benitoite comes from San Benito County?"

"Right. 'Meteor' means 'sky,' or 'high in the air,' and that's where each meteorite comes from. That makes it the rarest rock on earth, because it's not from here. It's a stone that's native to the sky."

He puffed on his pipe a moment, lost in thought, before continuing.

"Pallasite meteorites and pallasitic peridots are the only true cosmic gemstones on earth. There's plenty of them up there, I suppose. Just not down here."

The boy nodded again.

"Meteorites go way, way back, too," his uncle added, staring at the sky. "People forget that part of it. Meteorites are more than just space ships; they're time ships. They're the oldest rocks we've got. Most of them go back billions of years, to before our planet even existed. Heck, collisions of meteoroids, asteroids, and comets are what the planet probably formed from in the first place. Fragments, fused together by gravity."

Young Michael Miskulin followed his uncle's gaze and saw another falling star. Might that very object, or one of its extraordinary brethren, might somehow manage to survive the fiery descent, perhaps to find a home on his own world? To become one of those rarest of gems? At that moment, the full wonder of it dawned on him.

Which was, perhaps, exactly what he was supposed to learn.

SPEARS OF GOD

GHOST PEOPLE

>>>>>>

After a long, arduous climb, Doctor Michael Miskulin and Professor Susan Yamada finally came to the top of Caracamuni tepui, island of stone floating among clouds. Scores of the remote and inaccessible tepuis clustered where Brazil, Venezuela, and Guiana met. Tablelands perched atop vertical rockfaces hundreds and sometimes thousands of feet high, many of them remained unexplored. Most were home to plants and creatures endemic to a particular tepui—found only on that cloud-mesa and nowhere else on earth.

Yamada and Miskulin had left the half dozen hired porters of their expedition below the clouds and made the ascent by themselves. Alone together in the drifting fog and drizzle atop Caracamuni, amid the nearly two-billion-year-old ruins of ancient geology, Michael and Susan found themselves in a solitude sanctified by isolation in both time and space.

Crossing the high plateau the previous afternoon, Susan collected what she was sure were several sundews, pitcher plants, and assorted bromeliads previously unknown to science. She also identified what appeared to be an endemic clawed frog, a creature unable to swim. If it followed the same evolutionary history of clawed frogs on other tepuis, its kind had lived here since before the continents broke apart, and came together, and broke apart again.

"This place is incredible!" she said over a campstove dinner in their tent the previous evening. "I've heard of tepuis before, but being here is different from what I expected, or even imagined."

"I know what you mean. It's a lot chillier, for one thing. Especially after the heat of the sabana and the rain forest."

"No, that's not it. I mean, to be told there are places where the precip is so persistent it drives the nutrients from the earth—and creates a desert caused by rain—that's one thing. But to be hiking across a rain-desert island dotted with swampy little Edens full of carnivorous plants—that's a whole different story."

Michael nodded but said nothing. Later, however, once he was asleep in his mummy bag, the day's experiences shaped his dreams.

His nocturnal travels were as full of ancient stone black with endless drizzle as his gray daylight hours had been. Fog, rain, algae, and fungus shaped rocks into the columns and arches of a meandering dreamcity, a labyrinth of stone clouds hiding furtive people whose runneled faces and bodies were covered with lichens and mosses. . . .

The rain had stopped by the time he woke this morning. Outside their tent, the myriad soft-hard shapes of the eroded maze still stood about them—a dreamscape refusing to disappear upon waking. Already up and busy, Susan crouched in the midst of that landscape, packing her specimens. Michael stepped out into morning sunlight broken by high cloud. Susan stood and stretched, turning around and taking it all in.

"Even if your aunt's crazy stories about 'ghost people' turn out to be totally delusional," she said, "I'm still glad we made this little expedition."

"And that my uncle paid for it," Michael said, out of her sightline and urinating behind a boulder.

"That, too."

As he finished up, he stared absently at the surface of the rock before him, until it caught his attention more fully. Half a dozen types of lichens and mosses overlapped one another, and the underlying rock substrate, too—yielding a fractal frenzy of red ochre, yellow, white, slate blue, dark green, and black.

Doctor Rorschach, meet Jackson Pollock, he thought. He tried to remember what the splotchy palette reminded him of. Then, as he zipped up, it hit him: the encrusted stone looked almost exactly like the false-color satellite image his uncle had shown them of this very tepui viewed from space—right down to the cleft or abyss bisecting the labyrinth top into two convoluted hemispheres.

At the bottom of that midline depression were supposed to lie cloudforest and the entrances to a large cave inside Caracamuni, the home of the ghost people, if his aunt's stories held any truth.

" 'Ghost people' probably isn't what they call themselves," he said, helping Susan break camp. "If they really exist at all. That's what the Pemon down on the plains below call them."

" 'Spirit people,' 'ghost people,' 'sky people,' " Susan said, nodding. " 'Mawari' or 'Mawariton,' too. I did my research, you know. That's why I think they're mythical."

"Oh?"

"A reclusive tribe rumored to live on nothing but mushrooms and insects? Come on, Michael. That sounds like faeries or menehune, to me. 'Magical folk who peopled the land in days of yore.' "

Michael only grunted as he worked to smash the tent fabric into a stuff sack that always seemed too small for what it was intended to hold.

"It'd be great if they actually existed," Susan said. "A great ethnobotanical find, at the least. But I doubt they have much basis in fact—Pemon myths and your aunt's stories notwithstanding."

"We'll find out soon enough," Michael said, shrugging into his backpack and helping Susan on with hers.

Hiking under the broken sky of high cloud, he found the walk at least a bit warmer and drier than the drizzle that had prevailed the previous day. As he watched his feet move over the uneven ground, he found his thoughts drifting back to before they left the north.

Back home, he, too, had found the Mawari history—and his family's connection with it—improbable, if not outright crazy. There might be an occasional tribe somewhere in the deep backcountry still waiting to be discovered, but all the blank spaces had long since been more or less eliminated from the map. Or so he had believed.

Yet his aunt Jacinta had claimed to her brother Paul that she had discovered the people whose existence formed the basis of the Pemon legends of sky beings—a tribe that, despite the many names given them by others, had no name for themselves besides "the People." Except for confiding about the People to Paul, Jacinta had kept her turn-of-the-century discovery of them a secret from everyone. Paul, too, had apparently done nothing to prove or disprove his sister's claims, until now.

Unfortunately, Aunt Jacinta had also been documentably crazy.

From her late teens on, she'd been variously diagnosed as depressive, bipolar, or long-period schizophrenic. Whichever diagnosis was correct, the truth was that, up on Caracamuni, she went native in a most extreme fashion.

Before them now, a cloud-filled gorge came into view.

"Somewhere down there is where Jacinta's ghost people are supposed to live," Michael said, as he and Susan surveyed steep walls plunging away into mist.

"Obscured by clouds. How appropriate."

Together they swiftly descended into the fine cloudmist that blanketed the abyss. Walking through the increasingly dense undergrowth they came upon what seemed to be a game trail, though neither of them had seen anything on the tepui that would pass for game, big or small.

"At least we won't have to machete our way through," Michael said as he pushed foliage aside and plunged on ahead.

"What brought your aunt here in the first place?" Susan asked, sweeping a broken spiderweb away from her face.

"I think she first came to the tepui when she was a graduate student in anthropology. She also had a strong interest in your field, ethnobotany."

Susan grunted, preoccupied with making her way through the undergrowth.

"By the time she was a postdoc, she was convinced that a particular Pemon myth about the Mawari was true."

"Which one?"

"The one about ancient sky-gods who crashed their essence to earth as spores of the ghost people's totemic—and hallucinogenic—fungus."

Susan nodded.

"An undiscovered people possessing a potent medicinal plant not previously known to science. I can see how that might intrigue anyone interested in ethnobotany."

"It became something more than just an interest in a hypothetical plant."

"Oh?"

"According to Paul, my aunt felt she not only needed the Mawari, but they needed her, too."

Making their way into and under the tree canopy, through ever denser cloudforest growth, the two of them heard water flowing and falling with almost musical cadence. The air grew warmer, more sticky-humid, and thick with the smell of life and decay.

"What made your uncle suddenly interested in funding this expedition now, after so many years?"

"You've got me there," Michael said, holding a leafy branch aside so it wouldn't slash Susan in the face after he pushed it out of his way. "He's been obsessed with minerals and caves for as long as I've known him. It's what made him rich, after all. And Jacinta did tell him the Mawari fetishized a glassy mineral, stones of a particular 'tone,' which they required if they were to 'sing their mountain to the stars.' "

Michael held his breath a moment, wondering if Susan might ask him about his own interests in stars and stones. His fascination with rocks from the cave of the sky was even more widely known than his uncle's particular obsessions. Michael was relieved when she focused on something else.

"And that had something to do with their 'needing' her?"

"Jacinta felt it was her destiny to help the Mawari create some kind of crystalline shamanic machinery that would transform this mountain into, well, a spaceship of sorts."

Susan shook her head in frank disbelief.

"That sounds flat-out crazy. Your uncle Paul didn't strike me as the type to believe in such a wild idea."

"He's not, but he's more than willing to throw money in the direction of finding some unique stones."

They continued downward among misted and dripping plants. Susan identified them as lianas, orchids, epiphytes—seemingly of a thousand kinds.

"Some of these have to be endemics. Remind me to collect samples on the way out."

As the sound of a waterfall grew steadily to a roar, blotting out everything else, conversation became impossible.

Picking their way over the slippery downed trees that forded the torrent at the gorge's bottom, they both looked off to that place—somewhere not very far downstream—where the torrent-turned-waterfall thundered away into empty space, sending back up the gorge a twofold sound like an immense echoing heartbeat.

Stepping down onto the rightside bank, they continued east. Soon they found themselves moving along a track that was more and more obviously a footpath. Michael shot Susan a glance, which she pretended not to see.

After following the path for a time they came to what could only have been a trail made by humans. As the trail veered sharply up a small branch canyon, the thunder of the tepui falls at last receded enough to allow the insect and animal sounds of the forest to return. Susan and Michael walked on in silence, caught up in their separate thoughts.

Gradually they gained elevation, enough that the mist cleared around them and the jungle thinned perceptibly. The air had begun to cool again by the time they encountered several foot-trampled pathways converging on an earthen slope beneath a high cliffside.

In the cliff face were some half dozen holes or cave entrances from which a brisk breeze issued steadily. Out of the forest, powerlines and cables snaked—purposeful vines of black, gray, and red, all headed toward the cliffholes. They stopped and stared.

"I think this may be proof, beyond her own words, that Jacinta was here," Michael said.

"Why her, specifically?" Susan asked, still skeptical. "And why here?"

"Paul says her Mawari 'destiny' required that she squandered all her research money—and then all her personal funds—on high-tech equipment irrelevant to tepui exploration. I think all this may have something to do with that."

"Okaay," Susan said, still uncertain, "but where are the people, then? I haven't seen any."

"Me neither. How about taking a look inside these holes here?"

"Lead on."

He scrambled up the slope, toward the largest hole, into which the greatest number of powerlines and cables converged. Stopping at the entrance, the two of them took spelunking coveralls and caving helmets from their backpacks. They slipped the coveralls on over their hiking clothes and fastened on the helmets, each topped with an LED headlamp.

Making their way inside, they walked crouched over, descending into twilight. They soon found that all the cave entrances eventually came together in a single, larger tunnel. The green smell of the cloud-forest outside gave way to the scent of damp earth, then to the muddy stink of slow decay as their lights played on the cave walls and into pitch-dark side chambers.

In the first few side chambers they found only squeaking and rustling bats, the stench of their guano, and the delicate milk-on-Rice-Krispies crackle of meat maggots eating the flesh of nightfliers unlucky enough to have fallen to the cave floor.

Beyond where the bats dangled, they passed spectacular stone formations. Stalactites and stalagmites gaped like teeth. Farther on, those formations joined to become pillars and curtains of stone. Susan and Michael had barely finished marveling at them before they came upon more open spaces, and still clearer evidence that the aborted destiny of Jacinta and the Mawari might indeed have been real—or at least a powerfully shared delusion.

Susan and Michael found several pieces of high-tech equipment—an autoclave, two diamond saws, a foldout satellite dish, an uplink antenna, half a dozen each of camcorders, optidisk player recorders, and microscreen TV sets—presumably all items Jacinta had managed to get through the Gran Sabana and onto the plateau, before Michael's uncle Paul stepped in and stopped such craziness.

In the beams of their headlamps, Michael and Susan saw that the tech—once cutting-edge but now nearly two decades outdated—seemed to have never been used. It also looked almost too pristine, as if it had been maintained against the cool and damp of the cavern with an almost sacramental devotion.

The same seeming devotion had likewise been lavished upon piles of small shining stones, found wherever side tunnels came into the main tunnel.

Looking around him as his beam played about the chill damp darkness, Michael felt that in such a place as this, the range of both the probable and the insane were vastly enlarged. Here the boundary between the believable and the unbelievable seemed vanishingly thin.

That boundary broke completely when they came upon a great central underground room—and the first corpse.

An involuntary gasp of horror escaped each of them as they looked upon a young woman, her hands thrown up in a futile attempt to protect the remains of a face that had been blown away, leaving behind only a ruin of torn flesh and shattered bone. Lithe-bodied and auburn-haired, she was dressed in a purple-and-black loincloth and nothing else. As far as they could tell, she had been carrying no weapon when she was killed.

Shocked into silence, Susan and Michael shone their lights before them. Ahead, in the middle of what looked like a shallow lake—or perhaps a place where a slow-flowing subterranean stream broadened out into a wide channel—there stood a long low hummock or island.

All the way to that hummock they saw before them scene after scene of horrible carnage. A dozen or more corpses lay contorted and broken, spattered with ragged bits of flesh and bone. To the simple stone ornaments that had adorned these people in life had been added chaotic tattoos of their life's blood, dry upon their skins.

The two outsiders crouched on a bank beside the broad stream. Some of the corpses lay on the bank, some half submerged in the shallow water—more black- or auburn-haired people, dressed in varying amounts of that same woven fabric of purple and black. That they were also all barefoot only made them seem all the more vulnerable in death.

Abruptly Susan stood up and turned away. A moment later Michael heard her vomiting. He turned to see her leaning hard on her knees as she emptied the contents of her stomach. He fought hard against the same impulse, keeping down his gorge only by forcefully reminding himself again and again how much he hated the burning taste of vomit in his throat and mouth.

"Are you all right?" he said, placing a hand lightly on her shoulder.

"How could anyone seeing this be 'all right'?" Shrugging his hand off her shoulder, she wiped her bile-mucked mouth on the sleeve of her coveralls and turned away.

"It looks like they were armed only with stone-tipped spears," Michael muttered dully to himself as he crouched down again and examined the dead around them. "Shot and killed in a skirmish with attackers carrying modern weaponry—machine guns, mortars, grenades, by the looks of it. They've been dead awhile—more than three hours but less than three days, judging by the state of rigor."

"God!" Susan said, standing up. "I know you're a doctor, but how can you be so clinical? So dispassionate? This wasn't a 'skirmish,' it was a massacre! A genocide, if these people were endemic, like everything else on this hellish tepui."

Michael rose from the charnel mass of twisted bodies on the floor.

"I'm not dispassionate," he bridled. "Not callous. Clinical is the only way I can handle this. We owe it to them to find out what happened here. Find out who committed this . . . this atrocity."

They locked eyes for a moment, until Susan at last looked away and nodded in agreement.

"The attitudes of the bodies suggest they died protecting that low island, there."

Stepping carefully amid the bloody, broken, nearly naked bodies, they made their way to the low island, toward something even stranger than carnage.

In contrast to the chaos surrounding it, the island was crowded with carefully and lovingly placed dead, so many it seemed made of bodies, corpses preserved by the cave's stable environment. Fine masses of cottony white threads had spread and knit over the surface of each corpse's skin and over the island itself, covering both so thoroughly that it was hard to tell where one ended and the other began. Weird mushrooming stalks—convoluted like human brains but stretched anamorphically along the vertical axis—thrust up like alien phalluses from the corpses' open mouths, from their ears, their eye sockets. Particularly large specimens jutted up from the corpses' abdomens just below the rib cage.

Even Michael could barely keep from retching. He looked away.

"Some kind of traditional burial ground?" Susan offered. Michael nodded weakly in agreement.

They saw that the far more recently and unceremoniously deceased, in the shallow waters surrounding the island, were free of the fungal winding sheets, at least so far.

"They died defending the dead," he said.

"And maybe their totemic fungus too," Susan said, reaching toward the strange growths rising from the dead, as if to pluck one. She stopped in mid-motion, reconsidering her impulse. "Maybe your aunt wasn't so crazy after all."

Michael wondered dimly why the same forces of decay that ravaged the bodies of the fallen bats in the outer chambers had made no inroads here. Perhaps it was more than just the cave's stable environment that preserved even the much older corpses.

"Look," he said, pointing out to Susan the waffle-stomp of bootprints on one corner of the island. "The defenders didn't succeed, in the end."

"I don't think this was the end," she said, nodding her head in the direction she'd been looking. "Over there."

A trail of broken bodies led them onward, beside where the broad stream narrowed to a small whitewater river. The walls of the great room funneled down steadily narrower, toward where the river disappeared into a hole in the ground. Before that disappearance, however, the trail of bodies veered into a side tunnel that angled upward, into what looked like the last and most secluded alcove of the cave system.

Here, the greatest number of defenders had died. Most of them appeared to have been killed protecting a great blackish stone in the middle of the alcove. The stone was almost completely encircled by the bloody, torn, and broken bodies of its fallen protectors.

"Thank God your aunt didn't live to see this," Susan said. "It would have broken her heart, to see all the Mawari become ghost people—in fact as well as name."

"Jacinta didn't tell anyone about this alcove," Michael said, "not even Paul."

"Holiest of holies, maybe. A secret too deep to be shared."

From one section of the circle marking the tribe's last stand, someone or something had unceremoniously shoved aside several of the dead defenders, out of haste to get at the stone. Reluctantly, Michael moved his heavy boot-clad feet among the bodies, following much more slowly and cautiously that same despoiler's path toward the stone.

Having made his way as reverently as possible to the stone, Michael saw that those who came before him had not treated the stone itself so respectfully. A large chunk had been sawn from it and carried away—in the not too distant past, to judge by the gleam of the cut. He stared at the break, then took from his belt the magnifying lens and small but powerful magnet he carried with him from force of long habit.

"Well?" Susan asked. Beneath the glow of her headlamp, her face drifted moonlike above her spelunking coveralls. "What is it?"

"A meteorite," Michael said. The distance afforded by scientific observation and analysis granted him a peculiar, detached comfort amid all the horror around them. "Blackened and fusion-crusted, from the hot passage through the atmosphere. Oriented, too—shaped a bit like a squat cone, from ablation as it came in. A little over a meter tall, a meter and a half wide at the base."

"You said there are different kinds of meteorites. Any idea what kind this is?"

"Carbonaceous chondrite, maybe, but there seems to be significant iron present, too. Iron crystals and shaling in some spots. It's a strange one. Extremely well preserved, for something stored in a cave. This room must be drier than the rest. No seepage, see?"

He thought of the Mawari myth of sky-gods who had crashed their essence on Earth. Struck by a sudden inspiration, he made his way back through the broken ring of dead defenders far faster than he had come.

Clear of the endlessly staring dead, he took off at as much of a run as he could manage in the dark of the tunnel leading out of the alcove, along the way they'd entered.

"Where are you going?" Susan called from behind him.

"To the big main room," he called over his shoulder, "and those piles of shining stones."

By the time Susan caught up to him, Michael was examining a stone from a pile of the glittering things.

"Shocked quartz," he told her. "Meteoritic impact glass, likely coesite and stishovite."

"Of a particular 'tone'?" Susan asked. "Pitch or resonance, or whatever it was? Like their myth?"

"More like a particular lattice configuration. Coesite and stishovite are chemically identical to quartz, but they're both considerably denser than quartz. Their crystal lattices are different, too. That difference is detectable only through X-ray diffraction experiments, so far as I know."

He looked off, down the tunnel, toward the alcove. He thought of the broken meteoritic stone there. Then he looked toward the dead defending the isle of the dead. "Who would kill so many people, just to get at a meteorite?"

"You tell me," Susan said, something like anger and sadness rising in her voice. "You're the big expert, Doctor Meteor. Maybe you were expecting to find everything we've seen here? You're the one who told me about their spore crash myth."

"I didn't expect anything like this," Michael said quietly. For several minutes he could think of nothing more to say. His mind drifted far away, to where he'd found meteorites before, deserts both cold and hot—from Elephant Moraine in Antarctica to the Rub' al-Khali, the Empty Quarter, in Saudi Arabia. He thought how little in the way of skystones he'd expected to find amid the rain forests, savannahs, and tepuis of this trip. Now that he'd found this one, the horrendous circumstances of the stone's discovery had at last broke through his scientific detachment and prevented him from feeling any real joy in the find.

Susan drifted away, too, though not as far. Hearing the sound of movement in one of the side tunnels, she went to investigate. In an instant Susan found herself being stared back at by four nearly naked children, caught in the beam of her headlamp and momentarily transfixed by it. Dressed in purple-and-black loincloths of identical snaking patterns, the four stood in the side tunnel with their backs against the walls of tight niches, crude stone-tipped spears in their hands and cornered-animal fire in their eyes.

"Michael! I think you'd better see this."

The sound of Susan's voice, calling him from one of the side tunnels, pulled Michael back into the moment. Following in the direction of her voice, he soon saw the scene Susan's headlamp shone upon.

"I was wrong," Susan said, glancing at him. "Not all the Mawariton have become ghosts, at least not yet."

RELIGIOUS EXPERIENCE

"Joe Retticker," said the man, extending his hand for Darla Pittman to shake. "Pleased to meet you, Doctor." She shot a quick glance around her lab to make sure the man was talking to her. He was. Her lab techs were out on break with her postdoctoral research assistant, Barry Levitch.

Although he wasn't in uniform, from the man's ramrod bearing, close-cropped white hair and mustache—and the forceful way he pumped her hand—Darla suspected he was military. He was handsome, even somehow charismatic, in an Ooh-Daddy kind of way. It took her a moment to place his name, though, and tag a title to it. Major General Joseph A. Retticker, U.S. Army (Retd), director for operations, NSA/CIA joint Special Collection Service.

"This is a surprise, General Retticker," Darla said, running a hand through her curly blond hair as she collected her thoughts. "I believe you were on the DARPA board when I submitted my proposal—is that right?"

"Very good, Doctor Pittman. And congratulations on getting the grant. I was already a fan of your work, even before you submitted your paperwork to us."

Retticker turned to survey his surroundings, then began to walk about the lab as if he were a major shareholder in the place. Striding to keep up, Pittman supposed she couldn't much argue that point. The Combat Personnel Enhancement Program grant—$4.6 million, jointly administered by the Defense Advanced Research Projects Agency and the National Astrobiology Institute—would keep the lab running here in Boulder, Colorado, for the next two years.

"So this is where it all happened, is it? Where you proved it was meteorites that caused the Big Blow-Up of 1910?" The general peered curiously at a high-pressure liquid chromatograph.

"I found nonterrestrial components, trapped in fullerenes taken from the ash layer, yes," Pittman said. "Fullerenes are the fourth major form of carbon—after coal, graphite, and diamond."

" 'Metadiamonds,' you called them, in one of your comments to the press. Said something like 'I never metadiamond I didn't like.' Ha!"

Pittman reddened at his comment.

"That was a mistake—I'm terrible at humor. But the reseach was unmistakable. The forest fires broke out across eastern Washington, northern Idaho, and western Montana on August 20 of 1910. They were an unanticipated offshoot of unusually high meteoritic activity."

"A perturbation of the annual Perseid meteor shower's debris cloud," Retticker said, quoting her report from memory and turning away from the chromatograph. "As that cloud itself was affected by the 1910 passage of Comet Halley."

"You really do know my work," Darla said, glancing at the floor, embarrassed and flattered. "I'm gratified."

"A good deal of it, yes," Retticker said. "It was a high-profile discovery. Right up there with Miskulin's work on nonterrestrial amino acids. Pretty soon they'll be calling you 'Doctor Meteor' instead of him."

Darla winced. "I'll be more than happy to leave that title to Miskulin."

"Oh?"

"I can't say I'm impressed with his methods. About the best that can be said for his work on prebiotics and DNA precursors is that it's forced the specialists to pay more attention to *my* research."

The general smiled as he glanced out the window and noted the view of the Flat Irons.

"I see," Retticker said. "But there's more to it, isn't there? I gather some of your colleagues in the scientific community view Miskulin as . . . ambitious, shall we say?"

"He's a dilettante and a publicity hound is more like it," Pittman said, then she shrugged. "He's out of his league, and trespassing on our turf. I worked with him on a project for the National Science Foundation. Part of the ANSMET program—Antarctic Search for Meteorites. He was trained as an M.D. I think he actually snuck himself onto the project as the expedition physician."

Darla neglected to mention any of the more intimate activities she and Miskulin—he of the dark wavy hair and all-too-telegenic smile— had undertaken together during the nightless summer days of Antarctic deep-field work. That, however, had been years ago.

"Yet he has had some successes. . . ."

"Undeniably," Pittman admitted. From all this talk of Miskulin, she wondered if maybe she wasn't DARPA's first choice. Then again, she mused, they weren't likely to have wanted the kind of security risk Miskulin would have posed, given his views.

Putting such thoughts out of her head, she followed the general's gaze toward the upturned triangular slabs of the Flat Irons. She had free-climbed many a route on many a spire of that uplifted rock. One of her reasons for taking the job here at Colorado University, despite some internal department opposition to her appointment, was the campus's proximity to some of the best bouldering and rock-climbing country in the world.

"I'm not saying that Miskulin isn't a very shrewd researcher, in his own way," Darla added. "For all the controversy surrounding it, I think his work with meteoritic amino acids and DNA precursors is solid science. Still, he's not a professional meteoriticist. He's not even a geologist or geochemist. That's the real reason he's controversial."

"But he's not alone in being controversial, is he, Doctor?" General Retticker said, arching his eyebrows in a quizzical fashion. "Your ideas linking meteorites to religious dreams and visions—particularly Jacob's stone pillow, in the Bible—those haven't exactly passed unnoticed in some quarters. Pretty fanciful stuff."

Darla Pittman dismissed the controversy with a quick wave of her hand.

"There's nothing fanciful about it. There's solid documentation of persons who have experienced prophetic visions when they came into contact with, or even prolonged close proximity to, certain meteoritic stones."

"Other people have written about it besides you, then?"

"Just look at the publications of ethnographers from Mircea Eliade onward. The list of 'affective stones' is long. The Benben stone of Heliopolis in ancient Egypt, the hierophanic stones of Astarte in Tyre and of Cybele in Phrygia, the Sun-Stone omphalos at Thebes, the conical stone at the center of the Aphrodite temple in Byblos, the sacred stone that embodied the sun god Heliogabalus at Emesa, the oracular stones at Delphi, the Great Stone of Cronos, the Zeus Baetylos, the Chintamani stone purported to have 'telepathically guided' those who came in contact with it—"

"But those are all found in different parts of the world."

"Exactly! And despite that, they are all associated with instances of vision and prophecy. Among the ancient Nabateans of northern Arabia and Trans-Jordan, for instance, all the gods and goddesses were represented as stones or god-blocks. Aniconic rocks, monoliths and mega-liths, were worshipped throughout the ancient world. I've always thought the black monolith that set our shaggy prehuman ancestors on the road to becoming Homo sapiens in that old movie *2001: A Space Odyssey* nicely echoed the long tradition of vision-inducing god-blocks."

"An interesting speculation," Retticker said, suppressing a smile. "But when you start saying that some of the foundations of the Judeo-Christian and Islamic world religions—"

"Like Jacob's stone pillow dream," Pittman interjected wearily, "or the Black Stone of the Kaaba in Mecca."

"Right. When you say those foundations might have been built on 'sensations of disembodied euphoria and visionary insight' resulting from 'hydrocarbon outgassing by recently arrived meteorites,' well, it gives entirely new meaning to the idea of being stoned. You'll be lucky if they don't stone you for suggesting it."

"Frankly, I've heard more stoned-on-religion jokes than I ever wanted to hear, thank you. Both the jokes and the personal attacks are unimportant, though. My concern is what the facts point to. Even the Vatican has a substantial meteorite collection, for heaven's sake! The Latin word *vates* means 'prophet' or 'seer,' though the priests there will publicly deny any linkage between stone and vision. Determining the legitimate cause of that linkage is a perfectly appropriate area for scientific inquiry—denials notwithstanding."

"No doubt, no doubt."

"It wouldn't necessarily have to be ethylene outgassing, either. That was just one possibility. Even if you don't buy Miskulin's DNA-precursor push, it's long been known that meteorites harbor large numbers of various hydrocarbons—aliphatic linear ones and aromatic polycyclic rings—as well as exotic amino acids. Siegfried Haberer suggests even iron meteorites might play an affective 'spiritual' role, given Michael Persinger's work."

"What work is that?"

"Persinger has been very successful at artificially inducing religious experiences in his patients by exposing the temporal lobes of their brains to weak magnetic fields. Rotating fields in the nanotesla range induce the feeling of a 'sensed presence'—usually interpreted as God—in over eighty percent of test subjects. I have to admit that's pretty good, though personally I think meteoritic magnetism is probably a weaker explanation than the chemical one."

She turned and pulled a Bible from a bookshelf, where its tooled red leather binding made it look very much out of place among the more workaday scientific volumes.

"Just look objectively at this passage from Genesis twenty-eight: 'Jacob left Beersheeba and set out for Haran. When he reached a certain place, he stopped for the night because the sun had set. Taking one of the stones there, he put it under his head and lay down to sleep. He had a dream in which he saw a great ladder resting on the earth with its top reaching to heaven, and the angels of God were ascending and descending on it.

" 'There too stood the Lord, and he said, I am the Lord, the God of your father Abraham and the God of Isaac. I will give you and your descendants the land on which you are lying. Your descendants will be like the dust of the earth and you will spread out to the west and to the east, to the north and to the south. All peoples on earth will be blessed through you and your offspring. I am with you and will watch over you wherever you go and I will bring you back to this land. I will not leave you until I have done what I promised you.

" 'When Jacob awoke from his sleep, he thought, Surely the Lord is in this place, and I was not aware of it. He was afraid and said, How awesome is this place. This is none other than the House of God; this is the Gate of Heaven.

" 'Early the next morning Jacob took the stone he had placed under his head and set it up as a pillar and poured oil on top of it. He called that place Bethel. . . .' "

Professor Pittman snapped shut the red leather volume.

"Other sources specify that the 'certain place' where Jacob stopped was a shallow depression with other such stones scattered about, probably an impact pit or penetration hole at least, if not an actual crater. The crater interpretation is strengthened by the tradition of Jacob's Bethel altar-rock being found at the center of a *labyrinth*—meteorite in crater, stone at the heart of a labyrinth. His dream that he floated up an angel staircase and listened to God certainly sounds like disembodied euphoria to me. A number of traditions claim that Jacob's stone was located in its 'pit' or 'labyrinth' at what is now the Temple Mount in Jerusalem, beneath the Dome of the Rock.

"The clincher, though, is that Jacob uses what is in many sources called an 'oil received from heaven' to anoint the stone itself. And then he calls the place Beth El, the Gate of Heaven or House of God. Beth El is linked linguistically to the root of the word *Babel,* 'Gate of God.' Also to *baetyl,* the Greek 'House of God,' as in Zeus Baetylos. A *betyl* is a sacred rock that both manifests and houses the deity—and the root meaning of *baetylos* is 'sacred skystone.' "

"And the Black Stone of the Kaaba?" Retticker asked, turning from the window and peering over a suite of spectrometers.

"Al Hajar al Aswad," Pittman replied. "Sometimes referred to as the 'right hand of God' and the 'navel of the world.' Bayt Allah, to the Muslims. Another bethel-baetyl House of God. Most likely a meteorite, but also perhaps what's called a Wabar pearl—a type of impactite, impact glass resulting from a large meteorite strike."

"I've also heard it dismissed as an old hunk of touchstone basalt."

"If that's the case, then why should it become the literal touchstone of millions of Muslims on Hajj every year? The Black Stone was sacred in Mecca long before the Muslims got hold of it, too. It was worshipped with the moon god and his three 'sister' or 'daughter' goddesses from time immemorial. We can't know for sure what it is. Since the Black Stone's sacred, no one's ever been allowed to run experiments on the thing. We do know, however, that the tradition of kissing it during the Hajj actually goes back to pressing one's *head* against the sacred stone."

"Presumably to induce some sort of visionary experience."

"Exactly right," Darla said, fiddling absently with two small stones she had picked up from the top of a metal cabinet—one an iron-nickel meteorite, the other a stony iron. "Making them sacred does help preserve them, thank goodness, but it also makes them untouchable by science. What I wouldn't give to get hold of all those old holy rocks, and open them up!"

At that, Retticker glanced up at Pittman from the readout screen of a mass spec.

"We're pretty eager to find out what might be in those rocks, as well," he said, thoughtfully. "That's what interested us in your work, Doctor. If those meteorites possess valuable properties for chemically reactive armor, or mind-enhancing pharmaceuticals, say, then they could have important implications, from a military point of view.

"Since the recent unpleasantness with China, we've been following up on every lead that might prove to give us an advantage. Protective exoskeletons and musculature augmentation, drugs, hormones, microchip implants, even reworking the soldier's DNA—anything that builds up performance and locks out stress, fatigue, fear, or trauma. If the stuff that makes for these 'visionary' or seemingly 'magical' properties really exists, and could be harnessed, well, anything you and your skystones can contribute to our efforts will be greatly appreciated."

Darla nodded. There had been hints of a "recent unpleasantness with China" in the media, though not much in the way of particulars had been made public. That didn't matter to her, though, as much as the fact that she might make the current political climate work to her advantage.

"Any assistance you can offer in helping me gain access to those skystones," she said, "would likewise be greatly appreciated."

"Glad to hear it," the general said. "We've already collected some items we think you might be interested in."

Retticker went to the window and motioned to someone in the parking lot below. When he turned back to her, Darla gave him a puzzled look, but he only flashed her an enigmatic smile.

A few moments later a pair of clean-cut young troopers in crisp uniforms strode into her lab. Each held a handle mounted to a large case of polished wood.

At a nod from Retticker, the men stepped forward and hefted the wooden box onto a black-topped lab table. Judging from the way the men worked with it, Darla guessed that whatever was inside the case was pretty heavy. These men weren't exactly lightweights. After a moment, they snapped open fastenings and pulled the casing apart.

As she stepped in front of the two soldiers—who had moved aside and now stood at attention—her heart began to beat a bit faster.

Inside a sealed containment bag of clear plastic sat a pitted stone, ranging in color from reddish brown to charcoal black, and showing the clear presence of a fusion crust. It was a meteoritic, and a good-size chunk at that. She approached it, pulling a hand lens out of her pocket.

"An especially mixed specimen," she said, examining its surface through the plastic. "See the pressure marks that look like thumbprints? Typical of an iron meteorite. They're called piezoglypts, or regmaglypts. They're made by turbulent eddies in the superhot incandescent gases that passed over the meteor on its way through our atmosphere."

She turned her attention to where the hunk of skystone had been cut away from another surface.

"I think these are iron crystals. Sections of this rock might show very interesting Widmanstätten patterns, if you were to etch them with a nital solution. But there's a lot of silicate material here, too. A silicated iron meteorite? Maybe a mesosiderite? But those types are achondrites, and these look like nicely formed chondrules, here."

She walked around the stone, thoroughly oblivious to the rigid soldiers now, carefully examining it from several angles.

"Some of this material isn't far from microdiamonds," she continued, "of the type found in ureilites. Almost as if several space-rocks of varying types had smashed together and fused. Evidence of melt and brecciation too—a violent and very mixed history too indeed. I don't think I've come across this particular stone in the literature before."

"I don't believe you would have," Retticker said. "It's a new find."

"Really. What's its provenance? Where'd you get it?"

"A rather remote region of South America."

"General, the tradition is to name the stone after the town or landmark nearest to where the fall was found. Like the Murchison meteorite, or the Allende stone."

"Yes, I've gathered that. We don't know with certainty whether this stone originally fell where we found it, or was moved there. Let's just say it came from one of the high plateaus called tepuis. But you *do* think this ugly old rock has some scientific value?"

"Ugly?" Pittman asked as she continued to examine the surface. "Looks can deceive, General. Some of the ugliest meteorites—the carbonaceous chondrites—are among the most scientifically rewarding."

"Well, the more important thing is, it's all yours now."

Darla ran her hands through her hair and smiled broadly, hoping she didn't look too girlishly enthusiastic.

"The 'tepui stone' it is. Thank you, General. I'll do my best to make this fellow tell us what he knows."

"Very good," General Retticker said, extending his hand for her to shake. "Make the stones talk—that's exactly what we need you to do. We'll leave you to it, for now. I'll also leave my card and contact information with your department secretary. Keep in touch, and keep me in the loop. Good luck."

She rather regretted seeing him go. Kind of her type, if she were in the market for a little romance. Which she wasn't just at the moment. Too busy, especially now. As she gloved up and set to work, Professor Pittman soon found herself captivated with the stone they'd brought her.

HEAD TO HEAD

Animals in our shadows.

Those were the images Joe Retticker had in his head when he woke from a snooze on the flight back to California from Colorado. As the helicopter to which he'd transferred carried him through sunset light over the rumpled grassland and chaparral landscape of Camp Pendleton, he pondered what might have made such a thing pop up in his dreams.

Sounded vaguely enviro, now that he thought about it. Maybe it had something to do with the name he'd selected for this mission: Operation Star Thrower. In a biology class he took when he was at West Point, he'd read an essay called "The Star Thrower."

The professor who'd taught the course had been something of an environmentalist. These days he'd probably be branded as a fanatic, since successive administrations in Washington had succeeded in making environmentalism virtually synonymous with terrorism in the public's mind. There'd been nothing covert about that teacher, though. He'd been more than forthcoming with his beliefs. The essay, by Loren Eiseley, had been a good read, too—whatever its politics.

The thud of the helo touching down ended his reverie. Exiting the helicopter, he heard the sound of its rotors slowing over his head as he made his way across a grassy ridgetop. He was saluted by a jut-jawed, thickly muscled Army Ranger he recognized as Major Marc Vasques. He returned the salute and shook Vasques's hand.

"Good to see you, Major. How are the training exercises going?"

"If you'll follow me, sir, you'll be able to see for yourself. You're just in time."

In the deepening twilight, they walked toward a point overlooking a small box canyon. Vasques handed the general a pair of binoculars. Retticker saw that they were bimodals—for both day and night vision. Below their perch, a joint services training activity of the Enhanced Warfighter program, in cooperation with MERC, the Military Executive Resource Corporation, was about to get under way.

"The green team you see there just came out of the surf," Vasques said.

"Enhanced?"

"Yes sir. Power armor, full heads-up enhanced sensoria. They have to pass through this small canyon to reach their objective. Blue team plans to give them a bit of a surprise, though."

"Blue team enhanced, too?"

"Yes sir. SEALs, Rangers, special operations people on both sides— all new and improved."

General Retticker watched as the troops of green team advanced. He had just started to wonder where the blue team might be when a flash went off in the center of the canyon. He saw green team members banging their helmets with their hands or gun butts, then quickly flipping the heads-up visors away from their eyes.

"Focused mag-pulse bomb," Vasques said. "Takes out the heads-up electronics. Not big enough to take out the power armor, though."

Retticker nodded. As he watched, he saw the green team's advance go suddenly awry. Out of nowhere, fighters—the blue team—appeared, as if they had risen from the ground itself. Close-quarters battle followed, spectacular yet eerily quiet. "Kills," he saw, caused the power armor to go rigid, then collapse—quite effectively simulating a mortal hit.

Among those who hadn't been hit, a fantastic battle of supermen ensued. High-flying leaps and kicks and strikes everywhere, almost too fast to follow.

"Brilliant," Retticker muttered under his breath. Then, more clearly, "How'd blue team conceal itself so well?"

"The new chameleon camo, sir," Vasques said. "The stuff matches patterns in background temperature, as well as optical patterns. The temperature ranges and shadows at this time of the evening don't hurt either."

Retticker nodded, without taking his eyes off the tableau before them. "Yes, yes. If I recall right, that new camo muffles breathing, even the sound of the wearer's heartbeat. Very effective."

"Yes sir."

Below and before them, the leaps and falls and throws—all of the superhuman grappling between the soldiers—continued apace. Watching from this height, however, it was clear that the blue team had gained the upper hand, and would be mopping up before long—kicking butt and taking names.

"It's like watching a Hong Kong martial arts movie," Retticker said, turning now to face Vasques. "With the sound turned off." He switched the binocs to close-up mode.

"Yes sir. We're regular ninja masters, all right. And we don't need wires and harnesses for our tricks."

Retticker thought he heard something worth pursuing in Vasques's voice. He removed the bimod binocs from his eyes and peered at the major, who was no longer watching what was going on below.

"It sounds as if you're not impressed by your supersoldiers, Major. How so? I thought our recent field test for MERC was a success."

"They are impressive, sir, but—" Vasques paused. "Permission to speak frankly, General?"

"Granted—and welcome. As always."

"Sir, when we hit that tepui down there, we had every advantage. We had surprise on our side. We had night vision and the cave's darkness. Power armor and lethal firepower, against bare skin and spears. And we still lost two men."

"You were taking them on their own turf, Major. They knew the ground. They were the home team, fighting for their homes."

"Yes sir, but home court advantage should have meant next to nothing. It should have been a cakewalk."

"Any ideas why it was more challenging than you expected?"

"Nothing certain, sir. Just hunches."

"Such as?"

"Well, sir, it was like, from the moment we first stumbled onto one of them, they all instantly knew we were there. There was no way they could have spread the alarm—we made sure of that. Yet, for some reason, the silencers we started with didn't seem to silence *them.*"

"And?"

"The cohesiveness with which those people responded . . . it made me realize something, sir. Individual supersoldiers in supersuits aren't the same thing as a superhuman fighting unit. Heads-up displays and GPS can still only get you so far. That's why we had to kill so many of those tepui people—maybe all of them. We had no choice. They just wouldn't stop coming at us. They were of one mind, especially when it came to that rock of theirs. They were determined not to give it up, no matter what the cost. One of my men thought it might be some kind of meteorite."

"It is—at least according to the scientists who have it now."

"Sir, those plateau people seemed to think it was awfully important. Important enough to die for."

"Lots of people all over the world have thought certain objects were awfully important, at one time or another. Sometimes those objects have been meteorites. That's what the experts say, anyway. We don't know much about this particular rock yet. We're still in the early stages of the analysis."

Vasques glanced at his feet. When he looked up again, his voice was tight.

"It was almost as if they wanted to die. A bunch of soldier-assisted suicides," Vasques said. "Sir, the bodies we brought back for the docs, did they . . . did they find anything strange or unusual about them?"

Retticker smiled.

"There were a few anomalies. They all shared a rather unusual fungal infection. Rather outsized pineal glands, in the adults. Nothing that would account for the sort of cohesion you mentioned, though."

Major Vasques nodded, but he looked somewhat downcast.

"General, if your science wizards could come up with something to give us that kind of head-to-head connection among our troops in the field, added to our technical superiority, it would make for an unstoppable combination."

"Already part of the program, Major. Mind-machine action-at-a-distance—M^2A^3D. That's the tech. As for head-to-head telepathy, it's what the scientists call 'conjoint consciousness.' It'd certainly go a long way toward cutting through the fog of war, I'll give you that."

He glanced at Vasques.

"So far we've had more luck with M^2A^3D," he added ruefully.

"That about brain-machine links?" Vasques asked. "Joystick-trained monkeys, moving cursors and robot arms with nothing but a thought?"

"We're a good ways beyond that sort of thing," Retticker said. "It's not conjoint consciousness, though—that's a different story—but we're working on it. Anything else, Major? Any other 'hunches'?"

To Retticker's surprise, Vasques looked distinctly uncomfortable.

"There is something else, sir. I don't know, but it seemed that, at points during the fight, those people were projecting their pain back at us, right into our heads. It was all we could do to keep going. None of us like to talk about it, but I think all of us felt it at some point in the mission."

"Intriguing, Major. And certainly worth investigating further. Thank you for your input."

"Yes sir. I hope it helps, sir."

Darkness was falling, so they switched their bimodal binoculars to night vision and watched as, on the shadowed plain below them, small armies still clashed by night. As Retticker had anticipated, the blue team's members had overwhelmed their opponents at last.

Who knows what we might learn from what's out there in the twilight? Retticker thought, pondering what Vasques had said. From the crazy stuff, the wild stuff. From the animals in our shadows.

THE ARGUS SPIDER

Jim Brescoll sat quietly in his new office, so quietly, in fact, that to the uninformed bystander he might have appeared to be napping, his eyes safely hidden behind dark glasses.

Admiral Janis Rollwagen's office decor had been spartan—so austerely Scandinavian that the office hadn't looked all that much emptier when her furnishings were last hauled away. Brescoll had replaced those with the old dark wood of his antiques. He fully believed that more than just the furniture had been changed, however. He hoped he was already accomplishing the business of national security in a new way, as well.

The recently concluded Kwok-Cho affair had lived up to both sides of the ancient Chinese understanding of the word *crisis:* danger, and opportunity. That series of events had been dangerous enough in its unfolding, especially for Rollwagen, who had been revealed as a creature of the secret societies and shadow security apparatuses that had riddled the intelligence community for years.

For Brescoll, though, the precarious episode had proved to be a tremendous opportunity. At its most dangerous point, Jim Brescoll himself had been put under arrest by his agency's own internal security forces, the Emergency Response Team's Special Operations Unit. In an instant, however, the situation had flipped and he had gone from being a prisoner to being the first African-American—and first civilian—director of NSA.

History had left his agency with blots enough on its escutcheon, no doubt about that, but he'd willingly taken over the helm in hopes of steering it by a better star. His transformation and the transformation of his agency paled, however, in comparison with the change experienced by the secret architect of the revolution. Ben Cho had undergone a metamorphosis that seemed barely describable in human terms— Metaquantum Apotheosis, or Transcendence, or Singularity. Then he'd vanished utterly from the world stage. Perhaps human affairs were beneath his notice now.

Indeed, Brescoll supposed the Apotheosized One was busy enough with his own concerns, out there at the end of time, looking back like a distant guardian angel or bodhisattva over the vast ensemble of branching universes. To tell the truth, Brescoll found himself hoping that the

Transcendent One was out of the picture for good. He wasn't entirely comfortable with the intervention of superhumans in human history.

Life was so much simpler when it stayed within the smaller compass of the known and the familiar in a post–Peak Oil world. Once they'd learned the petroleum supply had most likely dropped past the half-empty mark, greedy nations seemed all the more eager to wage wars, greedy individuals seemed all the more bent on enhancing their personal power bases, and the president and the cabinet seemed more willing than ever to play musical deck chairs on Planet Titanic.

With a sigh, Brescoll peered into his AR glasses and pivoted down the mike, thus allowing him the luxury of voice commands. At least these new ARGUS blinks were more user-friendly than previous Augmented Reality glasses had been. Blinking into them and calling for selections, Jim pulled his messages and links out from peripheral vision and into the center of his visual field. He blinked on the first one.

Dear Director Brescoll:

Whether from minds under the influence of stars, or stars under the influence of minds, new constellations are coming into being. Just thought you'd like to know.

Best,
Karuna Benson
Cherise LeMoyne
Don Markham

Jim wouldn't have given the message much thought had it not intruded over his quantum crypto hardline. That was supposed to be impossible. His two chief scientific advisers from the Kwok-Cho days, Steve Wang of Princeton's Institute for Defense Analysis and Bree Lingenfelter from NSA's Laboratory for Physical Sciences at the University of Maryland, both assured him as much. Yet there it was.

The three signers had been involved in the Ben Cho/Jaron Kwok affair. They were reportedly still dwelling inside an underground powerhouse in California's Sierra Nevada—inside a mountain that was in turn protected beneath an impenetrable blister of exotic energy, a force-field dome. Several other impenetrable spots had appeared elsewhere across the globe—over what had been the Sun Yat-Sen Memorial Hall in China and in the South American Tri-Border, most importantly.

None of those domes were exactly your everyday street address, which also made the message harder to ignore, whatever the motivations of the three senders might be.

Markham and Benson and LeMoyne had attached several site-linked files, which he now brought before his eyes. One was a brief newsnote announcing that billionaire investors George Otis and Dr. Ka Vang were sponsoring research into spontaneous human combustion. Their goal, on the face of it, seemed to be to debunk the phenomenon once and for all.

Otis, an archconservative former cabinet member, and Vang, the computing mogul with connections to the discredited Tetragrammaton network, were a pair of odd bedfellows indeed. Jim wondered if there might be more to their "investments" than the curiosity of a couple of wealthy debunkers.

Although Vang and Otis's endeavor might just be a fluke or odd coincidence, he would keep an eye on it anyway, just to be safe. Tetragrammaton was down, but it was never wise to count someone like Vang out—at least not until you were absolutely sure.

As creator and CEO of ParaLogics, Vang had at one time run the largest specialty supercomputer firm in the world, a company whose biggest clients were the NSA and the CIA. Not bad for a guy born to a Southeast Asian peasant family in a village with a shaman and neolithic-level culture, recruited to service in a CIA-sponsored guerrilla army when he was just barely into his teens, and then, after Vietnam, retrained in California via an Intelligence-sponsored scholarship, to become an All-American success story in the information sciences.

No, Jim admitted grudgingly, it might not be smart to declare him a dead number just yet.

The second attachment was another news article, this one more extensive, describing a deal under which Victor Fremdkunst, meteorite hunter and self-proclaimed "fine art lapidary," had consummated a transaction with the curator of the Vatican's meteorite collection, handing over an undisclosed number of iron-nickel meteorites in exchange for what was thought to be a meteorite of lunar origin.

Related links led to sites chronicling the outcry against Fremdkunst for turning meteorites into a crass commodity. It seemed he was shaving thin slices from the skystones and applying lapidary techniques to highlight their unique features. Fremdkunst claimed thus to have succeeded in transforming the fallen stars from "artifacts" into "art." His creations had become modish conversation pieces fetching hefty prices among the wealthiest of the beau monde.

According to the news sites and hobby blogs, Fremdkunst's marketing success had driven up the worldwide price of meteorites to the point that it was becoming increasingly difficult for museums and research institutions to purchase new finds for their collections. With increased demand, there had come a spate of thefts as the black market sought to profit from the situation. Fremdkunst was blamed for the crime wave as well.

Jim always found it hard to determine how reliable this rumor-mill stuff might be. Undoubtedly some of it was valuable material, but much blogging and online reporting was less journalism than journal jism—not so much works of genius as jerks of wienius.

Through the various links, however, Jim was able to blink, in turn, to more solid news sites. There he found details concerning the disappearance and presumed theft of the antarctic Adelie Land meteorite from the South Australian Museum in Adelaide. He also read the happier story of how a security guard at the Smithsonian Institution's National Museum of Natural History had foiled an attempted burglary. There, too, the target was the museum's meteorite collections.

Other links Markham, Benson, and LeMoyne had sent him seemed less directly related to one another. The first was a brief news report on an apparently random suicide bombing that had led to the death in Israel of Enide Zaragosa, the daughter of Argentinian-Jewish meteoriticist Avram Zaragosa. Her father had been forced to leave a delegation that was accompanying the exhibition of Argentinian meteorites currently wending its way through a tour of museums and universities throughout the world. Israeli and Argentinian authorities, firmly maintained that Enide's death was unrelated to the exhibition or her father's work.

Stranger still were the reports from Santa Elena de Uairén, the largest town in the Gran Sabana region of the Venezuelan state of Bolivar. These news items cited statements by Doctor Michael Miskulin and professor of ethnobotany Susan Yamada. The two had apparently stumbled on the massacre of members of a tribal group recently discovered in the tepui country thereabouts.

Several linked sites revealed that the tribe's neighbors, the Pemon, had long described these tepui people—variously called Mawari, Mawariton, and Imawariton—as "tall, shadowy man-shaped spirits" who possessed the ability to "beam" their thoughts into the minds of those who encountered them.

The problem, Brescoll soon discovered, was that the Pemon were themselves far too Westernized. The more he read their accounts, the more and more they sounded like something out of *The X-Files,* with weird lights in the sky, sightings, crop circles, and abductions. The scientists Miskulin and Yamada, however, had at least managed to prove the existence of these Mawariton, if only to chronicle their extinction.

Strangest of all, however, was the link to a highly debated lecture by Miskulin himself, on directed litho-panspermia, or Cosmic Ancestry:

We should consider the possibility that most of the amino acids we've found encapsulated in fullerenes are not just the product of the partial combustion of meteoroids in the atmosphere, but function as prebiotic enzymatic material—prepackaged, as it were. The soccer ball–shaped, metadiamond cages of fullerenes make perfect packaging for such material, perhaps even for nanoparticles or nanobial organisms.

Complexity is the trick that life uses to overcome entropy, so once such prebiotic programmed space-seeds encounter a planet with habitats for life, these prebiotics continue their evolution to living cells. Perhaps, if they encounter a planet with the potential for more complex life, their job is to help organize that environment to support a further growing complexity.

There's the rub, though. Not even metadiamonds are forever. If Cosmic Ancestors sent out prepackaged prebiotics—space-seeds— on random trajectories, then it's likely that much of what they released into the vastness has fallen into stars and burned up, or has been drifting for aeons and become corrupted in other ways.

Human genetic material, for all the complexity it has already achieved, likely still possesses a great deal of unrealized potential—more than either evolution or genetic engineering have been able to yet tap into. The entire history of humanity, in fact, strongly suggests that our code is corrupted, that we are lacking some key puzzle-piece for realizing our potential as a species. But what if, out there among the stars, is the missing piece of genetic programming that is essential for some next step here on earth? What if there is a higher level of evolution available in those genes lost to us here on earth, but still remaining to be discovered out there?

Perhaps our fascination with the stars is in part a realization of a lack within ourselves. The good news is that the missing piece may still be available to us, not only around suns so many light-years distant, but also delivered 24/7 to our doorstep by Planetesimal Express.

Long before the clip ended, cautionary flags began to rise in Jim's mind. To him, panspermian hypotheses had always seemed prone to the cop-out of infinite regress: cosmic ancestors all the way down, the question of the origin of life endlessly deferred.

There was something else Brescoll found more disturbing than that, however. The emphasis on "next" or "higher evolutionary" steps. The emphasis on the darknesses of human history, too, as proof that the species was missing or lacking something.

Making up for some human "lack" or "flaw" was the sort of thing that had piqued the interests of secret societies throughout history. The Freemasons a few centuries back, Phi Beta Kappa in the 1700s, the Carbonari in the early nineteenth century, and, much more recently, the Instrumentality. That had nearly ended badly—very badly—even if it had put Brescoll in the position he occupied today.

The Instrumentality people, especially their Tetragrammaton wing, used to be quite fond of making those kinds of noises. About the humanity after humanity. Making up the "difference" had been a goal of the Tetra types, particularly. Which was, in the end, the source of the rift within the Instrumentality itself—between the Kitchener faction, bent on keeping "man as man," and the Tetra types, bent on fostering a cyborgized, posthuman humanity.

Jim shook his head, remembering.

As much as cosmic ancestor worship struck him as cargo-cult biology, however, machinic descendant worship struck him even more as cargo-cult sociology. He was glad the Tetra types had taken such a hit from the Kwok-Cho affair. Someone like this Miskulin fellow might have found their rhetoric of elitist saviorism more than a little seductive.

Maybe they'd already gotten to him? Tetra was too large and interwoven with the social order to be entirely obliterated, after all. With Kwok and Cho gone, might they still be around in some less organized fashion, working on a new project to while away the time?

But no; in this tepui incident Miskulin seemed somehow more a victim than a perpetrator. Jim could see how meteorites—stolen, or

market-cornered, or worshipped, or whatever—tied in to all that cosmic ancestor stuff. But how could it possibly be relevant to the machine-
descendant crowd?

When he at last figured it out, it all felt too familiar—and with good
cause.

Brescoll had, some months back, gotten himself appointed to the
joint committee charged with recruiting researchers for the DARPA
Combat Personnel Enhancement Program. He'd wanted to keep an eye
on any high-level posthuman push, and he figured *that* particular
camel's nose would show up in the supersoldier tent before it got in
under the tent flaps anywhere else.

He usually didn't have much trouble with such joint committee
work. DoD, State, they were generally okay with him, but there had always been something about the CIA. Too many operatives in the Company had too much torture-chamber time for him to feel all that
comfortable with career ghost-warriors—especially when the politicians
meddled with their work. Of course, the same could be said about the
covert "Strategic Support" and "Special Planning" offices at the Pentagon, and elements of NSA's own history too, particularly the presiden-
tially mandated "special access" electronic surveillance of the previous
decade, but those were aberrations within the overall structure. . . .

Wasn't one of the researchers recruited for the DARPA program
somebody already working on meteorites? Isolating exotic biologicals
from them? He seemed to recall such a job description.

Brescoll took off the AR glasses and rubbed his face. He stared at
the ARGUS blinks in his hand. He knew what the acronymn stood for,
of course—Augmented Reality Graphical User Spectacles, web-linked—
but it was still an odd name, when he thought about it. Wasn't the whole
thing about Argus, the hundred-eyed watchman of Greek myth, the fact
that he *didn't* blink? That at least some of his eyes were always open?

Planet Earth, it seemed to him, had increasingly become an Argus
planet, never completely closing all its eyes anywhere. The intelligence
community was no small part of that growing wakefulness—the
agency he himself headed, too, especially in the area of electronic intelligence. Pictures of many of NSA's older worldwide listening posts now
hung in the halls and on the walls of offices here in Crypto City—
images of nondescript government and military buildings surrounded
by satellite-dish chalices, by mushroom puffball and geodesic golfball
radomes hiding their eavesdropping antennas.

NSA's sky-eye builder, the National Reconnaissance Office, was also a big part of the Argus Effect, with its Keyhole- and Lacrosse-class satellites, its computers combining multiple-angle satellite imaging from both its photographic and radar sources among the sky-eyes and ears.

And the brains behind those eyes and ears. The human ones—the cryptolinguists and crypto computer scientists like Wang at Princeton, the physical scientists and infotheorists like Lingenfelter at the University of Maryland. Most important, the thousands of mathematicians and linguists, analysts and engineers and technicians, codemakers and codebreakers who took the off-ramp from the Baltimore-Washington Parkway to their everyday secret jobs in Crypto City, not far from the much smaller and less covert town of Annapolis Junction, Maryland.

The machine brains, too. The forerunners of an ultimate cryptoanalytic device, a "universal key" for breaking all codes. Out of the search for that grail had come all the strangeness of the Kwok-Cho affair. The whole dark side of the quantum cryptologic arms race and its assorted potential catastrophes. The conflict with the secret Special Computing Institutes, China's "Bletchley Park," driven by their goal of countering American hard-tech superiority through targeted "soft" or information-war programs.

Even the SCIs releasing hunter-killer programs against the human world's most advanced machine-intelligences, however, had been small potatoes compared to what had happened during Ben Cho's *almost* globally apocalyptic transcendence. The cover story Brescoll had himself helped cobble together—in the perhaps vain hope of explaining away the whole series of events—suggested that a number of short-lived "control failures" in military and civilian systems led to a bad synergy of computer warfare errors, which in turn very nearly brought on a genuine shooting war between the United States and China.

The two countries had sealed off their respective force-field blister zones and named them Mutual Assured Quantum Cryptologic Security Stations—the MAXX, as the guard troops called the one in California—the existence of which was supposed to guard against such "bad synergies" in the future.

True, the MAXX was somehow ensuring quantum cryptologic security, but no one knew how that was being achieved, exactly. Especially when—given this message Markham, Benson, and Le Moyne had sent him—those inside the U.S. MAXX, at least, could breach that same security at any time of their choosing. No one knew how they were able to do *that*, either.

If Brescoll knew how flimsy that cover story really was, he had to assume at least a few other people did, too. The world had dodged the big bullet, but who knew for how long? What if the whole affair wasn't just about the PRC and the USA anymore?

He put the blinks on his desk and rubbed his forehead, thinking of his predecessor, and of Argus. Janis Rollwagen was gone, taken out by the blind spot hidden in the very means she had used in hopes of avoiding all blind spots. She had become such a big spider in such a big web of information and intrigue that she lost touch with the reality to which that web was ultimately attached.

He didn't like killer blind spots himself—and the *terrae incognitae* under the force-field domes certainly showed a lot of potential in that direction. He hoped to avoid getting too distant from ground truth the way his predecessor had, but it wouldn't be easy. The web of things for Argus to guard was bigger than ever, and it was ever easier to become a spider trapped in a web of one's own making.

Much to do, and much to delegate—although how much it would be safe to delegate he could not yet say. Rollwagen's fate was a cautionary tale always warning him what might happen if too much of the hands-on part of this job was left in the hands of others.

NSA Director Brescoll had no choice but to keep all his eyes, ears, and options open. No choice but to treat as real this dimly emerging new constellation in the mind's sky. He set to work.

THE MADNESS OF THE WORLD

For a moment, Avram Zaragosa stared uncomprehendingly at the inscription. It stood on a heraldic banner, in the lower left-hand corner on the outside of a Book of Remembrances. The book was from his daughter's memorial service.

He will turn the hearts of the fathers to their children, and the hearts of the children to their fathers. Malachi 4:6.

His daughter Enide had been only seventeen—the same age as Fatima Halabi, the Palestinian girl with the explosive device strapped to her waist. The detonation had killed five and wounded twelve at the Aquarius Discotheque in Jaffa.

His estranged wife, Olivia, had opposed having their daughter join him on this trip, because of the danger. Enide, however, had been eager to go with him. He told Olivia that he didn't think his daughter should have to live in fear.

He assured her he had taken all the necessary precautions—he had himself lost a cousin to terror bombing, after all, so of course he was cautious. Security for the scientific delegation was absolutely solid. When they took trips separate from the group, Avram was always careful to take his daughter only on private tours, on private tour buses, to private tourist sites.

He knew full well that life in Israel had a roulette-wheel quality to it—these days much more than when he had visited as a boy. In that long ago time, Israel had been a secular and socialist state, and the kibbutz had stood as a proud pillar of national security. Or so he and his parents had liked to think.

Israel these days wasn't so very different from what his native Argentina had once been, after all. His homeland was infamous worldwide for having once been the haven of Adolf Eichmann and many other Nazis after World War II. Few people realized that it had also been home to more than half of Latin American Jewry, and the first choice of Theodor Herzl, the founder of modern Zionism, when he was contemplating a place for the Jewish homeland.

Avram's family were secular Jews rather than observant, yet they, too, had known terror. When he was a boy, the Argentinian military dictatorship that ruled from 1976 to 1983 had caused more than thirty thousand people to disappear. A disproportionate number of them, over two thousand, had been Argentinian Jews. His parents, always quiet academics and even more quiet leftists, had found good reason to be more soft-spoken than usual during those years.

In the last decade of the twentieth century the Israeli embassy and the building housing AMIA—the Argentina Israelite Mutual Aid Association—had both been bombed, with much loss of life. Avram's firebrand cousin Enide, for whom his own daughter had been named, had died in the AMIA bombing, all her passion and rage for justice notwithstanding.

In the first decade of the new century, the Libertard Synagogue in Buenos Aires had been likewise leveled. Hezbollah and affiliated terror groups had taken credit for the destruction.

Nor had it been unheard of for Argentinian Jews to die in Israel. Many who told the story of the brave fifty-one-year-old security guard, Julio Magran, and the fifteen-year-old bystander, Gaston Perpinal—both Argentinian and both killed in the same suicide bombing attack—spoke of it as if it had happened yesterday, rather than years and years ago.

Madness, all madness.

He had responded to those events with the same revulsion he once felt at the news that American-born Israeli Baruch Goldstein had walked into a prayer hall and gunned down dozens of Palestinian Muslim Arabs while they were at worship.

Yet for all his awareness of the world's madness, he had not thought that the terror would ever strike so close. Certainly not when he and his daughter parted on the street, Avram going to a bookstore for coffee and a paper, Enide going to the Aquarius for an hour with Ilana, a girl she had befriended on the tour.

Not when he thought he heard thunder from a cloudless sky, ten minutes later. Not when he knew it was an explosion.

Not even when he found himself running in the direction his daughter had gone, just a few moments before.

Running. Through a strange silence punctuated by the sounds of men yelling in anger and urgency, of women wailing in despair. Growing closer. Until he came upon the rubble of what used to be the Aquarius, transformed now into a nightmare land of horribly bloodied and wounded young people staggering about, dazed and in shock, gasping in a cloud of slowly settling dust.

Not even stopping when he saw the look in Ilana's eyes—Ilana the still living, tended by yellow-vested emergency personnel. Ilana, who had suffered the passage of ball bearings through her skull and brain. Ilana, once bright and independent, who would henceforth be neither.

Then, in a street strewn with blasted brickwork and bloody rags and body parts, he came to a dead stop. Because he recognized the shoe—the low-heeled sandal still strapped, the golden anklet above it still clasped, around a foot and ankle and lower leg still perversely perfect and young and vital, until it ended abruptly in ragged slaughterhouse meat and bone and blood, just below what would have been the knee.

The rest of the girl's body was simply gone, vanished, blown to pieces too small to readily identify.

He tried not to think that this was his daughter. He tried to look about him for other pieces of this poor unfortunate. Perhaps he could be of help to the emergency services people, the forensics people, the mortuary people. He was a geochemist who specialized in meteoritics and impact geology. He knew something about strewnfields, about blast patterns. . . .

When at last he could not deny any longer the great and horrible proof that lay before him, he picked up the severed leg, tenderly, tentatively. Slowly he turned it so he could see the gold anklet more clearly. The clasp was in the shape of entwined dolphins, the square golden letters spelled out ENIDE.

Embracing the severed limb, cleaving to it as if to force it to become part of his own body, he howled into the evening gloom reddened by dust and twilight. The emergency people could not pry the limb from him—no words either, beyond "My daughter, my daughter!"

Only when the forensics people came did anyone manage to finally free the remains of his daughter from him—a wrenching parting, for by then the blood from the leg, smeared into his shirt, had dried enough that it was almost necessary to cut his shirt free to take the limb away.

The wrongness of it all would not let go of him, even now. Sometimes he felt pressing into his chest that physical remnant of his daughter, a phantom limb from a body not his own. He expected to find stigmatic blood on his clothing whenever he looked down. It was never there, but his clean shirts were a palimpsest in which he could still read the wound.

He looked at the picture of his daughter on the first inside page of the Book of Remembrances. Blondish-brown hair, blue eyes, a bit on the chubby side with the last lingering babyfat of childhood. This book could be opened, but not her flat picture. All the memories that might have been—of college and career, marriage and family—were shut from her, and from him too, now. Her future life was a Book of Remembrances that would never be unsealed.

Children ought to bury their fathers, not fathers their children. Yet he had buried his daughter—enough of her brought home to Argentina to meet the requirements of Jewish religious law, anyway—and he was still here, continents and oceans away from the place where his daughter had been taken away from him.

The loss could not be taken away by distance. At the service, grief had overwhelmed even whatever desire for recrimination Olivia might have felt. For that time, at least, they were not estranged from each other, but simply aggrieved together.

The death had not brought them together beyond that day, however. Their divorce had been finalized only last week.

Waiting for his visitor now, Avram felt as if his life had become a wasteland—barren, empty, and dry. Like the Atacama desert of Chile, where once he had led an expedition searching for meteorites. He searched for nothing now. He was lost and he did not feel like finding anything, or being found. Why bother? Nothing good would ever come of anything anymore.

His friends and colleagues said it was survivor guilt, but there was more to it than that. No matter how strongly the authorities insisted that the suicidal attack that killed his daughter was random, he could not escape the feeling that, somehow, he was responsible. That this was no ordinary act of terror. His friends told him his fears were not rational, yet—

His doorbell rang. It rang again. He did not want to answer it. The past lurked behind that door, and possibly the future.

The doorbell rang a third time.

"Avram! Avram, are you home? It's me. Luis. Luis Martin."

Avram was stunned to hear Luis call out in English like that, even giving his name. The shock of it jolted him to his feet, but as he walked to the door, he realized that "Luis Martin" was probably not his visitor's real name anyway.

Perhaps solving the mystery of the man's name might help to explain why Luis often preferred, as now, to speak in English, though Avram was pretty certain, from the accent, that his first language was Brazilian Portuguese.

Avram opened the door, muttering apologies, and the madness of the world walked in, wearing a pale panama hat, a summerweight linen suit of matching pallor, and a mustache preternaturally dark for a man of Luis's years.

"Any reluctance you might have toward seeing visitors, Avri, I perfectly understand. My condolences on the loss of your daughter Enide. I was very much saddened when I read of it."

"Thank you, Luis. Please, sit down, won't you?"

Martin took a chair and sat, while Avram sat down more slowly on a sofa.

"Your cousin's name was Enide, too, wasn't it? Last time, the first time I mean, it was another Enide."

Avram nodded, but said nothing.

"You were only in graduate school then."

"Yes," Avram said quietly. "That was when I became involved in the study of meteorites."

Martin nodded. He took two cigars out of his jacket pocket and glanced expectantly at his host.

"None for me, but thanks," Avram said. "Feel free, yourself."

Martin lit his cigar in a manner that managed to seem both offhanded and ritualistic at the same time.

"You've come a long way since those early studies. Done some solid scientific work in Chaco Province, and in Brazil," Martin said after a few puffs. "Around Serra Geral, wasn't it?"

"Yes."

"Traveling back and forth through Tri-Border, you've also done some very good work for us, as well. I may have something more you can do—something that will take you away from your grief."

Avram only half heard Martin's offer, for he had let the mention of his old work flood his head with memories. The subtropical forests of Formosa province and Chaco. The National Park in the Distrito Chaqueño Oriental, its center and south covered by forests of quebracho colorado. The savannas of the west, with their Caranday palm trees. The Panza de Cabra Lagoon in the southeast, with its rich aquatic flora and fauna, so different from the Campo del Cielo, the Field of Heaven, the Sky's Land—dry, scrubby, treeless, and almost rockless.

"Yes, that was Campo del Cielo," Avram told Martin. "In Chaco and Santiago del Estero. There was a major meteorite fall in that area about five thousand years ago. Thirteen big iron-nickel meteorites had already been discovered there, in the four hundred and twenty-five years since the Campo was first visited by Westerners."

"I recall hearing something about an American gem and mineral dealer, arrested while trying to haul a big rock out of there," Martin said.

"That was Robert Haag, in 1992. He had made a deal with a local man to purchase a thirty-seven-ton meteorite. The Chaco meteorite, largest that ever fell in our country, and the third biggest in the world at the time. Haag bought the meteorite, but then the authorities arrested him for trying to make off with a national treasure."

"You were there in relation to that, then?"

"In a way. I was trying to determine whether any of the rocks at Campo del Cielo matched the Spanish historical descriptions of the Meson de Fierro."

"Ah yes, the great 'Table of Iron.' Now I remember. You proved the match, right? But how was that connected with the Serra Geral?"

"There are many legends of fire from the sky, among the indigenous peoples who lived in Chaco and Santiago del Estero provinces—" Avram said.

"The people who named Campo del Cielo, you mean?"

"Yes." Even if he was not yet ready to hear Martin speak openly of it, he was indeed secretly relieved to be taken away from his grief, if only for a few moments. "Among peoples in the littoral regions, the myths tell of a great flood that happened at the same time as the fire from the sky. I was in Serra Geral looking for geological evidence of that flood. I suspect it was a tsunami related to other, larger meteorites that fell into the Atlantic, about the same time that the Campo del Cielo stones impacted inland."

"Fascinating, fascinating," Martin said encouragingly. "I never realized how amazing it was, what you were doing there. For me it mainly provided a wonderful cover story for your trips back and forth through the Triple Border area."

Avram nodded. In the past, Martin had suggested that he was connected somehow with both Israel's Mossad and America's CIA, though Avram had never been able to pin down the exact nature of those connections.

Over time, he had come to suspect Martin's services went to the highest bidder. His money had always spent well enough, at any rate, and Avram had no trouble understanding the interest of international intelligence agencies in the Tri-Border Free Zone between Argentina, Paraguay, and Brazil. Those same intelligence agencies not only spied in the Zone but also recruited there.

The Zone itself was a sort of criminal United Nations, the haunt of warlords, revolutionists, counterrevolutionists, violent fanatics, drug smugglers, terrorists, arms dealers, money launderers, forgers, fugitives, and organized crime figures from Russia, China, Japan, Nigeria, the Middle East—just about anyone from anywhere who might have reason to be allergic to the law.

Looking at him now, Avram wondered whether Luis Martin might himself have once been a denizen of the Zone. Hell, maybe he still was. Perhaps he had just developed too high a profile, just become too well known. Hence the need for Avram, as a lower profile set of eyes and ears, a simple geochemist making a few extra Argentinian pesos.

"Your reports have prevented more than one terror attack, you know. A very fitting monument for your cousin Enide, despite the secret nature of that memorial."

"Thank you, Luis. I hadn't thought of it that way."

"You should. It may in some way help you to deal better with your current grief. I came here today because I think you can help us create an even more fitting memorial for your daughter, her namesake. One that involves your long interest in meteorites, and our long interest in the future."

"What do you mean? Which meteorites? Where?"

"Lots of places," Martin said, arching an eyebrow at him. "Stones in Israel, for instance. In the Empty Quarter of the Arabian Peninsula. Even one in Mecca, I'm told."

Mecca? He knew of no meteorites located there. Unless . . .

The stories of al Hajar al-Aswad, the Black Stone of the Kaaba! No one had ever proved it was a meteorite, despite the stories. Ambitious scientists and unscrupulous meteorite hunters had popped up abundantly in that context before—especially in crazy thriller novels—but surely no one, in real life, would have the audacity to go after a holy relic at the center of the Islamic world's greatest shrine.

Or would they? The idea of piloting passenger jets into monumental buildings had once been only the stuff of crazy thrillers, too. . . .

Luis Martin was staring expectantly at him now. Under Martin's gaze, Avram Zaragosa felt a new sensation burning across his chest, exactly where he had clutched his daughter's dismembered limb.

The bomb builder, the recruiter, and the driver for the "martyr operation" that had killed his daughter had all been arrested. Halabi herself had opted for martyrdom, an act of revenge for the death of her brother, Ahmed. There was no one left to blame for Enide's death, at least at the operational level, yet the madness continued.

In that moment, under Luis Martin's gaze, Avram's mind went red with the fire of a great hate, for all the billion-plus adherents to a worldwide religion. He was determined to make them all pay for what one of them had done to his daughter.

"Well?" Luis Martin said. "Are you interested?"

"Yes," Avram said. His eyes remained fixed on his visitor. "I'm very interested."

Martin smiled and stood.

He got to his feet, too. As they firmly shook hands, Avram Zaragosa heard the madness of the world speak his name.

SOUVENIRS OF A MADWOMAN

>>>>>>>

"It won't be for long," Susan Yamada said, glancing from Michael Miskulin to his uncle Paul, then to the Mawari children.

Dressed now in contemporary clothes to make them less conspicuous, they were also easier to tell apart. Three girls and a boy, they sat cross-legged in a corner of the room, preternaturally quiet and alert. As always.

"We brought them here because we need to continue keeping them out of the public eye," Susan continued. "Your compound here seems private, and Michael said you used to be a journalist, before you went into the sciences. We figured you might know how to fend off your former colleagues in the media if any of them came snooping around."

She glanced at Michael, who nodded in agreement and then stared hard at the man who stood before them. Uncle Paul had once sported a full beard and full head of hair, both sandy colored, but he had become increasingly bald, and his remaining hair and beard were abundantly flecked with white. Despite the years, however, his uncle still retained the character he remembered from childhood—impish, gnome-like, impulsive as always. At the moment, though, his expression was serious.

"I'll be glad to take care of them," Paul Larkin said somberly. "I bear some considerable responsibility for what happened to their people, after all."

"Oh, come on, Uncle Paul!" Michael protested. "Jacinta's been dead for years. The killing couldn't have happened very long before we got there. The massacre has nothing to do with you, or with her."

"I'm afraid I can't entirely agree with you," Larkin said, looking up from the glass of neat scotch he held in his hand, then glancing out the floor-to-ceiling windows that faced toward Lake Tahoe and the snow-capped mountains beyond. "This isn't about what 'might have been,' any longer. This is about what is. You see, when I funded your little expedition to Jacinta's tepui, there were things I didn't tell you. Things I was afraid might prejudice you."

"What do you mean?" Susan asked, sliding forward on the chair of plush leather into which she'd sunk. "What sort of 'things'?"

"Rather difficult to explain . . . here," he said. "I'll show you. Follow me." He turned toward the door.

Michael and Susan glanced at each other, doubt mirrored in their expressions, then they stood up and walked after him. The children, in their silent, quirkily observant fashion, each stood in turn, then followed the adults into the adjoining hall. All of them heard Larkin rummaging in the den down the hall before they reached him and saw what he was up to.

Once inside the room, the children sat cross-legged on the floor again.

"Maybe you could help me?" he said, pulling boxes out of a closet and handing them to the two adults. "What I'm looking for is a tiny white envelope, about the size of a theater ticket, sealed in clear plastic. Look through these, would you?"

Michael and Susan did so. Most of what they looked through was typical family memorabilia—a large crop of photos featuring Jacinta at various ages, news articles on her accomplishments going all the way back to science fair and high school chess team victories. There was a copy of her birth certificate, with the birth date—the sixth of June 1961—circled and accompanied by the scrawled annotation "Jung's death date."

"Jacinta made that note," Larkin said, glancing at the item in Michael's hand. "That particular synchronicity was a big deal to her. Claimed it had something to do with transmigration of the soul."

Michael and Susan nodded absently, then continued the search for the tiny white envelope sealed in plastic. Scattered among the memorabilia were even more esoteric materials. Michael saw clippings, notes, and Web printouts.

"Lots of information on quartz here," Michael commented.

"Yes. Jacinta thought the tepui people had an obsession with the stuff. Particularly important to their mythology," she said.

Michael nodded, but said nothing more as he continued to look through the yellowing papers. There were articles relating to the nature of the mineral, a silica fused from silicon and oxygen, harder than steel, fashioned into weapons for the past fifty thousand years, most prominently spearpoints and arrowheads.

Curious. Quartz was beloved by so many different people over the ages, from ancient Sumerians and Egyptians, Bedouins and crusaders and Oriental craftsmen, to electronics manufacturers, shamans and witches, alchemists and spiritualists.

"That's strange. There's nothing on shocked quartz from meteoritic impacts," Michael said. "Nothing on tektites or impactites. Nothing on coesite, or stishovite, or tridymite."

"Hmm! I'd only ever heard of shocked quartz in the context of 'blast glass,' " Paul said. "From nuclear detonations in the desert."

"It's a product of meteoritic impact, too," Michael said. "Several other high-pressure or high-temperature quartz polymorphs are connected to meteorites as well."

"I guess I missed that connection all these years."

Frowning, Susan glanced away.

"I thought we were looking for a little white envelope," she said, impatient.

Michael nodded. He knew that she still somehow blamed him for the murderous mess they'd stumbled on at the tepui. It had not so much caused a space to open up between them as broadened a gap already there—unfortunately.

His uncle cleared his throat.

"Myself, I never used to put much credence in the myths Jacinta was so keen on," he said. "Especially their genesis story. Just too implausible—that's what I thought at the time, anyway."

"Yet you've got lots of documents here that support her," Susan said, reading from clippings and other hard copies. "All this stuff on coelacanths, and cycads. Scorpions. Dragonflies. Ginkgos. Tuataras. Nautiloids, and Lingula clams. Relic populations of Homo erectus in Java and other Indonesian islands, even the indigenous Tasmanians and their supposed Mousterian Neanderthal toolkit."

Larkin nodded.

"Jacinta was fascinated by living fossils. I developed an interest, afterward. She claimed the people she found on that tepui might be an example of an Elvis taxa, or a Lazarus taxa."

"What?" Michael exclaimed.

"Species thought to be long extinct, but which suddenly reappear in the fossil record," Susan said, before Paul could reply. "That's legitimate science. This Mousterian Tasmanian theory, though, that sounds like the loonier fringes of cryptozoology, to me."

"Ah, here it is," Larkin announced triumphantly, holding up before him something slim and white inside a small plastic jacket. He broke the seal on the plastic, removed the ticket-size envelope, opened it, and removed a carefully folded sheet of age-brittled white paper, which he presented gingerly to Michael and Susan. Michael saw only a dusty blue image, like the photonegative of a brain.

"A spore print?" Susan asked.

"Exactly. I found two of those odd little envelopes buried deep in my backpack, after I emptied the pack on returning home from the foot of Caracamuni tepui. I'd just put a stop to her crazy shenanigans and foolhardy spending there. I've never understood her motivation, really."

"For the spending?" Michael asked, "Or for planting the spore print."

"Neither one, actually. When I confronted Jacinta, she denied having planted them there. She got very emotional, though, when I told her I would destroy them."

"Why did you want to do that?" asked Susan. "Destroy them, I mean?"

"I figured the fungus grown from such spore prints would be hallucinogenic," Paul said. "I know it may seem inexplicably severe, but I blamed Jacinta's descent into madness on such jungle hallucinogens— even if I didn't much believe her 'tepui people' stories."

He gave a long sigh.

"I didn't destroy them, as you can see. After she died, I couldn't bring myself to get rid of them, any more than I could destroy anything of Jacinta's stuff. All these years, and I've never been able to bring myself to set fire to it, or make public that spore print's existence, either."

"Why not?"

Paul paused thoughtfully before he answered.

"Jacinta didn't have all her mental access covers bolted down—that was more than obvious. Not just the Jung transmigration and odd gender stuff, either. She actually believed that a schizophrenic white girl and some forty or fifty tribal people were going to fly a mountain into the sky and become humanity's first ambassadors to the stars."

Paul took the spore print back from Susan, then continued.

"I've never been able to determine if *my* particular madness was to have believed her too little, or believed her too much."

"You're among the first to see those spore prints," Paul revealed as they settled back into the comfort of the living room. The children had taken up their places on the floor again.

"But not *the* first?" Michael asked.

"No, I'm afraid not."

"You didn't try to grow the spores out yourself?" Susan asked. "Or hire someone else to do it?"

"Not until recently," Paul Larkin said. "You mentioned my career change, from journalism into the sciences. I'm still something of an independent researcher. Money funds both independence and research equally well, I suppose.

"About two months ago I got in touch with Phil Damon, the professor who headed my dissertation committee when I was still in school. I was trained in the biological sciences, you know—even if that wasn't where I made my money. Damon's emeritus now, but he agreed to examine the spore print and have some of it plated out and grown by a colleague. I provided him with enough cash to ensure that it would be done properly—and quietly."

Larkin swirled the scotch in his glass, then took a sip.

"I gave this spore print envelope's twin to Damon and a mycologist colleague, to scrape spores from it to their hearts' content. I don't know that much about the specifics of what they were doing—it was all done in a chamber under a ventilation hood."

"Probably shook the spores onto a series of petri dishes filled with various growth media," Susan said, nodding. "Do you know what they plated out?"

"*Something* must have grown. I'm sure of that, now. Three weeks into his testing of the fungus, Damon called. I wasn't all too happy with what he had to say. He'd set up a meeting for me with a woman named Athena Griego, a venture capital agent. Despite my misgivings, I met with her. She said she represented a number of investors and pharamaceutical firms that might be interested in further research on the fungus. She struck me as a wheeler-dealer, an operator, you know?

A bit on the shady side. Eventually, though, she did manage to set up a meeting with Doctor Vang, of ParaLogics."

Michael whistled softly.

"Vang's a heavy hitter."

"Yes. Lots of money, and even more clout."

"He's mostly interested in cognitive enhancement drugs from what I've heard," Susan said. "That's why he's funded some very interesting ethnobotanical research, too."

"I gather he's had some setbacks recently," Michael said. Paul shrugged noncommittally.

"Maybe so, but he's still playing some sort of very high-level game, as near as I can tell. He and his people wanted the rights to experiment with the fungus. They paid handsomely for them. That money's come in very handy, lately. Your expedition was not without expense. . . ."

"But how much did you *tell* them in exchange for the cash, Uncle Paul?"

Paul shifted uncomfortably in his comfy chair.

"They wanted to know everything they could learn about its origins. I tried to keep a tight lid on it, only giving them enough to string them along, but after what you've told me about the tepui massacre, I'm afraid I may have told too much."

"Why were you even talking to them at all?" Michael asked. "And where do you think you slipped up?"

He sighed deeply.

"A number of organizations granted or loaned money and equipment to Jacinta, all those years ago. I returned as much of it as I could, but the folks who hadn't gotten paid came after me and your grandparents for a while, Michael. After her suicide, the suppliers and creditors finally wrote off both Jacinta and her failed expedition, under something called a forgiveness clause.

"She left a paper trail, though. Vang's people must have done some nosing around, and followed it through."

"Wait a minute," Susan said. "Are you actually suggesting that a respected businessman like Vang was behind the massacre of those poor people in the tepui?"

"Directly responsible? No. Not likely. He's too clever for that. I wouldn't doubt, though, that he has connections to corporate moneymen who have their own connections. Those connections might lead to military and intelligence contractors—what used to be called mercenaries and spies. Maybe even connections into the military itself."

"Who the hell would do all this just to get at a meteorite?" Susan asked, shaking her head.

"I don't know that someone like Vang is the answer to that question," Paul replied, "but even if he is, that still doesn't tell us *why* he'd take such drastic steps. What might someone expect to find that would lead them to countenance wholesale murder?"

"That's the more important question," Michael said. "Not who, but why. Why would someone do all this just to get at a meteorite?"

"You'll have to find that out for yourselves," Larkin said, gulping down the last of his scotch. "My job now is to look after these children. The only survivors."

"It's not like we're asking you to do it forever," Susan said.

Michael winced, wondering if he really heard the irritability and defensiveness he thought he heard in her voice. Children and marital commitment had been the no-man's-land between them for many months. He wondered if the situation with the Mawari children, the meteorite, and the massacre at the tepui were also all overlaid on that now, too.

"True, but as long as I have them we might as well make the best of all the assets I have on hand," Larkin said, putting an ancient cassette tape into a player and turning it on.

At the sound of the chantsong coming from the player, the hyper-alert children, up to that point silent as stones but for a certain nervous energy, began to whisper in monotones that still managed to sound excited. Soon the song had so enraptured the Mawari children that they were swaying and pounding the floor in time to it.

"What's that sound? That . . . song?" Michael asked, raising his voice over the noise of the children.

"It's a recording Jacinta made," Paul said, seeming strangely jubilant at the children's reactions. "I gather from her notes that it's a sort of 'nursery rhyme meets cosmogony.' Her translation is here somewhere."

Larkin scanned through several more pages from one of his sister's notebooks, and pulled loose a page for them to read. Mike and Susan read the words of the cosmogonic nursery rhyme's translation:

> In the cave of night, the seed of light
> bursts open in the dark.
> Out of the dark it grows the stars.
> The seeds which stars plant grow into worlds.

The seeds which worlds plant grow into life.
The seeds which life plants grow into minds.
The seeds which minds plant grow into songs
Of the All One who sleeps on the bed of forever
Whose mind is the cave of night
Whose dream is the seed of light.

"What's it supposed to mean?" Michael asked, studying the translation.

"I'm not certain," Paul replied, glancing at the children. He turned off the recording and the children grew quiescent again, almost as if he'd flipped a switch. "Jacinta claimed it was a children's version of their great myth, the 'seven ages of the Universe.' "

"Since the Mawari were—are—mushroom totemists, these 'seeds' in caves might more accurately be translated as 'spores,' " Susan suggested. "And the 'growing into' stuff sounds less appropriate to seeds and more appropriate to what mushroom spawn, the 'bed' of mycelium, does."

"Mushroom totemists, yes. Jacinta claimed the ghost people had a phrase in their language. She translates in her notes as 'A day is a mushroom on the spawn of time.' "

"Pretty complex ideas, even in that 'nursery rhyme,' " Michael said. "Parts of it could pass for physics, or biology, or theology."

"Or all of the above," Susan said, nodding.

"They seem to have been pretty complex people," Paul said, looking for and then finding a passage in another of his sister's notebooks. "Unusually long-lived, but also unusually low birth rates and fertility."

"Be fruitful—don't multiply," Michael said with a smirk.

"A good approach, if you're living on an isolated tepui," Susan said. "Sustainable in a marginal environment. But Michael tends to forget that our whole world isn't necessarily a marginal environment. And I wish you wouldn't keep speaking of these people in the past tense. They aren't extinct—at least not yet."

"Sorry," Paul said. Covering his embarrassment, he pointed to another passage. They both leaned in to see.

"Jacinta says here that, among the Mawari, language is for children, for only children have need of it. Speech as a mode of communication begins to sharply decline among them with the onset of puberty."

"These are already pretty uncommunicative," Michael said.

"What did you expect? They don't know our language!" Susan

said, frustrated. "And who knows what sort of shock they might still be in, given what they've seen?"

"I know, but even their body language and focus are different. Not much eye-to-eye gaze, or facial expression. Clumsy bodies, narrowly focused brains. Kind of like mild Asperger's or high-function autistics."

"There you go again, getting all clinical, Doctor. Are you talking about them, or *us*? Jeez, I know you're not big on kids, but even you must have been one once."

Michael glanced away, turning his gaze toward the floor. Them, or us? He could just as easily ask her the same question, though in the different context of children and marriage. He opposed the former, and she opposed the latter. He decided not to go there.

"I admit they're preteens from a completely different culture. Our armchair diagnoses—"

"Oh, for heaven's sake. They're not just some kind of living-fossil specimens. They're human beings who have seen every person they've ever known brutally murdered! We should be jumping for joy to see any hint that they still have *any* normal emotions, after what they've had to live through."

Paul cleared his throat and smiled awkwardly.

"I was very happy to see their response to the chant," he said. "Maybe, though, their lack of affect—and how we might deal with that—maybe it isn't only a response to trauma."

"No? What, then?"

"Maybe it also has something to do with what Jacinta's notes call 'full myconeural symbiosis.' She says adolescent and adult ghost people possessed that."

Susan shook her head.

"What I saw on that tepui didn't look like symbiosis to me. Those mushrooms sticking out of their bodies . . . it was horrific."

"She says in her notes that the fruiting bodies, the 'mushrooms,' only appear after the person dies. The 'sacred fungus' is a myconeural symbiont. They claimed it lit up 'a star inside the head' that allowed them to communicate mind to mind."

"I can see why you thought your sister was crazy," Susan said. "Telepathy is way out there in mystic woo-woo land."

"I don't know if I reject it as flatly as you do anymore," Paul said, "but she does make some rather extraordinary claims in her notes and comments, it's true."

"Such as?"

"She claimed the tepui people 'beamed' her. Planted thoughts in her head that didn't quite feel like her own. Said it was like someone else dreaming inside your head. You two haven't experienced anything like that while you've been in the presence of these children, have you?"

An awkward and uneasy glance passed between Michael and Susan again. Something about what Paul was saying seemed somehow familiar, though Michael couldn't quite put his finger on it. Then he remembered the dream of rain people in the stony maze, and later the dream of blood and death and fire underground, in the cave inside the tepui. Remembered waking up drenched in sweat—and that sweat turning chill when he learned Susan had just had the same dream.

He half turned toward Susan.

"No," Susan said firmly. "The ethnobotanical literature is full of shamans who claim to have such powers. That may be where Jacinta got the idea. But almost all those shamans were intoxicated or otherwise 'altered' at the time of their telepathic experiences, so their testimony is highly subjective at best."

"I thought the descriptions of her tepui experiences were rooted mainly in her own paranoid delusions, too," Paul said. "Voices in the head, and all that. I studied these notebooks, thinking they were the diary of her descent into the depths of schizophrenia, nothing more. I'm not so sure any longer."

"Why not?" Susan asked, perhaps a bit more pointedly than even she intended.

"Jacinta's most bizarre claims were linked to the existence of these ghost people and what they held to be true," Paul said, thinking it through as he passed a notebook to Michael. "But you see, they did—do—exist, after all. So maybe even something as strange as this 'mindtime' thing she writes about here—what she calls 'forays into sideways'—maybe there's some truth to it. Or maybe I want it to be true, at least."

" 'Mindtime'?"

"Seeing or living along alternate timelines, it sounds like," Michael said, looking over the notes. "All the 'what if' stuff of parallel universes."

"I'm sure almost every person who's lost a loved one wishes there were some place, some other universe where things turned out differently," Susan suggested.

"Yes," Paul said. "Maybe that's all it is. But I still hope it might be more than that."

Michael looked down. There had been no particularly upbraiding or admonishing tone to anything his uncle or even Susan had just said, yet he couldn't help thinking about the Mawari kids' lost loved ones and feeling obscurely guilty. Jacinta was his aunt and Paul his uncle. He felt a certain family responsibility for what had happened, as much as he would have preferred not to.

"Michael," Paul said, struck by a thought, "do you know of any precedent for mushrooms coming in from outer space?"

"Just listen to yourselves . . ." Susan interjected, smiling grimly.

"No confirmable precedent, no," Michael said, considering it seriously despite Susan's comment. "According to some researchers, though, Earth was overrun by fungus around the times of both the Permian-Triassic mass extinction, two hundred and fifty million years ago, and the Cretaceous-Tertiary extinction, sixty-five million years ago."

"How did they determine that?" Susan asked.

"The increased presence of alpha-aminoisobutyric acid, or Aib—an amino acid not found in the proteins of modern organisms, but found in a number of fungi and carbonaceous meteorites."

Paul Larkin laughed.

"Professor Yamada, there's more in heaven and earth than is dreamt of in your ethnobotanists' philosophies. Or even their hallucinations."

"Maybe," Susan said, sounding very much unconvinced. "But you are *sure* these kids will be safe here? I mean, I saw gates and cameras and fences on the way in, but no guards. I hope you're not relying on some sort of 'metaphysical' protection scheme for them."

"No need for that," Paul said with a smile. "I keep a security team on retainer, but that's mainly for when I leave the grounds. I have no need for lots of guards here."

"And that's because . . . ?"

"The gentleman who originally built this little lakeside estate was connected to the Vegas mob, so he had good reasons for being security-conscious. One of its later owners was a Bay Area electronic-surveillance mogul who was obsessed with the *Godfather* films and quirky enough to make Howard Hughes look like a regular Joe. Yet another was a rather corrupt Chinese diplomat with an extensive art and movie-poster collection. All of them added their bits to the security system. That history was a big selling point for me when I bought it."

"Really? Why?"

"Oh, chalk it up to a love of privacy. Or a family history of paranoia—whichever you prefer. But the fact is that this old place has security protections at all sorts of levels, from brick and mortar to motion sensor software. Any would-be trespassers or other prying eyes have a surprise or two in store for them. Those children will be safe here. Don't worry about that."

Larkin began putting away the notebooks and hardcopy collections.

"If there's even a remote chance I had something to do with the atrocity on that tepui, then I have a debt to pay, so let me pay it. And along those lines, if you two don't object, I'd like to keep you on my payroll to find out why those people were massacred—for what, if not for the meteorite, and by whom, if not by someone connected to Vang. I still think you should start with him.

"At least I can use some of that dirty money to find the responsible party—or parties," he continued. "The holidays are almost upon us. Indulge an old man. Consider my bankrolling your investigation, and my taking care of these children, as my early Christmas presents to you, and to them."

He stopped gathering and shuffling papers. Abruptly.

"You did bring a sample of the meteorite back with you?"

Michael and Susan looked at one another. Susan remembered Michael standing surrounded by the bodies of the dead tepuians as he carved off a slab of their sacred stone with a small diamond-impregnated saw blade. Had she not also believed so strongly in the importance of obtaining a scientific specimen, she might have seen what Michael was doing as an act of desecration.

"Yes, I did," Michael said. "It's bagged. I haven't begun working on it yet."

COLUMBUS OF THE BIOCOSMOS

Darla Pittman pushed her chair back and stared at the screen. She had been using every technique she knew of to make the tepui meteorite divulge its secrets. She'd called in a lot of favors to make it happen. She'd had no choice—this anomalous skystone wasn't quite fitting into any of the established categories.

She'd carefully run dozens of tests on her own, and had even more carefully farmed out to selected colleagues a large number of samples for an even larger number of tests. Variously sized pieces of the meteorite had been physically polished and etched, heated to 900° C, to 1000°, to 1200°, proton irradiated, acid isolated, neutron activated, ionized, demagnetized, hysteresized, microprobed, spectroscoped, epifluoresced, and chromatographed until the rock should have retained no mystery whatsoever.

The work was finally beginning to yield useful data. The meteorite's absorption of cosmic rays while in space had produced a wide variety of nuclides both stable and very slightly radioactive. Of course, 'highly radioactive meteorites' were a pop-astronomy urban legend—never actually discovered anywhere in reality, despite being so necessary to the creation of mutants in comic books, zombies in B-movies, and terrorist dirty bombs in adventure potboilers.

The actual radioactivity of meteorites was so slight that both the sample and the detector had to be put inside a thick lead container to shield them from terrestrial background radiation, including the uranium and potassium in the cinder blocks and cement of the laboratory's walls. From such faint cosmogenic radionuclide counts, however, Darla had a good sense of the meteorite's crystallization age, its terrestrial history, and the "flight time" between its initial formation and when it crashed to Earth.

Yet despite all she had learned, the rock still retained a not inconsiderable amount of mystery. Interrogating the stone with all those tests had not been cheap, and they'd taken time—time enough to make Retticker check up on her work and question both time and expense.

"Why so many tests?" he asked, bluntly—the same bluntness, charismatic confidence, and laserlike focus on his mission that she had found alternately charming and exasperating.

"Because the facts are always subject to interpretation," she explained, realizing she was walking a fine line. "There are skystones with no chondrules that are nonetheless classified as chondrites, and there are stones with chondrules that are nonetheless classified as achondrites, on the basis of more subtle mineralogical and chemical descriptors. The classification system is not so cut-and-dried as we might like it to be, especially in this case."

"But what's all that supposed to mean to the project, Doctor?"

"It means we've learned a lot and we're on track to learn a good deal more. We've just got some puzzle pieces that don't fit as of yet. But it's precisely in those places where the puzzle pieces don't fit that we're most likely to find something truly new—and perhaps militarily useful."

After that, Retticker backed off and left her to her work. Darla was still unable to fully classify the tepui stone, but she had become intimately familiar with it. She knew much more about the retention composition of its noble gases, the cosmic enrichments of its light rare earths, its volatiles and its refractories, its shock features of twinning, mosaicism, and impact melt pocketing. All of that told her not only that the puzzle pieces were more oddly shaped than she thought, but also that the puzzle itself was bigger and more important than she'd imagined.

Looking at the soft sky-blue fluorescence of a meteorite sample now, her mind drifted for a moment. She thought of another intimacy, on the blue-ice fields of Antarctica.

The South Polar continent had been a treasure trove for meteorite recovery since the 1970s. Meteors didn't become meteorites any more often over Antarctica than over any other continent, but as Antarctica's continental ice sheet moved slowly from the high plateau near the continent's center, downward and outward toward the coastline, it functioned as a long-distance, slow-motion conveyor belt, gathering meteorites over thousands of years and thousands of square miles.

Parts of the ice sheet came to a premature stop at surfaces where the ice backed up against a barrier, usually a ridge of mountains. Unable to continue its journey, the ice in these cul-de-sacs eroded faster than the meteorites the ice carried, thus depositing concentrations of them in meteorite-stranding surfaces. These surfaces were usually found on and near fields of blue ice swept mostly clear of snow by persistent strong winds.

Accelerated climate change had removed vast tonnages of ice, leaving still more meteorites exposed, so that nearly as many meteorites had been discovered in Antarctica in the last forty years as in the entire history of humanity up to that point—one of the few silver linings to the dark cloud of global warming.

The expedition she and Michael Miskulin had been part of had snowmobiled and powersledged for seven hours straight, over innumerable windsculpted ice dunes called sastrugi. When the expedition at last reached the particular blue-ice field it had been headed for, Darla and Michael were almost too tired to begin the search for meteorites.

Almost. Between the two of them, they still managed to find and positively identify no fewer than seven meteorites before they quit for the night—"night" being something of a fiction, given the twenty-four-hour sunshine of the Antarctic summer.

They retired together to a hexagonal army tent with opaque walls.

The blackout walls assured that inside the tent it was quite dark. Because the square groundcloth didn't quite fit the hexagonal tent, there were areas of bare snow on two sides. By lantern light, amid the real snow and the artificial dark, they ate a dinner punctuated with too many cups of reconstituted wine.

"Shooting stars are the trickster gods in an orderly heaven!" Michael had said, regaling her tipsily with some of his wilder ideas. "They're the Coyotes, the Anansis, the Lokis—the sublunary Dionysuses to the sidereal Apollos!"

They had laughed together at his trying to say "sublunary Dionysuses." After dinner, the two of them began to snuggle, but the lantern light was too bright for romantic ambience.

"Let me try something," Michael said, taking up some hot water left over from dinner. "Okay. Turn off the lantern."

Darla heard something sizzling and melting, and abruptly a beam of soft blue light shot upward, dimly illuminating the tent's interior.

"It's beautiful," Darla said. "What is it?"

"A physicist I met back at McMurdo calls it the Funaki-Yanai effect—after the people who discovered it, I guess."

"How does it work?"

"Look into it."

"Research it, you mean?"

"No, look into the melt-hole, in the snow. Over here."

Darla did so. As her eyes adjusted she saw that the snow was only about a foot deep, but it stood over ice many yards thick. The hot water had melted away the snow, exposing the surface of the ice below.

"The sunlight outside shines into the ice, which is really clear here in Antarctica," Michael said.

"But sunlight's got all the colors of the rainbow in it," Darla said, puzzled.

"The long path through the ice scatters and absorbs the other colors of the spectrum, leaving the light mostly blue by the time it comes out here."

The two of them set about heating more water and making more small, blue spotlights by melting holes in the snow. After half a dozen holes, they relaxed to enjoy the soft glow. One thing led to another, and they made love in a pavilion of soft blue light.

Darla snapped back to the present when Barry, her prematurely bald and excessively bearded postdoc, switched on the light. The blue glow on the meteorite faded away.

"Sorry to interrupt, Professor, but I think you need to see this." He gestured excitedly with the printout materials he held in his hand.

"If it's so important," Darla said, frowning slightly, "then let's take a look in my office."

"I just printed out these reports we got back from Lonsdale's and Chen's labs, via e-mail," Barry said, pointing out graphs and tables as he handed the documents to Darla. "The numbers of deuterium-enriched amino acids are the highest I've ever heard of. Over three hundred different species of amino acids—sixty more than even the Murchison meteorite! Hell, life on earth only uses twenty as fundamental building blocks!"

"I'm familiar with the established numbers," she said, preoccupied with the pages of readouts. Among the examinations of chirality and racemization and enantiomeric excesses, however, she found something Barry had apparently overlooked: two DNA-sequencing autoradiographs, accompanied by crystallographic images.

The gaps in the autoradiographs were puzzling. One suggested a six-nucleotide sequence, and the other a nine-nucleotide sequence. The restriction fragment length data were also strange, seemingly not the triplets of most gene units but rather sextuplets and nonuplets.

The crystallographic images appeared to confirm all of it.

No naturally occurring cell on earth made use of such sequences. Some synthetic biologists and artificial-life researchers had created such sequences, mainly for the sake of creating genetic molecules more stable and less prone to mutation than ordinary DNA. This had allowed them to reprogram cells to function as parts of the synbios' prototype "living machines"—when such prototypes managed to function at all.

There was just no record of the sort of sequences she was looking at, at least not anywhere on earth. Perhaps the images were artifacts, errors introduced in the process of making the autoradiographs. Maybe the restriction length figures were wrong, too.

Or maybe the general and his people had purposely contaminated the meteorite with synbiological molecules, to test her.

Turning to Chen's epifluorescence microscopy results, however, she got another surprise. Images of spheres, cylinders, rods, only fifty to a hundred nanometers on their longest axes. Chen's notes suggested they might be inverted micelles of organic material containing meteoritic components, or silica nanoparticles with organic components, but to Darla they looked like something else.

They looked like life.

Like nanobacterial or nanoarchaean spores, but also like tiny nonspore-forming gram positive bacteria. Microfossils? Or viable even now? And their size: so tiny!

Her heart beat faster. If the general and his people were testing her, they had gone to an awful lot of trouble. But that was precisely what claims of something extraterrestrial yet alive on a meteorite usually turned out to be: a lot of trouble. And the stuff of tabloids, pulp magazines, weird TV. Of H. P. Lovecraft's "The Colour Out of Space" and John W. Campbell's "Who Goes There?" Of *The Outer Limits* and *The Twilight Zone* and *The X-Files*.

Proof that we are not alone. That there is other life out there. So many people wanted to believe in that. Wanted it so much that it, too, often became a matter of faith rather than science. Still others felt just as passionately the need to debunk any and all such evidence of life beyond Earth.

She did not want this tepui stone to end up like the Tunisian Tatahouine stone, or the Australian Murchison stone, or the French Orgueil stone—each a lightning rod for scientific debate and disagreement that generated far more heat than light. Most of all, she did not want it to turn out like the Antarctic ALH84001 Mars stone, with learned NASA panelists endlessly and inconclusively arguing about microfossils versus terrestrial contamination and experimental artifacts.

Finding supposed microfossils would never settle such controversies. The only thing that would shut up all the debate would be to find something in the meteorites still capable of cell division. Grow 'em, scope 'em, and genome 'em!

But it was very difficult to create culture media to grow something truly unknown. It would be a shot in the dark, the medium as likely to kill the sample as grow it. As far as genoming nanoscale entities, well, if they were truly alien, she couldn't be sure even basic procedures like ribosomal RNA or DNA sequencing would actually work.

Up until now, all claims of extraterrestrial life had proven to be red herrings. Bacteria that had been recovered by astronauts on the moon had turned out to be Earth bacteria that had hitched a ride on a robotic lander. Yet those bacteria had survived on the moon for more than two years. *Deinococcus radiodurans* and *Micrococcus radiophilus* bacteria had been found living in the high atmosphere at the edge of space and growing in the hard-radiation environments of nuclear reactor cooling water.

Was the idea of something otherworldly and alive on meteorites just an old dream, or a far older memory? Long before Columbus "discovered" the New World, there had been mariners' tales from Norway to China telling of an undiscovered country beyond the sea. So, too, Darla felt sure, there had to be some truth behind all the old stories of sky-stones changing the fates of human beings.

Darla would give anything to know the truth of it. To be the Columbus of the biocosmos. To prove that "Life is endemic to Earth alone" and "The Earth is flat" belonged in the same dustbin of history!

And if she would give anything to know, she was sure the people she worked for—and others—would probably do anything to exploit such findings, if they could. Opening up a new world might also mean opening up a new world of problems.

Barry, however, was still rattling on about the amino acids.

"We should contact Miskulin with these results! We may have smoking-gun proof of exogenous delivery of genetic material here! The seeding of Earth, just like he's been arguing for years! We need to present at least our preliminary results at the big exobio conference in February—"

"We'll do nothing of the kind," Darla said, snatching the documents from Barry's hands. "At least not yet."

Miskulin, indeed! Embarrassing to think Barry should bring up his name, after interrupting her reminiscences of their time together. A relationship that would never have worked out, anyway. Not really her type, especially in the long days since they became competitors. If anyone would be eager to snatch the title of the new Columbus from her, it would be Michael Miskulin.

"But we're already presenting a paper at the conference! We'll be there anyway—"

"No buts. This meteorite came from a military source, for a military project. If all this pans out, do you want to be responsible for terrorists running around making some new kind of bioweapon based on what we've found? No. This has to be reported to—and cleared by—General Retticker and his people first."

Barry Levitch subsided, but she could tell he wasn't happy. So be it. She had more important things to worry about.

BRAIN STATES

Retticker looked at the back of Doctor Jeremy Michelson's head and its red halo of hair as Michelson led him down the chrome-and-white hallway of the Fort Mead Telemorphy Unit. Michelson, a biophysicist with NSA's W Group (Global Issues and Weapons Systems, in the Directorate of Technology and Systems), was on loan to the Combat Personnel Enhancement Program.

To Retticker, the owlishness of Michelson's looks—already suggested by the biophysicist's beaked nose and high forehead under his thinning, feathery red hair—was further exaggerated by his round oversized AR glasses and throat-mike combo, which he insisted on calling "ARGUS blinks." The fact that Michelson also compensated for his gawky height by stooping and bobbing his head slightly forward as he walked only made him look the Junior Birdman part all the more. Retticker, had had time to get used to the man's odd looks and ways when they had worked together during the Kwok-Cho episode, but his eccentricities still caught the general off-guard from time to time.

"It's peculiarly appropriate the Telemorphy Unit should be here at Fort Mead," Michelson said. "The army once housed its remote viewing program here, you know."

"No, I didn't know that," Retticker said, suspecting Michelson had programmed his blinks with Fort Mead's history and background and was now reading that material from his augments.

"Back during the cold war," Michelson said with a nod. "People who worked here went on to work with all the psi-spy stuff, at one time or another. Mental espionage. Clairvoyance, clairsentience. Precognition, postcognition. ESP, telepathy. Out-of-body and near-death experience—'oobies and endies,' as the researchers used to call them. Psychokinesis, micro-PK, all types of spooky action-at-a-distance."

Michelson opened a lab door and they walked inside.

"Of course, these days the work is much less focused on pseudoscience than on subtle science," Michelson continued.

"I see," said Retticker. "Wasn't it Hawking who said progress in science consists in replacing a theory that is wrong with one that is more subtly wrong?"

Michelson's face flushed pink.

"Yes, but a theory that's more subtly wrong is also more subtly right. What we're doing in these rooms is solid science—traceable all the way back to the work of Miguel Nicolelis and his colleagues at Duke University Medical Center."

"Perhaps," Retticker said drily, "but today I'm here to see your most *recent* work."

"Gladly. If you'll follow me . . ."

They entered a small room, about the size of a theater control booth. Through the large glass window at the front of the booth they could see a soldier seated comfortably in a streamlined recliner chair, on a slightly raised floor resembling a small stage or dais. The man was so still that Retticker thought he might be meditating or sleeping behind the gogglelike Bono shades he was wearing.

"Let's take a look at what he's looking at," Michelson said.

A screen showing a honeycomb of smaller screens lit up before them. From time to time one or another cell of the honeycomb would enlarge to cover most of the screen. Often this zoom-in would be followed by explosions of cars or buildings, or of human beings feebly attempting to flee the fiery onslaught—after which the enlarged cell would go dark and disappear, before cycling to another location. Retticker thought he recognized the imagery.

"Aerial reconnaissance?"

"Attack and reconnaissance drones, actually. UAVs At the moment Sergeant Phillips is monitoring about forty missions, mostly antiterror strikes against jihadist groups in Syria and Jordan. When appropriate, he has his drones fire missiles or strafe the targets. All without saying a word or moving a muscle."

Retticker arched an eyebrow.

"Impressive. How's it done?"

"Arrays of nanoelectrodes were injected into his bloodstream. They were then biochemically steered to attachment points in the command and control areas of his brain, mainly the frontal and parietal lobes. The faint signals from the nanotrode arrays are detected and analyzed by a computer system. The system recognizes patterns of signals that represent particular activities—concentration on something in the visual field, for instance. Or the muscular movements that accompany pushing a missile firing button, or pulling the trigger, on a fighter plane joystick."

"Hmm. This the stuff MERC helped fund?"

"Yes sir. Public-private cooperation. Military Executive Resource Corporation offset many of our costs, as did its corporate parent, Otis Diversified Industries."

Ah, Retticker thought. ODI was involved in everything from pharmaceuticals to weapons manufacture—magic bullets and plain old-fashioned ballistic ones. ODI involvement probably meant coordination with one of the stealthy strategic support offices at the Pentagon, too. Otis himself had lots of connections there. And with National Intelligence czar Ethan Watson, too.

"Good. But I don't see a joystick, or much in the way of 'muscular movement' here."

Michelson smiled broadly.

"When Phillips was training on how to use triggers or firing buttons on an actual joystick in a simulator, the researchers monitoring him were also recording and analyzing the output signals from his brain. Once the joystick and simulator were removed, Phillips quickly learned to assimilate the characteristics of the external devices. The properties of the telemonitoring, the drones, their flight and targeting systems—all have been incorporated into his brain's neuronal space as a natural extension of his own body."

Retticker looked thoughtfully at the quiescent soldier, then at the very active screens. Hard to believe the motionless young man was busily destroying things with his extended will.

"Did he need any particular talent to become proficient at this?"

"Not really. He was a decent video-gamer before he came into the program, but no better than tens of thousands of young men and women already serving in the armed forces. He says it's been like learning to drive, or to ride a bicycle, or use any other kind of tool."

"That makes sense. But how does it work, exactly?"

"The more we learn to use a tool, the more we incorporate the properties of that tool into our brains. That, in turn, makes us more proficient in using the tool."

"Practice makes perfect?"

Michelson nodded enthusiastically.

"In terms of brain-machine interfacing, it's more like practice shapes the neuronal space of the tool-user to more perfectly approximate the characteristics of the tool or device used. It works both ways, see?"

"Practice-effect feedback."

"Right. That's why the neurobiologists here have chosen to call what they're doing telemorphy, meaning to change the form, shape, or properties of something, from a distance—whether that something is tool or user or, most often, both."

"I suppose this telemorphy has other applications besides assassination drones?"

"Many, many others. A single soldier could potentially deploy the firepower of a robot platoon, or brigade, or army—"

"Watch it there, son," Retticker said with a laugh. He'd encountered this attitude of "technolatry"—technological idolatry—often enough to have thought up that private term for it. "You don't want to go telling the generals who fund your research that you plan to put them out of work!"

"I can show you other uses, in other labs here—"

"No, no. Not today. I take your point. Even if you could equip a soldier with more phantom limbs than a Hindu deity, though, that still leaves a problem."

"Yes?"

"I'm not certain that having a single soldier control dozens of drones or robots is really the best way to go. These sorts of things have their uses, certainly, but they're expensive to produce. And there's another potential problem, too."

"Oh?"

"I don't know as I'd want a single soldier controlling so much military hardware. What if he decided to go rogue against his own commanders? The more capability you put into the hands of one man—"

"The greater the danger he'll abuse it?"

"Exactly. Besides, human beings reproduce on their own readily enough to keep them far cheaper than any comparable robot. You know what one of my supertroopers said to me?"

"What's that, sir?"

"What would really turn individual supersoldiers into a superarmy would be what he called head-to-head connection."

"Conjoint consciousness," Michelson said, grimacing. "That's still a tough one. We've got a pair of nanotroded soldiers, and the neuronal space-state of one can be transmitted by radio to the other. Not conjoint consciousness yet, but we're—"

"Ah, but that, too," Retticker said, interrupting, "like your action at a distance here—it's all based on communicating data by wire, or radio, or other traditional methods?"

"That's correct."

"Well, radio waves can be jammed, wires can be cut. Radioed brain states can be neurohacked, right?"

"That's true enough, I suppose. But the problems of mind-machine action at a distance are not identical to those facing conjoint consciousness."

"But doesn't it boil down to the same thing?" the general said, trying to keep the impatience out of his voice. "We need a system that can't be jammed or interrupted or interfered with—whether that's brain to machine, or brain to brain."

Michelson blinked his owlish eyes several times in succession. Retticker wondered whether the man was accessing information through his AR glasses via such blinking, or whether he was suffering from some kind of nervous tic.

"I don't think that's possible, at least not at the level of classical physics," Michelson said at last.

"Then what about at a level that's more subtle, as you called it earlier? You know what I'm getting at, Jeremy. The quantum crypto stuff you were working on. Before the Kwok-Cho mess."

The biophysicist stood with his head cocked, pondering the possibilities with a stillness that almost matched Sergeant Phillips's. On one screen or another, vehicles and buildings continued to explode.

"Some aspects of quantum cryptography have proven to be impossible to break or interfere with," Michelson said at last. "As you'd prefer for military uses. Quantum neurocrypto. Hmm. That might still be an avenue. . . ."

Retticker clapped his hands together, almost shockingly loud in the quiet room.

"Now you're talking! You said yourself it's appropriate for this unit of the enhancement program to be housed here. Your science of telemorphy, as I understand it, is already taking old paranormal psi ideas and making them a reality."

Michelson looked down at the floor, almost shyly.

"You could think of it that way, yes. We have put action-at-a-distance and sensing-at-a-distance on a firm technological basis. In a sense we've already accomplished what the old ideas of telesthesia and psychokinesis were meant to describe."

Returning his gaze to the quiet soldier, Michelson continued to think out loud.

"Maybe what you're after is not PK or micro-PK, but quantum telemorphy. The same quantum entanglements that figure in qubit computing and qubit cryptography, especially quantum teleportation, might apply here, too."

Retticker stared narrowly at the man. He knew that neither of them was unmindful of how quantum computing and crypto had figured in the Kwok-Cho affair and all that Chinese unpleasantness. Still, he couldn't yet see where the man was headed. Best to draw Michelson out until he had explained his ideas enough to be understood by non-specialist nongeniuses.

"How so?"

"Well . . ." Michelson's voice trailed off, then his face suddenly brightened. "You could, theoretically, teleport not only the quantum state of particles but also of waves. Teleport the entire wave pattern, the entire quantum state description of a neuronal space. Pulse it through the quantum foam!"

Retticker shook his head. "I don't follow you."

"Think of an ocean made out of jittery foam," Michelson said excitedly. "The pulse could be a soliton—a standing wave, or wave of translation . . ."

"A wave made out of foam," Retticker said, smiling as he contemplated it. "So translating this wave . . . it would be like taking the pattern from one brain and imprinting it into another brain?"

"Actually, that's closer to what we're already doing with nanotrodes and radio waves."

"Sounds like turning your brain into a television set, except that both the transmitter and the receiver would be inside people's heads."

Michelson shook his head vigorously and negatively.

"This would be more subtle, more fundamental. Brain states are not exactly duplicable. This would be more like two brains sharing one state, for a time."

"How?"

"Think of each brain's overall state as an incredibly complex but coherent wave. Their state-sharing via the quantum foam would be like the kind of nonlinear memory that appears when two standing waves merge together, travel as one for a while, and then separate into their two former orders again."

Retticker glanced momentarily at the still soldier, still blowing things up with his extended will.

"Telepathy, then?"

"More than that. This is where neurobiology might really meet neurophysics! There are probably ways even far *less* subtle matter could be manipulated at a distance, through a similar method. What were once thought of as telekinetic, telesthetic, and telepathic abilities would cease to be mystical powers—"

Retticker gave the biophysicist a congratulatory whack on the shoulder.

"And they couldn't be hacked or jammed or otherwise interfered with?"

"I haven't heard of anyone being able to hack the quantum foam. If what was achieved was truly quantum-level neurocryptography, then there'd be no way to hack it or crack it."

"Brilliant, Jeremy. What would you need to accomplish it?"

Michelson gave it some serious thought. He seemed suddenly to deflate a bit, as if realizing how hard the task would be.

"I don't know that it *can* be accomplished. In some ways you'd have to be able to make the brain function like a room-temperature quantum computer. You'd need enhanced neural sensitivity throughout the cerebral cortex, for one thing. The kind of chaotic, spontaneous neural activity that's hypersensitive to quantum effects. In both the sender and the receiver."

Retticker frowned. He glanced again toward Sergeant Phillips, who continued destroying things and people at a distance while remaining steadfastly oblivious to his immediate surroundings.

"Sounds like drugs and consensual hallucinations again," the general said with a groan.

"On the contrary," Michelson said, blinking his eyes rapidly again in that manner which was either nervous tic or info-accessing. "If the quantum teleportation angle works, I think the telemorphic effects could be rendered rational, scientifically explainable, and predictable. It would be more a conscious alteration of quantum states than an altered state of consciousness."

Retticker smiled, thinking of classified Medusa Blue and Tetragrammaton research about which he knew a good deal, but of which Michelson, he was sure, knew nothing.

"Work on that, then," he said to the biophysicist, then checked his wristwatch. "My time's up. I need to be moving on, I'm afraid."

"I'm sorry to hear that, sir," Michelson said, looking genuinely downcast. "I haven't had much of a chance to show you our other work, or even introduce you to anyone else on staff."

"Another day, another time," Retticker said, shaking Michelson's hand. "It was good having this chance for a private briefing. Let's keep in touch, shall we? I can show myself out."

Waving farewell to Michelson, and to the undistractable Sergeant Phillips beyond him, the general walked away down the corridor. Retticker smiled, then exhaled a sigh.

He had been spending an awful lot of time lately inspiring these scientific specialists to look for the larger implications of their research, nudging them in practical, strategic, and tactical directions. People who'd been involved during the Kwok-Cho matter—even peripherally, like Michelson—were especially reluctant to look at the larger implications of their work. Once burned, twice shy.

Retticker hadn't thought such motivational and inspirational efforts would prove to be this challenging, but they had. A job of work, as his father used to say—and nothing easy about it.

THE MIRROR BETWEEN CHURCH AND STATE

"This place always reminds me of Stonehenge somehow," Dan Amaral said to the NSA director as they walked through the World War II Memorial. Dan was deputy chief of mission and chief political officer for the U.S. embassy in Cairo, but he was first and foremost an old friend and comrade in arms.

They had served together during Desert Storm more than twenty years ago. That in itself was enough to make Jim Brescoll more forgiving of his friend, despite Dan's affectations. His ever-present Sheik Abdullah mustache and goatee, his Anubis-headed walking stick, his clunky briefcase, his often unorthodox views—none of those much surprised Jim anymore.

"The pillared circle, you mean?"

"More that it's something out of another time," Dan said as they walked. "The America they fought for was so different from the one we live in now."

"Seventy, seventy-five years—that's long enough to change any culture."

"You know that's not what I mean, Jim. What they were fighting for was still pretty much a democratic republic, or a republican democracy, whichever you prefer. Then came the long militarization of America and Russia during the cold war, and everything began to change."

Jim glanced away into the middle distance of memory.

"Well, we won that one, anyway."

"You really think so? I don't know. Seems to me our country, in 'winning' that war, moved away from democracy and toward empire. Russia, in 'losing' that war, moved away from empire and toward democracy—at least for a while. A fun house–mirror symmetry if I ever saw one."

They both paused to take in a panorama that included the Lincoln

Memorial and the Washington Monument, but Jim's mind was elsewhere. The fun house–mirror reference reminded him of a meeting he'd had with Wong Jun, his opposite number in Guoanbu, the Chinese Ministry of State Security, after the Kwok-Cho affair.

Over dinner, Wong had maintained that during the twentieth century the world had been locked in a zero-sum game, with capitalism and socialism perversely mirroring each other.

"Reduced to simplest terms," Wong had said, "the capitalist makes a fortune out of someone else's misfortune—"

"—and the socialist makes a misfortune out of someone else's fortune," Jim said jumping in to finish Wong's thought. They had clinked glasses then, toasting to perfectly understanding each other.

Looking at Dan now, Jim thought that while they had not always perfectly understood each other, they had remained friends nonetheless.

"But we've entered the age of asymmetric conflict long since, ol' buddy," Jim said, taking a seat on the bench they'd stopped before. A short distance down the mall, a group of young tourists had their eyes closed and hands lifted to Jesus in prayer. Dan gave them a lingering look.

"Only in terms of hard-war tactics," he said, sitting down. "I've been serving overseas for a long time. Five years in Yemen, nine in Morocco, these last five in Egypt."

At his friend's glance, Jim nodded but said nothing.

"When I entered diplomatic service and got stationed in the Muslim world," he went on, "what struck me most wasn't the women in veils or the donkeys in the streets—it was the public presence of prayer. Men rolling out prayer mats and kneeling on the sidewalk to pray. The muezzin coughing or clearing his throat, unself-consciously, over the loudspeaker, as he got ready to call the faithful to prayer. Nowadays the call is mostly prerecorded, but you get my point."

"I'm not sure I do, actually," Jim said, peering at his old comrade.

"I thought it was all so different from America. In the old days you didn't see people praying out in public in the middle of a workday."

Jim followed his friend's glance toward the group praying nearby. Their minister or youth pastor exhorted them and they closed their eyes and held up their hands in praise of the Lord. Oh, I see. So that's what he's on about, Jim thought.

"In the old days it wasn't considered polite to talk about politics or religion in mixed company either, as you're doing now, Dan," he said. "Besides, I don't know that young people praying is such a bad change."

"Not in itself, no. To me, the sound of the muezzin's call to prayer is a beautiful thing, too. Like a hymn. The pilgrims turning in their orbits around the black-draped monolith of the Kaaba inside the Great Mosque at Mecca—that's a mesmerizing spectacle. I've only seen it on film. I can only imagine how it must be in person."

He looked away from the prayerful and back to Jim.

"But religion is best left private when people are outside their place of worship. Public space is always 'mixed company.' Inherently political. It's just not healthy—or polite—to mix politics and religion."

Jim glanced at him, but said nothing for all that the word *morality* hovered above his tongue.

"We're becoming the thing we fear," Amaral continued. "Just two sides of the same interrogation-room mirror. Fundamentalism is fascist religion, as sure as fascism is fundamentalist politics. Though none of them call it fascism or even fundamentalism anymore. They're all just 'religious conservatives' or 'Dominionists' now."

Over his AR glasses, Director Brescoll arched an eyebrow at his old friend.

"Man, you *have* spent a lot of time out of the country!"

"True enough. But whenever you wrap your God in your flag, you're bound to increase intolerance for your fellow human beings and their ways, and reduce respect for them as people, too. They say it just shows they have 'conviction,' but their convictions are making the world a more violent and hate-filled place. That's a disservice to both God and flag."

"These folks hardly seem the mirror-image of jihadists, though," Jim said, nodding in the direction of the praying tourists.

"Maybe not, but the type of god preached in fundamentalist madrasas, fundamentalist yeshivas, fundamentalist churches and schools—it's the same mirror-god of hate. For everybody who sees sex, or family, or religion, or nature different from how you do, well, just hate 'em, that's all. Hate, hate, hate. God's going to burn up all your enemies in the end-time anyway. They all agree on that."

"Hatred doesn't sound like God or Yahweh or Allah to me," Jim said. "That's just how people have twisted the message."

"I don't doubt it! The vast majority of Muslims, Christians, and Jews are moderates—and compassionate people of good intent. The

god of hate is a flag- or rhetoric-wrapped product of the fundamentalists' own fundaments. Nothing divine about it. They shouldn't call
where they pray 'churches' or 'temples' or 'mosques.' They're all really
worship-corporations fighting for market share. If we really believed in
the separation of church and state, we'd have taken away their tax-
exempt status at the first sign of their engaging in political advocacy—
and taxed them like any other business."

Jim smiled and shook his head.

"It's a good thing you've been overseas. You're just a little too
forthright in your views for the homefront."

"Yeah. I'd probably have needed diplomatic immunity in my native
country."

Jim laughed, but then grew more serious.

"They can still shunt you to a back desk or out of government completely. Just remember, old buddy: if you keep banging your heart
against the mountain, don't be surprised when it's not the mountain
that breaks."

Staring at the Anubis god-dog head atop his walking stick, Amaral
gave a world-weary shrug.

"Just traveled too far and seen too much, Jim," he said. "Sometimes
I think that if this planet were a restaurant the soup of the day would
be wingnut stew in hot petroleum broth. But so long as the holy folks
of whatever stripe don't damn me to their version of heaven or martyr
me for their version of paradise, then I'm quite content to live and let
live."

Amaral pulled a sheaf of documents from his antique briefcase.
"And I'll keep my job because I know what I'm talking about and I get
the work done. Which is how I found out a little more about this
fellow Fremdkunst and his meteorites."

Amaral handed Jim two reports, each of which prominently fea-
tured a list.

"Interesting character. Travels a lot between Israel and Saudi Arabia. I have some acquaintances in the state security apparatuses of both
countries. They helped with background on this one."

Jim nodded absently as he looked at the reports. He saw that, between them, the lists detailed Victor Fremdkunst's plane and train journeys between Jerusalem and Riyadh.

"Good work. Hmm. These documents say he was on business. Do
you know what kind?"

Dan leaned back on the bench and looked off into the sky.

"I dug a little deeper. He's set himself up as an artist and adventurer. I've always thought of those as low-paying occupations, but he's made surprisingly good money from them. He has quite the legitimate cover story, too, if that's what it is."

"Oh?"

"Says he's searching for meteorites, in places where ancient books and legends refer to catastrophic events. He apparently believes those cataclysms were meteoritic in origin."

"Where did they supposedly happen?"

"In Israel, at the Big and Little Craters, south of Jerusalem and the Dead Sea, west of Jordan. In his public interviews Fremdkunst claims the meteoritic material he's found there matches the probable time of destruction of the cities of Sodom and Gomorrah."

"Wait a minute," Jim said, doubtful but also intrigued. "I was raised Baptist. I read a lot in my Bible. God rained down fire and brimstone, as I recall. There's nothing to say brimstone couldn't be meteorites, but I don't think that's what the Bible says."

"Brimstone is what I remembered, too, and I was raised Catholic. So I did a little more research. Brimstone is burning sulfur. Seems there've been a considerable number of instances linking meteorite falls and the smell of sulfur. In fact, all meteorites contain varying amounts of a type of iron sulfide called troilite."

Jim glanced up into the sky, trying to see what Dan was seeing, but he saw only sky, not even any clouds.

"That's news to me."

Amaral nodded, returning his gaze to their more immediate surroundings at last.

"The clearest example I found happened in 1992. A 1980 Chevy Malibu got nailed by a twenty-six-pound meteorite in Peekskill, New York. When the eighteen-year-old girl who owned the vehicle reached down and touched the stone that had whacked her car, she said it was still warm and smelled strongly of sulfur."

Jim barked a laugh at the image of the poor young girl and her meteorite-bashed car.

"Hmm! Okay, maybe Fremdkunst has a point. What's he been doing in Saudi?"

"Exploring around the Wabar craters complex, in the Rub' al-Khali. There's an old story of a city there called Ad-ibn Kin, or Wabar, which was supposedly destroyed when God sent a rushing wind and fire from the sky to punish its wicked ruler." He twirled the head of his cane. "A related story also mentions a block of iron as big as a camel's hump, called al-Hadida. Or maybe that refers to the entire impact site, too, since that can be translated as 'the iron' or 'the iron things.' "

Jim leaned forward on his fist, unconsciously imitating of Rodin's *Thinker.*

"That's what Fremdkunst is after, then?"

"No, the iron camel's hump has long since been recovered. Fremd-kunst is not the first to look for meteoritic material in the Rub' al-Khali—not by a long shot. A Brit by the name of Harry St. John Philby led an expedition into the Empty Quarter as early as 1932, in search of the lost city of Wabar."

At Dan's glance to see if he was still paying full attention, Jim nodded but said nothing.

"Philby called himself Abdullah after he converted to Islam," Ama-ral said, stroking his mustache and giving Brescoll a sly look, as if daring him to make some kind of crack. "Interesting character. His son was, too: Kim Philby, the notorious British-Soviet double agent."

"But the father, he found the iron block?"

"No, not even him. The stories about the disaster from the sky, those differ. One is ancient enough to be a reference in the Koran, but the other probably refers to an event that is only about a century and a half old. Even when and where the city was supposedly destroyed is all confused. The city Philby was probably looking for was Ubar, not Wabar."

"Ubar—that *was* found, wasn't it?"

Dan nodded.

"Maybe, but the jury's still out. Through the use of satellite imaging, years after old Philby died, a trading center was found—a town that fell into a sinkhole when the cavern it was built on top of collapsed, and was then covered by desert."

"Not a happy ending for any city."

"No. Whether the satellite-discovered town was in fact Ubar is still being debated. The ending wasn't happy for Philby, either. All he found were a few craters, some fragments of iron, and black fused-silica globules. The tribesmen believed those black 'gems' were the jewels of the female inhabitants of the destroyed city. No ruins of a lost city for Abdullah Philby, and worthless 'desert pearls' for the Bedouins who led him there. Everyone was quite disappointed."

"No doubt," Jim said, hoping his expression conveyed adequate sympathy for the failed expedition.

"Yes, but like Dame Fortune's wheel, the sands of the Rub' al-Khali are constantly shifting. In 1965, Bedouin tribesmen found a forty-five-hundred-pound iron meteorite, which they claim is the Hadida. In 1966 an oil company engineer found another four-hundred-and-forty-pound fragment. I've seen both of them myself, actually, at King Sa'ud University in Riyadh."

Jim frowned in perplexity.

"If it's all been found, what's Fremdkunst after there now?"

"Apparently he doesn't believe it *has* all been found. Pieces of meteoritic iron continue to crop up there, and the scientific consensus is that there are probably other craters beneath the sands around Wabar. Nothing of the supposedly destroyed city itself has been found, if it ever existed. Fremdkunst could be trying to find more meteorites, or prove that Ad-ibn Kin is not the same as Ubar, or that a city actually was destroyed, perhaps not far from the Wabar meteoritic impact craters, but much earlier."

"Wouldn't that be a bit like lightning striking the same place twice?"

"It could happen," Dan said, shrugging. "At least it gives him a not-too-implausible cover story for being in Saudi, just as he also has for being in Israel."

Jim looked narrowly at his old comrade. From the way Dan had let that last sentence hang and glanced away, Jim knew there was more.

"But you don't think it's the whole story?"

"No. I followed up on some of the links you sent me. In cornering the meteorite market, Fremdkunst has pissed off quite a few people. Some of his critics hinted that he left the military under a bit of a cloud a dozen years ago, so I tried to find out more about that. Turns out one of his army buddies is a secular Arab-American who now works for State in Morocco, my old stomping grounds. I had a talk with him."

Jim shifted uncomfortably on the bench.

"And?"

"He said in his army days Fremdkunst strongly believed the U.S. government was out of control. All the usual reasons: the electoral process had been subverted, Congress was bought off, the administration was a gang of criminals, there was war profiteering by insiders, a right-wing-dominated United States with no viable internal opposition was well on its way to becoming the moral equivalent of Nazi Germany—but as the lone world superpower or hyperpower. Et cetera."

Jim nodded, remembering the strangeness of those days. Fringe right-wingers had come to the center of power, setting up special-plan "offices" in the Pentagon and White House, co-opting the top leadership of NSA and subverting its mission, churning out propaganda to subdue the national conscience so that no forceful American mass movement could rise against their plans—not only in opposition to the planners' preemptive wars and drive for empire, but also against their fully scripted first-strike use of American weapons of mass destruction against foreign nations and groups. That such use was projected to result in preemptive nuclear kill numbers that would have made Adolf Hitler blush with envy the New American Centurions readily justified in the name of national security.

Yes, everyone had lived through a paradoxical time—were still living through it, in many ways. A well-lit dark age, a gathering gloom made all the more profound by the ubiquitous screenglow. But things weren't that dark anymore. He hoped.

"A legitimate enough critique at the time, I suppose."

"Indeed. My source remembered very clearly that Fremdkunst described the government as 'coked up,' as in COKT, covert oligarchic kleptocratic theocracy."

"Your source has an impressive memory," Jim said, laughing. "Let's see. That would mean . . . what? Secret rule by a gang of wealthy thieves posing as moral and godly leaders?"

"Sounds about right."

"A certain wit to that, I must admit. And his solution?"

"He believed the military should take over. Because they were sworn to uphold the Constitution."

Jim shook his head in chagrined disbelief.

"That's a bit steep. Rather naïve, too. But all this is stuff from some years back in Fremdkunst's past?"

"Right. I suppose it could probably be written off as 'youthful indiscretion.' But my informant says there was weirder stuff, too."

"Such as?"

"Talk of Satanic fraternities at Yale. Murdered presidential sex-slaves. Major soft-drink companies hiding the fact that their products eat holes in the brains of consumers. Pharmaceutical companies forcibly numbing the minds of a populace already exposed to unknown diseases spread by unexplained chemtrails in the sky. And, of course, a 9/11/01

stand-down, along burning-of-the-Reichstag or Gulf of Tonkin lines—
jihadist attacks being part of a plan by CIA and Mossad to globally
export terrorist double-agents in order to drive up the profits of
defense corporations and the international bankers."

Jim raised his hands, as if to ward off more of the same.

"Wait. Let me guess. 'The international bankers are all Jewish, and
the Israelis have penetrated all aspects of our government and society,'
right?"

"Which they control through the Federal Reserve Board, the Council on Foreign Relations, and the Trilateral Commission. All the usual
suspects. More like youthful crackpottery than indiscretion, if you ask
me. Nowadays, of course, he gets along fine with everybody, including
the theocrats and oligarchs of both Israel and Saudi Arabia. A completely different man."

"Well, maybe someone finally took him aside and showed him that
the *Protocols of the Elders of Zion* was a forgery perpetrated by the
czar's secret police."

"Maybe. It's also possible he just got shrewder, less 'forthright' in
his opinions, to use your term. Understanding the seductiveness of
security—personal or national—does not necessarily render one im-
mune to its allure. Not even in my own case."

Amaral shuffled papers back into his bulky briefcase and snapped it
shut.

"At any rate, his interest in meteorites and impact geology has long
since put him in touch with a lot of geologists of all specializations, including those in the oil industry. Over the last decade, he's made some
very profitable investments. Some of them seem to have been on the
advice of George Otis, among others."

"Otis? Mister 'Godly America Fellowship'? Whew. Doesn't sound
like the ideological traveling companion of someone who once made
cracks about covert theocracies."

"Money and politics make for strange bedfellows," Amaral said
with a narrowed glance. "Fremdkunst has plenty of involvement in both
of those, too—and not only in Saudi Arabia and Israel. He's wealthy
enough to have bought a lot of friends, both military and civilian, in
our own government. His military records and ongoing connections
inside the armed services might bear some looking into."

Jim pondered his friend's advice. The odds on a Retticker-Fremd-
kunst connection were getting stronger all the time. But the possibility

of George Otis being involved, too—well, that was a new wrinkle. He was a heavyweight, lots of money and connections everywhere inside the Beltway, including with his own boss below the president, Director of National Intelligence Ethan Watson. Maybe it would be a good idea if he called in some of David Fahrney's clout on this, just in case he needed to even up the odds. Always a good thing to have a billionaire inventor, iconoclast, and brilliant autodidact in one's corner. A strange guardian angel, but he had proven *very* helpful during the Kwok-Cho affair.

He slapped his thighs and stood up.

"Thanks for the information and advice, Dan. I'll follow up. How about you, though?"

Dan Amaral squinted up at him.

"How about me what?"

"Would you be willing to go on my payroll for a while? As an NSA security liaison, overseas?"

Amaral paused, giving it some thought.

"I don't know if it's ever a good thing to work for an old friend," Amaral said, standing up more slowly. "This meteorite stuff at least has the appeal of novelty, though. Not what usually comes across my desk at the embassy. If you can arrange the posting, and State can fill my staffing duties, I'm up for it."

"Good," Brescoll said, smiling. "I'll get to work on it ASAP. Now what say we head to my house for supper? We can discuss your duties while I drive. I know Marion is eager to see you again."

THE PREROGATIVE OF FALLING STARS

The fifteen-hour journey from Riyadh to the Wabar craters complex— in a battered, ancient, sandblasted Zahid Trac Humvee—would have been strange and arduous enough by itself. Avram Zaragosa's driver, however, made it still more so. The man behind the wheel, Yuri Se-menov, seemed at first to be afflicted with the chattiness of a hermit who, having spent too much time in various deserts around the world, had at long last found a captive audience in Avram.

"This is nastiest of all," Semenov said, out of a mouth almost invisi-ble in its forest of bushy black-and-silver beard, beneath black bug-eye sunglasses and a floppy gray desert hat. "Empty Quarter is correct. Full of shifting seif dunes. Unpredictable sand cliffs, twenty meters high. Heat wave for this time of year—over 325 Kelvin during day, not much below 310 before midnight. Largest contiguous sand sea on earth. Broader than all of American Texas, where I live since becoming U.S. citizen. You'll see, you'll see."

Soon thereafter, a long camel caravan blocked their one clear way through a low pass among huge, horned, barchan sand dunes. The camel drivers refused to open up a space for the Humvee. Semenov honked the Humvee's horn and cursed the men and their beasts in Russian-accented Arabic.

"Ever since bilaterians invented anus," Semenov said, shaking his head when the caravan finally passed, "more and more assholes on this planet! Something biology books don't teach, but every field biologist knows."

"Aren't we supposed to be traveling in a caravan, too?" Avram asked. "For safety, I mean?"

"No need! We have food, fuel, water. We have radio. Most important, we have GPS."

Avram wasn't particularly reassured, especially when, a moment later, they began to bog down in the sand. Semenov adjusted the Humvee's tire pressure on the fly, however, and they continued on their way—up, over, down, and around dunes and cliffs.

They were in this for the long haul. Not that they had much choice. Wabar's remoteness, high ambient temperatures, and the surrounding soft and irregular dunes made the place inaccessible to fixed-wing aircraft or all but the most highly (and expensively) modified helicopters—and even such rare birds as those were most often restricted to dropping off and picking up, without landing.

When a sandstorm began to pelt them, Avram did notice that Yuri slowed slightly and detoured more often, to avoid plunging them over sand cliffs. Semenov also seemed to pay more attention to his treasured GPS as the storm worsened.

Avram rubbed the back of his neck. I'm GPSed too, he thought. That was the only real pain he'd had to endure for his mission so far. Luis Martin's technical people ("some new Tri-Border friends," as Martin put it) had designed a small capsule to be implanted under the scalp where it met the fleshy nape of Avram's neck, just about on a line with the foramen magnum. He hadn't felt much discomfort when they installed what they called "his own personal biopowered homing beacon," although it had occasionally proved something of a pain since then. An itch he couldn't actually scratch.

Wonderful. If he died out here in the desert, at least someone would be able to find his body. If they took the time to look.

"So, Yuri," Avram said, trying to make conversation to keep his mind off the worsening conditions, "what's a biologist like you doing out here, working with impact geologists at an astrobleme in the middle of the desert?"

Yuri smiled.

"Love that word—astrobleme. Means 'star wound,' you know? Not working with them, certainly. My research laps over theirs. I study ecologic and genetic anomalies linked to electrophonic meteors. You know electrophonic meteors?"

"I know many observers report a hissing noise, like radio static, during the sighting of a fireball. Sometimes even before seeing one. Since sound waves travel much slower than light, the phenomenon's never been satisfactorily explained."

Yuri shook his beard vigorously up and down.

"Da. Not just hissing. Snaps, pops, clicks. Rustling, rushing, roaring. Like great wind. Many sound effects, like thunder underground, in witness-eye records at Tunguska, before seeing bolide."

Avram nodded, though at the moment he would have preferred that Yuri pay less mind to conversational eye-contact and more to their journey. Better the man should have all his attention focused out the windshield, on the undulating gray-brown terrain through which he was maneuvering them. That landscape had grown increasingly indistinguishable from the very close, gray-brown sky swirling around them.

"So, you believe it was electrophonic?" Avram asked, glancing away from the desert and toward the driver. "The Tunguska . . . what? Stony asteroid? Comet?"

"Tunguska meteoroid, is it comet or asteroid? No one agrees. Call it Tunguska space body, TSB. Along flight path of TSB many ecologic and genetic anomalies. Accelerated growth, morphometric peculiarities in taiga trees, birches, ants. Even Rhesus negative, Rh-D gene—very rare among them—found in Evenki people along space-body trajectory."

Despite himself, Avram was fascinated by the way the man could drive such irregular and treacherous terrain while simultaneously expounding on his theories. It reminded Avram of a professor he had once studied with, a man who was most eloquent in his explanations when he was rather drunk.

"Hmm! How do you explain that?"

"Tunguska meteoroid's flight accompanied by powerful extreme low frequency–very low frequency electromagnetic radiation. ELF-VLF stressed local biota, triggered subtle mechanisms to release hidden genetic variation into phenotype. Some direct mutagenic factors, from ionizing radiation of lightning during explosion, cannot be prevented from inclusion also."

"Whoa, wait a minute . . . ," Avram said.

Yuri braked the Humvee to a near stop so suddenly it threatened to throw Avram at the windshield. Then, probably from the surprised look on Avram's face, he belatedly realized Avram had been speaking rhetorically. Yuri slipped the vehicle back into higher gear without comment and continued his dogged way through the sand-blind late afternoon.

It took Avram a minute to relocate his train of thought, and why he'd told Semenov to wait a minute to begin with.

"I'm not a biologist, Yuri. How does a fireball affect genes?"

"Many possibilities. Passage of fireball through atmosphere traps, twists Earth's geomagnetic field behind it. Strain energy of field releases as VLF electromagnetic radiation. Shock wave of meteoroid's catastrophic breakup propagates in plasma around meteoroid, making ELF electromagnetic transients. Tunguska blast force equals twenty megatons. Nuclear explosions similar in size generate much lightning. Lightning makes ionizing radiation to cascade. Explosive disruption of large meteoroid generates electromagnetic pulse also, and Joule heating."

"Without radioactivity?"

Yuri nodded. An annoying whine started up somewhere in front of the vehicle's dashboard. Yuri whacked the dash once, hard, with the palm of his hand. The whine subsided.

"Electromagnetic fields still at very low energies can induct—induce—heat shock proteins, HSPs. HSPs normally buffer genetic variation. In stable environments, HSPs, um, *ensure* phenotypic stability despite increased accumulation of hidden mutation in genotype. Understand?"

Avram nodded.

"But under catastrophic environmental stress, HSPs, um, are *overburdened* with job of chaperoning other molecules. No longer can they mask variations of genotype, so variations are released in phenotype. HSPs are capacitors of evolution. Ecologic and genetic consequences of Tunguska event, they are manifestations of latent mutations already present in Tunguskan biota. Stress response, due to increased electromagnetic radiation from TSB—ELF-VLF electromagnetic radiation from bolide, ionizing radiation from lightning to accompany explosion in atmosphere—that releases mutations already there but hidden, penned up—"

"Pent up?"

"Um. Okay. Thanks."

The whine from somewhere in front of the dashboard started again in earnest. Or maybe, Avram thought, the howl and rasp of the sandstorm had now decreased just enough that he could hear it more clearly.

"These genetic anomalies," Avram said, "they appear with statistically greater frequency along the TSB trajectory?"

"Da. And with greatest frequency at two points. One, where TSB trajectory would intersect Earth if meteoroid made it to ground. Other, at *point of extinction,* um, location in trajectory through atmosphere where cosmic velocity is lost, visible light goes out—"

"And remaining material falls freely due to Earth's gravity," Avram said, helpfully. "Becoming meteoritic upon reaching Earth's surface."

"Da. Is death-point of most falling stars blocked by atmosphere of Earth—at least for meteoroids under one hundred meters in diameter."

"But not so, if the meteoroid is sufficiently large."

"No. Then airburst detonation, heat and shock waves accompanying. Also lightning, thunder, electrophonic effects, do not forget."

The dashboard whine faded from Avram's consciousness as he experienced an epiphany—another realization of the wisdom that legends and oral traditions of peoples throughout the world contained concerning meteorites and impact events.

"So when prescientific peoples called meteorites 'lightningstones' and 'thunderstones,' they weren't just being ignorant and superstitious, after all."

"Not so wrong, no. Nejd meteorites, of same composition as Wabar stones and from trajectory of same fall, were reported seen falling in Wadi Bani Khaled during 'thunderstorm'—same day in 1863 as huge fireball headed in direction of Wabar site passed over mud-walled town that is now capital, Riyadh." Yuri jerked the wheel hard as a dune's sudden dropoff caught him by surprise. "But lightning-spark leaping in circuit of evolution is bigger than that."

Avram cocked his head in surprise.

"What do you mean?"

"Falling stars greater than one hundred fifty meters of diameter are not much retarded by passage through atmosphere blanket of Earth, no? They retain most or all of cosmic velocity. Point of extinction for them is within body of Earth itself. For objects greater than ten kilometers in diameter, point of extinction is not only catastrophic for meteoroid, is also catastrophic for to induce mass extinctions of many species on planet."

Avram nodded.

"Even an impactor of one kilometer in diameter produces effects powerful enough to potentially wipe out advanced civilization, if not the human species itself," he put in. "Fortunately, the bigger they come, the less frequently they fall."

"True, but evolution has created strategy to exploit even mass extinction. Stress of disaster overwhelms HSP buffer capacity, so hidden accumulation of mutation and variation is revealed. Survivors with more variation exploit disaster-opened niches faster."

For the first time, despite or perhaps because of the strangeness of the situation—traveling through blistering desert, up and down mountainous dunes, in a sandstorm, as night fell—Avram truly understood what the evolutionary biologists meant by punctuated equilibrium.

Earth was a palimpsest planet, the writing of life on its surface periodically but incompletely erased by enormous catastrophes. From the incompleteness of that erasure, life rewrote itself all over the planet again and again, scribbled itself anew across five great global extinction events—the Ordovician-Silurian, Devonian-Carboniferous, Permian-Triassic, Triassic-Jurassic, and Cretaceous-Tertiary—all of which had been linked to impactors from space.

"The latest great extinction event," Avram said, almost to himself, "is us."

Yuri gave him a quizzical look.

"The mass extinction we humans are causing is the only one not caused by the impact of a celestial body," Avram explained. "We've taken to ourselves the prerogative of falling stars."

Yuri nodded slowly. He seemed to weigh his answer before he spoke.

"But we have only partial success in this role, I think. We make many extinctions, but cannot make lightning of pent-up variation to leap gap from biochemical capacitors of evolution, as great thunderstones did."

The engine whine somewhere in front of the dashboard became a crackling snap, followed by a cycling of what sounded like broken pieces. Yuri smacked his hand against the dash again, this time in frustration.

"Dammit! Here's catastrophic failure. Desert duty today too heavy for heavy-duty air-conditioning—phooey! Night now, at least—and sandstorm is ending. Will get hot inside, but wait long as possible before opening windows, please."

"This has happened before?"

Yuri nodded grudgingly.

"Many times. Worst in bright day. So hot, have to snort water to keep brain cool. Snuffing, is called. I hate snuffing."

Trying not to think of heat so severe as to require such a ritual, Avram returned to their conversation for distraction more than anything else.

"If you're looking for ecological and genetic effects," he said, "then why Wabar? The ecology out here is about as sparse as you can get."

"True. And event here much smaller than Tunguska. Wabar-Nejd meteoroid probably only four thousand tons and one hundred kiloton of potential energy, to start. Lost most of energy during shallow oblique passage through atmosphere, maybe twenty to forty-five degrees from horizontal, before it hit desert floor. After airbraking in drag of atmosphere, largest impact only twelve kiloton, or one Hiroshima. But is recent—one-hundred-fifty-plus years old, not much older than Tunguska."

"Aside from the occasional camel or Bedouin, though, wasn't there pretty much nothing out here at the time?"

"Exact reason for research! We know which al Murra Bedouin were closest to impact. I have located descendants of people all along trajectory of Wabar-Nejd fall and am taking blood samples—both from people and camel herds. Collecting other medical records of descendants, too. Weighing them against general peninsula population. Looking for anomalies in numbers, statistics. In people I start with Rh-D gene, independent verification of Tunguska results. I do not stop there, of course."

It was growing incredibly hot and stuffy inside the vehicle. Avram, pouring sweat, was sorely tempted to open the window. When he touched the glass with the palm of his hand and felt how hot it was, he held off.

"What about the old stories of a destroyed city? Do you think it's under the Wabar astrobleme?"

Yuri shrugged.

"Wabar-Nejd is too recent fall. There have been other falls, though. Impacts of Wabar size may come once each decade, somewhere on earth. Most blow up over oceans, crash into water. Sooner or later, one explodes over or maybe impacts on modern city. Then what? Good to know effects, how to distinguish from nuclear blast. Do you know Koran, Sura forty-six, verses twenty-one to twenty-five?"

"No, I can't say I do."

"Mention, too, the brother of Aad," Yuri began reciting from memory, "when he warned his people in the wind-curved sandhills . . . : 'Worship none but God: verily I fear for you the punishment of the great day.' They said, 'Art thou come to us to turn us away from our gods? Bring on us now the woes which thou threatenest, if thou speakest truth.'

" 'That knowledge,' said he, 'is with God alone: I only proclaim to you the message with which I am sent. But I perceive that ye are a people sunk in ignorance.'

"So when they saw a cloud coming straight for their valleys, they said, 'It is a passing cloud that shall give us rain.' 'Nay, it is that whose speedy coming ye challenged—a destructive wind wherein is an afflictive punishment—it will destroy everything at the bidding of its Lord!' And at morn, nought was to be seen but their empty dwellings."

Yuri eyed him carefully.

" 'A cloud coming straight for their valleys,' " he said. "What sounds like that to you?"

"The dust trail or smoke train of a meteoroid," Avram admitted at last. "The 'wind-curved sandhills' does sound a lot like this Empty Quarter dune country, too."

"Exactly—and written in seventh century! Something else, also. Destructive wind comes as punishment in conflict between two brothers and their tribal groups there. Evenki people at Tunguska talk about TSB event same way: battle between shamans of rival but related tribes, one calling down destruction on the other. To call down, on enemies, disasters—bad stars—shows God on our side."

"The spears of gods or angels," Avram said quietly, the heat sapping his strength and attention. "In Central America, the conquistadors burned nearly all the Mayan bark books, but some that remain, particularly the Codex Borgia and Codex Vindobonensis, refer to the Nuhu. Star-entities, symbolized by spears and associated with meteoritic stones, particularly iron meteorites. The spears of God."

Unable to endure the heat any longer, Avram opened the window.

The blast of hot dry air made him think that now he knew what the clay pot felt like when the door of the kiln was opened. Yuri nodded as he rolled his window partway down as well. Surprisingly little sand blew inside.

"In Arab folklore," Yuri said, "angels hurl spears and other things at jinn sitting atop walls around heaven. Jinn are trying to eavesdrop on God's councils with angels, and angels are trying to drive them away, which is what makes shooting stars."

"All over the world, that association of meteorites and divine weaponry," Avram said, fighting a heat-induced lassitude. "Odin's spear Gungnir is made of uru metal from the heavens, from Asgard. The Hindu vajra, the 'diamond thunderbolt,' has many of the same attributes as Gungnir, too. And then there are the Spear of Lugh and the Spear of Luin, from Welsh and Celtic legends, which influenced the Arthurian material."

Yuri scratched at his beard, and nodded.

"Arthur's sword Excalibur comes from material that falls from heaven, as well."

"I've heard that. And he proved his right to kingship by pulling an earlier sword from a *stone*—a reference to forging the steel taken from meteoritic iron, some say."

"Weapons made from stuff of heaven," Yuri said, shaking his head. "Always same old story."

"Often the very same Arthurian story. Think of Hitler and his reported obsession with the so-called Spear of Destiny—the magically powerful Spear of Longinus, which pierced the side of Christ as he hung on the Cross—the one described in Wolfram von Eschenbach's *Parzival*."

"Same poem that calls Grail 'lapsit exillis'?"

"Ah, you've read it! I gather that phrase is derived from *lapis ex coelis* or *lapis de coelis,* both of which mean 'the stone from the heavens.' "

"Da. Or might be contraction of *lapis lapsus ex illis stellis,* 'the stone which came down from the stars.' "

Avram gave a weak laugh.

"No more. I know truths are hidden in myths and legends, but keep heading down that path and you end up looking for occult powers in Wagnerian operas. That way lies madness."

The energy-sapping heat and the potentially deadly tedium of traveling through desert terrain at last caused them both to lapse into silence. As their vehicle climbed updune, Avram saw over the Humvee's hood that the sandstorm had died away, enough that he could begin to see the stars. Soon, however, they were heading downdune again.

Before long he had fallen into a jouncing, sweaty sleep.

What jolted him awake at last was the end of their jolting ride. The stop in their motion put his mind back in motion, though only slowly.

"Ah, you wake. Good. Follow, please."

Still at least half asleep, Avram walked out into an otherworldly landscape of shelters that looked like a cross between a yurt and a dome—"yomes," Yuri called them—and craters that had been filling with sand for a century and a half, beneath stars now fading fast with the coming of dawn.

Following Yuri, he saw ahead of them in the clear early light a group of people dressed in white, working near the edge of the largest crater. As they got closer, he recognized their attire as environment suits— each rather like a cross between hazmat cleanup garb and a bargain-basement spacesuit—for working outdoors in the brutal climate.

He gazed across the crater they were working beside. It looked to be nearly completely filled with sand, yet still something over a hundred meters wide, judging by the rim. Given that an impact in sand generates a crater ten to twelve times the size of the impact object, he estimated that the impactor was probably close to ten meters across.

They were still short of the group in hazard white when he bent down to examine the stony edge of crater rim standing above the sand. From the uniform straticulations, he realized that the pale stony stuff must be impactite—sand transformed instantaneously into rock by the pressure of a meteoritic-impact shock wave. He also thought that the scattered stones along the crater rim—glassy black and shiny white— were probably tektites.

When he stood up, he saw that the sun had breached the horizon and Yuri was well ahead of him. He hastened to catch up.

By the time he reached the group, they had their headgear and flex-gauntlets off. A tall, square-jawed, sun-reddened man with piercing blue eyes beneath graying blond hair stepped forward. Beside him stood a dark-complected, dark-eyed woman with shoulder-length black hair.

"Welcome to Wabar, Doctor Zaragosa," said the man, thrusting out his hand for Avram to shake. "I hope Yuri 'Mister Toad' Semenov didn't give you too wild a ride to our digs."

Yuri gave Avram a smiling, squint-eyed look.

"No, not at all. We either slept or talked—me doing the former, and both of us the latter."

"Really? I'll bet Yuri could drive some of it sleeping. He probably did! I'm Victor Fremdkunst, the money behind this madness. Just visiting, actually. This is Professor Vida Nasr, your co-director."

"Pleased to meet you," Avram said. "I've read your articles on Libyan desert glass, from the Sand Sea strewnfield in western Egypt. Good work."

When Vida Nasr flashed a smile at him, he realized just how beautiful a woman she actually was. Just as quickly he reminded himself of his daughter's death, and of his own mission.

From her name and career path, he doubted this Nasr woman was a devout Muslim—secular Arab or Persian, more likely. Nonetheless, she, too, have a hidden agenda—she might be putting up as thorough a facade as he was himself. Best to be careful of her.

"The pleasure is all mine," she said. "Thank you. I know your own fine work at Campo del Cielo."

Fremdkunst laughed.

"Now that you two have finished with the official academic strutting and preening, grab yourself a cool suit, a personal locator beacon, and a magnetometer, Avram, and see if you can't help us find some meteorite spall."

As he walked away to find his gear, Avram wondered at Fremdkunst's suggestion. If he knew about Avram's implant, he would have realized that a personal locator beacon was rather redundant. Was Victor trying to hide what he knew about him? Or were there aspects of Avram's mission that exceeded even Victor's need to know?

INTERLUDE: A LATE-NIGHT HIKE IN DESOLATION

Under the moonless, starlit December night, Paul Larkin and the four Mawari children tramped away from Grass Lake in their snowshoes. This was supposed to be a short little nothing of a walk, he thought. Just a little snowcamping in the pristine white stuff from a recent storm. That was not how it was turning out, though.

He watched the kids moving ahead of him in the trail they had broken through the snow the previous afternoon. They were not just "the four Mawari children" anymore, he reminded himself. The kids had picked up English and other languages with astonishing speed. Not bad, coming from a people whose language apparently had no verb tense other than the present. They had already given themselves names extracted from what they'd learned on the Internet, too.

Paul was having less and less trouble distinguishing among them with each day that passed. He knew the youngest girl called herself "Ka-dalun" now, while "Aubrey Menehune" was the oldest, and the middle girl called herself "Ebu Gogo." The lone boy, more sullen and hard to reach than the others, called himself "Alii De Danaan."

Each had taken a name associated with disappeared fairy folk or little people from around the world.

Strange names, for strange kids. Too grown up and focused, and too young and clumsy, all at the same time. It was to get them away from the Web and the computers, from their endless soap bubble–blowing and marbles-playing, too, that he'd taken them walking in the woods—on day hikes down to Emerald Bay and along the Tahoe shore, as well as overnighters on the Rim Trail and up to the Echo Lakes.

Trekking into the southeastern edge of Desolation Wilderness for snowcamping had taken them just a couple miles inland from the south edge of Fallen Leaf Lake, with its lodge and lakefront cabins.

It should have been no problem.

No problem as they tramped that afternoon through the sparkling powdery snow, snow-limned pines, and crisp blue air. No problem as they set up a pair of tents—Paul and Alii in one, the girls in another—in an open spot under ponderosa and lodgepole pines west of Grass Lake. No problem as they fixed and ate dinner, before turning in for the night.

No problem, until the children's sense of disquiet and unease in the middle of the night led them to rouse him—and then, moments later, the sound of a branch snapping and displaced snow softly falling from trees.

As they moved through and over the snow, Paul wondered if their uneasiness had been some kind of sixth sense, something preternatural, or just kids afraid of the dark. The children had learned languages and tech so fast it was almost like four minds concentrating together on each problem or obstacle. Was this now something even more than that? Or was their hyperalertness just an overreaction bred of fear and suspicion?

He supposed such alertness wasn't too surprising in some ways, given that they'd seen their entire tribe killed off, and then been transported into a world that was (technologically at least) thousands of years into their future. A world populated by people who probably looked a great deal like the people who had massacred everyone they had ever known.

That would be enough to make anybody grow up fast and strange. Not to mention probably making them feel more than a little conflicted about their destroyer/benefactors.

They traveled on, under innumerable stars sparkling and cold as the snow about them, but far more distant and tranquil. Paul began to think that the children's uneasiness and the night sounds they'd all heard might be nothing after all. He felt sheepish that such late-night fears had led them to break camp at two in the morning and start back toward Fallen Leaf. He felt more than a little foolish, too, for having called in to rouse his security team with their concerns, and urging the team to proceed to his GPS coordinates.

A bright shooting star fell overhead, surprisingly slowly.

"Look!" Ka-dalun whispered, pointing—for Paul's benefit. The children all seemed to have seen it at the same instant.

"Geminid meteor showers are now," Alii said bluntly.

Paul nodded with enthusiasm, but said nothing. As a child he'd been fascinated by the sheer numbers of falling stars in meteor showers, the myriad quick sparks struck from the night sky. As he grew older, however, he'd looked for something slower, rarer, and more graceful: the long bright spear tipped with its diamond lotus of fire, blooming, flying, burning, dying.

Like this one.

Alii had just started to tell them that the Geminids were not, like most meteor showers, the debris trails of active comets but were instead the debris trail of 3200 Phaeton, which might be either a rocky asteroid or a very ancient extinct comet—when, in the starlight, little comet-tails began sprouting from the snow, moving closer to them.

Paul only had a moment to realize those were bullets impacting in the snowfield. He shouted "Run! Head for the rocks and trees!" before he was struck high on the right shoulder and spun around by the impact. A second impact, this one a blow to his left leg, knocked him and his snowshoes out of the snow and laid him down hard in a heap, poles all akimbo and snowshoes toes-up to the sky.

As he lay there, more stars fell overhead. He told himself to try to stay calm, to stay focused, to think about the children, but an all-too-comforting lassitude began to spread over him. Another meteor speared by overhead, a lit fuse dropping from the tall tapestry of the steadier stars. Fireworks, he thought dreamily. He waited for the boom, the starshell flash, the "Ahhh!" of the crowd. They never came.

Instead, sounds of something whizzing rapidly over his head caught his attention. His last thoughts, before he passed out, were of bottle-rockets, and whistling shells, and Ka-dalun and Alii and Aubrey and Ebu chorusing in his head "No! Don't let it happen again—"

At the chaotic borders of consciousness, Paul saw his grandmother shaking her finger and saying in his sister's voice, "It was *people* what turned Paradise into Hell!"

As he came more fully awake, however, the voice and words resolved themselves into the beeping of biomedical monitors and hissing of life-support equipment. He was surrounded by a rubber jungle of hospital bed equipment. He found himself catheterized and tanked on oxygen and God only knew what all else.

With a groan he removed the oxygen line clipped to the septum of his nose. A short blond woman dressed in nurse's scrubs entered the room, followed by a tall, thickset man dressed in uniform, removing his hat as he came in. It took Paul a minute to place him. Jarrod Takimoto, the chief of his security team.

"Glad to see you've rejoined us, Mister Larkin," Takimoto said, as the nurse checked his vital signs.

"Jarrod," he said. It was difficult to talk over the dry scratchiness of his throat. "Where am I?"

"Private clinic in Truckee. Caters mostly to those who've broken themselves skiing. We have the entire wing."

"Sounds expensive. The kids?"

"They're fine. Sleeping in shifts, waiting for you. They're in the lounge down the hall."

"That's a relief. How long have I been out?"

"Including surgery? About a day and a half. You'd lost a fair amount of blood by the time we got to you. One of the bullets was about this close to your femoral artery." Takimoto made a gap with thumb and forefinger that looked uncomfortably less than an inch wide.

The nurse finished up and left the room.

"Who came after us?" Paul asked quietly.

"Don't know for sure yet. They came in sterile—no ID. Five of them. Night vision, full body armor, silencers. We would have had a heck of a time stopping them. Luckily, someone else stopped them for us."

"Who?"

"I have no idea. But somebody killed all of the attackers."

"How? I thought you said they were in body armor."

"They were, but it didn't help them much. Blunt trauma took them out. The bulletproof gear wasn't pierced, but the forces of impact cratered everything down to four inches below the armor. Impact was right above the heart in most cases, unfortunately for them. Clean kills. Like somebody fired a heavy caliber slug into each of their chests."

" 'Like'?"

"Yeah, like," Takimoto said, staring at the hat in his hands, fiddling with its brim. "I had my people scour the area yesterday, but they found nothing worthwhile. No spent rounds, no shells, no slugs. No footprints, even. Found a few oddly shaped rocks, but you'd better ask a geologist about those. Nothing germane to the investigation."

Paul remembered the high, whizzing sound he'd heard, but tried to put it out of his mind.

"Somebody must have heard something?"

Takimoto shook his head.

"The assailants had silencers, like I said. Whoever helped you out must have had the same. If those kids know, they're not talking. Nobody heard anything. That's made it easier to keep all this out of the public eye, at least."

"What's the cover story?"

"If anybody asks, you've been hospitalized due to a skiing-related accident. Bad fall—broken leg and dislocated shoulder. So far nobody's asked."

"The staff here?"

"They're being paid enough to refer all questions to us, and to say nothing beyond that."

"Good."

"Mister Larkin? I've been waiting for word from you on whether I should inform the kids', er, guardians—Doctor Miskulin and Doctor Yamada?—about what happened."

Paul Larkin shook his head, vehemently and negatively enough to make stars flicker in his vision.

"You'll do nothing of the kind. They're off to Italy. Probably there by now. Our cover story is good enough for Aunt Susan and Uncle

Michael, if they ask, when they return. They won't have much time for it. Michael, at least, is going to some conference in Dubai, I think it is. Now, if you will, call the kids in so I can see them."

Takimoto left. Paul felt a pang at having to hide the truth from Michael and Susan this way. Cowardly and sneaky, but he had no choice. Who knew how they might respond, especially Susan, to news of his failure to take adequate security precautions for himself and the children? They might want to take the kids away, and he didn't want that at all.

Takimoto stepped back into the room and the children surged forward around him, each coming forward to give Paul a quick strong hug before stepping back from the bed.

Tears welled up in his eyes. These children were the last remnant of the people his sister Jacinta had so loved. The people she would have given anything to help. The people she had died for, because Paul had refused to believe in their existence all those years ago. Now he wanted fiercely to hold on to them, and never let them go.

THREE

ROCKS AND THE CHURCH

>>>>>>>

"Yo, Brother Doctor Guy!" Michael Miskulin called across the grounds of Castel Gandolfo. Aside from its hilltop position twenty-two miles southeast of Rome, the Castel did not look very fortified. Tall columnar Italian cypress trees were the only obvious sentinels standing beside the high square-cut hedges—the fortress's sole ramparts. Maybe that was part of the problem, given what had happened.

"Hello, Michael," said the bearded and bespectacled man coming toward them. He wore the black attire and white clerical collar of a Jesuit brother and looked to be in his early sixties. "I trust your flight was a good one?"

"Not bad, if you like hurtling through the sky in a pressurized sardine can with wobbly wings. At least my jet lag is better today."

"And this is Dr. Yamada?"

As Susan shook the Jesuit's hand, Michael introduced him as Guy LeConte, director of the Specola Vaticana, the Vatican Observatory.

"When I first met Brother Astronomer," Michael said, "he was only the curator of the Vatican State Meteorite Collection, in the Observatory Museum here."

"And you were only a rather pesky medical student, crashing an astrobiology conference," the Jesuit said with a broad wink. They walked together along one of the stone paths that radiated across the lawn like a sundial's hour-angle lines.

"I wasn't crashing it. I had submitted a paper for presentation. On survivability parameters for microbes in meteorite pores. It was my first conference presentation."

"And of course he presented the paper like an old pro," Brother Guy said to Susan. "Born to take the center stage. Ah, Michael, Michael. Indiana Miskulin and the Raiders of the Lost Aubrites. Always the high radar cross section—makes you easy to shoot down, my friend."

"You haven't exactly stayed out of the limelight yourself."

"No, that's true. But if you'd just followed a more traditional path in either medicine or impact geology, who knows where you'd be now?"

"Overworked as an internist or stuck among dusty rocks in a dustier academic department. You know me, Brother, I'm not good at office politics. That's why I never went to work for NASA."

The director of the Vatican Observatory gestured toward the telescope domes atop Castel Gandolfo's roofs.

"You were raised Catholic, as I recall. Too bad you never took Holy Orders. If you had, you could be funded by the Holy See, as we are here. No politics. Our only imperative is to do good science."

"I've never been good at following orders, holy or otherwise," Michael said, smiling and waving his hands in mock dismissal. "I actually thought I was called to the priesthood when I was in the third grade, but in the fourth grade"—Michael shot Susan a sidelong glance—"I began to realize what the whole celibacy thing might really mean."

Brother Guy gave them both a wry smile.

"Ah yes, sex," he said as they left the lawns and entered the Castel keep proper. "Nature has long used the pleasure of the senses to sell reproduction to her creatures. The way humans and all higher animals delight in such activity suggests to me that all creatures have always done so, to the degree they are capable—all the way back to single-celled critters that don't even reproduce sexually."

As they walked, dimly lit corridors and rough-hewn rock alternated with rebuilt modern interiors—crisp, clean walls and efficient lighting.

"Just imagine a microbe, say," Brother Guy continued, "undergoing all the contortions of pinching off and splitting into two more or less identical copies of itself. Then afterward both of them are smoking in bed, and one microbe says to the other, 'Was it good for me, too, baby?' "

Susan blurted a loud, surprised laugh as they walked down a hall lined with magnificent Baroque paintings.

"That's one of the better sex jokes I've heard in a while—and from a celibate priest, yet!"

"Brother, not priest. And I wasn't always celibate, you know. I came to my vocation rather late."

"Okay, Guy, you can stop flirting with her now. We need to get down to business—or to more blatant criminal activity, at least. The thefts from the meteorite collection, I mean."

"Killjoy. I'm very sorry Father Kunkel, our current curator of meteorites, couldn't be here to meet with you himself. He's rather busy with the police at present. Never fear, we're already on our way to the scene of the crime."

"Brother," Susan asked as they continued down a long hall, "how did the Vatican end up in the astronomy business anyway? After Galileo and all?"

"Those are probably the two most frequently asked questions we get. Yet, long before Galileo, astronomy was part of the core curriculum taught at the universities the Church itself founded, during the Middle Ages. Arithmetic, astronomy, geometry, and music were the 'top four,' the quadrivium, of the seven medieval liberal arts."

"What were the bottom three?"

"The trivium—grammar, rhetoric, logic. The Church's involvement with an observatory proper doesn't go all the way back to the Middle Ages, but it does go back to before the Galileo affair—to 1582, when Pope Gregory the Thirteenth asked Jesuit mathematician Christoph Clavius to improve the scientific data for the reform of the calendar."

"That the Clavius of moon-crater fame?" Michael asked, turning back from where he'd gotten ahead of Susan and Brother Guy.

"Very good, Michael. It is indeed. Much later, in 1891, Pope Leo the Thirteenth formally reestablished the Vatican Observatory on a hillside near the dome of St. Peter's Basilica. A signal to scientists and the faithful that science and religion had nothing to fear from each other."

Brother Guy picked up his pace and they strode past more spectacular Baroque depictions of the heavens.

"Light pollution drove us from Rome to Castel Gandolfo, here, in 1933. The same thing happened again as Rome grew, after the war. Since 1981 most of our real skywatching has been done in Arizona, through the Vatican Observatory Research Group, the VORG."

" 'Resistance is futile—' " Michael began.

" '—you will be assimilated.' The VORG is a partner in the Mount Graham International Observatory, which is where you'll find the Vatican Advanced Technology Telescope."

"And Galileo?" Susan asked.

Brother Guy heaved a sigh.

"Last time I checked, even the Church hierarchy was made of flawed human beings. Sometimes we make mistakes out of ignorance. The early seventeenth century was a very tense time for the Church— the Protestant breakaways gathering momentum for nearly a century, the ongoing madness of the Thirty Years War, all of that. Some very powerful prelates confused what makes us go to heaven with what makes the heavens go, as Galileo put it. The Galileo affair is not characteristic of the Church's attitude toward science as a whole, thank heavens."

"No?" Susan asked, not quite keeping the skepticism out of her voice.

"Think about it. The first chemist was a monk—Roger Bacon. The first geologist was a monk—Albertus Magnus. The founder of genetics was a monk—Gregor Mendel. The inventor of spectroscopy was a priest—Pietro Angelo Secchi—as was the first proposer of the Big Bang theory, Georges Lemaître."

"But . . . meteorites?"

"Oh yes, the Church has been in the vanguard even in meteoritics, the humble science of fallen stars! One of the great eighteenth-century scientific investigators of meteorites was a Jesuit priest, Father Domenico Troili."

"After whom the ubiquitous meteoritic mineral troilite is named," Michael said.

"Ah, can't fool you," Brother Guy said playfully. They followed him as he turned down a side corridor of the Vatican Observatory Museum.

"This place we're walking through, the Papal Palace at Castel Gandolfo, was originally built in 1590 for Maffeo Barberini. Barberini later became Pope Urban the Eighth, the pope who was behind Galileo's trial by the Inquisition. Since 1933 the same villa built for the persecutor of Galileo has been topped with observatory domes and has served as the home of the Vatican Observatory. I'm sure you both can appreciate the irony in that."

They stopped before a pair of policemen standing in front of a section of a modern, clean-walled, and efficiently lit hallway—blocked by crime-scene tape. Brother Guy spoke to the officers, who agreed to let them enter, but only if they gloved up, which they did.

Once past the tape, they stood before a wood-and-glass cabinet. Nearby were rank upon rank of drawers. Several of the drawers had been pulled out and left roughly stacked on the floor of the hall, and the doors of the cabinet were ajar. The floor was littered with plastic bags and the occasional glass vial.

"Looks like somebody was in a hurry," Susan said. "They certainly didn't bother to clean up after themselves."

"Yes, it would seem so. The collection, as you can see, is considerable. It contains fifteen hundred specimens from nearly five hundred different falls. It would have taken whoever did this quite a while to clean up—if they had ever intended to leave things orderly. Which I doubt."

"How did you get so many of them?" she asked, carefully picking up a meteoritic fragment in her gloved hand.

"The core of the collection was donated by the distinguished French agronomist Adrien-Charles, Marquis de Mauroy, mostly in the 1920s and 1930s. The de Mauroy collection itself is some two hundred years old. We have continued to add items to it here for over eighty years."

"When was the last time it was cataloged?" Michael asked.

"Before this recent unintended reorganization, the collection was cataloged twice—in 1983, prior to which it was in general disarray, and in 2008, when numerous additions to the collection's holdings necessitated a new inventory."

"Any pattern to what was taken?"

"After as much examination as the authorities will allow," Brother Guy said, nodding in the direction of the officers, "Father Kunkel has highlighted what we believe is missing—here, on this list."

Brother Guy handed him a printout of nearly forty pages of alphabetically arranged entries in what Michael quickly recognized as British Museum Catalog style. The entry for each specimen included the locality and date of the meteorite fall or find, its classification, weight, and a brief description. The catalog listed stones from around the world.

The first highlighted name Michael encountered was a famous one any meteoriticist would already know: "ALLENDE, Chihuahua, Mexico— Fall, Feb. 8, 1969—Carbonaceous Chondrite CV3—Specimens: Fragments, 5 gm, 5 gm." He paged through several more sheets listing mesosiderites, pallasites, octahedrites, hexahedrites, anomalous ataxites, and several other types of chondrites before he came to the next high-lighted item: "GROSNAJA, Mekensk, Terek, Caucasus—Fall, June 28, 1861—Carbonaceous Chondrite CV3—Specimen: Piece of thick slab in glass vial, 11 gm."

By the time he reached "ORGUEIL, Montauban, Tarn-et-Garone, France—Fall, May 14, 1864—Carbonaceous Chondrite CI—Specimens: Large fragment and many small pieces, 60 gm, Fragments 14 gm, 6.2 gm, 5.0 gm, 1 gm (Note: all specimens are in glass vials with cork stoppers)," Michael clearly saw the pattern to the highlighted entries. He stopped reading.

"All carbonaceous chondrites," he said. "Very important stones, but strange nonetheless."

Brother Guy nodded.

"Why's that?" Susan asked.

"If I were an ordinary thief," Michael said, "I would have grabbed the pallasites, since they're most readily convertible into gemstones."

"Or, if I were a collector gone bad," said Brother Guy, "I would have grabbed some of the lunar or Martian meteorites. We've got achondrite shergottite from the Shergotty fall in India, achondrite nakhlite from the Nakhla fall in Egypt, achondrite chassignite from the Chassigny fall in France—all benchmark Martian meteorites. Father Kunkel just traded several irons to Victor Fremdkunst for a lunar me-teorite, too. All very valuable. All untouched, as near as we can tell."

"I read about that swap with Fremdkunst," Michael said, shaking his head. "Sounded like a pact with the devil to me."

"Perhaps, but Father Kunkel thinks it was the devil who got burned on the deal. We worked out a bargain that was strongly to our advan-tage."

"Did Fremdkunst himself come here?"

"I know what you're thinking, Michael. The answer is no. It was all handled through intermediaries. And not even his intermediaries came to see the stones here."

"These carbonaceous chondrites," Susan said. "They're primarily of scientific interest?"

"That's right. Some would argue they're of *invaluable* scientific in-terest. Thank God what was stolen were only fragments. The rest of the stones are distributed in many institutions throughout the world—predominantly universities and museums of natural history."

"What about your security?"

"Medium level. More than a jewelry store, less than a nuclear reactor. Door control, alarm monitoring, closed-circuit TV in a few spots. Motion detection lasers and pressure sensors, though the latter have been switched off for years, after endless false alarms. Locks and keys for the cabinets and drawers themselves. A not-inconsiderable contingent of Swissers when the pope is in residence, which he isn't right now. Whoever took our specimens defeated all the safeguards."

"Maybe it was an inside job?" Michael suggested. "Even folks who've taken Holy Orders could have been following other orders."

"Not impossible. The police, however, have already found the ingress and egress paths of the thieves. They came from off the hill and returned in the same direction. The thieves also went to the trouble of either fooling or disabling all the security systems, real time. If they'd had somebody on the inside, I don't think they'd have had to go to that much trouble."

"Sounds like a very expensive professional burglary," Susan said, putting down a sealed plastic bag with a reddish-black stony-iron inside.

"Indeed it does," Brother Guy said, noncommittally but watching them carefully nonetheless. "Although what was taken were not pieces of the True Cross or splinters of the spear that pierced Christ's side, these cabinets were scientific reliquaries, as it were, and they've been violated."

"Somebody would have had to put a good chunk of money into planning and executing something like this," Michael agreed.

"But why do that," Susan asked, turning to the cleric, "if the stones were mainly of scientific interest?"

"We were hoping you and Michael might be able to tell us."

"Thanks for the vote of confidence, Brother Guy. But why us?"

"Precisely because of your high profile, Michael. We've largely managed to keep this crime out of the media, thus far. We're not sure we'll be able to do that for much longer, however. You're fairly well known, Doctor Meteor. If this blows up in the press, the fact that we've put you on the case will show that we're taking the matter seriously."

"Ah, I see. You're covering your ass, politically, despite your claim that politics isn't important to the science here."

Brother Guy gave Michael a wry look.

"I prefer to think of it in less colorful terms. Carefully considered public relations, as I see it. Actually, I wasn't the one who suggested hiring you. It came through some of our colleagues in Arizona, not long after they learned of the matter. The man at whose suggestion we recruited you is here on the grounds, though. Probably still with Father Kunkel and the police, looking at the escape route the thieves used. If you'll follow me . . ."

Brother Guy led them out of the violated meteorite display and the interior twilight of the Castel, into the bright sunlight of a Mediterranean afternoon. There they found a priest and police officer talking and gesticulating toward the steep hillside below them. Off to one side of them stood a man with a cane. He also wore a goatee and mustache trimmed in a style Michael thought looked somehow familiar, though he couldn't place it.

"That's the gentleman to whom you owe this assignment," Brother Guy said, sotto voce.

As they approached the brow of the hill, the man with the cane stepped toward them.

"Doctors Miskulin and Yamada, hello. Daniel Amaral, special liaison from the Department of State to the National Security Agency. The NSA director is an old friend of mine, and he has an interest in this case. He'd like to speak with you, once you've finished up here and have returned to the States."

CAUTIONS AND PRECAUTIONS

"It's beautiful here," Darla Pittman said as they drove down Fourth Street, through the small town of Hamilton, Montana. The Bitterroot Mountains formed a spectacular backdrop to the neighborhood of older but well-kept residential homes through which they were passing.

"Certainly is," said her driver, Biological Safety Officer Reg Singh. "I've become quite the fly-fisherman since I moved here. I understand you're a technical rock climber? There's great climbing in both the Bitterroots and the Sapphires."

Ahead of them she spotted a cluster of buildings, blandly functional in appearance. Given their location in a residential neighborhood, the structures might have passed for the campus of a high school or community college, with accompanying physical plant, were it not for the security-fenced perimeter, tall lights, and surveillance cameras.

"This is rather an incongruous place to put a BSL-4 biocontainment lab," Darla said.

"A product of history," Singh said with a shrug. "RML, the Rocky

Mountain Laboratories, started out in an old schoolhouse over a century ago. Rocky Mountain spotted fever was the scientific problem back then. The etiology of Lyme's disease was discovered here, too, in 1982. Of course, we've been investigating a lot more than ticks and fleas for a long time."

"I gathered as much," Pittman said as they pulled to a stop beside a guarded gate. The guard required that they both sign and date the logbook—actually a notepad computer—before entry.

"Under NIH's National Institute of Allergy and Infectious Diseases, we've prospered and grown," Singh said as he signed in and handed the stylus and notepad computer to her. "Especially since the Bioterrorism Response Act of 2002 paved the way for more top-level containment labs. RML's Integrated Research Facility here was only the fifth biosafety level-four facility in the country. RML-IRF is a major player in the fight against bioterrorism—despite the bucolic setting."

Handing back the log-in device with her signature, Darla Pittman nodded but said nothing. Reg drove them slowly into the secured facility.

Darla recalled with a twinge that, when she initially mentioned the bioweapon angle to Barry Levitch, she intended it as something of a canard. Upon relaying her preliminary findings to General Retticker, however, he had quickly gone to Defense Condition 1, at least in terms of containment. Ever since, she'd been threading her way through a vast bureaucratic maze.

It turned out that the national security community and its members had established and now sat on numerous advisory boards overseeing clinicians and researchers involved in viral diseases, bacteriological pathogens, biotech, immunology, and basic molecular biology. It was through Retticker's board-sitting friends that Darla had been allowed to pass through the acronymic labyrinth of government regulatory agencies—FBI, CDC, USDA, NIH, FDA, NRC, DHHS.

She'd had to learn more about biotech and bioterrorism than she'd ever wanted to. About "experiments of concern" and "designer diseases." About "restricted persons" who may *not* possess "select" and "novel" agents. About exotic pathogens and BSL-4 containment, in which nothing created or emerging within a laboratory should have any possibility of escape or direct contact with lab workers.

At CU, one of her colleagues in the biology department had been dragooned into giving her a crash course in microbiological laboratory practice, to brush up her skills. She'd been force-fed what she thought of as the Protocols of Bumble—BMBL, Biosafety in Microbiology and

Biomedical Laboratories. She knew all about the "dual-use dilemma," and about what was permitted and what was prohibited under the international Biological and Toxin Weapons Convention (BWC).

Worse, before she even left Boulder, she had to suffer many a hypodermic needle injecting various substances into her body as part of an immunization regime for work at RML-IRF. She endured almost as many more needles pulling things out of her—all sorts of baseline serum sampling—as part of the lab's serological surveillance program.

The pain and aggravation, however, seemed to be paying off at last.

"Here we are," Reg Singh said as they pulled up to the IRF proper. Flashing her a sly grin, he extended his hand for her to shake. "Congratulations on being named a principal investigator. As your biological safety officer, or BSO, I'll be keeping close tabs on you—same as I do with all the PIs on my watch."

Darla laughed and shook his hand, struck by how handsome Singh was when he smiled. His warm dark eyes just lit up, under all that wavy dark hair. She shook her head and smiled, too, as they got out of the car.

"If acronyms are toxic to microbes," she said, "then there isn't a bug in the world that will ever get out of our lab alive!"

Singh laughed politely.

"Fortunately we do not have to rely on toxic alphabet-soup bureaucracy for our real defense. We take almost as many measures to prevent the bad *guys* from getting in as we do to keep the bad *bugs* from getting out. Follow me, please."

As they approached the door, Singh tapped in a code. Someone buzzed them inside. In the IRF main lobby, they approached the man in control of the buzzer: an armed guard seated behind a counter with several closed-circuit TV monitors before him.

"Access control," Singh said, then introduced Darla to the guard. The guard handed them another logbook computer to sign and date. The guard then handed Darla a previously prepared photo-ID badge.

"That's all?" she asked, as they approached an elevator.

"Not quite."

She soon saw what he meant by that "not quite." They got into the elevator with no problem but, once inside, the elevator would not move. The elevator requested that each of them insert their ID into the card reader and then speak aloud their destination floor. At last, the elevator deigned to move. Darla gave Reg a look, but he waggled a finger at her.

The elevator opened into the corridor on the BSL-4 floor. A moment later they were confronted by yet another door. This one demanded a card to read, a retina scan, and yet another log-in before it would let them enter.

"Welcome to IRF BSL-4," Singh said as they walked into the anteroom of the lab suite. "We have both cabinet-lab and suit-lab facilities here. Class-three biosafety cabinets—glove boxes—and one-piece positive pressure suits ventilated by a high-efficiency particulate air filtration life-support system."

"So, HEPA-filtered air. That's it for acronyms and security, finally?"

"Not quite. The outer and inner changing rooms are separated by decontamination shower rooms. Once you've removed your street clothes in the outer change room, you'll be carded, DNA-printed, fingerprinted, and body-scanned before the system will let you pass into the shower rooms from this side. All outer and inner doors make an airlock, and the doors themselves are interlocking in order to prevent door sets from being opened simultaneously. We'll be meeting in the suit lab to unpack your specimens. See you there."

Darla walked into the Women's Outer Change Room and carded open a locker. She began stripping off her street clothes, hanging and folding them in the locker. Naked, she stepped up to the security console beside the door and slid her ID card into the reader, which took the card and kept it.

The system instructed her to place her thumbs on a pad that did both fingerprinting and DNA printing. When that was done, the system instructed her to step onto the footprint marks on the floor and stand very still, which she did. The system counted down from five to zero, then she heard the sort of mechanical sounds she usually associated with medical machinery—X-ray, MRI, and the like.

As she waited for some sign that she had passed muster, she thought about the relationships between security and freedom—and between biology and privacy. She'd heard of the biomanaged security state, but she'd never seen it as fully embodied as here, standing naked for machine inspection in a BSL-4 lab, in an otherwise nondescript building of a nondescript government-agency complex, in the middle of an old-fashioned neighborhood in a small Montana town.

Without fanfare the shower door gave a loud click. She stepped into the decontamination shower room and was blasted by very warm water. She wondered what chemicals and disinfectants it might contain. Singh could probably tell her, if she wanted to go into that much detail. She wasn't sure she did.

The shower shut down and she opened the door to the inner change room. There she found complete laboratory clothes—undergarments, jumpsuits, shoes, and gloves. Because she was going into the suit lab, she donned the one-piece pressure suit and hooked herself into life support as well.

She saw the pressure-suited Singh waiting for her in the corridor leading to the suit lab.

"That took awhile," she said to him, over the suit's comm link. "Is there any way in and out that's faster?"

"Under normal conditions, no. The BSL-4 lab can only be entered or left through the clothing change and shower rooms. The inner change rooms, suit lab, and cabinet lab are constructed as sealed compartments within an internal containment capsule. There is also an expedited airlock entry/exit system, but that's for use only in extreme emergency."

Darla nodded.

"The sealed internal shell facilitates fumigation and prohibits animal and insect entry. The floors are integrally sealed, and the sewer vents and service lines all have backflow preventers and HEPA filtering. The floor drains contain traps of chemical disinfectants appropriate to the particular microorganisms under study at the time. All access doors are self-closing and lockable, while the windows are all break-resistant and sealed. There's a dedicated nonrecirculating ventilation system providing directional airflow throughout the lab from areas of least to greatest potential hazard. Redundant supply fans, redundant exhaust fans. Exhaust air is multiply filtered in series, followed by incineration."

They entered the suit lab proper, where Darla saw her three pressure-suited assistants, including a broadly grinning Barry Levitch. They stood in a world built for ease of decontamination: plastic furniture, sealed and seamless benchtop workspaces.

"To prevent contamination of this inside world by the outside world," Singh continued, "or the outside world by this inside world, all supplies and equipment not brought in through the change rooms must pass through double-door autoclaves, dunk tanks, or fumigation chambers. All biosafety cabinets are heaviest duty, totally enclosed and ventilated, with arm-length gloves or half-suits attached to O-ring ports. We have redundant air compressors, alarms, and backup air tanks for all pressure suits. For the IRF as a whole we have autostart emergency power sources—backup generators—for the exhaust system, life support, alarms, lighting, entry and exit controls. You'll also find voice, computer, and fax communication hardlines from the lab to the outside world."

"Very good," Darla said, unable to think of anything else to say in response to the barrage of security info Singh had been hitting her with. She switched onto the common channel, which included the three assistants as well as Singh in the conversation. Everyone introduced themselves all around.

The assistants moved aside so she could see the transfer packages they had been awaiting. She recognized the packaging: durable cartons, labeled with biohazard symbols and infectious substances warnings. The packages came with attached sheaves of documentation—paperwork chronicling facilities, personnel, and "justification of need" for every stage of their journey.

At a nod from her, the assistants began opening the boxes, which were triple packed: heavy cartons on the outside, followed by absorbent and watertight secondary packaging, ending at last in the primary receptacles. In the case of the smaller box, the primaries were glass vials and bottles, while a containment bag of heavy plastic was the final line of defense in the larger box.

Such overkill, she thought, as the bag with what was left of their chunk of meteorite was lifted out of the larger container. The tepui skystone was less than one third the size it had been when Retticker had initially given it to her. True, a sizable portion of that reduction had been the result of the tests she had run or that colleagues had performed at her behest, but she was sure those tests accounted for no more than a quarter of the stone's lost mass.

Once Retticker had learned of her findings, he had divvied the stone far beyond her own distributing of it. He informed her that he was sending portions of it to his connections at the U.S. Army Medical Research Institute for Infectious Diseases (USAMRIID) at Fort Detrick, Maryland—yet another BSL-4 containment facility. Darla suspected that the general was now double-tracking the investigation, at the very least.

She wondered at all this belated caution. Who knew how many people had been exposed to the skystone on its way to her, its secret origins notwithstanding? She and Barry had long been exposed to the stone themselves, working with it for weeks without all these high-flown safety measures. She had been more afraid that she and Barry might contaminate the meteorite, than that the meteorite might contaminate them.

She was certain they had suffered no ill effects. No exotic face-melting infections, nothing even so much as a head cold—as she grumpily told the techs in Boulder while they were doing her baseline interview. They cheerfully informed her that the IRF's biomedical surveillance system monitored all employees for any lab-associated illness and that RML had facilities for quarantine, isolation, and medical care, in the unlikely event of exposure to a deadly pathogen.

No one in her university lab, it was true, had actually tried to culture anything found on the meteorite. Doing so might change everything, although she doubted it. Odds were all too overwhelming that what she and her collaborators had found in both the chemistry and the imagery was most likely fossil or artifact. Even if those nanoshapes were something potentially viable, how likely was she to stumble, at random, on the proper medium for growing such critters out?

"Hey, Doctor P," Barry said over the comm line, "there's a sealed envelope in here addressed to you."

Startled, Darla took the envelope from Barry. Opening it, she found a printed message from General Retticker.

Dear Darla:

I trust you are reading this inside a high-level containment lab—interesting twist on information security, eh?

There are some more facts you might like to know about your tepui meteorite. It was found in association with a tribe of meteorite cultists, who were infected with a fungal parasite. Their legends claimed the source of that mushroom infection was purposely crashed on our planet by their sky gods.

Make what you will of that. Your discovery of potential fossils or biologicals, however, leads me to think that it is perhaps possible that the meteorite may in fact be the original source of the tribe's endemic infection. For that reason I have also provided spore print material from their supposedly sky-derived sacred fungus. We gather from autopsies that the infection is limited to neural tissue and somehow involved in tryptamine chemistry. That might suggest to you some appropriate culture media and growing conditions.

I urge you in your research to verify the replicability or viability of any biologicals you might uncover. Whatever the truth of the tribe's legends, I feel that, should you succeed in growing out what you found in the meteorite, the risk of pathogenicity is strong enough that your work must be conducted in a top-level biocontainment facility. You're in Hamilton, Montana, primarily because that is the closest such facility to Boulder, Colorado.

I look forward to receiving further reports from you on your good work—and very soon.

Sincerely,
Joseph Retticker

Not exactly a love letter, but helpful and encouraging nonetheless. Darla glanced up from the note to find her colleagues in the suit lab looking at her expectantly.

"From General Retticker," she said, waving the note. "Wishing us luck and urging us to get on with it."

"What would you like us to get on with, exactly?" Barry asked.

"Take the samples we have here and locate all objects whose shapes suggest anything bacterial or nanobacteroidal. I'll come up with a list of polymerase chain reactants to determine replicability, and culture media appropriate for determining viability and growth rates."

Darla turned away from the group and situated herself before a flat-screen computer mounted flush with the top of the lab table. Bringing up a list of growth media on the display, she tried to puzzle her way through which media might be best. She stared at the note from Retticker again. What relevance could mushroom-infected meteorite cultists possibly have to her work? If the general wanted something in that line, he should have hired an ethnobotanist.

Maybe he had already done so. If, however, on the advice of just such a specialist, his people at USAMRIID were thinking they were going to grow something as complex as mushrooms from the nano-sized stuff she'd spotted, then she was sure they were off on a wild truffle hunt. No matter how viable the stuff might turn out to be, there was no way those nanoshapes could contain instructions for something as complex as mushrooms. They were just too small.

Given that neither she nor Barry had suffered any ill effects from exposure to the tiny things on the meteorite, she also doubted they would be able to infect humans directly. She'd have to test for that possibility, however—just to be on the safe side.

Then again, if the tiny things were living stuff, they might be able to splice some of their genetic material into more complicated organisms. Lots of viruses and bacteria possessed that capability. The mushrooms of the general's note might have served only as a vector for getting inside still more complex organisms, including humans.

And humans might serve as a vector for . . . what?

She stopped, realizing she'd only proceeded to that next step because of her time spent with Miskulin in Antarctica.

"The code for life on Earth did not originate on Earth," he'd insisted, in one of their argumentative conversations. "It seeded this planet from outer space. The life code came from space, and to space it must return."

"What's your proof?" she asked. " 'Seeded' is too purposeful. Why not randomly? And why 'must' it return to space? What are your sources? Where's your logic? We're not talking about salmon swimming back to their birthplaces, you know."

"You want proof? All you have to do is look at the deep genetic dynamic that's driving nearly all organisms on earth. Overpopulation, environmental destruction, aggressive territorial expansion. They're all part of—"

"Your usual litany of sins. I don't see it—not in every species, anyway. How do you know all that isn't just the result of human stupidity? You're arguing for some kind of biological essentialism. That's ideology, not science."

"No, this dynamic is truly universal. It's just that it manifests itself more clearly in some species than in others—in lemmings, for instance. Or in humans. Our fate is to swim the ocean of interstellar space, or die trying."

"Human beings as space lemmings? Doesn't seem like a very glorious end for carriers of your 'life code.' And how is this 'return' supposed to be accomplished, anyway?"

"It doesn't matter to the code whether it travels in starships, or in the corpses of deceased astronauts."

Typical Michael. Always had to have the last word. Still, Darla wondered if his ideas—ideological and illogical as they seemed—might still not be entirely wrong. She knew from the schedule for this year's exobio conference that he would be presenting a paper there. Might be good to pick his brain about "next steps"—in a circumspect and circuitous fashion, of course.

Staring at the list of culture media now, and checking off serum, cerebrospinal fluid, and mushroom mycelial media, Darla vowed that neither Michael Miskulin nor anyone else besides herself should have that last word, this time.

RENDEZVOUS IN THE BAY

Joe Retticker sat in the lounge of Victor Fremdkunst's ketch *Skyminer,* admiring the nautical brass, wood, and hemp-rope decor of the bar. It was much more ostentatious than his own bait-troller, the *Fish 'n' Reaction,* moored alongside. His own boat was a good deal more casual—and probably a helluva lot more fun, too—than Fremdkunst's.

He stood when Fremdkunst himself entered, clad in a bathrobe over swim trunks, toweling water from his hair like a bronzed blond surf god newly emerged from the sea.

"Hello, Joe. How's the fishing?"

A simple question, but there was something about the way Fremdkunst fixed him with his gaze that rendered every question weighty far beyond its apparent content. Maybe it was just the man's eyes—a luminescent blue Retticker had seen only one other place in his life: in the radioactively glowing coolant water of a cobalt-fueled nuclear reactor.

"Striped bass were hitting," Retticker said, as they moved from the bar to sit at a table. "Hit a nice boil of stripers an hour or so before you contacted me. How about you? How was the desert?"

"Hot enough to fry an egg on your forehead. Sandstorms. Surly laborers. At least the last member of our core team—the Argentinian, Zaragosa—he's on board. He strongly believes, as I do, that myths, folk stories, and religious tales of people throughout the world record more than a few meteoritic impact events. I think things should move ahead nicely now. Thanks for hooking him up with us."

Retticker gave a no-problem shrug. Just a stroke of luck, really. He knew Luis Martin from the old days in Tri-Border, and Martin knew this Zaragosa fellow.

The nautically-clad woman tending bar came out to take their drink order. Fremdkunst ordered a scotch, neat, while Retticker kept on with the screwdrivers he'd been drinking.

"Thank you, Vic, for the tipoff on the tepui," Retticker said. "Our experts are finding all sorts of interesting things."

"I'd love to take credit for that, but I can't. You can thank Doctor Vang and his people for the suggestion. I'm just in it for my share of the stone."

Ah yes. Doctor Vang. Personally Joe considered the whole Tetragrammaton organization only a shadow of its former self since the Kwok-Cho thing happened, but Vang still had lots of cash, clout, and connections. It was because Victor had dropped Vang's name that he'd taken Fremdkunst's "tip" seriously in the first place.

"I trust you're pleased with it?" Retticker asked, as the bartender brought their drinks.

"With the stone? Very pleased. I can see why your scientists should find it interesting. Defies current categorization schemes in a very big way. Most unusual. Pleased with my share of it, though? Never! Always too little."

Retticker had known Fremdkunst just long enough to realize that he was less than half serious. Still, he felt compelled to explain.

"Miskulin's expedition was close enough behind us that our tactical team was pressed for time. Those tepui people put up one helluva lot more fight than expected, too. Under different circumstances I'm sure we would have figured some way to haul their whole damned sacred stone out of there."

"Yes," Fremdkunst said, swirling the scotch in its glass. "Too bad you didn't. Miskulin's involvement was unfortunate, too. Those news reports on the massacre—"

"We had those squelched as quickly as possible."

"Yes. I was wondering how you did that."

"Spun it as conflict between new settlers in the savannah and indigenes in the hills. Very little, if anything, got out on their being meteorite cultists. We've got their national guard down there keeping any media people from flying or hiking to Caracamuni tepui—and there's been little enough interest, thank God. Feuds between Indians and settlers are ordinary enough so as to attract little media attention."

Retticker took a large sip of his screwdriver. For the vitamin C, he reminded himself.

"Once we're certain interest has completely died down, I'm sure we'll be able to go back in with an extraction team to pull the rest of the rock out of the cave. Then a heavy lift helo should be able to fly it out."

Fremdkunst nodded, shrugging his longish blond bangs from his eyes.

"Good. While you're at it, you might want to have your team see if there might still be some survivors."

"Vic, I already told you what the troops told me. None of those Mawari primitives were left alive. Our people found no survivors."

"I know, I know, but there's always a chance someone was missed. Humor me. Next time your people are down there, ask them to look again. All that loss of life disturbs me—really, it does."

As Fremdkunst contemplated his drink, Retticker wondered if the man might actually be sincere. He'd always assumed Fremdkunst was in it for the money and prestige of cornering yet more of the meteorite market. Maybe that wasn't enough to justify the massacre in his eyes, either.

"If by chance your people found someone still alive," he continued, "that might go some distance toward salving Doctor Vang's angst, also. He's obsessed with getting his hands on any living tepuians, you know. Even seems to think Yamada and Miskulin might have brought someone, or several someones, back with them."

Retticker nodded but said nothing, sure that Fremdkunst was fishing for info. Refusing to take the bait, he decided to change the subject.

"What do you plan to do with your share of the tepui stone?"

Fremdkunst put down his glass.

"Some I'll leave in its present state. The rest I intend to transform into art."

Retticker leaned forward, looking intently at Fremdkunst, trying to discern his real reasons for wanting a piece of that rock.

"And how do you do that?"

"You don't expect me to reveal all my secrets, now do you, General? I *can* tell you I'll microslice everything that's to be worked. Cut it for the best angles on the Widmanstättens, for the areas that show them. Etch up the detail. Polish it so any olivines and pyroxenes have just the right sheen. Seal it and sell it to a few discerning and discreet connoisseurs, when the time is right. Such a unique stone to work with! It has the potential to be my best work yet."

Retticker finished his drink. He hadn't much cared about such arcane rock art, but maybe he'd better develop a taste for it—or at least a knowledge of it—if he ever hoped to figure out Fremdkunst's agenda.

"Art for art's sake?"

"The money doesn't hurt, either," Fremdkunst said with a smile and a shrug.

"Sounds like a challenge worthy of your mettle, Vic," he said, slowly getting to his feet. "I'll let you get to it. I need to be getting back to port."

"I understand," Fremdkunst said, also getting to his feet. "Let me walk you up on deck."

The walk was short, but the sun topside was bright and the wind brisk enough to make Retticker squint.

"Oh, by the way, Joe," Fremdkunst said, pausing in his farewell handshake to blast him with that radioactive-cobalt gaze of his. "There is something you might like to know. Doctor Vang's people inform me that someone by the name of Amaral has been looking into my doings in Israel and Saudi Arabia."

"I don't know anyone by that name."

"Ah, but he may know you, or at least *of* you. This Amaral is an old war buddy of NSA Director Brescoll. I'm told Vang and this Brescoll fellow had a bit of a run-in during that intelligence community shakeup last year."

The general felt his brow furrowing, quite unhappily.

"Let me get this straight. Are you telling me I should grab my ass and keep it tight when I'm around Brescoll?"

"I think that sums it up quite succinctly. Be on your guard, at the very least."

"I'll do that," Retticker said, turning toward the ladder that led to where his troll-rigged powerboat was moored alongside. "In the meantime, you take care of yourself out there in the desert."

"Nobody gets to choose who they'll share space with on the obituary page," Fremdkunst said with a smile. "I've never liked that. Death the great leveler, and all. A bit *too* democratic. I intend to stay out of that part of the paper for as long as I can."

"Glad to hear it. I'll do the same."

Before he could climb down the ladder and board his boat, however, a small but needle-sleek vessel pulled up alongside, farther toward the bow. A single passenger—a compact, square-jawed man with perfect alpha-male silver hair—bounded aboard Fremdkunst's ketch while his driver waited below. Fremdkunst introduced the man as George Otis.

"Hello, General," Otis said, giving Retticker a firm but somehow perfunctory handshake. "I believe some of my companies are doing joint work with your people. Nice to meet you in the flesh."

"The same," Retticker said, hoping his tone wasn't so cool or his handshake so stiff that they might betray his dislike of the man. From having encountered them in various media over several years, he recognized Otis's face and clipped Texan accent. One couldn't really call it a drawl, since there was nothing drawn out about it.

The accent, however, wasn't what Retticker found offensive about the man. He wasn't fond of Otis's mix of religion and politics and especially disliked the way Otis had metaphorically dragged the corpse of his favorite nephew—one of the 9/11 dead—into the political arena in order to advance his own agenda and career.

"I was just leaving," he said, and bid farewell to Otis and Fremdkunst.

Otis nodded absently and turned toward Fremdkunst as if Retticker were already gone. As he moved to unmoor his boat from *Skyminer* with the help of Fremdkunst's crew, he overheard Otis say something to the effect that one of his associates, a Mister Fox, wanted to talk about some misgivings he had about a rock.

Out of the corner of his eye, Retticker was surprised to see Fremdkunst respond to Otis's seemingly offhand comment with a snap-to-it urgency. He wondered just what the relationship of the two men might be.

The *Fish 'n' Reaction*'s engines started with a deep thrum and he pulled away from Otis and Fremdkunst. As he left, however, only Fremdkunst's crew was waving to him. Fremdkunst himself was talking on a satellite phone while Otis looked out over the estuary, as if pretending not to listen.

His mind was in a welter as he left them in his wake. This potential trouble with Brescoll was not something he had looked for. Not at all.

Dammit, he thought. Vang had reeled him into this, by suggesting something from that tepui might be "a great leap forward" toward the grail of military materials science: namely, a source for an ultimate protective material, perfect for creating sensitively reactive armor—the kind of stuff that would make troops in Kevlar look like tin soldiers.

That was why he was involved in this. And maybe Fremdkunst was in it for the art, or the money, or both. And maybe, just maybe, Vang was in it for some lingering Tetragrammaton "forcing" of human evolution. But what about Otis? Clout and cash and connections like Vang's, yet otherwise those were two people with agendas about as different as could be. What could possibly have made them buddy-up?

Motoring back toward the Potomac and his home berth, Retticker contemplated the list of people he should trust least. Brescoll might have the top spot for the moment, but Fremdkunst and Vang and even Otis were not far behind.

SKYROCKS AND CAT'S PAWS

Jim Brescoll entered the Smithsonian Institution's National Museum of Natural History via the Constitution Avenue entrance. He checked in at the guard station, as he had been instructed. He showed one of the two guards his picture ID. Without comment, she swapped the ID for a behind-the-scenes identification badge that would give him access to areas of the museum not open to the public.

He hoped this meeting would be worth it. He'd had to clear a sizable chunk of his schedule to get away long enough from headquarters to get together with these two.

"You'll be working with the Mineral Sciences unit, is that right?" asked the other guard, a man who looked to be in his fifties.

"Yes, Department of Mineral Sciences," Jim said, impressed by the unexpectedly rigorous security procedures. "United States National Meteorite Collection."

"Please sign the guest register of the host unit, here," said the male guard, showing him a map and presenting a form to sign, as the female guard made a call. "Thank you."

"I'll escort you to the first-floor rotunda," said the young woman after she'd gotten off the phone. "The curator of the meteorite collection will meet us there."

They rode the escalator from the ground floor to the first-floor rotunda. The moving stairway deposited them in front of the African elephant that was the static centerpiece of the domed space. To Jim's left stood the Mammals Hall, while to the right he could make out dinosaurs, fossils, and creatures of ancient seas in the Early Life Hall.

"Jim Brescoll?" asked a boyish-looking, clean-shaven man in retro horn-rimmed AR glasses. Jim nodded.

"Richard Phares," said the young-looking man, shaking Jim's hand. "I'm curator of the meteorite collection."

Phares nodded to the guard, who nodded back before returning to her station via the down escalator. Jim belatedly realized that he had been handed off to another employee escort.

"Are you familiar with the collection?"

"Can't say that I am," Jim said as they walked toward an elevator.

"Ah, then you're in for a treat, if you have a minute or two before your meeting."

Jim checked the time readout on the edge of his ARs.

"I suppose I could spare a couple of minutes," he said, as the elevator door closed.

"Good," Phares said. In a moment the elevator doors opened, and they were on the second floor. To the right stood the Hope Diamond, in the prime foot-traffic space of the Janet Annenberg Hooker Hall of Geology, Gems, and Minerals.

"We have one of the finest and largest museum-based collections of meteorites in the world. Many of our best specimens are on exhibit here, in the Moon, Meteorites, and Solar System Gallery of Annenberg Hooker Hall."

Jim nodded, his eyes passing over the many exhibit spaces in the gallery. The myriad upright glass display cases, housing a rainbow of important and exotic gem and mineral specimens, hit him with a momentary wave of sensory overload.

"Meteorites have been part of the Smithsonian from the beginning," Phares said, smoothly shifting over into full museum-guide mode. "Given that he was a chemist and mineralogist, it's not surprising that James Smithson included meteorites in his original collection. He donated those specimens to the Smithsonian, along with the funds to found the Institution.

"Sadly, Smithson's meteorites were lost in an early fire. Ironic, really, that they should have survived the scorching trip through the atmosphere from outer space, only to be destroyed by a fire in a place intended for their preservation.

"I think we've more than made up for it, though. Since 1870, when the modern meteorite collection got under way, we've gathered more than seventeen thousand specimens of more than nine thousand distinct meteorites. The collection is strongest in iron meteorites like these you see here, but we have pieces of every type of space rock. We're particularly proud that more than half of the known Martian meteorites are housed here."

"I always thought of meteorites as just blackened stones," Brescoll said, as he gazed at a thin wafer of rock with several inclusions. It looked rather like a slice through a shiny amoeba of liquid mercury and amber, flash-frozen and mounted in glass. "These are beautiful."

"Yes, that's a Willamette III AB iron. Thin sectioning allows us to study the rocks' mineralogy and texture. The national collection houses over seven thousand polished thin sections. If you'll follow me, I'll show you more of those."

Phares ran his badge down a keycard slot beside a door labeled RE-

STRICTED ACCESS AUTHORIZED PERSONNEL ONLY. Jim sensed that they could speak more freely and directly, now that they were out of the museum's public space.

"Those thin sections," he said to Phares as they walked down the hall. "That the sort of stuff Fremdkunst does?"

"His work is much more spectacular. Our thin sectioning of iron meteorites is mainly for classification purposes. Neumann lines and Widmanstätten figures for the irons. Petrologic type—degree of chondrule metamorphosis—for the chondrites. What we do is knapping a flake off a stone, basically, to make sure it's flint or chert or obsidian. What Fremdkunst does is more like working those stones to a perfectly finished spearpoint. The same basic processes but, in his case, carried many steps further and finer."

"He's that good, eh?"

"One of a kind, really. He has an incredible eye for seeing the beauties hidden in meteorites—and an even more impressive knack for bringing out those beauties in his finished pieces."

"Then why's he so controversial among collectors?"

Phares sighed as he opened the door to the Meteorite Verification Laboratory and signed in on yet another guest register.

"As scrupulous as Victor Fremdkunst may be as a craftsman, he's even more unscrupulous as a businessman and collector."

"Good at what he does," Jim said, "but what he does ain't good?"

"Yes. I'm afraid his successes as an artist don't make up for his failures as a human being."

Ahead of them, Jim saw a thirty-something couple examining some of those seven thousand polished meteoritic thin sections housed in the collection. Most of the sections they held up seemed to be encased in glass or some sort of clear thermoplastic resin. Watching the couple, it took Brescoll a moment to recognize them from the pictures he had already seen of the two.

"I gather you haven't met before," Phares said. "James Brescoll, this is Susan Yamada and Michael Miskulin."

As Jim shook hands with them, Yamada seemed polite enough, but Miskulin struck him as a bit standoffish.

"Michael and Susan were telling me about their visit to Castel Gandolfo, to investigate the meteorite thefts there. Very unfortunate losses. We're lucky one of our security guards was on his toes and caught our would-be meteorite thieves before they could do any real damage here. We beefed up security for our collection after the attempted theft."

"I noticed!" Brescoll said. "Too bad you'll probably have to maintain that heightened level of caution."

"Given the rash of thefts from meteorite collections recently, we plan on it."

"Any word on the thieves your people caught, and their motives?"

"From their arrest records I would guess they apprenticed in breaking and entering, then branched out into knocking over jewelry stores."

"Low-level hirelings, then?"

Phares nodded.

"Yes, unfortunately. They seem to have been recruited in a rather circuitous fashion, too. A labyrinth of ephemeral cell phone numbers, anonymous e-mail remailers, clandestine money drops—so much so that they can't say who actually *did* employ them. I have the card of the police detective I've been getting updates from, if you'd like to find out more about the investigation."

"Thanks, I'd like that," Brescoll said, then turned to Miskulin and Yamada. "What about the thieves who broke into the Vatican Observatory?"

"They haven't been caught yet," Miskulin replied, in a terse and not particularly friendly manner, continuing to look at slices of meteorites.

"But their profile might be similar to the thieves here," Yamada said, as if obscurely embarrassed by her partner's short answer. "The curator said his collection had medium-level security."

At the mention of security, Brescoll looked quickly around the room, then gave Phares a questioning glance. The curator got the point.

"Well, I can see you three have a good deal to discuss," said Phares. "No one will be using this lab for at least the next half hour, so you'll have some privacy. If you have any questions, I'll be down the hall in my office. You can stop by for the detective's card when you're through, Director Brescoll."

Jim thanked him and Phares left.

"Thank you for agreeing to meet me here," Jim said in as casual a tone as he could manage.

"No problem," Miskulin said, still riffling through the slices of fallen stars. "I always enjoy seeing the National Meteorite Collection."

"Ah," Brescoll said, picking up an attractive cut stone of his own, "but you don't particularly enjoy seeing someone like me, is that it?"

Miskulin glanced at Yamada, who suddenly became interested in the flooring.

"Look, let's cut to the chase," Miskulin said, putting aside the rocks from space. "Big secretive corporations, big secret government agencies—I don't trust either of them. NSA means 'No Such Agency.' Wasn't that what they used to say? Some kind of iron hammer inside a velvet computer, but it still means spies."

"I wouldn't exactly agree with that description," Jim said, "though that *is* an interesting image."

Miskulin looked at him narrowly, then nodded, the feathery spikes of his red-tipped dark hair following (slightly out of phase) the motion of his head.

"I gather you're more subtle and abstract about your spying than other agencies are, but I'd bet your people have been involved in their share of atrocities. All excusable, since 'national security' is part of the name, right? Why should we even consider working with you?"

Jim contemplated his response. He supposed it wouldn't matter much to Miskulin that he was the first-ever civilian director of NSA, the budget of which came entirely out of the Department of Defense. Or that, since assuming the directorship, he'd begun steering NSA away from the militarization of intelligence that had come to dominate the intelligence community over the last two decades. Or that, in standing up to the secret-society and cryptofascist types within his own country's intelligence community during the Kwok-Cho affair, Jim had not only put his long career in government service on the line, but also his freedom.

No, not even Jim's having been arrested for taking his stand would redeem him in the eyes of someone like Miskulin. Somebody always has to be the truest of true believers, even holier than the holier-than-thous. Miskulin seemed to want to play that role. So be it. Replacing the wafer of stone in the tray from which he'd taken it, the director decided directness would be the best course.

"If you're finished with your rant, I will simply tell you that I actually agree with much of what you've said. I'm not an elected official, so I can tell you that yes, my agency has in the past been responsible for needless bleeding—and may well be again. We're a sword wielded by the Commander in Chief. It's a big world, and a very dangerous one at times. Even in an organization mainly made up of mathematicians, linguists, engineers, and codebreakers, intelligence gathering is not always bloodless."

Miskulin looked as if he were about to respond, but Yamada cut him off.

"I'm still trying to figure out what meteorite thefts have to do with national security," she said.

"Very little, ordinarily. Depends how you define national security. Well-placed sources, though, have suggested to me that these meteorite thefts might be linked to a number of other suspicious activities that *will* directly impact our security."

"Oh?"

Brescoll nodded. "An informant on a special operations team has provided details that particularly seem to confirm that connection."

"You still haven't answered my question," Miskulin broke in. "Why should we even consider working with you?"

As he answered, Jim Brescoll looked at him as blandly as he could manage.

"Because we've learned that a private military corporation covertly engaged U.S. military assets in an operation that resulted in the deaths of a tribe of meteorite cultists inside an obscure South American plateau."

Miskulin and Yamada were both startled at the revelation. Jim was pleased to see that he now had their full attention, and continued.

"Because, by working with us, we may be able to learn not only who did the killing, but who gave the orders, and why."

Jim picked up another of the carefully vacuum-sealed star slices.

"Look, I know you're Paul Larkin's nephew. I presume he has kept you on his payroll to find answers to some of the same questions that interest me."

No startlement this time. Neither Miskulin nor Yamada gave any sign either confirming or denying that statement. Jim guessed his hunch was right, however, when another of those meaningful glances passed between them.

"Okay," Miskulin said. "So maybe we do have a convergence of interests. Maybe."

"What would you want us to do?" Yamada asked.

"What you have been doing, only more so. You're scheduled to make a presentation to this year's Exobiology Conference on the Origins of Life, aren't you, Doctor Miskulin?"

"Yes. I'm giving a lecture at ECOL."

"What's the topic?"

"The role of meteorites in circumpolar shamanism."

"Not on what happened at the tepui, though?"

"That's still too preliminary. We need more data, more evidence."

"Probably a good idea to keep it low profile for the time being. I gather you're not attending, Professor Yamada?"

"It's in Dubai. Not exactly cheap to fly or to stay there, you know."

"Well, I may be of some assistance. In addition to what Larkin is already paying you, we will channel you funds for any particular needs you might encounter."

"Taxpayer money?" Miskulin asked sourly.

"Don't worry, the funds are legitimate," Brescoll assured him. But he resisted any temptation to elaborate.

"You said 'particular needs,' " Yamada said quickly. "I assume that would include flying to and staying in Dubai."

"Yes."

"In exchange for . . . ?"

"In exchange for funding and information, I'd like you two to serve as a cat's paw for me, in what will also be an internal investigation of sorts. I can't offer you all the details yet, but rest assured your help will be invaluable."

" 'Just trust us—for we are benevolent and all-knowing,' " Miskulin said skeptically. "Come on! Give me a break."

"I don't expect you to trust me blindly," Jim said, smiling despite himself, "and I'll tell you as much as I can. One thing I can reveal is that a retired military officer of high rank has been observed in the company of one Victor Fremdkunst."

"Fremdkunst!" Miskulin said, then turned to Yamada. "See? I was right. I knew Fremdkunst had to be involved somehow!"

"How do you know this officer wasn't just an art lover interested in Fremdkunst's work?" Yamada asked Brescoll. "Or something equally innocent?"

"We can't rule that possibility out completely, it's true. But this officer has no history as either a collector of meteorites or of meteorite art. Yet, even before the events at the tepui, he had already seen to it that a meteoriticist would be employed by DARPA, in their Combat Personnel Enhancement Program. That could be circumstantial, too—just another coincidence. But the coincidences are starting to pile up. They're beginning to look less like accidents and more like parts of a plan."

"Who's the meteoriticist?" Miskulin asked. "Or is that a top secret, too?"

"Her name is Darla Pittman," Jim said. He was surprised to see Miskulin flick his head back, then glance sidelong at Yamada. "You know her?"

"We were involved, in a meteorite collecting expedition in Antarctica. Years ago."

It was a subtle thing, that pause after "involved." Miskulin's exculpatory little shrug didn't soften at all the line forming on Yamada's brow, either.

"I do seem to recall reading that you two were colleagues there, now that you mention it. So much the better."

"For your cat's paw?" Yamada asked.

"Precisely. We've learned that there's been a request for an ethnobotanist to join Pittman's team, too. I'm going to put both your names forward, as candidates to work on the project. If someone lobbies against your candidacy, that may tell us something."

"And if it doesn't?" Miskulin queried.

"That may confirm some other possibilities. The same is true for Pittman. We'll make sure your services are offered on very favorable terms. If Pittman doesn't want either of you working for her, it may prove that she's already working with materials taken from the tepui, or that she at least knows something about them."

"Or it may prove nothing," Yamada said. "We made our story about the massacre of the tepui tribe public, but it disappeared from the news way too fast. Hidden in life, and hidden in death. Those people deserved more than that."

Jim Brescoll nodded.

"I completely agree. A special ops team with connections to our military appears to be deeply implicated in the killing of those tepui people. I want to find out why they killed them, if they did, and I want to bring the killers to justice, in any case."

Yamada, at least, seemed to feel he was sincere. Jim pushed on.

"Maybe Pittman is innocent. Maybe she's genuinely ignorant of the tepui, or of the massacre, or even of your reporting of it. Maybe not. It's often difficult to distinguish feigned ignorance from the genuine article."

"Especially when the person has had a lot of practice, hmm?" Miskulin said. "You've had a great deal of personal experience in that, haven't you?"

"I won't deny it," Jim said, averting his glance briefly.

"Let me make sure I understand what you're proposing," Susan said. "You want us to spy on this Darla Pittman person, to learn more about her work for the government? And, in so doing, find out what your own people might be up to?"

"Indirectly, yes."

"And this military officer already happens to be a professional spy.

Someone who should be able to spot amateurs like us a mile away. Sounds like it's out of our league. I don't think we're qualified for the sort of thing you're suggesting."

"I don't want you to act as professional spies, Susan," Brescoll said, picking up one of the meteorite slices. "What I'm asking you is whether you think you can play dumb, act smart, and keep your eyes open long enough to get some answers."

"For whom?" Miskulin asked.

"For all of us, on all of this," he said, taking in the meteorites with a gesture. "Everyone who might be concerned about meteorites and their impact on human history—folks like Paul Larkin, among others."

"That sounds like some sort of conspiracy," said Yamada.

"I prefer Doctor Miskulin's term—a 'convergence of interests.' Well? What do you say?"

Yamada turned to Miskulin.

"Maybe it'll keep Paul from harping at us about Vang, at least for a while."

Jim startled at the name. He wondered if he'd heard right.

"Did you say Vang? Doctor Vang, of ParaLogics? What's your connection with him?"

"We don't have any," she said, "but Michael's uncle thinks we should be very careful of him."

"Why's that?"

"My aunt Jacinta passed some specimens from the tepui, spore prints, on to Paul, before she died. My uncle ended up providing a sample to people connected with Vang. Paul thinks he might have let too much slip—maybe enough to have revealed the tepui's location."

And thereby set the stage for the massacre, Jim thought. He nodded. Running background, he'd learned a little of the crazy sad story of Jacinta Larkin. He would have to learn more.

As he collected contact info from the two of them and began to say his good-byes, Jim realized he had already learned more from Miskulin and Yamada, in less time and at less cost, than he had any right to expect.

FALCON AND FALCONER

The plane flew out of the desert, sinking through darkness, toward the magic carpet of latticework and light that was the United Arab Emirates.

"In Arabic, one of the many words for 'desert' is also the word for 'labyrinth,' " Vida Nasr said to Avram, turning from the window beside her. "I think it should also be the word for city."

"For Dubai, you mean?"

"Not Dubai in particular, as much as cities in general."

"I suppose you can get lost in both," Avram said. "Cities and deserts, I mean."

Glancing out the porthole window again, Vida shook her head.

"It's more than that. Human beings were originally nomadic, right? Even before we were anatomically modern humans, we were nomadic. Hunters and gatherers. Then herders, eventually. Mobility, open spaces, small populations—I think that's what allowed us to coexist with each other."

Avram nodded. He found nothing particularly objectionable in that idea, but then paleoanthropology and archaeology weren't his strongest fields of expertise.

"As soon as agriculture rooted us into a smaller compass and our populations began to swell, though," Vida continued, "we started to build alleys and streets, courtyards and walls. We trapped ourselves in mazes—for privacy, for protection. Psychological reasons, too."

That sounded to Avram like aspects of biology he did know something about.

"Like coral polyps building reefs," he suggested. "Or the free-living forms of immature clams, secreting shells after they settle down."

Vida nodded.

"If you include the arid zones of the poles, more than half the land surface of the earth is already desert," she said. "With our help, the deserts are growing by at least fifty square miles a day—even more if you include broader global climate effects, induced by human activities."

Avram looked at her narrowly.

"It almost sounds like you're saying we 'grow' deserts."

"Exactly so. A world culture of exponential growth against finite resources. Where people go, deserts follow, because we bring the desert with us. The city is its domesticated form, like dog is of wolf, or wheatfield of grassland. A labyrinth whose paths we think we already know, but maybe don't. What the desert is to the Bedu in their tents, the maze of walls and streets are to city dwellers in their apartments. If the future of humanity is in cities, then the future is a domesticated desert."

"Did you learn such ideas from the Bedouin—the Bedu?"

Vida gave a light, tinkling laugh.

"Hardly. Maybe I should say what the desert *was* to the Bedu. In Saudi, Oman, and the Emirates, most of them have long since given up the nomadic life for a more comfortable existence in the markaz settlements. Our last experts in wild wastelands are steadily joining the rest of us in adapting to the domesticated deserts."

"Probably not the smartest idea for us as a species," Avram said. "Especially if the wilds make a comeback."

"No, maybe not so smart. That's what's been happening, though, all over the world."

Glancing out the plane window as well, Avram tried to see what she was seeing. Whenever he had previously approached cities by air at night, he had thought of them as oases of light surrounded by deserts of darkness. He wasn't so sure of that now.

"Where did you learn this stuff, then?"

"From observing high-tech counterculturists, actually," she said, smiling. "Ever hear of Burning Man?"

"I don't think so."

"The Burning Man Project, officially. Started out as a performance art happening and evolved into a neotribal experiment in art, free expression, and voluntary community. A free-play zone for grown-ups in a clothing-optional, temporary autonomous theme city. Culminating with a human effigy figure many stories high, and the platform it stands on, both being burned together, via tons of fireworks and incendiaries."

Avram arched an eyebrow in surprise.

"Sounds like a pyromaniac's dream come true. Where could you do that sort of thing without getting in hot water with the fire authorities?"

"I think it started on a beach near San Francisco. The summer I went, they'd long since moved the whole event onto a gypsum playa, a dry lake bed in Nevada's Black Rock Desert. The same place a British team first broke the land speed record at faster than the speed of sound."

Avram nodded, familiar with such terrain.

"I've hunted meteorites on desert dry lakes. They're not bad places to find stranded stones."

"That was one of the reasons I went, too. I was interested in meteorites even then. I didn't find any—didn't get a chance to look, actually—but Burning Man as a whole was a crazy, wonderful spectacle."

Avram smiled, and tried to make himself more comfortable in his seat. In their time at the Wabar digs, he'd begun to find Vida's company altogether too pleasant. Almost dangerously so. Absently he rubbed the spot at the back of his neck, beneath which his implant lay, still presumably ticking out his location to those who knew how to listen for it.

Luis Martin and his anonymous backers most likely. The ones who had roused him from his violent despair at his daughter's death and set him on this road—from Argentina to Wabar and now to this conference.

Sending him to Wabar had at least taken him closer to what he supposed was his intended target. He wasn't quite sure how "The Money"—Victor Fremdkunst—fit in with what Luis Martin had offered him. Even less clear was how this conference fit in with the plan of his larger mission. What was he supposed to learn there? Was he supposed to make some sort of connection? He seemed headed in the wrong direction.

As a professional meteoriticist he was interested enough in the conference speakers and panels, but he felt adrift, a puppet whose master had put down the strings. He'd been left to rely more and more on his own choices and chances, precisely at the time when he was becoming more unclear as to what those were. He had to remind himself more and more frequently that his mission was too important to be sidetracked or absorbed into any other plans or longings. It wasn't easy, especially with Vida looking at him.

He snapped out of his reverie.

"Spectacle, yes. Sounds like it would be," he said, "though I must admit I'm having trouble visualizing such an event."

Vida looked off into the middle distance. The engines of the jet throttled back as they fell through the night.

"Picture forty thousand nomads who have driven to the desert in cars, trucks, and RVs. Or flown onto the playa in private planes. They park, pitch their tents, build domes and shade pyramids and other temporary structures. Hundreds and hundreds of little camp-neighborhoods pop up, each one its own temporary little world in the temporary city. Within the city and across the playa, they travel mainly on bicycles and by foot, during the day. At night, art cars depicting everything from UFOs and dragons to pirate ships and riverboats—and decorated with twinkle lights and lightwire and neon—cruise all over the dry lake bed. At the center of the city is the giant effigy Man lit up in blue or yellow neon. Are you visualizing that?"

"I think so."

"Okay, now picture that the city these technomads and artists create only appears on the desert for a week or so, then disappears for the rest of the year. The city, the people, their bicycles, their art installations, their fires—they all vanish like a mirage. During the rainy season the playa remembers again that it was once a lake and floods, erasing the tire tracks and almost all other traces of the spectacle."

Avram tried to wrap his mind around it in a way that made the oddness of it seem more familiar.

"Brigadoon at Black Rock," he said at last.

Vida nodded, her eyes glinting as she smiled at his description.

"Right. Exactly like a giant Etch-a-Sketch, erased first by fire and then by water. The first time I saw them burn the Man, the fire generated multiple firestorm vortices—tornadoes of flame that circled all the way around the pyre more than once before the whole installation collapsed and a crowd of tens of thousands of people surged forward to dance in a great counterclockwise circle around the burning remains."

Avram whistled softly through his teeth.

"That's an incredible image. Crazed spectacle, indeed."

"Very surreal. It made me think, though."

"About what?"

"About how cities began, or maybe how they'll end. Like I wasn't seeing just the event itself, but maybe an aftershock of something from the distant past, or a foreshock of something from the distant future."

Avram shifted in his seat again, and glanced at her narrowly.

"What was your role in all this?"

"The first time, I was a volunteer firefighter stationed about halfway back toward Center Camp. That far back, I didn't get caught up in the crowd surge. I did get to see the embers and firebrands of the Burn drifting about a hundred feet over my head, though. Against the band of the Milky Way in the desert sky, the flying embers looked like constellations of slow-motion falling stars. I'll never forget that."

Through Avram's mind flashed the memory of a shooting star streaking behind a horizon lined in pines, over ten thousand feet up in the mountains, during a Perseid meteor shower years before. At the time he'd thought of the idea from the Kabbalah that, at the beginning of the world, the vessels intended to channel the celestial light shattered with the force of that light, such that some of their sparking shards fell to earth and became trapped in the material world.

According to the great Kabbalist Isaac Luria, the job of human beings was *tikkun:* to embody the process of celestial repair by leading a holy life, thus raising the sparks out of their entrapment in matter so that they might be restored to divinity.

Avram didn't believe anymore that such a restoration was possible. He stopped believing when his daughter died.

"I'm confused. You were a firefighter for an event whose centerpiece was a ritual inferno?"

Vida smiled awkwardly.

"Like being an air-traffic controller for kamikaze pilots, I know. I'd just started my senior year at UCLA. My boyfriend was an anthro major and volunteer firefighter. That's how I ended up staying at the Black Rock City Volunteer Fire Department Fire Camp. I was helping him put out unauthorized blazes set by freelance pyros, and any spot fires from the Burn's flying embers."

"Put them out? Why?"

"You wouldn't want the city catching fire, or unprotected burns on the playa, either. The second time I went—the last time—I was there as a civilian, just enjoying the freedom of the city."

"You never went again?"

"Couldn't. The event was on government land, Bureau of Land Management property. A Bible-thumping Texas billionaire by the name of George Otis got himself put in control of BLM, mainly so he could help his cronies exploit mineral and mining rights. Otis considered the whole festival inspired by Satan. One of the first things he did was get the event banned on public health, safety, and environmental grounds."

"That seems plausible enough," Avram said, his voice trailing off as he saw the look on Vida's face.

"But it wasn't! The reasons for the shutdown were all a sham. The playa's a giant gypsum deposit five hundred feet deep. Impervious to most things you could throw at it. And the surface areas under all the big burns were lined with fire-resistant material—year after year—to prevent the heat from vitrifying even a small section of the desert underneath it. Any part of it you turned into glass would be a pain to remove and restore."

She gave a quick, sharp shake of her head, without breaking eye contact with him.

"No, what was anathema to Otis was the idea that adults are not six-year-olds. That they should be allowed to think as they wish and play as they please, so long as all their play and work is done by mutual consent. That radical notion was the real reason for the shutdown."

"Freedom is dangerous," Avram said, "and must be carefully watched."

"If not destroyed outright in the name of safety," Vida said, nodding. "I've heard rumors the festival might be coming back, though. Who's to say that, given world enough and time, Black Rock Desert might not become a new center of pilgrimage? Like the Vatican, or the Temple Mount, or even Mecca?"

Avram was startled to hear her mention that last pilgrimage destination, but just then their plane banked sharply, covering his startlement. Thinking of how his mission forced him to keep the fire of his revenge alive, yet at the same time banked down, he understood how the giant effigy Man might feel, waiting to flare into a final blaze.

An enormous structure loomed above the city before them, an immense, tapering pile of slender, softly glowing cylinders like a dream tower painted by a science-fiction illustrator. Its appearance stunned Avram, but Vida took it in stride.

"Wow! That's a helluva skyscraper!"

"That's the Burj Dubai. I think it might still be the tallest building in the world. I'm not sure."

"Burj? Isn't that where our conference is being held?"

"No. Another Burj. Our conference hotel is the Burj Al Arab. It's the one that looks like the lateen sail of an Arabian dhow. There, see it? Not quite so new or so tall, though it was once the tallest hotel in the world. Most buildings in Dubai were once the tallest or the most luxurious in some category or other. The buildings themselves are not as ephemeral as their original claims to fame, is all."

"You sound like you know the place well."

"I've been here a few times. I have family here."

"Really? I thought you were Egyptian."

"My family is originally from Iran. My parents were both born there. They and their relatives were scattered in the Iranian diaspora, after the mullahs came to power. Some of my cousins ended up here. Our parents and aunts and uncles taught all of us how to speak Farsi, in addition to Arabic. Maintaining tradition, you know. I can teach you a bit of that language, if you'd like."

"Yes, I'd like that." Might come in handy, too, he thought.

Their jet touched down. Amid the hurry of deplaning and meeting the limo that would transport them to the hotel, they had little time for further personal revelations or meditations. Their pace didn't slacken until they had arrived in the marble-and-gold ambience of the Burj Al Arab's lobby, where Avram saw a discreet sign welcoming conferees to this year's meeting of ECOL, the Exobiology Conference on the Origins of Life.

They made their way between hotel registration and conference registration, through an identifiably academic crowd in casual-professional drag. The men tended to be balding, bearded, and bespectacled, and the women looked to have spent more time in the laboratory and the library than the spa or the salon. Avram thought that the more tanned and lean among them were either recently returned from sabbaticals or from research in the field.

"There's Yuri, talking to Darla Pittman," Vida pointed out. "I think he got to ride in with the boss. He's actually giving a paper, and not just attending, like us."

"I read the abstract in the preprogram," Avram said. "Heat shock proteins, hidden mutations, evolutionary capacitors, the meteorite falls at Wadi Bani Khaled, Nejd, and Wabar—all that. He told me not to worry about attending his presentation, since we'd already heard it informally on the dig."

"About half a dozen times!" Vida said with a smirk. "Considerate of him. Victor isn't giving a presentation, as far as I know."

"Not according to the latest update, no," Avram said as he perused the conference schedule in the program book. "There are several presentations about the ongoing spate of meteorite thefts and proposed security protocols for protecting collections. I'm sure he won't be very far away from that discussion, whether he's physically present or not."

Vida flashed him a wry smile, but then was distracted by something.

"Look, Michael Miskulin's here. With his latest flame, too, the ethnobotanist, what's her name."

"Yamada," Avram said as he looked back to the list of speakers, guests, and attendees. "Strange . . ."

"What is?"

"The astrobiologists and exobiologists here are from all over the world," Avram explained. "I haven't attended all *that* many conferences, yet I know many of them personally and nearly all of them from their published work."

Vida shrugged back her dark hair, and thought about that.

"We're not a big community, when you come down to it. Almost everybody knows almost everybody."

Avram contemplated the idea of a small town's worth of people with the same professional obsession, scattered all over the planet. Everyone he knew in that community seemed supercompetent in their fields, most of them surprisingly young and very bright. Yet as he looked about him, he also wondered why so many of them—so many of us—were so screwed up, socially. Unmarried or divorced because they were unable to maintain more settled and domestic relationships. More comfortable looking at mediating screens than unmediated faces. In some ways this conference—and others he'd attended—was like a meeting of Academic Asperger's Anonymous, but without the obvious therapeutic function.

And with *agendas*—besides the official ones listed in the program. Who was working—and/or sleeping—with whom? Whose star was on the rise? Whose career was cold and dead as a distant planet?

Victor Fremdkunst waved them over and introduced them to one of the conference's keynote speakers, Dr. Monica Grady of the British Natural History Museum. As they chatted, Avram quicky realized that Fremdkunst was playing bad-boy outsider to Grady's doyenne of meteoritic studies.

So it went throughout the evening reception, people meeting and greeting, bobbing and weaving, noshing and kvetching and catching up on each other's work, a social gathering of bright people who tended to fail unpredictably in social gatherings, before awkwardly retiring to their rooms, there to continue partying in small groups, and a few just to sleep.

The following morning Avram overslept enough that he was twenty minutes late to the initial Welcome and Introduction. Because he knew he would not see Vida, or Yuri, or Victor except in passing as he made his way to a full schedule of panels, he and Vida planned to get together for brunch before the conference got into the full, multitracked swing of its panels and presentations.

Avram sat down to brunch on a terrace overlooking Jumeirah Beach, its main hotel, and the Wild Wadi Water Park. As he waited for Vida, he perused the conference schedule on his AR glasses, blinking on items he thought might be interesting.

Discussions about the genomics of extremophile organisms found in solfataras, hot springs, and hydrothermal vents. Lecture presentations on Arctic sea ice and Antarctic Lake Vostok—buried under miles of ice for hundreds of millennia—as analogs for the intra-ice biological niches of Jupiter's moon Europa. Panels on relative likelihoods of microbial contamination of Earth by meteorite-borne extraterrestrial life, versus microbial contamination *of* meteorites *by* terrestrial life.

Looking away from the conference schedule, Avram soon became more interested in watching and chatting with a friendly South African falconer in slouch hat and safari togs. The man paced the grounds before him, working his bird up and down the great lateen-sail face of the Burj Al Arab, his falcon eliminating any pigeons or other nesters it encountered.

Avram hadn't been watching the falcon and the falconer long before Vida sat down at his table and Avram returned to the varied presentations and keynote speeches on the schedule.

"See anything particularly noteworthy?" he asked, noting that Vida was engaged in the same winnowing process.

"The stuff on cryptoendolithic communities of fungi and photosynthetic microbes, hidden in layers beneath the quartz surfaces of stones in the Dry Valleys of Antarctica," Vida said, looking over the marked items on her own conference specs. "That looks like solid science, though not particularly new. Same with the panels on extraterrestrial volatiles and microbes making it onto habitable planets: impact delivery of organics to Earth, Mars, and Europa; microbial survival in solar system space; the usual. This one here, though—arguing that Earth's oil reserves are much older 'fossil' fuels than is generally accepted—I hear that's going to be controversial."

" 'Oil from Heaven.' Interesting title. Why that one?"

"Word is the presenter plans to argue that the world's oil reserves were not the result of plant and animal remains being altered by geological heat and pressure. He claims they're the product of kerogenous substances initially brought to Earth through billions of years of meteoritic impacts. Maybe some of the geologists will come to blows with him, if we're lucky. How about you?"

"Nothing so exciting as that. I thought I'd end my day early with Miskulin's talk, 'Of Lemmings and Life Codes,' before I get woozy with conference overload. Miskulin ought to be plenty controversial enough."

"I wanted to see that, but it's the same time slot as the one on oil," Vida said, puzzling it out. "You'll have to give me a full report. Hey, what about this one—Miller's lecture on those star-spear things?"

Avram blink-scanned through the schedule until he found the listing of a presentation by American anthropologist Karl Miller. Judging from the title and synopsis, Miller would be arguing that the Aztec gods Tlaloc, Huitzilopochtli, and Quetzalcoatl were related to the meteoritic star-spear entities called Nuhu by the Mixtecs.

"The Nuhus?"

"That one."

"No, I'm afraid I can't make that one. Same time as the one on microbial contamination."

"I'll check the Nuhus out, if you'll take notes on the Miskulin presentation for me."

"It's a deal. I—"

He was interrupted by the sudden stoop of the janitorial falcon. At something over two hundred miles per hour the raptor easily took out a pigeon a couple of meters from them—close enough that they clearly heard the crack of impact. The falconer could not help smiling slightly at their startlement, even as he apologized.

"Like a feathered shooting star, that bird," Avram said, shaking his head.

"More like a feathered cruise missile," Vida corrected, frowning slightly. "One of my Dubai cousins is something of an aficionado, when it comes to falconry. If you want to see why it's such a big thing here, I'm sure he could set up a hunting trip for us, if you'd like."

"Yes, I'd really enjoy seeing that."

"What's your schedule later this afternoon?"

"Not much, other than the Miskulin talk."

"Good. That's over pretty early in the day. Maybe my cousin can set something up."

"Now, I wouldn't want to impose on his hospitality . . . ."

Vida laughed.

"I doubt he'd consider it imposing. He'll grab at any excuse that lets him get out into the desert with his birds, especially during bustard season. Be back here at two-thirty or thereabouts. The odds are good my cousin Umar will be waiting here with me by then."

Avram agreed to rendezvous with Vida on the terrace at the specified time. She left ahead of him while he finished his coffee. Gathering his papers and stuffing them into his small briefcase, Avram startled as the falcon landed on his shoulder. As he watched, the bird stood on one sharp-taloned foot and extended the other leg toward him. Wrapped around that leg was a small scroll.

Avram looked beyond the bird to the falconer, who touched his slouch hat in recognition, then motioned that he should take the scroll off the bird's leg and read it. A bit perplexed, Avram did so.

My Dear Doctor Zaragosa—

Events are beginning to break in Jerusalem, about which you shall soon hear. How they sift out may affect our timetable. We will, however, have an in-country meeting together before too very long. In the meantime, you might want to sit in on Dr. Miskulin's presentation today.

Persevere—
Luis

PS: I thought you might appreciate this method of communication.

The falconer whistled off his bird and turned away. Avram watched it go, then looked about for Luis or anyone who might be watching him for his "employers." He saw no one who might fit that description.

Avram pondered. Perhaps not puppet and puppeteer, but falcon and falconer instead? Avram was not certain how reassuring he found that idea, but he now had no doubt that the falconer was still watching the falcon, and the falcon could still hear the falconer.

The rest of the morning went along normally enough, until Avram got a bit disoriented and lost after the microbial contamination talk. As a result, he arrived late to Miskulin's lecture.

By the time Avram snuck in at the back of the hotel ballroom where Miskulin was making his presentation, Doctor Meteor was already well along in talking about the elaborate mythology Inuit shamans had built up around the "One Who Falls from the Sky"—the literal meaning of *qilangmiutaq,* the word for "lemming" in Inuktitut, the language of the Inuit people.

Miskulin dismissed as "facile and fundamentally racist" the anthropologists' anecdotal explanation for such lemming-names found throughout the circumpolar north—that "primitive" peoples, seeing the sudden explosion in local lemming numbers, simply assumed the creature had fallen from the sky. Miskulin's countertheory was the product of his experiences during a summer appointment at the Flash-line Mars Arctic Research Station (FMARS)—or so he claimed.

Long publicized as "Mars on Earth," FMARS was a Mars-analog habitat and scientific facility situated within the frigid and arid environs of the twenty-three-million-year-old, twenty-four-kilometer-wide Haughton Impact Structure, the most northerly meteor crater on any of earth's continents.

There, besides helping to test environment suits and habitat structures for an eventual Mars colony, Miskulin said he came to a better understanding of the boom/bust cycles of lemming populations. He connected their extreme aggressiveness during periods of exploding population to a similar dynamic of overpopulation, environmental destruction, and aggressive territorial expansion in humans.

At FMARS he also first encountered the story of Uvavnuk, the nineteenth-century Inuit woman who became a shaman and poet after reportedly being struck by a ball of fire that fell out of the sky. Some of the tribal witnesses claimed it was a meteor, others thought it was ball lightning, still others that it was a "spear of God," but all agreed Uvavnuk was immediately possessed by a tupilak spirit—something of a "cross between a shooting star and Tinkerbell," in Miskulin's words—who gave Uvavnuk her life-song.

Avram jotted down Uvavnuk's song as Miskulin recited it in translation:

> *The Great Sea has set me in motion, Set me adrift*
> *And I move as a weed in the river.*
> *The height of sky And strength of storms Encompasses*
> *   me,*
> *And I am left Trembling with joy.*

According to Miskulin's Inuit sources, forever after her encounter with the fireball, Uvavnuk had strange powers over—and affinities with—lemmings, to the degree that she was also known as Lemming Woman.

Even the story of shamanic healer Uvavnuk and her meteor-assisted metamorphosis, though, was only a launch-point for Miskulin's larger argument that a great amount of reliable astronomical observation had been encoded in such legends—a basic approach with which Avram very much agreed.

Avram didn't give it the same biomedical spin Miskulin did, however. Doctor Meteor boldly argued that the traditional association of comets and meteors with shamans, priests, and healers, on the one hand, and with pestilence, disease, and contagion, on the other, was not superstition but was based in experience.

He cited a long tradition of "bad stars." Comets or meteor showers had reportedly been seen in the skies about the time of the final collapse of Rome and the plunging of sixth-century Europe into the Dark Ages. They had also been observed contemporaneously with the appearance of the Black Plague during the first half of the fourteenth century, and the spread of the Spanish Flu during the early twentieth.

Miskulin read them all as proofs that organic compounds and organic life of nonterrestrial origin had in the past traveled to the Earth in meteoritic material. Coupled with arguably extraterrestrial fossil bacteria from meteorites, and with evidence that various types of hardened spores could travel through deep-space-like conditions and yet remain viable, such oral traditions convinced Miskulin that, throughout its geologic history, the Earth had been periodically exposed to prebiotic and protogenetic material from off-planet, both from within the solar system and from the depths of interstellar space.

For him, the heretical idea of "germs from space" seemed entirely plausible. He ended his presentation with the proposal that historical records ought to be reexamined in light of this, and that shamans and traditional healers from throughout the world ought to be interviewed and questioned about their myths and legends concerning transient celestial events and meteoritic impacts before such information was lost forever, trampled out of existence by the global march of Western biomedical orthodoxy.

No sooner had Miskulin finished than the room erupted into questions. As the questioning ran long, Avram quietly made his way out the nearest door of the ballroom, in order to keep his appointment with Vida and possibly with her cousin the falconer. Yet as he walked, he wondered. True, he had already been planning to attend Miskulin's presentation, but why had Luis wanted him to attend that one in particular?

He shrugged. Perhaps it was not always easy for the falcon to divine the falconer's intentions.

INTERLUDE: FOX GOES TO GROUND

Amid explosion, fire, and gunshots, through bodies of the faithful blown to pieces, they had entered the building. The bespectacled, rail-thin man who traveled with them stayed focused on his mission, intensity of purpose seeming to cloak him in an impenetrable aura. Fire and noise of clashing forces notwithstanding, he made his way swiftly to the raw rock protruding from the floor of the shrine.

Despite the frenetic chaos around him, he patiently lifted the earth-penetrating sonar-scanner from his shoulder and set it gingerly down on the floor, before carefully wiping the dust from his eyeglasses. Looking at the rock, he nodded to himself, satisfied. Powering up the scanner, he lifted it to his shoulder and began methodically playing it—back-forth, up-down—over the rock before him.

A lull in the chaotic noise opened up around him, but Avigdor Fox barely noticed it, so intent was he on his scanning of the rock. Nor did he notice when the noise of gunfire intensified again, for by then he had located what he was looking for.

Removing hammer and chisel from his belt, he crouched on the raw stone and began chipping methodically away at a small area of the stone, working a depression into a hole.

The gunfire grew loud enough that even he noticed it now. Just a few more minutes, Fox thought. A few more good whacks—I'm almost there!

Abruptly, the only sound in the building was his hammer hitting chisel, chisel chipping away at stone. Then hurried footsteps from behind him.

"You will come with us, please," said a voice coming from the same direction as the footsteps.

"Just a minute—a minute!" Fox said, far too preoccupied to turn and see the speaker. "I'm almost there!"

A single pair of footsteps came toward him.

"You will come with us. Now."

A gun barrel—hard and quite warm—prodded him at his left temple. As he dropped the hammer and chisel and slowly stood, he seemed to fall back into his body. He tasted dust and smoke in his mouth. He smelled chipped stone, burnt gunpowder, and cordite. He heard sirens, booted footsteps, and masonry falling. He saw the bodies of those who'd been killed defending the shrine. He saw the fire at the entrance through which they'd blasted their way in, the ancient doorway still burning. Those who had cracked the place open for him also all seemed to have died.

As he was marched out of the shrine by antiterror SWAT units of both the Jerusalem Police and Wakf Islamic security, the many misgivings Avigdor Fox had had about this enterprise, everything he'd managed to push out of his mind these last few hours, all came crashing in on him.

LABYRINTH IN AIR

As Avram walked onto the terrace, Vida and a short wiry man with wavy black hair stood to greet him.

"This is my cousin Umar," Vida said.

"Pleased to meet you," Avram said, shaking the man's hand.

"The pleasure's mine. You want to see falcon hunting, yes?"

"That's right."

With a sly smile, Umar gestured for them to follow him. When they came to Umar's Jeep parked in the Burj Al Arab's lot, Avram saw that there was a hooded bird of prey on its perch, facing them out the back window.

"Saker falcon," Umar said proudly. "She's a strong, smart bird. Aggressive. Good endurance."

They got into the vehicle and drove mainly west for nearly an hour, then turned north. Avram filled Vida in on the Miskulin presentation, and Vida did the same for him regarding the Nuhus. Glancing at her notes from the lecture as they bounced along increasingly rough roads, she told him about Miller's interpretations of the red-and-white Nuhu symbols from a number of bark books or codices. He mentioned the Colombino-Becker, the Zouche-Nuttall, and the Ríos, but focused especially on the Codex Boturini with its history of the Aztec migration into Tenochtitlan, the Tira de la Peregrinación.

"The Tira tells how the 'god' Huitzilopochtli—who also seemed to be a Nuhu, from the red-and-white symbols associated with him—was discovered in a cave," Vida explained, as Umar went off the road completely and jolted them along through the desert. "Inside a place depicted as Curl Mountain in some codices and Flower/Fruit Mountain in others.

"Huitzilopochtli was reportedly carried on the back of a priest with the glyph-name of Serpent," she continued. "The priest with Huitzilopochtli on his back led the pilgrims who founded Tenochtitlan. When the travelers became discouraged on their long road and would go no farther, the priest insisted that Huitzilopochtli spoke to him and said he wished them to continue their journey."

"That's all well and good, I'm sure," Avram said, over their bouncing ride. "Sounds somehow like the Exodus from Egypt—but what does it have to do with stars and meteorites?"

"Huitzilopochtli had to be carried by a *yahui,* or priest, because, although he could speak, he was a bundle without feet. Miller said these speaking bundles without feet, like Huitzilopochtli, were never human beings in any form. They were instead objects treated not so much as 'gods' as simply 'sacred' or 'belonging to the gods.' "

Umar plunged into a wadi flat as a highway, and their ride was a bit smoother for a time.

"In the Codex Telleriano Remensis, what are called Nuhu by the Mixtec are generally associated with a *yahui*-priest, who is in turn connected to celestial bodies referred to as fire serpents. Those are usually glossed as *cometas*—as comets, or meteors, or both.

"Thus the priest with 'serpent' as part of his name," Avram said, "in the story of Huitz-his-name?"

Vida smiled.

"Right. Miller suggested the Nuhus were part of a meteorite storm that struck the Americas, leaving 'magical' magnetic stones and pebbles in the mountains and on the plains. That storm's context supposedly also explains the continuing myths about strange lights seen near sacred caves in the mountains."

"How so?"

"Streaks of light coming from the Orionids, Perseids, or Leonids are said to be the *yahui,* who leave their caves only at night. The *yahui,* like the Aztec god Tlaloc, were believed to reside in mountain caves that were miraculous treasure houses filled with all that was needed for wealth and prosperity.

"The descriptions of the caves in the Mixtec Nuhu tales and the Aztec tales of Tlaloc are identical in their emphasis on an abundance of food and wealth. Many codices show the same mountain for the place where Huitzilopochtli was discovered: a mountain with a whirlpool inside, and things like white flowers and fruit trees blooming on top. Miller said that's due to impact geology."

"Caves? Impacts? Whirlpools? What's the link?" Avram asked. Umar turned out of the wadi and zigzagged up a hillside so erratically that Avram wondered whether their driver might be lost, too.

"If a meteorite hit a mountainside, it could create a cave, large or small depending on the structure of the mountain and the size of the impactor," Vida said. "Miller believes that a magnetic stone, later named Huitzilopochtli, was found in what the codices show as Curl Mountain Cave. Able to indicate north, or 'speak,' the stone was carried on the back of a priest and helped guide the people during their migration to Texcoco and Tenochtitlan, to found their new nation."

"I'm a big believer in the idea that meteorite histories are often shrouded in myths," Avram said as they rolled past mounds of dry desert brush and stone outcroppings, "but a rock that talks? That sounds like a stretch."

"In our terms, yes, because we understand 'speak' as indicating sounds emitted from the mouth of a person or an animal. In the ancient Mesoamerican world described in the codices, though, the scrolls coming out of a mouth as 'speaking'—"

"—in fact only imply a transmission of information," Avram said, suddenly getting what she was getting at, "like captions under pictures in a newspaper or in a comic strip, which can be 'thought bubbles' as well as spoken words."

"Right. A magnetic iron meteorite—shown in the codices as a sacred mummy bundle, but without the feet seen on depictions of human mummy bundles—such a stone would have the ability to 'speak north,' " Vida said. "Its opposite end would then 'speak south.' "

"Still seems like a bit of a stretch to me."

"Maybe. Some people in the audience thought it didn't stretch far enough. Darla Pittman, for one."

"Oh?"

"She wanted to know whether the stone's speaking to the priest might indicate something other than magnetism. If 'speaking' simply meant information transfer, then she thought maybe the priest himself might be hearing voices, due to some psychoactive effect arising from his proximity to the meteorite."

"That sounds like Pittman, all right," Avram said, nodding, his head moving more vigorously than he'd intended as, just then, they moved over bumpier ground once more.

"Psychoactive skystones are her hobbyhorse, yes," Vida agreed, her voice vibrating oddly with the bounce of Umar's driving.

"And she rides it whenever she can. Anybody else in the audience get up on their horses and ride?"

"I don't know if it is *her* hobbyhorse, as you say, but Susan Yamada was quite enthused about meteorites inside mountain caves, especially with all that stuff about a whirlpool inside a Mountain of Fruiting Flowers, or whatever. She thought that might be a reference to some psychoactive agent, perhaps in fungi associated with those particular caves."

"That makes sense, too," Avram said, trying to ponder the possibilities despite the jouncing ride. "I mean, given that she's an ethnobotanist. What about the connection with Quetzalcoatl?"

"Miller thinks a number of the codices are really describing Huitzilopochtli as a star that fell from the skies under the auspices of Tlaloc," Vida said, her ride-jounced voice breaking up her pronunciation of the Aztec words. "Under other aspects, Tlaloc is also known as Quetzalcoatl. Miller said the name Quetzalcoatl, 'feathered serpent,' also has associations with comets and meteors."

"Like the priest with 'serpent' in his name glyph, again?"

Vida nodded.

"In Aztec or Mexica art, fire was often depicted via images of feathers, so feathered serpents, like fire serpents, were also sometimes images of comets and meteors. Quetzalcoatl shared similarities with earlier Maya meteor gods, particularly the brother-gods triad at Palenque. . . ."

They had to stop speaking then as, bouncing through a heavily folded countryside of brush and rock and dry wadis, conversation became too difficult to continue. It seemed to Avram that he'd been spending an awful lot of time in such bad-shocks and rough-road conversations since he came to the Arabian Peninsula. Thinking about what Vida said, though, he was struck by the image of a great meteor as a stone fletched with flames, trailing a feather boa of fire.

Before too much longer, Umar pulled up alongside three other off-road vehicles. Relieved that their bladder-jolting, kidney-punching ride was over at last, Avram took the time to notice that each of the other off-road vehicles also had a falcon perched in its back window.

"Like guns on gun racks," Vida remarked, "in pickup trucks of the American South."

"Maybe it's not so glamorous as a Bedu on horseback with falcon perched on his gloved hand," Umar said with a shrug, "but we have fun in ways the old Bedu could hardly imagine."

Umar didn't elaborate further as he went to greet his friends and fellow falconers, to whom he also introduced his cousin Vida and her guest, "Ibrahim."

Umar and his friends spread out. They tossed lures—bustard wings sewn together, with a small piece of meat attached to each—into the warm air of late afternoon. Their birds dove on the lures, hitting them with an audible crack.

As he warmed up his female falcon, or hurr, with the lure, Umar explained that though it was late in the hunting season, some of the saker's favored prey, the houbara bustard, were still in the area. He also went into extensive detail on how he had trained his bird, always trying to walk the fine line between making her tame enough to control, but not so tame that she would lose her killer instinct. Vida cracked wise about falconers' treatment of their female birds resembling their attitudes toward woman generally, but Umar chose to ignore that.

When Umar felt the bird was ready, he donned a pair of what looked like goggles and sent the bird out on a long arc. After a few moments, some distance toward the horizon, Avram saw Umar's hurr fold her wings and drop like a stone. Below her, a rather stout, gray-brown bird broke from cover, twisting and turning in low, wing-pumping, darting flight.

Almost before Avram had time to gather that the plump but extremely agile ground-hugger was a bustard, Avram's bird made some adjustments in its trajectory and nailed the bustard a few feet off the ground, even as the prey was trying to execute a further evasive maneuver. Umar, Avram, and Vida walked to where the saker stood over its downed victim, the hurr's wings hunched over the bustard as if to protect her prize from rivals.

"I told you before we have fun in ways the old-time Bedu could not imagine," Umar said, handing Avram the goggles. "This is what I mean. Here. Put these on."

As Umar and his friends whistled their birds off down the wind, Avram put on the eyegear. He was surprised to find that the goggles were telepresence gear, but even more surprised to discover the point of view from which he was watching the world through them.

He had a literal bird's-eye view, and that bird was Umar's female saker falcon, on the hunt.

It was a dazzling and dizzying experience, just to hang suspended in the air like that. The view became even more impressive, however, as the falcon rose in a widening gyre, tracing a labyrinth in the air.

Suddenly the hurr spotted a bustard and started into a stoop, the ground rushing up at much more than a hundred miles an hour, the bustard darting and weaving in a brief aerial dogfight, wild maneuvers arising from its wild attempts to dodge the oncoming feathered bullet, then at last the crack of impact as the hurr hit her target—

"Wow! This is great!" Avram said. Once the hurr stood crouched on her target, he handed the telepresence goggles back to Umar.

"Nano-optical feed," Umar explained. "Years ago, people began implanting falcons with microchips in their chests to identify the birds and their migration routes. Then someone got the idea of using the falcon's eyes as optics for telepresence. Some Western people go so far as to put implants in their falcons' brains, so they can control them like RC cars or planes."

One of Umar's friends, overhearing, spat and began a disparaging rant about how everything started going to hell once the Qataris put those little Swiss-made, remote-controlled titanium robot-jockeys on the saddles of their racing camels, in place of the young boys who had traditionally served in that role. Umar nodded throughout, until he finally cut the man off.

"We do not do that. We like to look through our birds' eyes, but not control their minds. These birds are our heritage. We do not use them so much to hunt our food anymore, but their freedom is still part of their beauty, to us."

Avram found that he was absently rubbing the back of his neck. He quickly stopped doing so. This talk of implants seemed to have the power of suggestion, at least for him. He hoped that was the only unconscious power his own implant had on his mind. He, too, appreciated the beauty in freedom, especially his own.

As the sun set, they enjoyed a Bedouin feast of houbara bustard and hare, and much Bedu talk of birds, freedom, and heritage. They were getting ready to break camp when a helicopter came arrowing in low through the twilight, ruffling the feathers of even the falcons behind glass in their four-wheel-drive palanquins.

Once the helo landed, Avram and Vida recognized the man who jumped out of the machine and came striding, bent over, toward them.

"There's emergency," Yuri Semenov shouted to them. "Attack on Dome of Rock, in Jerusalem. Considerable damage. Fremdkunst wants to meet with you both, for safety reasons. Right now."

"How did you find us?" Avram asked.

"Activated frequency on GPS PLBs—personal locator beacons Fremdkunst makes us wear."

"But why *our* safety?" Vida asked. "Who attacked the Dome?"

"Early reports say ex-American Israeli settlers connected to Kach-movement Kahanists and Christian Zionist end-timers. Others say Arabs blew up own holy site to unite Muslims in war against Israel. Fremdkunst says meteoriticist also perhaps involved, so safety concern for us."

As they headed for the helicopter, Avram was already thinking about the Dome of the Rock, racking his brains for everything he knew about the Temple Mount. Most of all, however, he feared that security, heightened in response to the Mount events, would make his own mission to Mecca all the more difficult.

Events are about to break in Jerusalem, Luis had written. How had he known?

In his mind's eye flashed the falcon's-eye view of the target bustard dodging and weaving. For all the bustard's maneuverings, however, the bird of prey had nailed it from air to ground. Avram found that thought strangely reassuring.

FOUR

HILL OF BEANS

>>>>>>>

Images from a thousand miles away cast a pall over the final day of the ECOL gathering. Pictures of the smoke-cloud from the Dome of the Rock billowed up on every screen, followed not long after by another cloud—more smoke and flames, this time billowing from a counterblast's explosion and fire at the Western, or "Wailing," Wall of the Second Temple.

If there were any silver linings to the dark clouds of the situation, Michael thought, it was that neither the Dome nor the Wall were as severely damaged as either might have been.

Susan couldn't bear to watch it. She was still dutifully attending the remaining panels and lectures of the conference—more out of avoidance of the news of the world than anything else. Michael, fearfully fascinated, was glued to any news about the disaster from any screen he could find, so much so that he was giving the rest of ECOL a pass.

The same pall darkened the informal interview he had scheduled with Darla Pittman. Her response seemed to be somewhere between his own fascination and Susan's avoidance. Darla's mind was clearly somewhere else—much nearer Jerusalem—and the interview, in the quiet bar off the Burj Al Arab's main lobby, was perfunctory in the extreme.

Sitting beside her, in tall chairs at a high table, he didn't know whether to stay or go. So he kept drinking. Whenever he turned away from the news reports, however, even he couldn't help noticing the furtive glances being tossed their way—most particularly at Darla.

"They took the Beth El!" a man said to his female companion at a table nearby. Michael recognized them vaguely as conference attendees.

"If that's true," said the woman, "there'll be riots, or worse."

"And all because of her and her crazy ideas!" said the man, staring in their direction, speaking just loud enough to make sure he would be heard.

The woman shushed him, but the barb struck home. Michael pushed back his chair, intending to go over and confront the guy, but when he saw the way Darla winced it stopped him.

It was all over the breaking news. Avigdor Fox, the meteoriticist taken into custody during the incident at the Dome, had apparently been obsessed with Darla's work on the Beth El, or "Gate of Heaven." Copies of her articles, much annotated and decked with marginalia, had been found in a raid by security forces on Fox's apartment. Darla was feeling the heat of Fox's involvement, all right.

Michael was torn. If Darla was connected somehow to the tepui assault, then she might already be a party to genocide. Who was to say she might not in some way also be deeply connected with what had happened in Jerusalem?

Yet, as they pored over reports together in the English-language *Dubai Times* and on the small flat-screen monitor mounted in the table's surface, he did some furtive glancing of his own. Darla seemed so genuinely distressed by what had happened that he felt more inclined to comfort than to castigate her.

"It says here," he began, putting his arm lightly around Darla's shoulder, to reassure her, "that, according to an ancient Semitic tradition, 'the bare rock atop the mount was held in the mouth of the serpent Tahum and was the intersection of the underworld and the upper world.' And here: 'Other traditions hold it's the site where Abraham built an altar on which to sacrifice his son Isaac.' See? Lots of interpretations of what the place means. Why should any of them concern you?"

Darla shook her head, frowning.

"Thanks for trying to distract me, Michael, but you know as well as I do it's not that. Read on."

"What? 'Others say the patriarch Jacob used a stone from that same site as a pillow. Upon waking from his famous dream-vision, Jacob anointed the stone pillow Beth El, with oil he received from heaven. Then the stone sank deep into the earth, to become the foundation stone of the great temple that would later be built by Solomon.' So?"

"Oh, quit dancing around it, Michael. Here: 'Scientists have weighed in on the site's significance, too, most notably meteoriticist Darla Pittman, who claims that the stone which induced Jacob's dream was a meteorite.' "

It was a no-win situation for Miskulin. In the end he said nothing, only nodded his head in the affirmative.

"Some who have read my work," Darla said, "don't seem to be above crashing the Gate of Heaven."

"He was a researcher of only minor note, Darla. More an adventurous collector than a real meteoriticist, even worse than me! Maybe he was crazy enough to think this was his ticket to the big show."

"No one sets out to be a minor meteoriticist," she said with a sad smile, leaning a bit more heavily against him. "No more than someone sets out to be a minor poet, or a minor painter."

Almost before Michael was aware of doing so, his arm had moved down her body and was around her waist.

"So, maybe, after reading what you wrote," Michael said, his voice a bit more slurred with alcohol than he'd expected, "someone tried to extract rock of the celestial dome from the celestial Dome of the Rock. That's still not your lookout."

"And why not?" she asked, turning more fully into him, seeming more than a little grateful for the companionship.

"We just put the ideas out there, Darla. We aren't responsible for how others interpret them, or what they might do based on their interpretations."

As she looked up into his eyes, everything about her seemed so open and willing. The sometimes hostile distance between them, the years since their ice-blue love affair in Antarctica—all seemed to sublime to merest vapor in the heat of the moment. The remembered taste of her lips flashed with dreamlike vividness into his mind. He would have kissed her right there had he not seen, out of the corner of his eye, Susan approaching the bar from some distance away.

Instantly Michael's hand was off Darla's hip, his arm away from her waist. Hand raised, he waved for Susan to see him, to come over and stand with them at their awkward high table. As Susan approached, he wondered how much she had seen, and how she might interpret it.

Darla, her expression somewhere between inscrutable and obtuse, played off what just happened between them as if it *hadn't* happened— so flawlessly that Michael wondered if anything *had* actually occurred.

"Sorry to interrupt," Susan said neutrally, "but I was wondering if your interview was finished."

"I'd think we're finished for now—Michael?" Darla asked.

"I think so."

"Well then, Doctor Yamada, I know it's hard to think about something like a job interview at a time like this, but if you're up for getting it done, we'll do it."

"Thank you, yes. Just so long as we don't have the news monitor on in the table, and I don't have to watch it on the screen," she said. Darla politely blanked the tabletop news feed as Susan moved her chair around, to sit with her back to the bar's larger hanging screen. "Oh, and Michael, I took a call from your uncle Paul on the satellite phone. Sounded important. You should probably call him ASAP."

"I will," Michael said, trying not to appear too abrupt as he moved away from the table. "Bye for now, Susan. Darla."

As he walked away, he wondered how the interview between Susan and Darla would go. All very professional and impersonal, no doubt, despite the informality of the setting. Who knew what might be going on beneath the surface of that businesslike veneer? He hoped he hadn't provided grounds for too many subtexts.

Then he thought of how perfunctory his own interview with Darla had been, in the face of the growing world crisis, and realized he was thinking too narrowly. He thought of Bogart's Rick, in *Casablanca,* saying how the problems of three little people don't amount to a hill of beans, and he smiled.

In an alcove not far from the elevators, Miskulin grabbed one of the Burj Al Arab's satellite secure-phones, put in a call across the world on it, and charged it to his room. Paul Larkin answered almost immediately.

"Ah, Michael, glad you called. There are some fascinating things happening here. Your friend Brescoll has been in touch. And with these young people you left in my care . . . just some amazing things going on. You and Susan need to get back here at your earliest available opportunity and have a look-see. Got it?"

"Will do, Uncle Paul. Susan will be particularly glad to hear it. She thought you were putting us off a bit, not letting us see them before we flew out here."

"Nonsense. I was just being sensitive to the fact that you two had your itinerary too crammed already. When do you fly out?"

"Tomorrow morning. I don't remember exactly when we're scheduled to land in San Francisco—datelines, and all."

"No problem. Beam me your updated itinerary and I'll have a helicopter waiting to shuttle you out here from the airport."

They said their farewells then and Michael made his meandering way back through the lobby. Looking in on the bar he had left only a brief while earlier, he saw that Darla had left and Susan was sitting alone, nursing a drink. Michael tried not to think how unlike her that was as he sidled up next to her.

"What's the word from your uncle?" she asked as he sat down.

"He requests our presence ASAP. Wants us to see the kids' wonderful progress."

"About time."

"How'd the interview go?"

"Pretty well, but short. She seemed preoccupied."

"The Jerusalem crisis is weighing on her—more than on the rest of us."

"Maybe so. She had a meeting scheduled with her postdoc, too. Barry somebody. I guess I have the job, if I want it. Same with you?"

Michael nodded, then looked at her more carefully.

"You don't look particularly celebratory about it, if you don't mind my saying so."

She looked at him as if she were about to say something pointed, then turned away and spoke to her cocktail glass instead.

"Do you remember the psychoanalyst who presented at that interdisciplinary conference we attended in San Francisco? The one who said that, psychologically speaking, the essence of the scientific method is paranoid alienated voyeurism?"

"I remember how bogus I thought that idea was," Michael said with a smirk.

"Maybe. But what we're doing for Brescoll feels like scientific investigation gone bad."

"How so? I thought you were the one who was gung ho on all this, when we had that little meeting at the museum."

"I don't like to be in situations where I have to constantly worry about whether I can trust the people I'm talking to. With Darla, for instance. I was wondering if she was being too lax, considering I was interviewing for some kind of top-secret work. Then I thought maybe she'd already done a thorough background check. So then I wondered what her ulterior motives might be in hiring me. Or in hiring us."

"That *does* sound paranoid," he said, trying to laugh it off.

"Yeah, but I don't like having to hide things from people. Or wondering whether they're hiding things from me. You know?"

Mainly to give his hands something to do, Michael activated the flat screen mounted in the table. Reports from Jerusalem continued, images of a golden dome scorched black on one side, and of an ancient wall charred by recent fire.

". . . subsequent violence by the Al-Jafari Freedom Brigades," the newscaster intoned, "claiming in an e-mail message to Islamic television and radio outlets that the attack on the Western Wall was only a first response to the brutal attack on the Dome of the Rock. Meanwhile, the State of Israel has condemned the Dome attack as an act of terrorism. Most of the attackers appear to be Israeli citizens, however. . . ."

Michael switched off the sound, then gestured at the destruction.

"That's the way the world works, much of the time."

"Maybe. Or maybe that's the work we've made of the world."

"And quite a piece of work it is," he said with a chagrined smile. Yet as Susan turned back to her glass, Michael couldn't help wondering whether her talk of secrecy and mistrust had more to do with the small world of personal relations across a single bar table than with the big world of international relations they saw on the screen.

INTERLUDE: FOXHOUNDS, FOXHUNTER

Three police officers Avigdor hadn't seen before opened the door to his cell. Armed with submachine guns, they marched their manacled and chained prisoner down the detention center's long hallway.

"Where are we going?"

"You're not going to be our problem anymore, Doctor Fox," said one of the men. "You're being transferred to the custody of the Israeli Defense Forces."

The man looked at him as if he expected Fox to start shaking in fear, but Avigdor actually felt strangely relieved. He had been doing a lot of thinking. He had screwed things up royally, but maybe, just maybe, he might live long enough to tell the truth and set some things right, in the end. At the very least, if he told the right truth at the right time to the right people, he might be able to take down with him some of the powerful men who had led him into this maze.

He had taken unusual risks and beaten the odds before, to locate and recover unusual meteorites. Yet he had never gotten the recognition his discoveries deserved. Always the praise had gone to well-spoken media darlings like Michael Miskulin. The powerful men who'd brought him in on this had known what he wanted. They snared him with the promise of meteorite hunting on a remote mesa in South America—the sort of adventure he most preferred, and one that might at last make him the front-page phenomenon he had so long desired and deserved to be.

He should have known something was up when they switched the target from South America to Jerusalem. The South American operation didn't require an on-site meteoriticist, they said. That was the first betrayal.

But the Jerusalem target—far more dangerous, but potentially far more important. Avigdor knew Darla Pittman's work very well. Even he, however, was not so audacious as to think that it might be possible to snatch a sample of such an ancient sacred stone and subject it to scientific investigation.

That was the glory they had offered him. He had been unable to resist.

How he wished he had resisted, now, even as he offered no resistance to the police officers marching him toward whatever destiny awaited him in IDF custody. Ahead, the hallway opened onto what looked like a loading zone. From beyond the doors there came a low sound, a distant roaring.

His heavily armed police escort pushed open the great doors and the roar rose to deafening crescendo. Camera flashes lit up the air around him, so powerfully that for a moment he was blinded. As his eyes adjusted, he saw media everywhere. Ahead of him, at the end of the concrete ramp, waited an armored IDF van.

Is this the attention I desired? Avigdor wondered grimly.

He felt himself struck painfully, sharply, by a force so powerful it turned him halfway around. Before his eyes a man rose up, with curly black hair, white shirt, dark pants, camera, and photo-ID press credentials hanging on lanyards about his neck.

The man appeared to have leapt up onto the ramp from the crowd beyond. He had a gun in his hand, and he was firing.

Avigdor felt himself struck in the side, then in the chest, then in the chest again, before he fell to the ground.

Now he heard sounds—of shots, and perhaps of struggle nearby. Soon he could not tell whether the sky above him was night or day, but he knew he was dying. Only one thought filled his mind as the whole of the universe shrunk down toward a squirming red line, then a crimson point.

Is this the attention I deserved?

STONE CODE

Darla was many hours into a long, sleepless Bangalore-Beijing-Seattle flight back to the States, watching on the airline seatback screen the endless coverage of the tit-for-tat monument attacks in Jerusalem.

"It's easy to dismiss those responsible for the counterattack on the Western Wall of the Second Temple as the usual suspects: jihadists and intifadists," said the talking head with the requisite news anchor mane of silver hair, switching to full commentator mode. "Those responsible for the initial attack on the Dome of the Rock, however, are not so easily handled.

"They now seem to have been a diverse group. Members of the racist Kach movement founded by Meir Kahane. Displaced settlement hilltoppers. Flannel-wearing, M-16-toting radical Jewish nationalists. The money to fund the attack, however, appears to have come from radical-right Christian Zionists in the United States. Some of those groups counter that it was actually the Palestinian Arabs who launched the initial attack on the Dome, in order to exploit Arab furor for a war against Israel.

"Like their hard-core Israeli fellow travelers, the American Christian Zionists believe—as do Muslim jihadists too, oddly enough—that a global war between Muslim and Jew is a necessary prelude to the unfolding of their particular end-time scenarios—"

A special bulletin interrupted the program she'd been watching. Indeed, she soon saw, special bulletins were interrupting the programming on all the news channels, as she flicked among them.

"—lone survivor of the attack on the Dome of the Rock—"

"—meteoriticist Avigdor Fox has been killed—"

"—being transferred from Jerusalem police to Israeli Defense Force custody—"

"—assailant Ismail Hijazi—"

"—Arab Palestinian born and raised in Israel—"

"—used forged press credentials—"

"—access to the transfer for a photo opportunity—"

"—reportedly distraught over the attack on the Muslim shrine—"

"—shot the meteoriticist not with a camera but with a nine-millimeter—"

Darla wondered if her jet-lagged mind might be dreaming or hallucinating all of this. Once past the initial hallucinatory feel of the news, she was for a moment perversely relieved. Both her name and her theory about Jacob's stone pillow were now much less likely to be blazoned across the media in connection with the Dome attack than they would have been, had Avigdor Fox lived to stand trial.

Then, almost immediately, she felt guilty for having felt relieved.

Watching the ongoing churn of special reports and bulletins, however, she began to wonder if this latest turn of events was what it seemed to be at face value, or whether it might conceal a larger aspect. She didn't doubt that Avigdor Fox had been shot dead, but the fact that he had been killed before he could talk struck her as just too convenient—and not just for her and her reputation, either.

A dead man's secrets would be forever beyond the reach of both judge and torturer. If Hijazi killed Fox, Fox wouldn't have the opportunity to break under pressure. Fox was the one person who could tell the world who might really be behind this whole mess, and now he was dead—how very handy.

Such reasoning, however, inevitably turned her to the "who" question: Who might Fox have ratted out? What were they working on? And why were they doing so?

Darla wondered if the answer to that much bigger "why" would ever see the light of day. Like the truth of so many other geopolitical incidents in which powerful interests had converged and contended, it was far more likely the truth of this episode would also disappear beyond some impenetrable far curtain, some event horizon of history.

She wished she could be content to live inside the black memory-hole, like nearly everyone else, but she was beginning to suspect that she and her own work might already be somehow involved in that larger convergence of historical forces. She wondered which might be the largest possible Russian doll here, the one containing all the others in a long series of dolls-within-dolls . . .

How much did the general know about all this?

She thought she knew the extent of his involvements in her research on the mysterious tepui stone. She thought none of his interest went beyond the supersoldier program, but now she wasn't so sure.

She knew that, among other things, he was looking for some super-protective, subtly reactive material capable of shielding the wearer not only from ballistic and stabbing weapons, but also from blast, shock, and heat effects—perhaps even the whole range of nuclear, biological, and chemical agents. Certainly that had piqued her own interest—that, and perhaps other, more obscure forms of troop augmentation.

Was that all he was after? Or were his efforts connected to something larger? Perhaps to those ongoing thefts from meteorite collections? Reluctantly, Darla began to consider the possibility that she might herself be the recipient of stolen goods.

She glanced again at the news as it continued to churn away. Might the general perhaps be connected somehow even to the assault in Jerusalem?

She turned off the news. The jet hurtled between the star-spangled ocean of night far above and the wave-crested Pacific far below. Darla saw no shooting stars out the window, though they were very much on her mind. Turning from the window, she looked about the cabin of the jet, where most of her fellow passengers were sleeping, including her lightly snoring postdoc research assistant, Barry Levitch.

Shards of stone falling ablaze from heaven. What was their true relevance to human history, to all the events that had contributed to the ranks of humanity now obliviously sleeping in neat rows around her?

She had long believed those otherworldly shards were broken vessels, and that those vessels sometimes contained substances or properties that affected everything from terrestrial chemistry to mental states in individual human minds. She heard nothing at the conference to dispel that belief.

She had no doubt, for instance, that Miller's meteoritic Nuhus—spears of the gods or spears of God, whichever—had exerted a psychoactive influence on those who came in contact with them. It was just too much like the stories about the Central Asian Chintamani Stone and its powers. Even if the action of such stones had been purely magnetic—à la Michael Persinger's "divinity inducing" rotating magnetic fields—she was sure the stones' effects were more than just to point north.

DARPA, she knew, had been experimenting for years with TMS, transcranial magnetic stimulation, as a performance enhancer for military personnel exhausted by those protracted field operations that deprived troops of sleep for days or weeks on end. Given how many hours straight she'd been awake, she could probably use a pulse of TMS herself right now.

In the next occupied seat over, beyond the empty seat beside her, Barry turned in his sleep. She envied him. She always had trouble sleeping on flights, no matter how long her travels kept her in the air.

She thought back on the conference, and then on that whole geopolitical chain of Russian dolls Avigdor Fox's death triggered in her mind. She couldn't help but remember that Russian fellow Yuri Semenov's presentation, too. He had talked about physiological effects of electromagnetism connected to meteoroids and meteorites, effects that were a lot bigger than just magnetic stones pointing north, or tweaking a few neural networks inside a shaman's head to make a new lightbulb flash on there.

In his concluding remarks Semenov speculated that the tremendous burst in species diversity at the beginning of the Paleozoic—the "Cambrian explosion"—might somehow have been precipitated by a literal explosion. He suggested that burst might have resulted from yet another great skystone impacting the earth. No impact crater had been identified as of yet, however, and Semenov did not propose a specific mechanism for that explosion of diversity.

If Darla was right, smaller sacred skystones opened up minds for a potent change in perceptions and the generation of new ideas. If Semenov was right, the wrath-of-God impactors opened up genomes for a potent change in trait expression and the generation of new species.

Yet none of that exactly fit what she'd seen with the tepui stone. Or fit the larger issue of the meteorite thefts worldwide, either. Up to the present she had not pressed General Retticker on the provenance of the tepui stone and the tribe that had worshipped it. About all he had offered, besides the occasional cryptic note, was a warning to her, before she left for the conference, not to mention the stone specifically in her conversations and interviews. She was particularly not to mention it to Yamada and Miskulin.

She hadn't done so during her interviews with them. Still, she would be more than willing to tolerate having both of them on her team, if it meant she could find out something General Retticker himself didn't particularly want her to know.

Learning more about the stone's original setting was not something on which she had planned to spend much time. So much of experimental science was, after all, about examining the object independent of its context. Now, though, she realized she might need to take that context into account.

She knew a good deal about the context of the sacred stones of the Old World, but she didn't know all that much about the context of meteorite worship in the New World. She would have to play things very close to the vest, but hiring Yamada in some sort of consultant capacity might help her puzzle out the larger background of the thing.

She would have to be careful. For someone like Semenov, she supposed there would be little purpose in gathering such shards, since he saw meteoroids and meteorites as essentially solid projectiles. If the tepui stone was in fact only one of many stolen meteorites, however—and if those stones were being gathered in order to piece together some greater puzzle, some great mosaic—then whoever might be trying to piece together that larger whole must be after something more than ballistic information.

Those mosaic-makers and puzzle-solvers also seemed willing to countenance anything to achieve their "big picture" goal, including murder and, it seemed now, even the risk of global religious war. Reassembly on such a scale and at such a cost had to be for some deeper reason. But what?

All that effort only made sense if the fragments still contained some other information, in much the same way that a vessel once filled with oil, even after it has shattered, still retains some drops of the original liquid adhering to its shards.

What if the catastrophic rocks from space not only freed up the expression of mutations and variations by overwhelming the chaperone capacities of heat shock proteins—as Yuri Semenov contended—but also injected nonterrestrial exotics into those opened genomes while their guards were down? Gathering stones together then made a definite sort of sense, if someone was in fact trying to piece back together genetically coded material that had been broken into fragments, or otherwise corrupted by passage through vastnesses of time and space.

Such ideas brought her perilously close to Michael Miskulin's notions that the life-code did not originate on earth but in space—and that, unfortunately for everyone, life on this planet had gotten a corrupt copy.

Barry woke up and looked at her as he rubbed sleep from his eyes.

"You look deeper in thought than I was in sleep," he said. "Mind if I ask what's on your mind?"

"I was thinking about Miskulin's idea," she said, glancing down. "That life on earth started from some incomplete copy of the cosmic life-code, floating around out in space."

"What about it?" Barry asked, stifling a yawn.

"Microbes from space might have helped in the initial genesis of terrestrial life," she began, "but I don't really see how they might be all that implicated in anything that happened later."

"Single-celled critters were the dominant life-forms on the planet for three quarters of the history of life on earth," Barry agreed sleepily. "From four billion to one billion years ago, the single cell was pretty much the whole story."

"Right. Just adding more single-celled bacteria to the mix probably wouldn't have changed things much, until the Cambrian explosion hit and multicellular organisms evolved. Even if the exotic bacteria did come from space. It was almost all microscopic life."

"Yep. The planet'd look a lot different without the plants, animals, and fungi we can actually *see*."

Barry's mention of the fungi reminded her of Retticker's note on the meteorite cultists of the tepui, and her own research on the tepui stone. Looking about her, at the plane full of sleeping passengers, she wondered how freely she could speak of her work. She decided to take the chance.

"Yet the prebiotic and potential-genetic material we're working with in Montana seems to be hopelessly redundant and meaningless," she said, almost to herself. "I don't see how an injection of such junk could have affected the evolution of multicellular life, much less the minds of modern humans."

"What if it's not junk?" Barry asked.

"What do you mean?"

"Everybody used to think the majority of DNA was junk because it didn't obviously code for proteins. They thought the introns were just segments of meaningless DNA that sat between the genes that coded for proteins. Then they found out that the Group Two introns could insert themselves into host genomes and later splice themselves out once they'd been expressed as RNA."

Darla saw what he was getting at, especially in conjunction with the spliceosome, an odd little complex of catalytic RNAs and proteins.

"Peculiarly parasitic bits of RNA and DNA," she said, thinking it through. "Introns in general, working with the spliceosome, could proliferate, mutate, and evolve. Over time the intron 'junk' developed RNA-mediated genetic functions that evolved independently and in parallel to proteins."

Barry sat up straighter in his seat, realizing what their conversation might be tumbling them to.

"Parasitic nucleic acids and spliceosomes sound like the sorts of things that might well have come in from space . . ." he began.

Darla, however, was already thinking several steps ahead of him.

"In much the same way that parallel processing works in the brain, the successful injection of such components into the single-cell world could have resulted in the development of new RNA-based genetic operating systems and regulatory networks—"

"—communicating regulatory information in parallel to protein-based systems and networks," Barry said, nodding eagerly.

Darla, however, was still far ahead of him. Semenov hadn't seen the mechanism, she realized. Having examined the tepui stone, though, Darla thought she could now see the outlines of the system through which the machinery of life on earth interacted with the vaster machinery of the heavens.

"There's some basis for believing the nucleus is itself a molecular-parasite immigrant," she said. "Something like a large and persistent DNA virus that made a permanent home within prokaryotes, allowing them to become eukaryotes."

"Couple that with the development of a new RNA-based control architecture, which could have resulted in a tremendous burst of new molecular evolution—"

"—and together they'd likely be enough for the Cambrian explosion's blast of diversity."

"Bingo! I think you're on to something, Doc!"

It didn't stop there, though. Now that she thought about it, the affects of newer architectures for both generating and controlling organismal complexity kept popping up. Large-scale changes might be related in time to the great impactors punctuating the overall equilibrium of evolution, yes, but smaller-scale changes might also be related to smaller meteoritic events.

"Genetic objects such as transposons and other repetitive elements are also considered molecular-parasite 'immigrants,'" Barry said. "They supposedly colonized the genomes of various species in waves, at different times during evolutionary history. They used to be thought of as genomic junk, too."

Darla nodded.

"And now they've turned out to play a key role in genomic regulation and epigenetic inheritance."

"Some of those might also be nonterrestrial in origin!"

She knew that one such formerly "junk" element was involved in adenosine-to-inosine editing of RNA transcripts. These "editor" components overwhelmingly occurred in repeat sequences, called Alu elements, within noncoding RNA sequences.

Alu elements were found only in primates, and A-to-I editing was particularly important in brain activity.

The colonization of the primate line by Alu elements made possible the development of a new level of complexity in RNA processing, allowed more flexible and dynamic programming of neural circuitry, and laid the foundation for memory and higher-order cognition.

She wondered again at that old space movie, with its black monolith from space, and ancient primates embarking on the long journey to becoming human.

"Doc, do you think maybe the repetitive prebiotic material and what looks like nucleic acid junk we've found in the tepui stone . . . do you think that might not be junk after all?"

Darla pondered it, possibilities flashing through her mind.

"Far from being just junk, it might be a sample of a vastly expanded and highly sophisticated regulatory architecture. One that, in bits and pieces, has been manifesting itself throughout life on earth for a billion years."

Barry whistled softly, but Darla barely heard him. Caught up in her thoughts, she was not inclined to further discussion. Barry seemed caught up in his own thoughts too, but eventually he turned on the seatback screen in front of him and watched the reports and bulletins on Jerusalem for a time.

Someone knows about all this, Darla thought.

Someone who knows that explosions in complexity occur as a result of advanced controls and embedded networking.

Scattered throughout the meteorites of the world, there just might be the whole code of a most important program, a design system not only for the generation and control of higher levels of complexity, but also for self-reproduction and self-programming of complex systems generally. The full unveiling of such a code could have tremendous implications, not only for General Retticker's search for chemically reactive armor or performance-enhancing drugs, but perhaps for all life on the planet.

She thought of the stories of the Nuhus, of the *yahui*-priests, and of the abundance of food and wealth hidden in the caves associated with them. That jogged in her mind the old tales of the Grail as *lapis ex coelis,* the stone from the heavens, which also provided food and wealth in many of the stories of the medieval Arthurian romancers.

Scattered across time and space in new world and old, might those images of abundant food and wealth stand for *something else* in those stories—something far more than mundane, that could only be described in mundane terms? Was that "something else" the reason why someone (or more than one someone) was going after all the pieces? A new kind of philosopher's stone—a black stone, exiled from the sky, which nonetheless enabled a transformation far more important than that which turned base metals into gold?

Near her, Barry snorted. Startled, Darla stared at him.

"Sorry. I was just watching these news reports on the Temple Mount mess. I wonder if the physicists' talk of all their alternate worlds and parallel universes would have made a difference in that nightmare."

"I don't follow you."

"What if, in infinite universes of infinite possibilities, there might be an earth somewhere where Moses never lived, and Jesus never lived, and Muhammad never lived? Would it make any difference? Would there be no religious relics or monuments for people to build up or tear down? Or would people still be blowing things up in Jerusalem?"

"If not there, probably somewhere else," Darla said, fighting the slide into glumness as she thought again of Avigdor Fox and the Temple Mount. "I guess if all the religious impedimenta—the relics, the shrines disappeared, it might give everybody pause, for a while. But people and monuments are easier to get rid of than ideas. Might as well throw in Buddha, Hitler, and Einstein never existing, while you're at it."

"Okay, done. Go on."

"I think ideas like theirs would still probably pop up one way or another, with or without them."

Barry gave her a skeptical look.

"Ideas floating around in the ether, destined to manifest themselves independent of particular individuals? That's too Platonic *and* too fatalistic for me." Barry switched off the seatback screen in front of him and turned over in an attempt to get back to sleep. "G'night."

"Have a good sleep," Darla said, wishing Barry what she was unlikely to experience herself. She stared out the window again, wondering about things to say to General Retticker and things not to say to Yamada. She wondered, too, about what had happened between her and Miskulin— once again, for a very brief moment, after that brief interview.

Odd. She supposed she could write it off to her feeling low at the time—and any port in a storm, as the saying went. Michael really wasn't her type, she knew that. Had known it, for years.

Certainly Freud would have had something to say about the fact that she'd always preferred stronger, quieter, older men to those of her own age or younger. Men like the general, if he had thrown her a sign in that direction. Or if she had had time to throw him one.

Staring into the night she almost hoped she might see out there the faintly glimmering outlines of some architecture of infinite possibility, a constellation of fate or destiny. All she managed to see were a few distant stars, fading as the earth turned this side of itself into the light of a star much nearer.

BRIGHT MENISCUS

"Welcome to Temple Mount," Victor Fremdkunst said, shifting something that looked rather like a large video camera onto his left side in order to shake hands with Retticker. "Thirty-five acres of the hottest real estate on the planet—or at least the most contested."

Joe Retticker nodded as he looked at the heavily guarded precincts around them.

"I know how zealous the parties are about defending their turf here," Retticker said. "Things must have reached a pretty pass for them to be willing to 'reassign' the management of this crisis to multinational forces."

Fremdkunst led Retticker through the late afternoon light, away from the desert-painted Humvee in which he'd arrived.

"Both the Israelis and Wakf, the Islamic Trust that oversees the Dome, were more than happy to turn this situation over to the UN," Fremdkunst said. "The 'Dome intifada' this whole thing has caused is putting all previous uprisings in the shade."

Retticker nodded. He had seen the reports. The Muslim world was up in arms. Riots in Pakistan and the Arabian port city of Qatif. Massive street protests from Morocco to Syria to Iran. Not a good time to be a a blue-helmeted peacekeeper in this neighborhood.

Tools jangling on his tool belt, Fremdkunst in full meteorite-hunter mode led the way along a cypress-bordered allée toward a broad plaza, paved in slabs of pale stone, surrounded by pillared and colonnaded structures.

"What's that gadget you're carrying?" Retticker asked.

"Netsonde side-scanning earth-penetrating sonar unit," Fremdkunst replied. "The latest tool of the trade."

Retticker was going to ask what trade, but then he saw, dead ahead, the vault of the Dome of the Rock, blackened on one side. The portico leading to the nearest entrance of the Muslim pilgrimage site was gutted and broken.

"Thar she blows," Fremdkunst said. "The Dome itself. Over that way is the Western Wall plaza, where the Jewish First and Second Temple once stood. The center of spiritual life for the Jews in Israel. The Second Temple is where Jesus taught and overturned the moneychangers' tables, where he was tempted by Satan while floating in the air. Beyond the Dome that way is the Al-Aqsa Mosque. The Stables of Solomon, or what's left of them, are over that way, and the Mount's Golden Gate is off there, too."

Around the shrine of the Dome stood a sea of blue-helmeted soldiers. Fremdkunst and Retticker flashed their credentials and the blue sea parted for them. As they got closer to the shrine, Retticker thought he recognized some of the troops in the innermost rings as enhanced warfighters. Beyond them, amid the rubble of the nearest shrine entrance, stood a man in what looked like a desert-camo business suit.

"There's the gent who got you assigned as an adviser to the multinational force," Fremdkunst said, nodding his head in the man's direction. "He must have pulled a lot of strings. I believe you've met before, aboard my boat *Sky Miner?*"

In the midst of what Retticker was now sure was a contingent of MERC supertroops, there stood George Otis himself, a corporate emperor surrounded by his praetorian guard.

Unlike all the grim-faced troops and officials they'd encountered, the silver-haired power broker was smiling broadly. Retticker got the distinct impression that Otis would have been practically skipping with happiness if the rubble and debris he was walking through offered more solid footing. Fremdkunst reintroduced the two of them.

"So, Mister Otis," Fremdkunst said as they surveyed the damage, "what do you think?"

"Splendid, splendid!" Otis said, beaming. "What with the blast at the Western Wall, some of my friends in the Knesset are calling for the annihilation of the 'House of Esau' and the 'Amalekites,' biblical names for the Palestinians!"

"Annihilation?" Retticker asked. "How?"

"Surgical fuel-air bombing strikes. It'll be like hitting them with mininukes but without the downside of radiation overspray. The Israelis are at last realizing that the two-state solution is not final enough. Obadiah fifteen to eighteen may very soon be fulfilled!"

Although he didn't recall the scripture verse, Retticker knew well the power of fuel-air bombs. They were more appropriately known as MAD FAE, for "mass air delivery fuel-air explosives." He had seen them in action on the battlefield—big canisters filled with ethylene oxide or aqueous ammonium nitrate mixtures, descending by parachute and detonating just above the ground, producing blast overpressures of hundreds or even thousands of pounds per square inch, disintegrating everything within tens to hundreds of yards. They were nothing to be toyed with, especially if one were considering effective tools for a civilian genocide.

Some of Retticker's misgivings must have shown themselves in his face, for Otis quickly qualified his enthusiasm.

"I'm sure no one takes any pleasure in such pronouncements of extermination. I know I don't. As the Bible says in Ezekiel eighteen thirty-two, 'For I have no pleasure in the death of him that dieth, saith the Lord God.' This isn't about some simpleminded hatred of the Palestinians or of Islam. This is about God's Plan. Believers can rejoice in the hope that the unchurched, seeing such calamities and catastrophes breaking out, will realize all this as prophetic fulfillment of a twenty-five-hundred-year-old verdict from a judging God—and will turn to Jesus Christ for salvation in the face of it!"

Blindsided by Otis's smugly smiling self-righteousness, Retticker could only nod. Flanked by his MERC supersoldiers, Otis turned on his heel as Fremdkunst led them into the damaged shrine.

With the sun declining outside, it was cool and damp and rather gloomy inside the structure. Retticker looked about them, but many of the finer details of the structure—its ornamentation and calligraphy—were becoming lost in shadow.

That sensation of cool dampness only grew as they approached the spot where naked rock protruded out of the shrine's floor. As the three of them stood looking down at the stone, the troops fanned out into defensive positions around them. With the troops deployed, the gloom of the damaged shrine took on a surreal air.

"The sacred stone of Mount Moriah itself," Fremdkunst said quietly. "The presence of a town on the south side of the Mount goes back to at least the late Chalcolithic and Early Bronze Ages. A heckuva lot of human history and prehistory dial down right to this spot. Five thousand years' worth, at least."

"The town was originally called Urusalim," Otis said, nodding as he knelt down and reverently touched the exposed rock. "A Semitic word meaning 'Foundation of Shalem' or 'Foundation of God.' Jewish tradition says the rock here at the top of the Temple Mount was the first rock laid down as the foundation of the rest of creation. The rock where the world began, and also where it will end."

Otis stood and walked to another part of the rock before kneeling and touching it again.

"When King David captured the city from the Jebusites about three thousand years ago," he continued, "he made it the capital of the Jewish kingdom and changed its name to Jerusalem, 'City of Peace.' The Ark of the Covenant was brought to the Mount around 950 BC, but it was also here, much earlier, that Abraham built the sacred stone altar for the sacrifice, in faith, of his only son Isaac. Also where Jacob used one of the stones as a pillow and had his great dream-vision of angels going up and down a ladder or stairway to heaven. The same stone later became the foundation stone, the *Even ha-Shetiyah,* of Solomon's temple. It was on that same stone that they set the Ark of the Covenant.

"According to one Kings eight, the *Shekinah,* the Divine Presence, descended onto this place. Ezekiel eight four and eleven twenty-three tells us it was from this same place that the Divine Presence departed. Ezekiel forty-three, lines one to seven, says it will be to this same place that the Divine Presence will return."

Barraged by the biblical sound bites of such proof-texting, Retticker could say nothing in reply. The light continued to fade inside the shrine. To Retticker, the gloom seemed filled with both the promise and the menace of long history. A small electromechanical whirring began as Fremdkunst powered up his earth-penetrating sonar device.

"Where do people pray in here?" Retticker asked at last, looking about them.

"Anywhere they like, I suppose," Fremdkunst said, bringing the screen of his sonar-scanner up to his face and panning the device slowly over the stone. "This isn't a mosque or a temple. It's a *Mashhad,* a shrine for pilgrims. First this was a Jebusite holy place, then it was the site of the two Jewish Temples.

"Under the Romans it was a sanctuary dedicated to the Roman god Jupiter. Then it became sacred to the Muslims because Muhammad stopped here during his Night Journey. From this stone, the As-Sakhra, the Prophet ascended to heaven on a ladder of golden light. That's why the Muslims capped it with the Dome of the Rock—Qubbat As-Sakhra, in Arabic."

Fremdkunst changed the direction of his sonar scan, then began slowly panning over the rock from a different angle before he took up his history again.

"For a few years it was the primary sacred site of Islam, until Muhammad quarreled with the Jews of Medina and Allah directed him to shift the still-point of the turning world to Mecca. When the Christians controlled the city, they turned this place into a shrine called the Templum Domini. Then it went back to being the Qubbat As-Sakhra after the Muslims regained control of it."

Retticker and Otis watched Fremdkunst perform his sonar-scan ritual. It was getting dark inside the shrine. They would need to use flashlights or headlamps before long.

"Beneath the sacred stone is a cavelike crypt called the Well of Souls," Fremdkunst said. "According to ancient folklore, you can sometimes hear the voices of the dead and the rushing of the rivers of paradise in the crypt."

"Sounds like everyone has wanted to own a piece of this rock," Retticker said. "Whose turn is it now, science's?"

"Perhaps," Fremdkunst replied. "Wait a minute. I've got something here."

The meteorite hunter stepped onto the rock and, after a brief zigzag of misdirection, narrowed in on his target. To Retticker it looked as if Fremdkunst was paying more attention to his scan readout than to where he was placing his feet. With considerably more care and caution, Otis and Retticker followed. Standing over the spot on the stone the screen had led him to, Fremdkunst pulled the sonar scan away from his face and looked down.

"This is where Fox was working," he said. "The stone's newly broken here, see? According to my scanner, he was only centimeters away from reaching the embedded stone when his work was interrupted."

Fremdkunst handed Retticker a small LED keyfob light.

"Here. Press the button on this and keep the light focused on this hole here."

Retticker did as he was told. Fremdkunst grabbed a hammer, chisel, and small miner's pick from his tool belt. Taking up and putting down the tools as needed, he widened and deepened the hole in the sacred stone. His pick at last made a hollow sound, as if he'd struck the rock wrong.

Immediately a scent filled the air around them, a fragrance like incense or perfume but with an earthy organic undertone like mildew or mushroom. Fremdkunst stopped digging but Retticker kept the light shining on the darker stone embedded within the rock outcrop before them.

Abruptly something seemed to twist the LED beam, to make the brightness lenticular above the hole itself, like a meniscus of surface tension between oil and vinegar, like a lens-shaped bubble rising through water or a fingernail sliver of moon coming over the horizon. Ghostly as a glowing mushroom cap, the bright meniscus rose a foot or so into the air. Abruptly it burst, leaving a smear of wetness on the stone as its only trace.

"Jacob's stone and the oil of heaven!" Otis said, a bit too enthusiastically for Retticker's taste. "This is a sign from God, that He is well-pleased with our work!"

"Maybe," Fremdkunst said, "but I think the jury's still out. We can each make up our own minds about this, and each make up our own opinions about it, but I don't think we can each make up our own facts. I'm going to look for a scientific explanation."

"What about contamination?" Retticker asked.

"Us by it? Or it by us?" Fremdkunst said, smiling as he scraped up samples of the smeared stone. "This rock's been here a long time. Many other people have likely been exposed to it—without recorded harm."

Humming happily to himself, Fremdkunst chipped loose pieces of the stone from which the strange perfume had come. He tapped them gently into specimen vials while, standing over him, George Otis prayed with eyes closed, repeating "Thank you, Jesus! Thank you, Jesus!" like a chant.

Watching them, Retticker had no idea which ritual—scientific, or religious—might be the more appropriate response. He was sure, however, that he had come a long way from where he'd started. A blissful, druglike lassitude settled upon his thoughts.

This was all beginning to feel like a lot more than just investigating potential soldier-enhancers for tactical advantage. While searching for possible superarmors and perfected unit cohesion, he had somehow stepped onto a battlefield bigger and deeper than he had ever imagined, one whose lines were drawn in ways he did not yet understand, and whose boundaries stretched far beyond his view.

PROPHECY AND CONSPIRACY

Jim Brescoll grimaced. The government-issue sedan, of which he was the unlucky driver, was a bucket of sludge when it came to handling the curves of the mountain road. Not that the road, as it climbed into the central Sierra, was particularly tortuous: California Highway 168 was a full four lanes, at least along this stretch of it. Yet the sedan was sloshy on the turns and underpowered on the uphill grade. Ever since global oil production peaked and started on the downslope, nearly all government vehicles were required to be alternate-fuel hybrids, but this one didn't even have the virtue of being particularly fuel efficient.

The bright sky and snow on the distant peaks reminded him of another winter trip to California, years ago. He wondered what it would be like to drive this road in a high-powered sportster, with a tight rally suspension and steering package. Or perhaps even taking this highway on a crotch-rocket motorcycle, an adventure of which his wife would never approve—

His satellite screenphone rang for his attention. He put on his augmented reality glasses and answered. Dan Amaral's mustached and goateed viz, narrowcasting from Israel, appeared in faux 3D in the doubled readout screens in the upper-right corners of Brescoll's glasses.

"Hello, Jim. Doesn't look like you're in your office, judging by the background."

"I'm on the road in California," he said, thankful that this land yacht he was driving at least had a secure videoconf line compatible with his AR specs. Even that compatibility, however, could not compensate for a chat carried on halfway across the globe. The signal time-lag punctuated their conversation with hanging silences.

"Ah. Off to meet your mysterious sources inside the mountain?"

"Right you are."

"I thought you weren't going to be doing any more of the legwork on this. What about Steve Wang and Bree Lingenfelter? This would seem to be up their alley. I mean, you *are* the director, after all."

"Not a 'red-shirt,' as my predecessor used to say. I know. But on this one my sources would meet only with me."

"Then I hope for your sake they're not playing ninepin and drinking heavily when you rendezvous with them. Ethan Watson and the administration won't hold your job open if you get Rip van Winkled for ten or twenty years. Such things happen to people who meet strange folks inside mountains, you know."

Jim smiled.

"I'll be careful. No bowling with strangers, I promise. How about you? I've gotten full reports on the intifadists who attacked the Second Temple's Western Wall. What about the others? Any progress on those Temple Mount incidents and the dead meteoriticist?"

Amaral puckered up his face in distaste.

"Nothing but the clash of fundamentalisms here—'religious conservative' Jewish nationalists, 'religious conservative' Muslim intifadists, 'religious conservative' Christian Zionists."

Amaral glanced away. Brescoll guessed he was consulting a PDA or laptop computer.

"The radical Jewish nationalists were mostly hard-core settlers living in broken-down trailers in the Samarian mountains. Zealots who think the Palestinians are the current incarnation of the 'Amalekites'—eternal enemies of the Jews the Bible says attacked Moses and his people on the Exodus from Egypt. The Christian Zionists believe the Bible predicts the ingathering of the Jews into a Greater Israel extending from the Nile to the Euphrates. Once the Jews have achieved this Greater Israel, all of them will convert to Christianity—or 144,000 will convert and the rest will be left behind to die in the Tribulation with the rest of us, depending on whose scenario you follow. In either case the Jews will cease to exist as Jews."

"I wouldn't think Jewish Zionists would be particularly happy about the ceasing-to-be-Jews part," Jim said, trying to rein in the buttcushion sedan's oversteer on a long curve.

"No, they're not. One of those niggling end-time details, where the apocalyptic Jewish and Christian zealots part company. The radical Jewish nationalists have no problem with the Greater Israel aspect, though. They've been more than willing to accept the funding lavished on them by their fellow apocalypse addicts in the U.S. The Christian Zionists believe the ingathering and conversion of the Jews signals that all the CZ hopes for the End of Days are about to be fulfilled. Armageddon, Rapture, the Return of Christ to rule for a thousand years on earth—the whole scenario."

"And that's relevant to what's happening at the Temple Mount?"

"Right. Members of the Jewish Temple Mount Faithful believe the Torah obligates Israel to rebuild the Temple whenever it becomes possible to do so. Heaven will not send the Messiah as a sign of redemption until there has been a national repentance and the task of rebuilding the Temple has begun."

Brescoll nodded, but Amaral seemed to be consulting his research oracles via the Web again, so it took him longer than time lag to continue.

"Israel gained political control of East Jerusalem nearly fifty years ago now. The main obstacle to the rebuilding is that most rabbis and archaeologists believe the Temple stood precisely where the Dome of the Rock stands today."

"I can see how that might present a problem . . ." Jim said, trailing off as he rounded a bend in the road. Around him he saw that, after a long stint among foothill oaks and manzanita, the highway was beginning to rise into heavy pine forest.

"And how. Many Muslims believe that Jews are already intent on destroying some of Islam's holiest sites to make way for the Third Temple of the Jewish people, and the fulfillment of the future prophetic program for Israel."

"But what do Christians have to do with a Jewish Temple?"

"That's a little more convoluted. For some Christians the construction of the Third Temple is an important sign that the 'time of Jacob's Trouble'—also known as the 'Tribulation'—is at hand."

"No construction has been done yet, though?"

"Yes and no. For more than a quarter of a century now, the Temple Institute, aligned with the Temple Mount Faithful, has been creating a 'Temple-in-waiting.' They've produced ritually appropriate vessels, priestly garments, all the paraphernalia needed for rites and worship at a rebuilt Temple. They've also run computerized visualizations and drawn up blueprints for the Third Temple."

"An interesting mix of high-tech and ancient tradition," Jim said thoughtfully, "but I still don't see how that makes American Christians cough up money."

"For certain Christians," Amaral explained, "all these contemporary physical preparations and political demonstrations by Orthodox Jews point toward a restored Jewish Temple. According to some Christian interpretations of the Bible, a still later rebuilding will be the Messiah's Temple, which will appear when Jesus comes to reign on earth for a thousand years."

Jim shook his head. He was raised Baptist himself, but he'd never thought too much of end-time speculation. A friend of his had once referred to it as Christian sensualism: as a believer, you were strongly discouraged from engaging the services of a prostitute, but you could still fantasize all you pleased about the Whore of Babylon.

The highway he was driving narrowed from four lanes to two, and in more and more places the narrowness of the road-cut reduced the shoulder to nothing. Enclosed on both sides by tall pines, the number and severity of the highway's twists and turns increased.

"What about this guy Hijazi who took out Fox? That whole thing sounds way too familiar."

"How so?"

"Like somebody did a cut-and-paste on a couple of pages out of the old Kennedy Curse playbook."

"Yes . . . ?"

"Hijazi's the silencer," Jim said, "like Jacob Rubinstein—aka Jack Ruby, the mob-connected nightclub owner—supposedly was."

"Conspiracy theory," Amaral replied, with a wry smile. "About the only thing these Kahanist Jews, Mudayyinist Muslims, and Christian Zionists all agree on is that God plans a terrible war in the Middle East as the kickoff to the apocalypse that'll cleanse our decadent world of all its evils. They're all working toward that. Co-conspirators, without knowing it."

"The interests of powerful forces do sometimes intersect," Jim said. "If Ismail Hijazi's grief and anger were exploited, if he was 'allowed' to get past security and express his rage in a way that resulted in Avigdor Fox's death, then who made straight the way for him? And why?"

Amaral paused, longer than required by the satellite time lag, long enough to suggest he was giving those questions considerable thought.

"I think the latter question is easier to answer," he said at last. "At least superficially. Dead men tell no tales. Who might have set that up, that I can't say."

"Look into it, would you? See if you can't find out who both Fox and Hijazi might have been meeting with in the days leading up to the incidents at Temple Mount. A good place to start would be with phone records, electronic transfer records, anything that might establish times, places, connections. I'll have some of my people get to work on the telecommunications and e-commerce ends of it and share with you whatever they manage to find."

"Sounds like a plan. I'll get cracking."

"Good. I think I told you about the tip I got on this Avram Zaragosa person. Any word on him?"

"The meteoriticist whose daughter got suicide-bombed while visiting here," Amaral said, nodding. "Yes. I've checked with sources both here and in South America. He's dropped out of sight. No one appears to know Mister Zaragosa's whereabouts."

Jim pondered that. He didn't like loose ends, but he'd have to let it go, for now. Too much else to deal with.

"We need to see whether the Temple Mount situation might fit into the broader puzzle of meteorite thefts worldwide," he said, "and where all of that might be heading."

"You haven't said much about these people inside the mountain, Jim, but I gather they're great prognosticators and makers of scenarios . . ."

"Where'd you hear that?"

"I have my sources in your world, too, you know. How about it?"

"They're good. Maybe the best."

"Ah. 'If you can look into the seeds of time and say which grain will grow, and which will not, speak to me, who neither beg nor fear your favors nor your hate.' *Macbeth*. Banquo's words to the three weird sisters—the witches. Banquo ends up dead, by the way. Murdered. You might want to be careful yourself."

"Not that I'll be meeting with witches or weird sisters, but duly noted. You're in much more the global hotspot than I am, after all. So take your warning to me and double it for yourself."

"I'll be happy to leave all this behind, believe me. Listening to these people, you'd think the world's been going to hell in a handbasket for the last five thousand years. I wish it would just get there already—Armageddon tired of the End of the World!"

Jim groaned at the bad pun.

"Ouch."

Amaral smiled and they signed off.

As he drove on—more serpentine road-warring through the sea of pines—Brescoll remembered to voice-message Wang and Lingenfelter on the East Coast to share their telecommunications and e-commerce intelligence on Fox and Hijazi with Amaral. When he finished, he saw that, outside the car windows now, there was still snow on the ground at this elevation.

At last he made his way through the multiple townlet-islands that loosely made up the burg of Shaver Lake. Turning off the highway, he drove past the marina at the northernmost end of the hydropower lake. Soon he turned onto a recently plowed private access road, snow-banked on both sides. The road had been previously owned by Southern California Edison but, since the Kwok-Cho affair, it had been deeded over to the U.S. government and administered by Central Security Services, NSA's military wing.

As he drove through the parklike pine forests of snow-limned trees marching to the frozen shore of the lake, Brescoll found the road very scenic. It was also heavily surveilled, gated, and multicheckpointed, he knew, though this was his first visit to the Mutual Assured Quantum Cryptologic Security Station, the MAXX.

At each checkpoint, he slowed and stopped. The identification and biometric security procedures became more involved and redundant. In addition to signing in and presenting his ID badge for scanning and photomatching, he soon had to submit to having his retinas, finger-prints, voice, and DNA printed and matched.

At the end of it all, he pulled into a cul-de-sac parking lot empty but for plowed-up mounds of snow. Before him, oddly free of snow, rose what from the air might have been mistaken for an usually symmetrical, smooth, and pale granite dome. In the days immediately after the Kwok-Cho affair, it had often been mistaken for exactly that. No one was allowed to make that mistake these days, however, because no one was allowed to see it from the air anymore.

For ten square miles, the atmosphere above the dome was the type of no-fly, off-limits, highly restricted airspace that usually prevailed only over the most secret of defense installations—what military pilots called Dreamlands. True, it could be seen from satellites in space, but from such distant heights it was even more the featureless landscape-feature that presented itself to Brescoll's eyes now, from less than a dozen yards away.

Brescoll got out of the car and into the crisp air to take a better look. Surveying it at close range, Brescoll could see that the thing wasn't made of granite, or rock, or any solid substance, for that matter. From the way it bent the air slightly about its curved surface, Brescoll could clearly see that the thing was a pearl gray dome of force. It sheltered everything for a thousand yards around the actual granite of the mountaintop.

Brescoll knew that, before the Kwok-Cho affair ran its course, there had been, just about directly in front of him, the mouth of the tunnel that led into the mountain. The road inside that tunnel made its way more than a mile into the rock, and at its end was an automated powerhouse tucked into an artificial cavern. The manmade cave was shaped rather like a loaf of bread, one hundred feet high and three hundred feet long, buried a thousand vertical-feet below the surface of the mountain.

Under the dynamited and shotcreted dome of this cavern, beneath the granite dome of this mountain, beneath this dome of force, beneath the dome of the sky, something was undeniably going on. Whether what was happening beneath all those domes and rocks was fit for a holiest of holies—or an unholiest of unholies—no one on the outside knew.

Markham, Benson, and LeMoyne, on the inside, had messaged him that they would know when he had arrived on their doorstep. No secret passwords or codes would be needed.

For a moment, Jim wished that he weren't standing here alone, that maybe he could have brought Steve Wang and Bree Lingenfelter along, to lean on their knowledge. Just in case.

He pushed that thought out of his head. Too late to change things now.

Although there was as yet no door to be seen, Jim Brescoll stepped forward, hoping to learn how events at the Dome of the Rock, half a world away, might be connected to other domes and other rocks.

CONVOLUTIONS OF HISTORY

Avram knew something big was afoot when Fremdkunst's connections suddenly sent in two helicopters. The smaller chopper dropped workmen at the Wabar digs, who began putting up more yomes. A much larger heavy-lifter dropped a modular building and installation crew onto the site. No sooner were the workers finished than they were he-licoptered out, never to be seen more.

Although the modular looked like a cross between a double-wide trailer and a temporary classroom, Avram soon learned it was a mobile quarantine laboratory facility.

Along with Vida and Yuri, he found himself spending less time ex-amining Wabar meteorites and impact glass, and much more time teaching deep-desert survival skills to a half dozen new arrivals. Five of these new arrivals turned out to be high-powered scientists: a pair of biochemists, a pair of molecular geneticists, and a twofer—a binotech-nician amply overqualified in both biotech and nanotech.

Avram found the sixth new arrival more of a puzzle. A bearded and bespectacled young Saudi, he introduced himself as Mahmoud Ankawi. He specialized in the teaching of Arabic, Arab culture, and the compar-ative religions of the peoples of the Book—Islam, Judaism, and Chris-tianity. Ankawi had no need of training in desert survival skills—being already expert in such matters, apparently—and he was also an avid amateur meteorite hunter.

A curious skill set, Avram thought. When he talked with the man, however, Ankawi's meteorite "hobby" history sounded legitimate enough. He, like so many others, claimed to have gotten involved in his "interest" by looking for coins beneath the sand with a metal detector, before graduating to the sky-iron currency of fallen stars.

By the time Fremdkunst showed up at camp again, the three senior investigators had more than a few questions for him—especially since he brought with him scores of new meteoritic samples. They had time to ask those questions, too, for the desert was enduring a spate of rain and mud when Fremdkunst arrived—an inconvenient wonder in the Rub' al-Khali, parts of which see no rain for years on end.

"Victor, what's this all about?" Vida asked, when she, Avram, and Yuri finally cornered Fremdkunst in one of the secured rooms inside the quarantine lab.

"Sit down. I'll show you."

Avram watched Vida and Yuri take seats around the lab's confer-ence table. Avram reluctantly followed suit, despite the fact that Victor remained standing.

Bright blue eyes flashing, Victor glanced around as if he didn't wish to be overheard. When he was certain the airlock was sealed, he took a vial from one of his pockets and twisted off its cap.

"This," he said. "Here. Take a sniff."

As Victor passed the vial beneath their noses, Yuri, Avram, and Vida did as he'd suggested. To Avram it smelled quite pleasant, if also a bit odd—a combination of perfume and mushroom subtly mixed.

"That's one of the divinest scents I've ever smelled," Vida said, eyes closed as she continued to savor it.

"Glad you like it," Victor said, screwing the cap back on the vial and placing it on a nearby shelf, where it stood among many others. Avram began to feel a vague euphoria mixed with lassitude. He wondered if whatever it was Victor had swept before their noses might have a mild psychoactive effect of some sort.

"But what is it?" Vida asked.

"A little gift from the Temple Mount."

"What?" Yuri asked, incredulous.

Vida gave Fremdkunst a suspicious look.

"Victor, what was in that vial?"

"Something quite possibly of extraterrestrial origin."

"Exposed to air?"

"Air? Yuri, he exposed *us* to it! Are you nuts, Victor? How dare you expose us to that so callously, so cavalierly—"

"Relax, relax. It doesn't seem to have done any lasting harm to Jacob all those thousands of years ago, if this is from the same rock. Or to anyone else who might have been exposed to it since then."

"But why?"

"Because, like our friend Avram here, I believe many myths and stories of ancient peoples actually describe celestial and meteoritic events—and their consequences. How about you, Vida?"

Vida was caught off guard by the question.

"Yes. I suppose I believe that, too."

"We're not the only ones," Avram said. "At ECOL, Miskulin suggested the scientific community ought to build up a global chronicle of shamanic responses to transient celestial events and impacts. I guess that's part of what he was doing in his presentation on the Inuit and lemmings."

"So I've heard," Victor said. "And seen—I've viewed a video recording of that presentation. What happens in lemming-year events has analogs in overpopulation, environmental destruction, and aggressive territorial expansion associated with humans. A number of scientists believe that, not just Miskulin."

"What does that have to do with meteorites?" Vida asked.

Avram was about to say something about Miskulin's life-code theories when Victor beat him to it—with something much more specific.

"The same 'junk' nucleic acid sequences that code for the lemmings' protein and hormonal changes during lemming-years," Victor said, "also show up in organic material extracted from meteorites. Even more interesting, though, is that there are recurring legends associating meteorites with human territorial expansion, particularly the founding of a tribe or nation."

"The Nuhu," Vida said. "The spears of the gods. They guided the founders of Tenochtitlan. Miller talked about it at ECOL."

Victor nodded.

"I'm not too familiar with that one, but it sounds right. There are many, many others. The best known is probably Jacob's dream-vision, in which God makes all those promises to him about how numerous and important his descendants will be."

Avram stroked his chin, thinking.

"Miskulin said that the life-code *programs* species to expand and explore the spatial dimension, because that serves the code's goal of re-turning to space and propagating itself throughout the universe."

"Too simplistic," Victor said, shaking his head.

"Sounds not so simple to me," Yuri said. "What makes you say simplistic?"

"Because the human response to celestial events is much more com-plex than that. It reflects who we are as much as what happens in the sky, but it's deeper even than that," Victor said, leaning on the table, staring from one to the other of them with eyes so bright and penetrat-ing they seemed almost radioactive. "You'll have to excuse me if this sounds a little weird. I've just gotten back from spending a good deal of time with a billionaire fundamentalist and a big military honcho at the Temple Mount. Frankly, I'm also a bit stoned, as they used to say. So, I would guess, are the three of you, right now."

Avram, Yuri, and Vida glanced sheepishly at each other, confused. His colleagues grinned awkwardly at Avram, and he back at them. He also felt some apprehension beneath his own smile, and sensed the same from Vida and Yuri.

As Victor toyed absently with one of the other vials from the shelf, his smile seemed to have no such underlayer of fear or worry.

"All of us are quite literally *stoned,* then, since the source of our psychic alteration is a stone beneath the Dome of the Rock. My mili-tary acquaintance had the same response you did. Contamination, and all. Almost didn't let me carry my samples away with me.

"My biblically literalist friend responded differently. For him this is all glorious proof that the Antichrist must appear before Christ appears at the Second Coming. End-time destruction must come before divine transcendence. The shadow of the bad and catastrophic runs ahead of the light of the good and creative."

"What do you mean?" Vida asked. By way of answer, Victor put on a pair of augmented reality glasses and slid each of them a pair. Picking his pair up, Avram noticed that they were some of the fancy new ARGUS blinks, with slender pivoting throat mike and all.

"I looked up the root of the word *apocalypse*," Victor said, blinking them to a prechosen website. "It's from the Greek verb *apokaluptein*, meaning 'to uncover.' Revelation, in the sense of unveiling. The ecstasy of dream or vision that lifts the veil of waking illusion, to reveal a deeper reality. That was the original meaning."

"That's not what apocalypse calls to mind when I hear that word," Avram said.

"No," Victor continued, calling sotto voce for selections and blinking them to other sites—with wonderfully vivid graphics of hellish oranges and reds. "The popular meaning, now, emphasizes the rending of the veil of this world. Global destruction brought on by end-time catastrophe—a necessity, if the world is to be renewed. So, which one do you think rocks from space are really about? The 'apocalypse within' of individual ecstasy, or the 'apocalypse without' of worldwide catastrophe?"

Avram, Yuri, and Vida glanced at one another.

"Catastrophe," Vida said. "At least in the case of doomsday impactors."

"Yes," Avram agreed. "They've made Earth a palimpsest planet."

"Oh? How so?"

"The extinction impactors are like big erasers. Older life is mostly erased so newer life has a place to write its own story over the old one."

"Da," Yuri said. "That's your pattern: catastrophe, then new world. New worlds for old. Clear decks. Clean slate. Darkest before dawn. If all end-time visions share deep echo, genetic grammar of punctuated equilibrium, then apocalypse outside might also make apocalypse inside—in genes, neurophysiology."

"What about a rock that more directly causes 'apocalypse inside'?" Victor asked. "There is a precedent, you know. The lapis. The alchemical philosopher's stone."

Vida frowned deeply.

"What are you saying?"

"On my way back to the desert," Victor said, calling up more pre-selected images, "I saw a TV program giving background on the Temple Mount attacks. It traced the connection of the Knights Templar to the Mount, and to alchemy. The original purpose of the Templars was to guard the Temple Mount precinct."

"I thought these graphics looked familiar!" Vida said. "Did this program suggest the Templars discovered the Ark of the Covenant in the ruins of Solomon's Temple? And that the Ark contained a stone from heaven, or a meteorite, similar to the Black Stone of Mecca?"

"The same. You saw it too, then? What do you think of the theory?"

"Pretty unlikely, since the Ark disappeared from the temple about twenty-seven hundred years ago—long before the Templars showed up."

"True, but what about a discovery of skystones *like* those contained in the Ark?"

"I don't follow you," Avram said.

"I've been researching it pretty furiously since my experience at the Temple Mount," Victor said, calling for selections on Jerusalem and Mecca, then blinking them to those sites. "These sacred stones have a convoluted history. Some historians say what the Templars found in their excavations at the Temple Mount was a fragment of the same Black Stone as that found in the Kaaba. The Hajar al-Aswad."

"I have heard Jacob's pillow-stone might be under Dome of the Rock," Yuri said, "but this is new on me."

"Some historians argue the Black Stone is a meteorite of ancient Bedouin provenance," Victor said, calling up more images from the Mideast and blinking through them. "Others say it's a meteorite stolen from an Egyptian pyramid or temple, where it was the throne of Isis. Anyway, the Black Stone eventually ends up in the Kaaba, the Cube temple in Mecca."

"Then how did part of it also end up at the Temple Mount in Jerusalem?" Avram asked, uncertain curiosity contending in his thoughts against certain confusion. "If it did, I mean?"

"Some say the Black Stone might originally be from the same fall as Jacob's stone pillow," Victor said with a wry smile. "One thing you can count on: when everyone wants a piece of the rock, the rock doesn't stay in one place happily ever after."

He blinked them to what were obviously historical illustrations.

"Long before the Templars rose from their ranks," he said, "the mad Caliph al-Hakim gave Pope Sylvester's order of chronicler-monks the run of the Mount. Al-Hakim was himself the great-grandson of the Fatimid Caliph al-Mansur, who was the first and only person since the Prophet known to have had close personal contact with the Black Stone over a prolonged period."

"So?" Yuri asked.

"So the stone stayed in al-Mansur's presence for several months—after it was presented to him, and before it was returned to the Kaaba. No one knows just how much of the stone was 'lost during shipping and handling' by him, and by the Ismailis."

"Wait, wait . . . I know something about this," Vida said. "The Qarmatians, the people the Nizari Ismaili Shiites came from, lived in Persia. The Heysessini, the so-called Hashishin, or Assassins, came from the Nizari Ismaili sect of the Shia."

"What do you know about these Qarmatians, these Ismailis?" Victor asked, striding around the lab, examining the samples. "I've read that they were allies of the Templar knights."

"I've heard that, too. Some Islamic scholars say the Ismailis may have kept a piece of the Black Stone themselves, before they passed it along to al-Mansur. Speculation. Not all that much is known about them. They had an exotic theology—equal parts Koran, astronomy, and Plotinean Platonism. Some scholars suggest there was also a Kabbalistic component to their worldview."

Victor gave her a quizzical look at that, but said nothing.

"What happened to the sect?" Avram asked. Vida took over, calling up sites on the Ismailis and blinking to them on all their AR specs—more historical images, including photographs of ruins on a rocky, mountainous perch.

"Nasir al-Din al-Tusi, the great scientist and writer, reportedly betrayed the Nizari fortress of Alamut to the Mongols, who destroyed the place, along with the last of the Heysessini. During the thirteenth century, I think it was."

"The whole period of the Crusades was steeped in power politics like that," Victor said, returning to the conference table and leaning on it once more. "You think that, just maybe, the Fatimid Caliph al-Mansur might himself have decided to keep a piece of the Black Stone . . . as part of that politics?"

"When the stone came back to the Kaaba it was a lot smaller than when it went out," Vida said with a shrug. "That's well documented. Since it was only removed from the Kaaba for those few brief years during al-Mansur's time, any carving or splitting of the stone would most likely have been done at that time."

Victor smiled wickedly.

"Some historians speculate it was al-Hakim's possession of his great-grandfather's chunk of the stone that drove Hakim mad."

"Made mad from a rock?" Yuri asked, with much indignation and bravado, it seemed to Avram. Understandable, given what Victor had exposed all of them to, and its possible source. "How?"

Vida blinked them to a site dealing with al-Hakim.

"Shi'ite tradition claimed that, at the turn of the fourth century after the Hejira, the Maudi or savior would appear and convert the entire world to Islam as a precursor to the Day of Judgment. In the year 400 AH—After Hejira—al-Hakim was the most important Shi'ite leader. He declared the Maudi had arrived, and that he himself was that divine personage."

"And the rock explains this . . . how?"

"Say al-Hakim had a piece of the rock," Victor said. "Then say that, maybe, he was reminded of its great importance by the envoys of the pope. Maybe spending a lot of time in the presence of the rock induced some kind of recurrent hallucination, or more prolonged mental imbalance. Enough to convince him of his own divinity."

"Sounds like some of Darla Pittman's ideas," Vida said, swiveling the mike away and propping her blinks on her forehead. "Which I didn't give a whole lot of credence to, before today. Even *if* this stuff we sniffed is harmless enough that we can converse more or less lucidly, I'm still not fond of having my head experimented with—without warning or prior permission. Any idea how long this altered state we're in will last?"

"A couple of hours. Don't worry. I've already been through it," Victor said, taking off his AR glasses, his toothy smile and striking blue eyes flashing mischievously. "Doctor Pittman wasn't quite right, you see. The 'head change' she's been touting as the primary cause and effect of so much, it's only secondary, really. A by-product of the 'stone of transformation' being exposed to the elements. The heart of the mystery lies elsewhere. That's what we need to stay focused on."

"Whatever the explanation for al-Hakim's madness, some historians of the period suggest he might have feared the stone's power enough to hide it in the Dome of the Rock, within the ruins of Solomon's Temple in Jerusalem. A place that apparently already housed rocks of similar type."

"Interesting," Avram said, trying to focus his thoughts. He felt almost too lucid, the orbit of his imagination expanding so that, a moment before, he had wondered which would vanish last—the lightning of Fremdkunst's smile, or the flash of his eyes—if the meteorite collector were to disappear Cheshire-cat style. "What does it have to do with alchemy, though?"

Avram didn't learn the Cheshire-cat answer, for Victor dropped his blinks back down over his eyes and flipped the mike back into command position.

"The chronicler-monks evolved, in conspiracy theory, into the hoaxed-up 'Order of Our Lady of Mount Sion,' " Victor said, taking up the thread of his discourse again, calling up search selections and blinking them to painted illustrations of crusaders, then woodcuts of alchemists. "The Knights of the Temple were real, however, and were initially the military wing of that earlier monkish order. A number of later alchemists with Templar connections believed the Black Stone and Jacob's stone pillow were archetypes of the lapis, the philosopher's stone. Still later, alchemists wrote that nothing could be accomplished in the Great Work without the right *prima materia.*"

"And what the chronicler-monks may have found in the ruins of the Temple of Solomon—"

"—was the best *prima materia* possible. Pieces of the alchemists' 'black stone.' Pieces of a sacred skystone or several such stones, whether from Mecca, or Egypt, or right there in the Kingdom of Jerusalem. That's why I was intrigued by your mention of Kabbalistic elements in what the Hashishin believed, Vida."

"Why?"

"Because there's a great deal of overlap between Kabbalah and alchemy," Avram said, guessing what Victor was getting at. Victor seemed content to let him explain. After a moment figuring out the fancy ARGUS blinks, he was able to call up the right search selections and maneuver them to appropriately illustrated sites.

"The first Kabbalistic text, *Sefer ha-Bahir,* was eventually put together and edited in Provence, in France, during the twelfth century. *Sefer ha-Bahir* combines the ideas surrounding the work of creation— the animating of matter—with the concept of celestial projection as a way to return to the divine source. That combination of ideas lies at the heart of alchemy as a mystical science. Systems like Kabbalah provide software for understanding and programming the universe-hardware."

"Exactly," Victor agreed, blinking them from alchemists and Kabbalists to images of King Arthur and his knights. "What the alchemists were after—transmutation of elements, panacea for all ills, the elixir of life—are the same characteristics found in the Grail for which the Knights of the Round Table supposedly went questing—the actual chalice of the Last Supper, not the later Holy Blood and Mary Madgalene theory of sacred and profane history. It's no coincidence the first great story of the Grail was authored by Chrétien de Troyes."

"What's the connection?" Vida asked.

"Troyes was the capital of Champagne," Victor said, calling up sites that, as he blinked them through, turned out to be illustrated with sumptuous twelfth- and thirteenth-century paintings of royal courts, knights, ladies, and minstrels. "Chrétien's patroness, Marie de Champagne, was the daughter of Eleanor of Aquitaine, who was herself the daughter of Guilhelm the ninth, count of Poitiers, duke of Aquitaine, and first known troubadour poet.

"The troubadours came out of Provence, which was also the seat of Kabbalistic learning," he continued, calling up more sites and blinking them onward through images of poets reading, rabbis praying, and knights battling. "Courtly love poetry, Kabbalism, and Templar influence all moved northward via Eleanor at Poitiers and then through her daughter Marie at Troyes. By the time Chrétien wrote his *Perceval*, Troyes not only had a strong Templar presence linked to the Middle East, but also a very active Sephardic Jewish community with roots in both Provence and Muslim Spain."

"And Grail in *Parzival* is alchemical, too," Yuri said. "In late twelfth century, Wolfram von Eschenbach refers to Templars as keepers of Holy Grail, and describes Grail chalice as miraculous stone—as *lapsit exillis*."

"A pun," Victor said, blinking them through pictures of stones and chalices accompanied by Latin phrases. "It suggests the exiled stone of Matthew—the stone that was rejected by the builders but has become the cornerstone. Perhaps punning on the alchemical 'lapis elixir' of the philosopher's stone, too. Transmutation of lead into gold is not so very different from transubstantiation of wine into blood."

"Does this writer Wolfram say anything about the stone's supposed powers?" Vida asked.

"Quite a bit," Victor said. "In *Parzival,* it can supposedly heal and nourish and enrich those who possess it—"

"Sounds like wish-fulfillment," Avram said grumpily.

"Well, why do many cultures wish upon a falling star? There's some sort of collective folk memory behind that, I'm sure of it. *Parzival'*s meteoritic grail even has the ability to communicate its wishes."

"Like the Nuhus!" Vida said suddenly.

"Oh?"

"When the Mixtecs, the Maya, and the Mexica were describing their meteoritic god-spears in the Mesoamerican codices, they'd had no contact with Europeans, yet the descriptions of the Nuhus' powers are almost exactly the same as those of the Grail!"

"A spear that heals and communicates also figures prominently in the Grail stories, too—the spear that pierced Christ's side," Victor said, calling up and blinking them through a series of increasingly cryptic engraved illustrations. "There are other puzzle pieces, too. The Black Stone, the Hajar al-Aswad or Hajar al-Fehm—the 'stone of wisdom'— is set in a *corner* of the Kaaba. It's not only Matthew's but also the Mason's 'Cornerstone.' The stone of the Coalmen, who refer to themselves as the Fehm or 'Perceivers.' The stone of the secret Italian society known as Carbonari. The mysterious black 'stones of power' in the ships' ladings of English explorer Sir Martin Frobisher's 1577 expedition to Baffin Island and beyond—stones most likely meteoritic, and eagerly awaited by Frobisher's tutor in navigation, the alchemist and magus Doctor John Dee. . . ."

Avram gave a sour laugh. The others looked at him.

"Templars, assassins, Grail knights, Kabbalists, alchemists—they're all doubtless fascinating, but I don't think there's much scientific basis to any of this. Remember what I said when we were driving across the desert and this came up, Yuri?"

" 'That way lies madness.' "

"Right. Conspiracy theories rush in where historical facts fear to tread."

They smiled, but Victor was having none of it.

"I'm no irrationalist, but sometimes much madness is divinest sense, people. What I've seen recently has forced me to be open to unusual possibilities. Just because someone or something is outside the ordinary mind-set doesn't mean unsuspected patterns might not actually *be* there. Symbols, metaphors, analogies—they're all 'not real' but they're also usually connected to some pattern that *is* real."

He sotto voced and blinked them into a welter of alchemical imagery.

"The lapis as philosopher's stone is traditionally a symbol and agent of transmutation—not for changing lead into gold so much as for transforming the soul of the human individual into something higher. According to the alchemists, their work was the work of the lapis, which was also the work of Christ: to awaken the god asleep in matter. In the Arthurian material, the cup of the Grail that held the blood of Christ is paired with the Spear of Longinus which pierced his side, causing that blood to flow—the bleeding spear that wounds but also heals, and which, some sources claim, had a spearhead of meteoritic iron, the *prima materia*. As late as the sixteenth century, alchemist Gerhard Dorn was telling his students that the goal of alchemy was that they should transform themselves into *living philosophical stones*."

This time it was Yuri who laughed. The others stared at him.

"I was thinking of something else you said when first I brought you here, Avri."

"What's that?"

"Latest great extinction event is us. Human species is now extinction impactor."

"See?" Victor said. "That's it! What we extract from these sky-stones says as much about us as it says about them. Will we as a species collectively embody the global doomsday rock, or individually embody the ecstatic lapis? The sky is our touchstone—the streak we make across it will attest to our true quality."

"Whichever that might be," Vida said, taking off the AR blinks. "And you still haven't fully answered my question. What are these labs and all these new samples about?"

"They are our wake-up call, Vida. Our reveille. Which Rock of Ages are we? My people are gathering together shamanic and priestly 'power objects' ranging from Inuit knives made of meteoritic iron to talismanic skystones from Papua New Guinea. We're building up the chronicle of shamanic and priestly responses to celestial and meteoritic events, just as Miskulin suggested. From all of that we just might be able to extract and put back together what it is that made these things grails in cultures throughout the world. That which wounds the shaman also allows him to heal—himself, and others. The heart of the mystery!"

Vida stood and walked to the racks of samples and specimens on the nearby shelves.

"Where did you get all these?" she asked, examining them.

"I have a not inconsiderable collection, as you may recall," he said, taking off his AR glasses. "Some newer sources, too. I'm afraid I'll have to swear all three of you to secrecy on this while our research is going forward."

"Why?"

"Because I don't know exactly what we'll find. The priests of the old mystery religions believed that what is revealed must be reviled, or it will be reviled. There's a lot of truth to that, I think."

Vida wasn't completely satisfied, Avram noticed. As their conference broke up, however, he turned to contemplating the fact that "reviled" spelled backward was "deliver." He'd always enjoyed palindromes, but in the state of mind in which he now found himself, they were a diversion more pleasant than ever. Reviled Eve deliver. Deliver Eve reviled. He was sure he could blink himself to dozens of sites running such mirrorings, if he really wanted to. He thought again of spear and chalice, and wondered why.

Avram took off his blinks and shook his head, trying to shake his thoughts back into their accustomed patterns. The effect of whatever it was they'd inhaled from Victor's vial was still very much alive in him. His palindromic woolgathering lingered long enough that Yuri and Vida were already out of the lab before he got out of his chair.

"Avram, may I speak with you before you go?" Victor asked. Avram nodded.

"I find it interesting that you are so much an unbeliever in conspiracies," Victor said, "when, as near as I can tell, you are part of one."

"What do you mean?" Avram asked, fighting to become more alert despite the lingering effect that breathing the stone's outgassing, or whatever it was, still had on him.

"Relax. Let's just say that I know something of your friend Luis. The one given to wearing panama hats and pale linen suits?"

Avram said nothing.

"I don't know all that much about him, admittedly. He does have interesting connections. I think our specialist in all things Arab and Islamic, Doctor Ankawi, is one of those connections. Perhaps he's here to help you prepare for your own particular Grail quest? Whatever that might be, I wish you luck. Farewell."

Before Avram had a chance to ask a single question, Victor was gone. Avram's many questions, however, did not leave with him.

INTERLUDE: LAUGHING SOLDIERS, SORRY LUCK

Dan Amaral regained consciousness to find his arms bound behind him, his head throbbing, and his shoulder crusted with dried blood. He looked around the room. In the harsh light from the ceiling's bare-bulbed fluorescents, he saw two other men, similarly bound, and what looked to be a metal door with a tiny, wire-reinforced glass window in it.

Everything came flooding back.

He'd been following up on the webwork of links surrounding Fox and Hijazi on the run-up to the Temple Mount incidents. He'd promised Jim Brescoll he would do, that before the NSA director himself disappeared on his increasingly extended "leave."

The mass of intercepts and general intel sent him by Brescoll's underlings, Steve Wang and Bree Lingenfelter, had contained a few grains of wheat amid their mountains of chaff, after all. In developing the background of times, places, and connections for Hijazi and Fox, Amaral had noticed an interesting link that even Lingenfelter and Wang had missed.

Phone intercepts showed a call from Avigdor Fox to Victor Fremdkunst. Electronic transfer records showed a link between Ismail Hijazi and one Hassam al-Wahari, a wealthy financier. Rumors of the dubious provenance of al-Wahari's personal fortune—money made smuggling guns and drugs across a frontier ranging from the Druze valleys to the Khyber Pass—hung about him like a taint, though the truth or falsehood of such rumors remained undecidable.

No apparent link existed between Fremdkunst or Fox and al-Wahari, however.

And then there it was, right next to Dan's morning cup of coffee and his copy of the English-language *Amman Times,* with its daily tally of rebel suicide-, car-, and roadside-bomb deaths.

An enterprising reporter, noting the involvement of a meteoriticist in the Temple Mount incident, had looked back through the paper's files and found a local connection: Hassam al-Wahari, whose Life/Style Profile a few years earlier showed the silver-bearded millionaire standing in front of his collection of "meteorite art."

The reporter had newly interviewed al-Wahari for his response to the Temple Mount incident, which the financier had roundly condemned. Of everyone reading the *Amman Times* that morning, however, perhaps only Amaral knew enough about Victor Fremdkunst to recognize that the unidentified meteorite art in the years-old file-photo was the work of the master's hand.

Dan had made occasional press reports from his various postings in the Muslim world. From those he still had legitimate-enough media credentials. True, the credentials were for his pseudonym—he'd never written those reports under his own name—but editors had been fine with that, since he was giving them real on-the-ground reports, and not just hotel-bar journalism.

He now made use of his pseudonymous identity in requesting an interview with al-Wahari regarding the worldwide traffic in stolen meteorites. To his surprise, the financier had agreed: "If you can get here, I'll sit for the interview."

"Getting there" was the problem. The predominantly Anglo-American occupation of Jordan—following the overturning of an Islamist coup that had itself overturned the previous elected government—was extremely unpopular with the locals. So unpopular that even the police forces the occupiers had organized to protect Jordanian civil society against the militias were themselves thoroughly infiltrated by Mudayyin militiamen.

Through Brescoll's people at NSA, however, Dan at last managed to hook up with the Brits in nominal control of the area east of Amman, where al-Wahari kept his primary residence. British intelligence personnel had gotten Dan a ride in a lightly armored Land Rover with a couple of SAS COPs—Special Air Services Close Observation Patrollers.

Despite being scheduled to take them through Jordanian militia territory, not far outside the city, the trip was still supposed to be a milk run. Harris and MacGillivray, the special forces boys giving him a ride, were a couple of grimly humorous chaps with the counterterrorism squadron based out of Hereford.

Dressed in Arab mufti, they delighted in mocking the "yessir, nosir, updown, ticktock" of the regular-army types. They were also well pleased to inform Dan that they had satellite link to top SAS intelligence officers at their UK headquarters in High Wickham.

"Pretty high-level cooperation, eh?" MacGillivray said, giving Amaral a sly look. "You get that when you're pilotin' a carful of explosives."

Seeing Dan's discomfited expression, Harris laughed.

"Now don't you worry, sir. Just 'breaking yer balls,' as you Yanks say. The noisemakers are real enough, but we promise to get you to your destination in one piece—more or less!"

The laughter stopped, however, as they approached a Jordanian police checkpoint. The two men grew instantly serious as the policeman demanded identification. Dan handed his press ID to the SAS men, who handed it along with their own to the police officer. The policeman didn't seem satisfied, however, and signaled to his men to come forward.

"Look here," Harris said, "why don't you gentlemen just give your commander a call? He's been informed of our mission. We've got clearance—"

MacGillivray cursed under his breath as the police came forward, guns drawn.

"Balls! I recognize one of 'em—he's Mudayyin!"

Small-arms fire erupted from inside and outside the Land Rover. Harris slammed the vehicle into reverse and smashed the gas pedal, rocketing them backward with such force that Dan was thrown forward against the back of MacGillivray's seat and flung to the floor of the car.

He heard two of their vehicle's tires blow out on the spike plates the police at the checkpoint had laid out behind them—a different kind of bang than the ambient gunfire. Around the corner of the front seat, Dan saw MacGillivray shooting with the heavy handgun in his right hand while shouting for aid and assistance into the satellite phone he held in his left. Harris was similarly multitasking with gun, steering wheel, and shifter—slamming the stick into forward even as he kept firing.

Dan thought they might actually escape their pursuers when the other two tires blew and they careened into the side of a building. Harris raised his hands in surrender while MacGillivray kept calling for aid on the phone, even as their captors banged opened the doors and dragged them out of the Land Rover.

One of the policemen, either too adrenaline-pumped or too moved by bellicose high spirits to much consider his actions, slammed Dan in the head with his rifle butt, knocking him out cold.

"How long have I been out?" Dan rasped to his fellow captives in the bare room, everything seeming somehow blue-green and submarine under the sickly fluorescent. Despite being bloodied and battered, his fellow captives were still quite recognizable as his COP buddies, MacGillivray and Harris.

"A good long while," Harris said, spitting out what looked like a piece of a tooth. "We were beginning to worry about you."

"Where are we?"

"In jail is my best guess," MacGillivray said. Harris nodded.

"What do you think they'll do with us?"

Harris laughed.

"Full of questions, aren't you? Depends who 'they' are. If it's just the police, they'll probably make a big stink with our governments for shooting at officers of the law, but eventually they'll let us go. If we're in the militia's hands, who knows? Shoot us as spies, maybe."

At that, both MacGillivray and Harris laughed. Most incongruously, Dan thought.

He didn't want to ask any more questions after that. His shoulder stabbed him when he moved wrong—annoyed from whatever laceration or shrapnel had lodged there. His head hurt from concussion, and hurt even worse when he considered his predicament.

He didn't know whether what had happened was personal or not. Had al-Wahari set him up, ensnaring the two SAS men along the way, purely by accident? If so, had someone higher up influenced al-Wahari to such action? Who might that someone be?

Or was this all just random bad luck arising from being in the midst of insurgency and asymmetric "low intensity" conflict?

His boss, Jim Brescoll, had gone missing, and now Dan Amaral supposed that he himself had, too. He felt unprotected, vulnerable, scared. He kept feeling that way until the throbbing in his head and jabbing in his shoulder eased enough to allow him to sleep.

He awoke to the sound of distant roaring and explosion, followed by shouting and yelling, much closer at hand. MacGillivray and Harris had managed somehow to inch their way up the wall to a standing position, where they waited, quiet and alert.

A face appeared at the tiny window for a moment, then disappeared. After a moment, a voice commanded "Stand away from the door, please!" in Glaswegian-accented English.

The door blew inward, and British commandos in desert-urban camouflage swarmed into the room.

The same man who had commanded them to stand away from the door now called out their names: "Harris? Amaral? MacGillivray?"

When they had each responded, troops cut their bonds and medics looked to their wounds.

"This got a bit infected," the young corpsman said to Dan, out of his face-paint, as he examined Dan's shoulder. "Your head wound is clean, though. Looks like you'll be going home, sir."

Yes. Home. He was glad to be no longer missing—and he was willing to bet that Hassam al-Wahari would no longer be available for an interview. At home, too, there was somebody still missing—someone who would have to be found if he or Dan were going to determine whether what had happened was a plot directed against him, or the mere workings of perverse fortune.

SCISSORS, PAPER, ROCK

Michael was glad of the noise the helicopter made while shuttling them to his uncle's compound beside Lake Tahoe. It provided an excuse for him and Susan not to have to talk to each other. They had in fact not talked to each other during most of the transcontinental flight back from the ECOL conference, without any particular excuse. Susan had seemed pensive, and he was loathe to break into her thoughts.

Departing the helicopter after it settled on the helipad, they found Paul Larkin waiting to greet them, and tell them about the several long-distance "information exchanges" he'd had with Brescoll.

Watching his uncle talk about that, Michael felt that Paul seemed older, his face more drawn, as if something had knocked the wind out of him—something from which he was only now recovering. Paul mentioned no health problems, however, and Michael felt it would be impolite to ask. Besides, the man was like a cat—he could lose one life and seemingly still have the energy of eight more to draw upon.

"How are the kids doing?" Susan asked, breaking her silence at last as they moved out of the propwash.

"Extraordinarily well. They have names now, you know. Gave them to themselves."

"They're speaking?" Michael asked. "English, even?"

"Long since," Larkin said, nodding. He led them down a garden path, away from the cold winds of the helipad. "More than a dozen languages, between the four of them. I thought we were going to be studying those kids, but I think it's more accurate to say they're studying us."

They passed between terraced landscape beds just beginning to pop with overly optimistic spring bulbs. Mainly crocuses, Michael noticed, of about a hundred different colors.

"Who's 'us'?" Susan asked.

"All of us. Everybody outside their tepui. Humanity. The whole crazy contemporary world."

"How're they managing to do that?"

"Came from my following a hunch that maybe my sister's crazy ideas about them actually might have some validity. Apparently they do."

As they walked toward the guesthouse Larkin had set aside for the children, he tried to explain.

"I still doubt the Mawari would have ever been able to 'sing their mountain to the stars,' but I suspected Jacinta must have had some reason for spending all that money trying to get all that telemedia and computing equipment up to the top of that damn tepui, all those years ago."

"The equipment we saw?"

"And much, much more. The portable solar and gasoline-fueled electric generators, the thousands of feet of power cables—that must have been intended mainly to power the equipment. The way I figure it, the foldout satellite dishes and uplink antennas were supposed to plug the tribe into the worldwide infosphere—leapfrog them from Paleolithic to Postindustrial."

He slowed, glancing at the early flowers, bulbs forced by the January thaw.

"No need for most of that gear here," he continued. "My compound is online and on the grid. The key thing has been to get these remnant ghost people as much access to as much of the world's distributed information as possible. To that end I've set up the best computing and telemedia facility I could for them."

"But why that?"

"I owed it to Jacinta," Paul said as they approached the guesthouse. "Back then, I stopped her from completing that project, or fulfilling that prophecy, whichever way you want to look at it. Over the past couple of months, I gave the kids a little initial training on the machines, but pretty soon they didn't need my help anymore. They took to that tech like they were born to it. Their learning curve has been incredible. So far they still share my distaste for those AR glasses, but I don't know how long that will last."

"Any evidence of Asperger's-ish stuff, like I suggested?" Michael asked.

"I guess you could say they're superfocused. Fascinations with certain things—the physics of games like marbles, or the dynamics of soap bubbles and snow globes, for instance. Not much interested in social interaction or social cues. I think they find games and ideas a good deal more interesting than people. Or that they're more interested in people in the abstract than in concrete examples."

"The waves on the ocean of history," Michael suggested, "rather than the droplets."

"Right, but if they're savants of some type, then they're prodigious savants. Not narrow. They've immersed themselves completely in the whole infosphere of our contemporary world. Deep, in many fields, I'll say that for them."

Larkin opened the heavy oak door in the stone wall of the guesthouse and they walked inside.

"What have they been doing with what they've learned?" Susan asked.

"All kinds of things. That's why I don't think Asperger's or highfunction autism describes them. They went through a phase where they wanted to know everything about us—you, Michael, me. They particularly enjoyed the old story of our benitoite mine adventure, Michael."

Michael shook his head and smiled, but said nothing.

"After that, they went through an intense gaming phase, then an intense language-learning phase—particularly impressive, since their own language seemed so simple. After that they compulsively watched movies in all sorts of languages, particularly superhero and martial arts films, as I recall. Since then, they seem to be mainly devouring facts and absorbing experiences—at least those you can render digitally and zap around the world."

"Have they gotten any exercise at all?" Susan asked. "Any time outdoors, in the fresh air?"

"I've taken them hiking on the Tahoe Rim Trail and a bunch of other trails in the Desolation Wilderness," Paul said. "Lots of day hikes—around Emerald Bay, along the Tahoe shore, jaunts to Fallen Leaf Lake and the Echo Lakes. Even a couple of overnighters."

"And what about security when you've been on these hikes?"

Paul gave Susan a long awkward smile Michael couldn't quite fathom.

"Oh, you can count on that! I've also hired a private tutor in the martial arts, to give them a dose of reality in those disciplines, since they seemed so fond of the screen's fantasy versions."

The three of them approached a voice-activated wallscreen computer. Paul accessed it through his voiceprint.

"They know I keep a record of what they're accessing. Here, I'll show you some excerpts."

The screen lit up, showing one of the girls blowing a soap bubble while also intently watching a French television documentary on Han dynasty artifacts. Another of the girls did the same while watching an American news broadcast about an Indian monsoon. The boy absently flipped a snow globe, saying the word *Rosebud* while sampling musical forms from various times and places: madrigals and hip-hop, Tibetan temple gongs and rock 'n' roll, Sufi chants and technopop and worldbeat. The last of the girls gave her full attention to a poetry jam performance in which a pistol-packing poet in a rising voice pronounced "I was born a gun / You loaded me with words / Why the surprise when I SHOUT?"—and fired off the gun just at the end of that last word, so that "shout" also became "shoot."

In a later sequence, having apparently gotten beyond their fascination with bubbles and globes, all four sat before screens showing sacred and pilgrimage sites from around the world—Machu Picchu, Teotihuacan, Cahokia Mound, Newgrange, Stonehenge, Notre Dame, Saint Peter's Basilica, Delphi, the Great Pyramid, Jerusalem, Mecca, the Ganges, the Potala Palace, Angkor Wat, and many more which were less immediately recognizable.

Then they scanned screens running what looked like extremely complex mathematical equations—at unbelievable speeds—somehow able to manipulate the elegant flow of that process, while apparently never communicating with one another at all. In yet another sequence, what looked to be star charts and astrogation data darted across screens in front of the children.

"Wait!" Michael said. "Pause it there. Yes. Right there. I thought so. Do you know what those are?"

"What?" Susan asked.

"Those are orbits. For the Apollo and Aten asteroids. Rocks from space on Earth-crossing trajectories."

Paul smiled.

"That would fit the pattern. They've spent one helluva lot of time checking out meteorites, meteors, asteroids—lots of other stuff involving space, too."

"Such as?"

"I sent some of it off to an astronomer friend of mine, Michael. She said that several of the ancient sacred sites they focused on have astronomical alignments. The deep-space info was mainly regions of the sky, first between the constellations of the two Dippers, and then specifically Eridanus and Cancer. I have no idea what it means."

Susan gave him a piercing look.

"Did you ask them?"

"Of course—and the discussion immediately degenerated into snippets of their usual 'cave of night/seed of light' myth-talk. When I pushed them, they tried to explain it to me in terms of a fungal life cycle: spore and spawn and some kind of mushroom-stone thing. Incredibly frustrating. I've tried, believe me. I even had them do a project for me."

"On what?"

"I asked them to dramatize that genesis story of theirs—animate it with computer graphics, cull images from the infosphere, collage it together."

"And?"

"I've seen their little movie. It makes some sense when I see it, but less when they try to explain what it means."

"Could we view it?" Michael asked.

"I don't see why not. I'm sure they'll be happy to show it to you."

Paul led Michael and Susan into what had once been the living room of the guesthouse but was now a combination media lounge, computer center, and children's playroom. When the adults entered, the four kids looked up from their flat screens and leapt to their feet, smiling.

Michael knew they were preadolescents, between ten and twelve years of age, but they struck him as also much older now. The way they greeted "Uncle Michael" and "Aunt Susan"—and quite formally said how glad they were to see both of them again—*that* bespoke not only rapid language acquisition but also an adult sophistication far beyond their years.

He wondered how much of this his uncle might have pre-scripted.

He was soon sure, however, that that sense of premature maturity was not something Paul could have imposed on them, especially when the next moment one of them, shyly as any ten-year-old, was informing Michael and Susan that they had names now.

"Oh? And what are you calling yourselves?" he asked.

"I'm Ka-dalun," said the shortest girl, with the briefest flash of an impish smile. Now that he was looking at her, Michael thought she might be the youngest. Awkwardly, she reached out her hand for Michael and Susan to shake.

"Alii De Danaan," said the boy, also shaking hands in the same formal but awkward fashion.

"Ebu Gogo," said the middle girl.

"Aubrey Menehune," said the tallest girl. After Aubrey formally greeted them, all four children went back to whatever they were working on or playing at via their screens. Michael couldn't quite figure out what that something was, or whether they were all doing the same thing, but whatever it was it involved lots of flashing, frenetic activity on the monitors, and a spot in what looked like the South Atlantic, judging from the map display on one of the girls' screens.

The oddness of the children was unsettling. They struck him not as inhuman so much as extrahuman, like child geniuses or prodigies. He supposed their history of massacre and ten-thousand-year leap forward might have made them mature early, though certainly not completely. Such a background was all too likely to leave some gaps and blank spots in their socialization.

"Fascinating names, no?" Paul said, turning to his adult companions.

"Fascinating names, yes," Susan said. "All refer to myths and folktales about lost peoples, if I'm not mistaken."

"Absolutely correct. All are 'fairies' or 'little people' who have disappeared from around the world—as named by the cultures that displaced them."

Susan nodded eagerly.

"Some anthropologists think such stories are a sort of 'survivor guilt.' Collective memories of later metalworking invaders who drove their stone-tool-wielding predecessors to extinction. At least that's the theory."

"Or even the collective memory of us anatomically modern humans wiping out our Erectus and Neanderthal predecessors," Michael said, watching the preoccupied children. "Their interest in such things . . . it makes a certain sense, you know?"

"Why would it even surprise you?" Susan asked.

"Why do you say that?"

"Is this interest in lost little people out of their guilt from having survived when the rest of their tribe is dead? Or is it to remind us of our tribe's guilt for having killed them?"

Michael's only answer was to shrug his shoulders and lift his empty hands. Why she still continued to blame him for somehow causing what had happened to the tepuians—just because he was a meteoriticist, and just because his scientific search had led him to that place—was beyond him. His uncle was nominally more responsible, yet Paul was never as much the target of Susan's ire as he was. No use arguing with her, in any case.

"Maybe when the machines rule the world after we're gone," Paul mused, breaking their stalemate, "they'll think of us the same way we think of the fairy folk."

"If they think of us at all," Susan said. "I'd prefer not to believe in any such 'machinifest destiny.' "

Larkin smiled. He turned from them and addressed the boy, who answered without looking up from his screen.

"Alii?"

"Yes?"

"Would you be so kind as to show Michael and Susan the movie you and the girls made about your people and the stars?"

"Yeah!" said Alii, breaking away from the screen for a moment. He popped their movie into the slot of a projection-screen laptop and let the movie play against the nearest wall. Michael soon saw that it was anime, intercut with stock film footage.

Something spherical appears, against a background of stars. Flashcut to the hollow, spherical, flagellated colony of the protozoan *volvox.* Zoom in on the sphere's surface, covered with more complex features, somehow machinic and organic at the same time, ancient stone beneath overlapping finely machined wings of moths, or butterflies, angels—or demons.

Zoom out. Miragelike shimmer of force about the sphere. Glinting, lambent brightness of myriad wings beating against the bright wind from a star almost near enough to be called a sun. Flashcut to great masses of monarch butterflies, balls and bunches of them gathered in a eucalyptus grove near the California coast, opening and closing their wings in the winter sun of a cold morning.

Zoom out. Passing between the Scylla of a red giant star and the

Charybdis of a newly formed black hole, the peaceful journey of the winged stone ship morphs into a tale of shipwreck—the craft ripped into, by forces powerful and invisible.

Zoom in. Many of the winged things upon its surface crumple and die in the accident, gaping holes break into the hollow stone beneath their wings. Crippled, the ship falls toward the sun.

Zoom out and pan. Carried by the strange angels, sections of the sphere break apart and go into orbit around the sun—first farther out in a wilderness of floating ice islands, then among the rubble of an aborted planet.

The remainder of the broken sphere continues to fall sunward, toward an Earth that's all right, and all wrong—continents misshapen and in the wrong places.

Zoom in. What's left of the still-living ship calves and breaks up. Tattered wings carrying stones through sunlight wind catch fire as they plunge into atmosphere—angels burning across the sky, petaling away like blowtorched roses and melting into the surface of their burdens, leaving only the stones to strike the unfamiliar Earth as meteorites.

Flashcut to fungus fruiting in incredible profusion around craters. Clocks with millennium hands spin in a corner of the screen. Millions of years pass. Other graphs in the bottom of the projection show incident radiation and corresponding mutation rates.

Time-lapsed imagery proliferates, as does what grows from crash sites throughout the world: the same something, changing, evolving, denaturing, until it is no longer the same something at all, but thousands and thousands of species ever more distantly related. Only in a few shielded biomes—caves, particularly—does anything like the original strain survive.

Long zoom in from satellite space to anvil-shaped mountain floating among clouds. Caracamuni tepui. A charred skystone in a cavern room. A child's-eye view of lost parents, lost people, lost world: all golden, wonderful, larger than life, a tribe happy in their own skins and wearing little else, all sitting on their shins in a great circle around a skyburned stone, singing and reaching with their arms toward it, arms and upper bodies swaying in tune as if the stone in the center were a lighthouse and the people themselves were the ocean drawn up in waves by the passage of its invisible beam.

A shattered skull, a smashed fungus, both spattered with a red more vivid than paint or ochre. Then darkness.

"Thanks for letting us see the movie," Paul said quietly. Alii,

Aubrey, Ebu, and Ka-dalun each nodded stiffly, and the latter two smiled shyly. They quickly returned to their computers, to whatever work or play so obsessed them in the infosphere.

"Where did the kids get that stuff?" Susan asked, a palpable excitement in her voice that Michael felt just as strongly. The adults were seated at the far end of the room, having cleared the children's work and play things from a sofa, love seat, and rocking chair.

"Like I said, the imagery is either computer-generated or culled from material available on the Web. As for where the narrative originated, your guess is almost as good as mine."

"Almost?" Michael asked. Paul Larkin nodded.

"I have access to my sister's notes, after all. According to Jacinta, the ghost people of the tepui claimed that the spawn of the mushroom they found in that cave 'remembered' how it got there. In the time-before-time, their 'mushroom stone' brought the spawn, or so they claimed. Their myths claimed the stone came 'from the sky.' "

"This is very strange," Michael said, rocking slowly in the chair. "Still, it's just possible that their myths may be telling us something. I mean, Caracamuni plateau is shield rock, one point eight billion years old, so it's certainly old enough to qualify for being around since 'the time before time.' A puzzle, though, nonetheless."

"What about it, in particular?" Paul asked from the sofa. Susan sat forward in the love seat suddenly, popped a pair of blinks over her eyes, flipped down the throat mike and began fiddling with her hand-held PDA. She panned and tilted her head around for the best signal from the nearest wireless connection port.

"I always thought the dispersal of life-code materials would be essentially random," Michael said. "Unguided at all stages, like evolution itself. If what those four kids put together echoes the truth, then that changes things."

"How so?"

"That thing that looked like some kind of winged viral starship," Michael said. "What do the kids say it is?"

"A 'contact ship from a sixth-age civilization' is the best I can squeeze out of them," Paul said. "If Jacinta was right about their cosmogony, I think that's the stage where what we might call 'interstellar travel' first pops up."

"So this ship or whatever it is apparently gets into trouble, right?

Out beyond the edge of what I'm thinking must be our solar system—
out beyond the Oort cloud. Then the crew appear to sacrifice themselves amid what seems to be the Oort cloud. Then again near what I'd
be willing to bet are the Kuiper and asteroid belts. Then finally on a
world that looks like it might someday harbor intelligent life—one that
has me racking my brains trying to remember what Gondwanaland
and Pangaea were supposed to look like.

"The kids' movie doesn't suggest anything about what happened to
the ship remnants in the belts or the cloud, but it sure seems like a plan
for vectoring in *something* on comets and shooting stars."

"That's way too guided and directed for my taste," Susan said, continuing to scan through the infosphere on her blinks but not so preoccupied that she'd let that statement go unchallenged.

"If that's the reality, though, then I'll have to change my hypotheses
accordingly," Michael said. "Even if, seeing those winged things, I had
to force myself not to think of Tinkerbell or tupilak."

"That reminds me," Paul said. "Do other myths and folklore show
any association between meteorites and mushrooms?"

"Way ahead of you," Susan said. "I'm connected to an ethnobotanical Web database. Here we are. A few things do pop up. Take a look."

She turned the PDA screen toward them and together Paul and
Michael crouched over it as Susan called up and blink-scanned them
through lists of abstracts. Michael saw some interesting associations
involving fungus lore and natural atmospheric and astronomic phenomena. Apparently, for the ancient Greeks and Romans, when a
thunderbolt or thunderstone struck the ground, it was believed to
cause mushrooms—boleti, puffballs—to arise from it. Both bolt and
stone were considered "fiery progenitive spears of God."

Susan blinked farther down the site's linklist. In silence they jump-
scanned through synopses of numerous folk stories about shooting
stars or meteorites as the putative cause of a yellowish jelly-fungus,
Tremella lutescens, popularly called "fairy butter" or "star jelly." Also
listed was the dye-maker's false puffball, *Pisolithus tinctorius*—often
readily misidentified as a stony-iron meteorite lying on the ground.

Susan called up other sites and blink-scanned on, until she located
another entry she found particularly interesting. According to that
source, both lightning strikes and "fiery dragons"—the latter associated with meteors—had been cited in folklore as causes for fairy rings
since at least medieval times. In the Austrian Tyrol, the dragon whose

fiery tail-coil created the fairy rings was said to appear at Pegasids on August 10 and Martinmas on November 11—dates matching the Perseid and Leonid meteor-shower maxima, for the very time period when that bit of folklore first became popular.

Susan blinked to a final site, which was short enough that she summarized it for them.

"Several types of jellylike fungi, slime molds, and the alga Nostoc are traditionally identified as 'star-slime' or 'star-rot.' Many other, similar folk names, found throughout medieval to early modern Europe, almost always describe this jellylike stuff as the remnants of a fallen shooting star."

"All this could just be a coincidence, though," Michael said. "I mean, European fungus fruit most commonly with rains and cooler weather, right? That means they would most likely pop up from late summer to early winter. Which happens to coincide with the stronger concentrations of meteor showers during the year—for the last couple millennia, anyway."

"But that might be more a proof than a refutation," Susan said, taking off her blinks. "There might just be something to the 'fireball hits ground, fungus springs up' connection. Certain mushrooms fruit only in disturbed or burned ground, for instance. A number of others, like morels, fruit most prolifically the spring following a forest fire. Mushrooms are among the first organisms to colonize areas devastated by recent volcanic eruptions, too."

"When you wish upon a spore," Paul half-sung, "then you really know the score?"

They laughed, but Michael shook his head.

"I think we may be missing a deeper evolutionary advantage than just fruiting when the competition's been reduced by fire. Say it's not about something as complex as mushroom spores coming in on meteorites. Say what's coming in is simpler."

"Such as?"

"Something that can take over the controls of a cell the way a virus does. In most places in the world, the most ubiquitous inhabitants of soil—those more complex than bacteria, anyway—are the mycelial structures of fungi, the underground horizontal 'trees' from which the mushroom 'fruit' forms."

"You've lost me."

"If something comes crashing in from the sky, the slightly higher organism it would be most likely to encounter first would be white thready stuff—fungal mycelium. That 'something simpler' than a spore might explain what these meteorite thefts are really all about, too."

Paul laughed.

"Now you've lost me, too."

"Maybe, if you get enough pieces of meteorite, you can put together enough of that simpler material to create a sort of 'Rosetta keystone.' One that will work for the purpose of multiplicity reactivation and phoenix phenotype."

"Too much jargon," Paul said, laughing. "Layman's terms, please."

"I'll do better than that," Michael said, putting on his own blinks and borrowing Susan's PDA. He would have just gone blink-to-blink with Susan, but Paul eschewed the AR specs-tech, so Michael proceeded in this more cumbersome way—as Susan had—out of politeness. In a moment he had searched the infosphere and had up on the screen a little computer-animated movie, showing Paul and Susan the very processes he was talking about.

"Say you take a bunch of double-stranded DNA viruses and destroy them, inactivate them, using ultraviolet irradiation, the way they do here. If you infect a cell with a lot of those inactivated virus particles— infect the cell with a very high multiplicity of disabled virions—you'll often see reactivation of viral function."

"How is that possible, if they're all dead?" Susan asked.

"The disabled viruses cooperate in such a way as to literally re-assemble the viral genome from spare parts found in a bunch of different viral particles. See? A process called complementation allows the viruses to grow initially, since genes inactivated in one virion may still be active in one of the others."

He called up another website at a university medical school, and blinked to another sequence of images.

"The fascinating part is that the various parts of the genomes can sometimes provide individual genes that act together to resurrect full function without necessarily re-forming a single full or autonomous virus. With replication and recombination of genetic elements, even the full function of the wild-type virus can be regenerated.

"If you have enough of the pieces around, a phoenix phenotype can arise from the ashes of its own previous destruction. If I were trying to come up with a way for a life-code to survive destruction or corrup-tion, I think the ability to regenerate whole function from spare parts would be a handy capability to have. The exotic amino acids and nucleic acid precursors we've been seeing in meteorites for years—the very stuff the experts have been dismissing as 'space-junk DNA'—may turn out to be neither space junk nor junk DNA."

"But how is that relevant to the Mawaris' mushroom?" Paul asked. "Or to the properties Jacinta suggested it gave the people?"

"Think of the fully functioning pattern as something more even than a potent prebiotic programmer-molecule. Think of it as a 'metaphage,' acquiring or binding to information about its environment, analyzing that information, and executing a response that feeds back into what it binds to. The metaphage is constantly feeding upon the world and itself and generating new components in an expanding explosion of creation. It changes what it 'eats' and 'eats' what it changes. A recursive pattern or program that's lively but not, strictly speaking, alive."

"Like viruses?" Paul asked. Michael called up and blinked them to another series of microbial images.

"Existing like they do in the overlap between biology, biochemistry, and biophysics. Exerting pressures on the course of evolution, not from outside but from within the web of life, like they do. But much more powerfully. Cybernetically, like some sort of quantum DNA computer virus, or a quasiviral supercomputer—"

"Whoa, whoa," Paul said. "I've always had trouble understanding how quantum computers are supposed to work. Can either of you geniuses explain that to me?"

"Think keys and locks," Michael said. "A classical computer faced with many billions of possible keys for a lock must try each key in the lock, one after the other. A quantum computer, however, can try all the keys in the lock simultaneously. The physicists of the many-world or multiversalist school see the quantum computer as actually billions of quantum computers, each machine in a separate universe, each trying just one key."

"For the many-worlders," Susan explained, "the answer arises from summing over billions of parallel universes, each with its own machine."

"All those parallel worlds sound a lot like what Jacinta calls 'mind-time' in her notes on the people of Caracamuni," Paul said.

"That I don't know about," Michael said, "but I do think a metaphage variant, with a good percentage of the entire pattern, might well have taken up permanent residence in their mushroom, which then took up residence in the Mawari. The culture of those tepui people may well have been a response to that. If we don't take it literally as some kind of directed evolution, then maybe the 'accident' the kids' little movie showed might be some kind of analogy or metaphor."

"For what?" Susan asked.

"For evolution exploiting the disasters that punctuate its usual slow course. For metaphages encapsulated in metadiamond cages, released by the cataclysm of their fall from heaven. For the pure strain of whatever came down from the sky dying out, over time, nearly everywhere on earth except in a few chambers underground—if we're to believe their movie, and their memories even if it *is* a bit of a stretch."

"And the metaphage that invades the mushroom that invades the Mawari that makes them want to sing their mountain to the stars, to complete the whole cycle—that *isn't* a stretch? Come on! Scissors-paper-rock meets animal-vegetable-mineral is way too broad, as an interpretive model for evolution. Mystic woo-woo, again."

"Perhaps not," Larkin said, picking up a disk. "Aubrey—think fast!" he shouted, even as he unaccountably threw the disk across the room, directly at the young girl's head. As the disk flew through the air, Michael realized that not even a supercoordinated child could catch the thing, and each of these kids was anything but supercoordinated.

And she didn't catch it. Just as unaccountable as Larkin's behavior in throwing the thing, the disk itself came to a hovering stop a foot short of the girl's head. Aubrey turned in her desk chair, picked the disk out of the air, and put it on her desk as she turned back to her screen.

"Did she just do what I think she did?" Michael asked. Larkin nodded.

"Discovered it almost by accident," he said. "A hunch about some oddly shaped rocks. That it panned out was the reason I called you at your conference."

"But how?" Susan asked, incredulous.

"Jacinta's notes suggest that the fungus inside the Mawari is a symbiont. Apparently it takes until at least the onset of puberty for it to fully develop, but as it does the nerves and fungal mycelia together create what she calls a 'myconeural complex.' Her guess was that the complex allows for consistent high-level brain activity without burnout or any apparent ill effects—and with parapsychological phenomena as an upshot. She didn't understand the mechanism, but she hypothesized it might be mediated biochemically through what she calls 'adaptogens.' "

"Have you discovered the mechanism?" Susan asked. "As an ethno-botanist I'd really like to know how such a thing might be possible—I mean, if it wasn't just some kind of sleight-of-hand trick we saw. If it *really* happened."

"I've run those poor kids through a battery of tests with all the doctors and technicians I think I can trust," Paul said. "MRIs, NMRs, PET and CAT scans, tracer-dyes, the works. Partly to follow up on what Michael suggested in terms of Asperger's or high-function autism. Our preliminary results make clear it's something more than that."

" 'Preliminary results'?" Susan asked.

"What they suggest," Paul continued, "is that, after someone ingests the fruiting body, the spores germinate and the spawn forms a sheath of fungal tissue around the nerve endings of the central nervous system. Some of the fungal cells penetrate between the nerves of the brain and brain stem, without damaging them. Believe me, I was hard-pressed to keep a couple of our good but worried doctors from dosing the kids with broad-spectrum, systemic antifungals. Anyway, this myconeural complex is involved in the enlargement of the pineal gland in the brain and somehow circumvents or at least alters the activity of the raphe nuclei."

"Amazing," Michael said. Seeing Susan's questioning look, he explained. "The dorsal and median raphe nuclei in our brains function as a sort of 'governor' on the level of brain activity, keeping it down to low percentages of total possible activity. It's your body's way of stepping on your mind."

"And the pineal gland?"

"It's involved in sleep and dreaming, particularly through the processing of tryptamines, the conversion of serotonin to melatonin. It also plays a role in the timing of sexual maturation, via gonadotropin hormones. It usually begins to shrink with the onset of puberty—and calcify, with age."

"I think I recall reading somewhere that the 'imaginary friends' of childhood are related to the child's very active pineal gland," Paul said. "Is that right?"

Michael nodded.

"Some researchers have claimed that, yes. Oh, and the pineal is light sensitive, even though it's way inside the brain. The 'third eye,' in a lot of spiritual traditions. The 'eye of the mind' and 'seat of the soul.' The 'chakra door' that opens into the astral planes."

Susan rolled her two more mundane eyes at mention of that, but said nothing.

"In her notes on the Mawari," Paul continued, "Jacinta suggests that the parapsychological phenomena she found among them—clairvoyance, second sight, forays into what the Mawari call 'mindtime'—might correlate with consistently high levels of brain activity. Almost as if the Mawaris' bodies weren't stepping on their minds."

"You've used that word *mindtime* before," Michael said. "What's it supposed to mean, again?"

"I'm not exactly sure. From her notes I gather it involves a sense of the patterns of possibility backward and forward in space and time—alternate timelines, possible worlds, that sort of thing. Which you now tell me is increasingly accepted science." Larkin shook his head. "If it's real, then whoever attacked the Mawari to get at their holiest of holies must have been surprised by the resistance those people were able to put up. They probably had some sense that an attack was coming."

"Still, their crystal ball must have been pretty cloudy," Susan said. "They're all dead, except for these four. The attackers apparently got what they wanted."

"We don't know that for certain," Michael said. "Or not all of it, at least. Paul, you said Aunt Jacinta's notes referred to a mushroom stone, right? Do you know of any examples of such a thing?"

"I looked into it, because of Jacinta's mention of it. The Maya and other Mesoamerican peoples carved things the anthropologists call mushroom stones, but I don't see how they might connect to this."

"You're both being too literal," Susan said. "Think like a botanist, and you'll realize there's another term for 'mushroom stone.' "

"Oh?"

"What is it?"

She called up search terms and blinked them to an appropriately illustrated site.

"The Latin is *sclerotium,* from the Greek word *sklerotes,* meaning 'hardness.' A dense, hard mass of branching filaments, called hyphae, found in certain fungi. Sclerotia can remain dormant for long periods. If the tepui people's culture was as centered around their sacred mushroom as your sister claimed, Paul, then it's likely they were quite familiar with the mushroom stones we call sclerotia."

Michael jumped up from his seat and began to pace a bit as he thought.

"That's brilliant, Susan! That info you showed us before, about how some kinds of fungus were mistaken for meteorites? What if, at the tepui, it wasn't a mistake? We've got to get more work done on our own chunk of the tepui stone!"

"Why the sudden push on that?"

"Because it might be the metaphage in sclerotium form. Part space rock and part dormancy stage! That would explain why the tepui stone doesn't fully fit into any established category of meteorite—"

Susan scowled.

"I thought we were supposed to be finding out who massacred the *people* at the tepui. And working for Mister NSA. And possibly even working with Darla Pittman."

Before Michael could say anything, Paul Larkin replied.

"Yes, you certainly seem to already be juggling a lot of balls in the air, but I suspect it really is all part of the same ball."

As they left the room, Larkin tried to explain to Susan what he suspected. Exiting with them, Michael noticed that the Mawari children were still working busily in front of their screens—and that now all four of them were looking at something in the sky over the southern Atlantic, between Africa and South America, called Argus Point. Must be some kind of game after all, he thought. He still thought that, during their flight to Montana, and the entire time there with Susan and Darla.

CLIMBING SIDEWAYS

Darla Pittman was working late in the cabinet lab at Rocky Mountain. She needed time to think, and she found she often thought better alone. She also wanted to avoid running into Susan Yamada and Michael Miskulin yet again. They had been on-site for briefings the past week and more. Playing things close to the vest had already proven more taxing than she'd expected.

Following her hunch and bringing Miskulin and Yamada in on her project had almost seemed more trouble than it was worth, especially given the security questions it raised for her. Less risky candidates could readily be found. Still, her hunch and its risks were paying off.

Feigning ignorance of any connection between the materials in her possession and their source in a particular tepui—and making sure that Barry did the same—had been a pain. As a result, though, she'd learned from Yamada and Miskulin a great deal about what she was now sure was her stone's provenance.

It was truly *her* stone, for she was the only one cleared to work directly with the tepui materials in any new experimental processes or procedures. She'd issued those security guidelines herself.

During the day she usually worked in the suit-lab facilities—at least partly to set an example for Barry and the rest of the laboratory staff. There was no one else in the lab to set an example for at this time of night, however. She happily stayed out of the awkward pressure suit and worked through the glove boxes, the Class III biosafety cabinets. Not having to fuss with the pressure suit also freed up more mental disk-space for thinking things through.

Normally she did some of her best thinking while rock climbing— time away from her busy schedule that she zealously guarded. This past week, however, she'd sacrificed some of that solitary time to take Michael and Susan with her and give them an introductory lesson in climbing on one of her favorite local rock-routes in the Sapphires.

Not just for the exercise, but for the privacy, too. Her rock-climbing routes tended to be remote and therefore not eavesdropped upon or otherwise surveilled. A good thing, in case the awkwardness of socializing with Michael and his current flame unexpectedly blew up in her face. An even better thing, if the mission she had in mind—serious and important enough to make her risk more than awkwardness—panned out as fully as she hoped.

Eyeing the rock face, she chose what she considered an easy route for her novice partners to follow—one with lots of cracks and holds, nubbins to tiptoe on and finger-cling to, even a line of protrusions, called "chickenheads," big enough to grasp and dyno back and forth from, through the final chimney and stemspots. She figured the route she put together was only 5.6 or 5.7 in difficulty, so she climbed in gym shoes, leaving the sticky boots and electrostatic surface-bond tech to her less-experienced partners.

As she lead-climbed for them, Michael and Susan gave her a lot to think about, mostly unintentionally. As always, Darla found it relaxing to lose herself in solving the vertical, three-dimensional chess problem of the climb before her. She popped stoppers and nuts into cracks and wedged her camming "friends" and "protection" into spaces with an almost thoughtless ease. Michael and Susan were snap-linked onto her rope line and freed up, as they passed them, the anchor-pieces Darla had set ahead of them. The two novices talked almost incessantly, trying to cover up their nervousness at slipping and falling—and catching themselves from slipping and falling.

As her companions scrambled upward against gravity (while also trying to avoid looking down through the empty air to the treetops below them), Darla found it much easier to glean information from them than they did from her. In that other chess game—their conversation— she clearly had the advantage.

Darla smiled, remembering. She hadn't thought of rock climbing as a form of interrogation, but it seemed to do that job well enough. Michael and Susan had occasionally caught themselves and switched back to speaking in more general terms, but by the time the three of them hauled up and carefully coiled their off-belayed ropes, Darla had heard their harrowing tale of the genocidal extinction of the tepui's mushroom-cult inhabitants. Equally disturbing, in some ways, was their tale of Jacinta Larkin's discoveries, her madness, and the connection of both to that lost tribe's myths and supposedly mythical powers.

It had taken the whole of the length of the walk back to the car, but gradually Darla realized just how successful she had been. Michael was still competition to be wary of in the fame game, but Susan seemed convinced by the day's climb that Darla had no immediate designs on "her man"—if that's what Michael was. Hard to say. The two of them seemed to Darla less like lovers and more like longtime friends.

Call it a bonding experience, but for a while, too, it seemed as if the three of them were able to put aside all the agendas of those they secretly worked for—Michael and Susan, as well as herself—and just be who they were. Although none of them trusted either of the others totally, each of them trusted the other through at least a broad range of scientific objectivity.

On the walk back, that was where she'd scored most of all—in the science, the one area where they'd all felt comfortable enough to let their guards down more than a bit. Despite the sometimes circumspect nature of Susan and Michael's hints, she'd learned that they believed the reason the tribe's tepui stone might not fit into established meteorite categories was because it might be what Susan called a sclerotium, a mushroom stone—part meteoritic rock and part dormancy stage of what Michael was calling a "metaphage-fungus mutualism."

Darla's feigned ignorance and amazement at that idea verged on the genuine. Following up on what Susan and Michael's ideas had suggested to her during their rock-climbing jaunt, she reexamined the plated and test tube versions of what she had already grown from the spores Retticker had provided.

Although the search for bacteroidal and nanobacteroidal components in her sample of the stone had proven largely a dead end, the search for "space-junk DNA" in the tepui stone and skystone samples from throughout the world had proven to be anything but inconclusive.

Chen's description of "silica nanoparticles with organic components" had turned out to be more right than he could have guessed. Fullerenes were involved, too, as Miskulin had suggested. Metadiamond cages apparently surrounded silica nanoparticles laced with organics, which in turn encapsulated DNA. The electrical charges of the silica nanoparticles held and compacted the DNA, while the organic components made the normally rigid silica nanoparticles more flexible and capable of releasing the encapsulated biomolecules.

It seemed a mechanism almost tailor-made for vectoring prebiotic and potential-genetic material, without the need for bacteria or even viruses. A mechanism also quite capable of setting up the entire "phoenix phenotype" and "metaphage" scenario Miskulin had suggested, in his roundabout way—including the transfer of that metaphage replication information to living cells.

Especially fungal ones.

On media combining cerebrospinal fluid, serum, and neuronal matrix, Darla had succeeded in growing and running genetic analyses on that meshwork of mycelium and neurons Jacinta Larkin had called "myconeural complex." Some very interesting stretches of code appeared, especially those higher-order nucleotide sequences that looked like the products of synthetic biology and artificial-life research.

Self-binding space-junk nucleic acid from the tepui stone helped her sort and confirm which parts of those sequences might have been delivered by the stone itself. Allowing "junk" sequences from her other meteoritic samples to bind with the stone-derived code, she had now succeeded in quickly generating a more complete biochemical program than even the stone itself provided.

Looking at one such augmented myconeural colony on a petri dish in the glove box before her now, she saw that all her extractions and recombinations were simply the same thing Nature was always doing, only much faster and in a more directed fashion. Her efforts at accelerated evolution had already produced something new—something of which she was undeniably proud.

Qualms about the general's ultimate motivations notwithstanding, she'd already reported her latest findings to Retticker. He was perhaps the only other person who might fully understand them. She had wanted to wow him, and had succeeded amply. The general was not only impressed but also very enthusiastic.

An alarm sounded. Startled, she dropped the petri dish she was holding—still in the glove box, fortunately. She swiveled her head about the lab to see where the alarm was coming from. Then she saw the readout.

Someone was coming in through the expedited airlock entry/exit system—the route no one ever utilized, the route to be used only in extreme emergency. But what was the emergency? Other than the small spill she'd just made in the biosafety cabinet, nothing seemed amiss. The alarm had begun to sound before the glove box accident happened, too.

She still had her hands in the glove box when intruders in what looked like armored black environment suits broke into the cabinet lab and raked her and the glove box with automatic weapons fire. Her face crashed against the crack-spidered lid of the box. As she began to pass out, she saw that the interior of the biosafety cabinet had been compromised in the worst way. Her own blood was mixing with the spattered myconeural matrix from the petri dish she'd been holding.

After that she saw nothing more, but she could still hear, in a disembodied sort of way. She thought she heard a male voice over a suit intercom say "She's gone," then felt someone carefully picking through the contents of the glove box. Other sounds—of the lab being ransacked?—grew fainter. At last the only thing she heard was her own voice in her head, telling her she was dying, telling her that someone—the people behind Miskulin and Yamada? or the general?—had betrayed her.

Then everything *shifted*.

She found herself on a pine-scented mountain ridge, looking down on a white ocean of cloud. Near the shoreline of that fog ocean, the tops of lower mountains and foothills protruded, islands in the sea of clouds. On all the nearby "islands" she saw the glint of what she somehow knew were the open-domed mansions and compounds of the healthy and wealthy, the Fog Makers who ruled this world.

She knew, without knowing how she knew, that the whiteness of that cloud-ocean concealed something much darker beneath. That deep mist, both manufactured and meteorological, was constantly monitored by Weather Control. Manipulating temperature inversions and domes of high pressure, Weather Control locked down ground-moisture in large long-lasting fog banks—as vapor reservoirs to fall back on, between the ever-briefer but more intense large-scale rain events. Inside this nearly perpetual toxic fog, the pocked and tumored masses of an impoverished humanity lived their empoisoned and imprisoned lives.

The poisoned poor, their every moment overseen and overheard by surveillance cameras and microphones, their every step noted by ubiquitous tiny spy-blimps, had even more reason than the wealthy to want to escape. To fire off rockets to other planets, or live in faux-medieval baronial splendor, as the healthy and wealthy did. To be anywhere but the here and now of their goggled and filter-masked daily lives in the undercloud. She knew too that, for the vast majority of the population, such dreams could remain only dreams.

The fog that confused and enthralled them was not only water vapor but also a bright electrochemical mist of words, images, and socialization drugs. The people beneath the white cloud-ocean feared cancer less than arrest or execution should they fail to work their mandatory overtime. Which was necessitated by the need to feed mandatory overconsumption. Which was necessitated by the need to spur mandatory economic growth. Which was itself necessarily over-taxed to pay for mandatory imperial overstretch. Which was made necessary in turn by mandatory resource scarcity. Which was made necessary by mandatory overpopulation in order to overwhelm and subjugate neighboring nations. Which was, of necessity, promulgated through mandatory hyperattendance at family-worship services hammering home the bromide that "God is on our side." Which was all made palatable with the help of mandatory overmedication and media saturation.

Such endless obsession with exponential growth kept the Fog Makers' heads well above the same toxic clouds that were the foundation of their wealth. For now.

She knew how the pearly mist-clouds—bright by night, gray by day—had, for the vast majority of humanity, hidden the sun, moon, and stars behind a heavy veil. She knew about the billions who put in legally required viewing time in front of their control screens, mind-numbed by food and drink that by law were laced with requisite doses of Corzap U4X (sulprexasol) and its family of tweaked-supertryptamine behavior-modification pharmaceuticals.

She knew of the perils awaiting those who refused to wear their biometric-monitoring corporate association apparel, because she had long refused to don such a CAAP foghat. She knew about the hell that came of continuing to believe in the apocalypse that failed to happen, and continuing not to believe in the apocalypse that was already under way. She knew about the superdroughts, the spreading deserts, the endless border wars beyond the tenuously controlled climate zones of the foglands, drizzletowns, and mist cities. She had lived all of that.

"The rich on their hilltops may be living like kings," sang a voice in her head, so distant it seemed to come from another world, "but even folks in the fog are saying the craziest things. Although scenarios of our case may not yet have reached worst, just remember: when the storm finally comes, it strikes the high places first. . . ."

As Darla came back to a world of pain both more and less familiar, she raised her head from the lid of the glove box. She was in her lab again, yes, but the place was shattered and broken, a ruined remnant of its former order. She stared at her hands, where the smear of blood and myconeural complex was drying on her broken-fingered biocontainment gauntlets.

As security personnel in pressure suits poured in, she contemplated what she had just experienced. She thought of Albert Hoffman in his Sandoz lab, three quarters of a century earlier, spilling a previously unknown but extremely potent hallucinogen on his hands, and then enduring the unprecedented psychedelia of his bicycle ride home through the streets of Berne.

What she had just lived through, however, seemed less an altered state of consciousness than a slip sideways into an alternate universe—one significantly different from, yet somehow also frighteningly similar to, her own life in this world.

She continued to gaze at the drying smears on her hands while pressure-suited paramedics examined her. Staring at her bloodstained fingers she realized, with growing awe and wonder, the most familiar yet unfamiliar sensation of all.

She was still alive, when by all odds she should not have been.

Almost dying was an experience life-changing enough that, as the paramedics ministered to her, she began to question what she had been doing that almost got her killed.

Maybe her supposed friends might not really be so friendly, after all. Maybe her supposed opponents might not in truth be her enemies. Maybe she'd found out things she wasn't meant to know. Maybe, just maybe, being a firmly independent observer might be the best way to proceed, from now on.

SELF-HEALING

Once they were alone together in Darla Pittman's private and guarded hospital room, Joe Retticker pulled up a chair beside her hospital bed. He felt glad of the chance to travel into the hinterlands of Montana, away from the Beltway, away from the ongoing crisis in the Middle East. He was more than a bit surprised at Darla's first words to him.

"You caused this, General," she said, sounding both angry and distraught. "You betrayed me."

"I assure you I've done nothing of the kind. What makes you think I would?"

"You were the only one who knew the most current status of my research."

"And for that I'd want to invade your lab and kill you? Think, Darla. What could I possibly gain from smashing up your lab and its work? How would I stand to benefit from destroying a project I helped set up myself—and from which I've already been getting results?"

"Maybe our work was moving too fast," Darla said, "or not fast enough, or in the wrong direction. Maybe the attack on the lab was intended to be just a theft, and I happened to be in the way. Or maybe it was a test."

"That's a lot of maybes, Darla. How would shooting up the lab and killing you constitute a 'test'? What kind of results would I supposedly have been looking for, on that test?"

"I'm not sure, but my survival has provided a lot of data for your project, I'd bet."

"I don't deny that. Your survival is an almost miraculous example of self-healing."

"And self-healing is a capability that supersoldiers could certainly use, wouldn't you say, General?"

Retticker looked away.

"Yes. Like flatworms, I suppose."

"What do you mean? You wanted to cut me in half to see if I'd grow a new head? Or a new body?"

"I 'wanted' nothing of the sort. Just an old joke among those of us in the warfighter enhancement business—that such regeneration would be a neat trait to splice into the soldier genome. But no one's ever managed to make a higher organism self-heal or instantly regenerate that way, not even by manipulating injected stem cells. A fatally wounded soldier—or chief scientist—is not a cut flatworm or a lizard that's lost its tail. Why would I want to risk killing you, when past experience would predict so little chance of a positive outcome to such a 'test'?"

He could see Pittman pondering his question. Good. She seemed to be getting past her anger, at least a bit.

"Darla, I realize you must find it hard to be dispassionate and coolly logical about this when you nearly lost your life. Still, the more clearly you can think about what happened, the more likely we are to get to the bottom of this."

Darla flashed him a cynical smile.

"Like your intelligence types have gotten to the bottom of Fox getting blown away by Hijazi?"

Retticker gazed down at the pattern in the blanket on Pittman's hospital bed.

"I'm sure that will be found out, too, with time."

"Oh? Personally, I don't want to have to wait around until the records are unsealed, since by that time all the principal actors will already be dead. I want some questions answered first."

"Go ahead."

"I want to hear you admit that tepui stone is from the same place Miskulin and Yamada found all those people massacred."

"Yes, that's where it's from," Retticker said. He decided not to mention the young survivors he'd learned of. "Things weren't supposed to turn out the way they did. They put up more resistance than expected."

"And your supersoldiers were involved?"

"You know I can neither confirm nor deny that. I'd guess you already have the answer you want, though."

"Those people who penetrated our lab and shot me . . . I'd be willing to bet they were supertroopers, too."

"Maybe so, Darla. But they were not mine. And they didn't do it under orders from me."

"If not yours then whose? If you didn't betray me, then who did?"

Retticker sat back in his chair.

"I suspect that whoever betrayed you also betrayed me."

"Oh?"

"Because you were right: I should have been the only one to know of the current status of your work. The intruders in your lab apparently knew what they were looking for. My guess is that our communication channels have been compromised. I don't think they expected to find you in the lab at such a late hour, however."

"Collateral damage to their raid?" Pittman asked, eyeing him narrowly. "Or a victim of friendly fire?"

"The former, I think. Whoever ordered this is no friend to either of us."

"Any candidates?"

"Too many," he replied, pondering it. He lapsed into silence, as did Darla.

Fremdkunst? he wondered. No, he didn't have this kind of reach.

Brescoll? He did have the long arm of Central Security Services. NSA's military wing was essentially a small covert army, navy, and air force—and at Brescoll's disposal.

If this had been NSA work, though, Retticker was sure he would have heard something about it. He had many connections in Crypto City—sources from whom, in fact, he'd heard the rumor that Brescoll had himself been MIA for weeks now, inside the MAXX in the mountains of central California.

Brescoll could have set such a raid in motion before his disappearance. Or maybe his disappearance was more apparent than real. The way the raiders had come stumbling upon Pittman and shooting things up, though—CSS even at its worst would have been more subtle and shown more due diligence than that. No, probably not Brescoll.

Vang, maybe? He was after some superenhancer of his own out of all this—remnant Tetragrammaton or Instrumentality scheming, Retticker was sure. Vang had the money and connections to suborn personnel, compromise systems, and send in mercenaries, too, but he was shrewd. He wasn't the type to resort to force-scenarios until all other options had been exhausted.

His money and influence had, for instance, easily overcome the medical confidentiality protections that were supposed to govern the doctors and technicians who had seen Paul Larkin's four young houseguests. Those techs and docs had all claimed they'd passed on privileged information about the children only out of concern for the poor, fungal-infected kids, never out of a concern for money. Of course.

Yet even with that information in hand, Vang and his people had not gone off cowboying on their own. They had instead passed the word along to Retticker, for him to take action on it or no. So probably it wasn't Vang behind the lab raid, either.

That left George Otis. With all the public-private and defense intelligence cooperation surrounding the supersoldier program, his people had at least as many opportunities to suborn personnel and compromise systems as Vang ever had. Probably more.

Given that Military Executive Resource Corporation was paying a lot of bills for warfighter enhancement research—and that even more money was flowing from MERC's corporate parent, Otis Diversified Industries—the strong possibility of compromised communication channels might actually be the least of Retticker's worries. The shoot-'em-up raid at Rocky Mountain felt very much like something the MERC cowboys might have been in charge of.

Otis and his people had opportunities, all right, but what about motives? When he was in politics, Otis had been noted for his ruthless, take-no-prisoners style.

Then again, the same thing could be said about the way the raid on the tepui had turned out, under his own watch.

Retticker took no particular pleasure in what had happened there. It was duty, and it had been discharged. Yet he remembered Otis's almost fanatic joy at the mess swirling about Temple Mount.

And the day they were all aboard Fremdkunst's boat, hadn't Otis and Fremdkunst both taken a call from somebody named Fox? How deeply might Otis and Fremdkunst have been involved with Avigdor Fox's final days, or even his assassination by Hijazi?

Otis was a hard-core Christian Zionist, true, but was he so hell-bent on bringing the Rapture that he would betray even his allies in the name of fulfilling some obscure end-time prophecy?

Retticker suddenly saw Darla Pittman and the quizzical look she was giving him. He shook his head.

"Sorry. I was just going through the list of suspects in my head."

"And?"

"Plenty of leads," he said, standing, "but no smoking gun yet. I'll keep at it, and I'll be back in touch. I promise. Anything else I can do to help?"

"Get me released so I can get back to work. I'm in perfectly good health, now."

"For someone shot six times, I suppose you are. The doctors are intrigued enough by your case to want to keep you here longer than you might need to be, but I'll see what I can do."

He shook her hand, much more warmly than he had in the past, genuinely relieved she was still alive and apparently healthy. Her own handshake, however, was more reserved than he'd expected, as if some unspoken and unspecified connection between the two of them had weakened.

"I'm off to talk to the directors at Rocky Mountain," he said. "Any messages?"

"Tell them I'm ready for work, and I expect the cabinet lab to be ready, too."

"Yes, ma'am," Retticker said, giving Pittman a mock salute that managed to make even the frustrated scientist smile.

A knock sounded on the partially open door. Retticker turned to see a man and woman in the doorway as the door swung wide, both of whom looked to be in their thirties. The man was carrying flowers, and the woman a card.

"Michael! Susan! What a nice surprise!" Darla said. "General Retticker, this is Michael Miskulin and Susan Yamada. They're consulting on the project."

"I don't believe I've had the pleasure," Joe Retticker said, feeling awkward but glossing over everything with his friendliest, folksiest, don't-mind-me smile.

"I hope we aren't interrupting . . . ?" the woman said.

"Not at all. I was just bidding farewell to Darla, here."

Retticker left the room and headed down the hallway of the small local hospital. Glad to have slipped out as smoothly as he had, he exhaled slowly and pondered his options. So was Darla chumming up with Miskulin and Yamada, now? Or was she just milking them for information? More variables to put into the equations.

Brescoll's apparent disappearance had allowed Retticker to learn, through his connections at NSA, that one of his own supersoldiers had leaked information to that agency. That would have to be dealt with . . . and soon. Best to strike before the director showed up again, or his replacement got a firm grip on the reins.

Best to keep Vang satisfied and everyone else in the dark, as well. Get those tepui kids at Larkin's place under better observation and control. Abduct them to a safe house, if necessary. Getting the rest of their holy stone helicoptered off Caracamuni tepui might be a good idea, too.

If Brescoll reappeared then, playing Vang against him would be simple enough. Playing them both against Otis might be more of a challenge, if it came to that. How the tepui stone—and now these survivors, too?—might fit in with Otis's doings in the Middle East, Retticker couldn't yet say. He rather hoped he wouldn't have to find out.

Fat chance of that. There was a lot more at stake, now, than even self-healing for supersoldiers, valuable as that might yet prove to be.

OUT FROM UNDER THE UNBREAKABLE BUBBLE

Jim Brescoll stepped back into a world bristling with weapons pointed at him, or at least toward him. The soldiers of Central Security Services stood poised and at the ready with a quite impressive array of armaments. He was so much reminded of a scene in *The Day the Earth Stood Still* he almost laughed.

It took him a moment to recognize that the man approaching him was Dan Amaral, one arm and shoulder in a sling.

"Jim! Thank God you're all right! You are, aren't you? All right, I mean?"

Jim nodded slowly.

"We've all been worried," Amaral continued. "Especially your wife and kids. Despite my reassurances. Despite the messages from Benson and LeMoyne and Markham. What have you been doing in there all these weeks?"

Funny, he felt as if no time at all had passed, but also that years had passed, too. He realized slowly that something was different. Ah, the snow was gone. As he turned toward where Dan was pointing, he couldn't really remember much of anything, until he saw the MAXX in its bubble of force behind him.

Bubble of force . . .

The memories came back so powerfully he tottered on his feet, then collapsed to the ground.

Inside the cavern, inside the powerhouse mountain. In the auditorium-size wonderland of the latest high tech, hidden beside the main generator room with its great enclosed sideways waterwheel of a turbine, forever turning. Computer monitors and projection screens hanging in front of the blasted and shotcreted walls. Bent-air holographic projection tables. Real-time holographic remotes, haptics on full-sensorium feedback virtuality units.

Don Markham, Karuna Benson, and Cherise LeMoyne—quite something other, now. They didn't so much "communicate" with him as share their dreamtime, the kaleidoscope of microcosmic universes, the panoply of parallel worldlines with which they interacted. Were they themselves glowing and winged and many-limbed? Or was that just some distortion of time in their kaleidoscopic realm?

The three did not so much "show" him things as drop him into events. He got the sense they knew exactly which events he wanted to see, but they were going to make him experience others of their own choosing, first.

The damaged mirrorball starship made of wild glowing angels, luminous butterfly octopi, all breaking up, slow-crashing stones through the solar system. Sky-scattered pieces orbiting, returning again and again, burning through the sky, plummeting to earth. Broken stones, rare and precious, scattered through time in cave and mountain, shattered forest and ocean floor, icefield and desert plain.

Stones driving ancient artists to paint their worlds inside caves. Stones reverenced in the desert, raised by hands onto platforms and hidden in tents. Carried on the shoulders of nomads, the shatter cones and oriented skystones of the goddess's breast, the god's right hand, the holy object generating the holy place generating the holy city.

Mushroom-worshipping, hunting-gathering, insect-eating, dark-haired and bright-eyed people of the tepui, dressed in purple-and-black loincloths or robes of the same intricate knot-weave, the same snaking double-helical pattern.

Caracamuni tepui, but not the same. A Caracamuni where Paul Larkin's sister Jacinta completed her mission. Where she did not commit suicide. Where the ghost people were not massacred.

The forests far below the tepui tossing like waves in a storm. A vast song of human voices filling the air, and a great ring of dust forming halfway up Caracamuni's height, the tepui itself growing taller—not growing but separating, top half from bottom half at the ring of thinning dust, until a space of clear sky stood between the sundered halves of the ancient mountain. Rising on song like a mushroom in the night, drifting away like a ship slipping from harbor toward open sea, open sky, the flat-topped mountain ascending in a bubble of force, a pale fire like inverted alpenglow beginning to shine from the sphered mountain itself, increasing in intensity until in a brilliant burst of white light the mountain disappears, silently and completely as a soap bubble bursting in a summer sky.

Jim realized, in some distant way, that he was being loaded on a gurney and trundled toward an ambulance. He heard nothing of the voices around him, however—saw only their silently shouting mouths. His ears were still filled with the memory of a tremendous blast like thunder sweeping over the world, as the tepui departed from a universe not his own.

Disappeared. From a universe where the Mawari genocide never happened.

The paramedics spun the gurney and he saw once again the bubble of force in his world, around this powerhouse mountain that had never taken flight, yet was also a world removed from his own. The medtechs bounced him into the womb of the ambulance, birth in reverse.

That other universe shown him by his contacts within the mountain held darknesses of its own. In that far other world, into the world the flying mountain left behind, Paul Larkin had unknowingly carried a spore print back with him, from which was grown an obscure South American fungus, *Cordyceps jacintae,* from which the covert operators of that world's Tetragrammaton cabal had in turn extracted KL 235, a supertryptamine intentionally misnamed ketamine lysergate or "gate."

In that universe, they had payrolled ob-gyns to pump their patients' wombs with KL during the embryonic development of their unborn children. To encourage the development of paranormal talents useful to Medusa Blue, the psi-power enhancement project within Tetragrammaton. To facilitate computer-aided apotheosis, the translation of human consciousness into a machine matrix, the seamless mind-machine link Tetra had sought for decades.

Instead, in that universe they succeeded only in turning out myriad Medusa Blue babies, children who possessed only "latent talent" at best, or were possessed by lifelong madness ending in suicide, at worst.

As the siren began to sound and the ambulance to move, Jim realized he had returned enough to this world to hear its sounds once more. He realized, too, that crazy things not so very different had happened in his own universe.

Like doping up your own soldiers on BZ without their knowledge or consent. Like dropping LSD on your own unsuspecting citizenry. Like nuking your own citizens. Like looking for latent talent by other means.

Latent talent . . .

The question wasn't what *had* been done to unknowing and unconsenting employees and citizens—by governments in the name of international insecurity, and corporations in the name of bottom-line profits—but what *wouldn't* be done by such organizations in the name of such things. In his own worldline, too, there seemed no bottom to how low corporations would go to protect the bottom line, no government atrocity indefensible in the name of national defense.

Of all the things the three inside the mountain had shown him, the strangest was the way those alternate universes seemed to parallel the possible pasts and converge upon the possible futures of his own world. *This* world, in which Jacinta Larkin had been prevented from helping the tepuians sing their mountain to the stars. In which the tepuians themselves had been massacred, despite their ability to travel in "mindtime."

This universe, where the spore print that Paul Larkin indeed possessed, and the mushrooms grown from it, had at least not had KL 235 extracted from them—at least not yet. Although there had been no KL here, there had been other covert projects for manipulating what went on inside the womb, also in the hope of activating "latent" paranormal talents in the kids.

Those projects had involved long-term twin studies, and the inducing of dissociative identity disorders. He had learned of them from Janis Rollwagen herself, in this world, in which so many forces also conspired toward that next step of apocalypse, or transcendence, or apocalyptic transcendence. The world in which, if those forces could not bring humanity to the stars, then they would somehow have to bring the stars to humanity.

The world in which Jaron Kwok—even more ethereal than Markham and Benson and Le Moyne, and more powerful—had decided to stay behind, he now knew, as Ben Cho's vicegerent, his "governor of the change." The world in which those four had given Jim—via the mindtime he'd experienced inside the mountain—what he had been after all along, without really knowing it. The most likely outcomes, the most plausible futures, on his own particular worldline amid the great ensemble of branching universes.

The strangeness even of those closer realities. The latent talent behind childhood's baby talk of imaginary friends, behind stories of fairy lands. The sensitivity to leakage from universes next door, only hinted at in all the mad visions of demons and angels, all the schizoidal, schizophrenic, multiple personality, autistic or dissociative identity disorders, in all the symbol-capable but dysfunction-prone brains chronicled throughout history.

A talent now to be exapted—by catastrophe. Split-kids pushed through a genetic and evolutionary arch of experience inside themselves, until they could access the quantum-computing capabilities latent in their own DNA. Until they could at last become tesseractors. Ravelers and knitters of the fabric of reality. Superpeople able to unlock all the doors of all the universes.

And all it would cost would be the intentional inducing of deep suffering in them. Treating them as subhuman in hopes of making them superhuman. Again and again.

The ambulance trek was shorter than he'd thought. He wondered distantly why they'd stopped.

Kids. Children . . .

The Mawari survivors. The mushroom cult and its mindtime. The stone from the tepui. The Black Stones. The meteorites pilfered from all over the planet. The *prima materia* to be tortured until it yielded answers.

Maybe not giving the answer sought or expected.

Fiery small stones burning out of the sky, streaking toward other streaks rising on columns of cloud by day, pillars of fire by night. Great bursts of forking lightning, and flashes above *any* clouds—seen from space. Claps of thunder and stones falling from the sky. Monuments and monoliths rising—or mushroom clouds roiling—into the air.

The sound of a helicopter approaching. Doors of the ambulance opening. The gurney rising. Medical evacuation.

"The Mawari kids," Jim Brescoll said, reaching up suddenly and pulling Amaral, beside him in the ambulance, down to his face by the man's good arm. "The spore print. Larkin has them. The tepui stone. We must secure them all!"

He fell back on the gurney, remembering too late to ask Amaral whether he had located Zaragosa. Then he was troubled by memories no longer.

THE SACRED AND THE SECRET

Avram was winched into a helicopter and flown to Riyadh. There he was to collect samples from the forty-five-hundred-pound iron meteorite Bedouin tribesmen called the Hadida, and from the additional four-hundred-and-forty-pound fragment found by an ARAMCO oil man. Victor said he wangled these chips off the big blocks on "long-term loan" from King Sa'ud University. Yuri, too, had shown a considerable interest in the specimens. Avram suspected a good chunk of money probably changed hands in the course of getting those "loaned" chips released to the foreign researchers' custody.

He was glad for the chance to get away from the Wabar digs for a while. The "yome, sweet yome" life he shared with Yuri in the desert was cordial enough, but still cramped. Lately he found himself more and more distanced from the work, now that the scientists of the small and the very small—the biochemists, molecular geneticists, and nanotechnicians—had come into their own. The focus had shifted from local field collecting at Wabar to what those lab rats could extract from the various stones Victor Fremdkunst had collected from throughout the world.

The digs continued, but more as a pretext for all of them being in the Empty Quarter than out of any urgent scientific need. Other than Vida, no one seemed to notice the increasing amount of time Avram was spending with Professor Ankawi—his tutor in conversational Arabic and Arabian culture, as well as all things relating to Islam.

That tutoring had kept him from learning as much Farsi from Vida as he might have liked, but he had probably learned enough to get by. Arabic was likely to prove more important—so much so that Avram never troubled Ankawi with any mention of his interest in the language of what had been Persia, Islam's other great ancient center of culture.

Under such circumstances it was getting harder for him to maintain his facade of straightforward scientific researcher, with no ulterior motives for being in the region. Secretly, he felt like a fraud. He wasn't a professional liar or actor or politician. Only by dint of tremendous mental effort had he been able to hold in all the words and thoughts of revenge for what happened to his daughter. Even that effort, in itself, might have cued the people around him (especially Vida) that something was askew with him.

Helicoptering back to camp now, in sunset light over an endless monotony of scrub giving way to an endless monotony of dunes, he sighed.

He was reminded of other flights, other sunsets, other challenges. Of something that had been itching at his mind ever since flying with her to the ECOL conference. And of a conversation he and Vida had had, while walking in the desert at sunset, a week ago now.

"You once said that place in the Nevada desert, Black Rock City, might someday end up a pilgrimage site like Mecca," he said to her. "What made you think that?"

Vida looked away into the seemingly lifeless distance, gathering her thoughts.

"A few things. The firestorm vortices, the way they whirled like flaming Sufi dervishes around the Burning Man's pyre. The temporariness of the tent city in the desert, like the thousands of encampments in the Mina Valley during the Hajj. A 'Black Rock' figuring prominently in both—though in Nevada that was the name of the place where the festival happened."

"Just a coincidence, don't you think?"

"Probably. I guess it was mostly the way the thousands of people surged forward and began to circle-dance around the pyre after the Man collapsed. Counterclockwise—the same direction the pilgrims in the Great Mosque at Mecca orbit around the Kaaba. Seven circuits. Like the visible planets around the sun. But maybe that's just another of your coincidences, too."

"You've been to Mecca?"

"No. I've always wanted to go—and always wanted not to go, if you know what I mean."

"No, I don't, actually."

Vida smiled.

"I was raised in a secular manner, but my cultural background is Muslim. It'd be intriguing to see the Black Stone up close, maybe find out whether it is a meteorite or not. I don't know whether that would make it more sacred, or less sacred, for me."

"That's why you do—and don't—want to go?"

"Only part of it. All the hajjis, everyone I've ever met who has gone on pilgrimage to Mecca, they all say the Hajj was the climax of their religious lives. It changed their lives. That intrigues me, but I don't know if I want my life changed that way. Not if it means I'd have to transform myself into a much more traditional Muslim woman."

They walked in silence for a moment before she finished her thought.

"Your friend Professor Ankawi could probably tell you a lot more about the Hajj. You seem to have been picking his brain a good deal lately."

Avram shrugged.

"The allure of the unknown. And the unknowable, most likely."

"Oh? Well, Ankawi's a fairly mysterious fellow himself. I thought I overheard him say something in Farsi to one of the workers from the Gulf yesterday. Flawless Farsi. I wouldn't mention our little language lessons to him. You might embarrass me."

Avram nodded, grinding the toe of his boot absently into the sand.

"I haven't, and I won't. Didn't wanting to seem a dilettante. Ankawi's not the unknowable I would be interested in, anyway—Mecca would be."

"Why's that?"

"You know, the guarded checkpoints, the 'Entry Prohibited to Non-Muslims,' all of it."

"I don't know if I agree even with that policy," Vida said, glancing down. "I know the reasons for such exclusivity, of course."

"Yes?"

"Mecca is the holiest city of Islam," she said, staring off again. "The whole focus of Mecca is Islam. Those who don't follow Islam have no reason to be in Mecca. No tourists, only pilgrims. No one but believers, in a city and countryside consecrated to belief."

"Which probably makes the place feel all the holier," Avram said. He had seen tourists even in Saint Peter's Basilica in Rome, and on the Temple Mount in Jerusalem.

"Yet there's always that 'no one but' part to it," Vida said. "That's the rub. The whole interlock of sect, sacred, and secret."

Avram turned away from the setting sun and together they headed back toward camp.

"Freedom of association to those on the inside means guilt by association to those on the outside," he agreed. "Maybe if nothing was secret, nothing would be sacred."

Vida smiled in surprise at him.

"The dream of science. Its heretical potential, too."

"That's why the fundamentalists hate evolutionary theory," Avram said. "It lets out of the bag that the *process* of evolution is older than *belief* in religion!"

She laughed politely, but soon grew serious again.

"More to it than that. More to it than even Victor's 'revealed, re-veiled, reviled' shell game. Have you ever had an experience that just couldn't be scientifically explained, Avram? Or know someone who did?"

Avram thought about it. With great difficulty he checked himself from mentioning the odd episodes that had followed his daughter's death, but he still had to say *something*.

"I know someone. A bachelor uncle, who was still living with my grandmother when she died. They were cleaning the awnings on the family house together when she turned to him and said, 'Marco, I don't feel well.' Then she collapsed. He tried performing CPR on her, but it turned out she'd suffered a massive pulmonary embolism. He always maintained, afterward, that he felt his mother's—my grandmother's—spirit pass through his body as he held her dying in his arms."

"Did you believe him?"

Considering his answer, Avram could not help but think again about Enide's death. When he held his daughter's severed leg in his arms, he had felt no spirit of his daughter, whole or partial, pass through him. Only smeared blood drying into his shirt.

If a soul could be obliterated like the body it inhabited, then a soul certainly wasn't what everyone said it was. Since his daughter's death, he doubted such a thing existed at all. It was no more real than the phantom limb he'd thought he felt pressing into his chest afterward, or the invisible stickiness of blood that he could never find on his always clean shirts. None of that was real. Just his mind playing tricks on him.

"No, I didn't believe him. Marco may have *thought* he felt something, but I don't think what he felt actually existed, objectively."

Vida nodded slowly as the desert faded toward night.

"That's what makes it a tough call. How can you say to someone that what he is sure he felt was actually not real? That he didn't actually feel what he felt? Who would know better than the person involved? There'll always be that reasonable doubt."

Together they watched the last sliver of the setting sun's light flash, then slip below the horizon.

"The larger the continent of knowledge, the longer the shoreline of mystery where it rises out of the sea of ignorance," Vida said as the twilight deepened around them. "Something will always be sacred to us because it will still be secret to us, right? The allure of the unknown, as you said yourself."

Avram smiled sadly, remembering. The ghost—no, the memory—of his daughter and the way she died would always prevent any real intimacy, or even deeper friendship, from developing between him and Vida. In his waking life as well as dreams, the attraction between a bright and beautiful unmarried woman and a recently divorced man would always be there. The denial of that attraction, however, had turned their relationship, though friendly enough, into banter and joust, constant questioning, the perpetual need to be on guard.

Wearying, to be so guarded in his responses all the time, but probably also a good thing, given his mission. It had served him well when Luis Martin surprised him in Riyadh today. He was just leaving the science building at King Sa'ud University, having picked up the meteorite samples for Fremdkunst and Semenov.

"Hello, Avram. I hope you haven't forgotten our work?"

"Not at all," Avram said as they walked together down the steps outside the building. "I've been studying very diligently with Professor Ankawi."

Avram noticed that Luis was wearing a more paramilitary, desert-camo version of his usual attire. With his sunglasses and preternaturally dark mustache he could have passed for a political strongman in many regions of the world. He had exchanged his usual panama hat, however, for a traditional red-and-white-checked kaffiyeh-cloth headdress, and so looked more appropriate to the Middle East than to his own actual roots. He was also carrying a case exactly like the one in which Avram himself was carrying the meteoritic samples.

"Not too distracted by your attractive colleague, Vida Nasr?" Luis asked as they made their way onto and across an open, spacious quad. "Not spending too much time with her?"

"No more than professional collegiality dictates," Avram said, hoping he didn't sound too wary. How it was possible for Luis to communicate a sly look from behind those sunglasses, Avram couldn't figure. Something to do with arching the eyebrows, he supposed.

"Glad to hear it! Pop-quiz time. Define *tawaf*."

"Means 'turning.' The rite of circumambulating the Kaaba in seven circuits during the Hajj—the annual pilgrimage required at least once in a lifetime of all Muslims of sound mind, maturity, and the financial stability to afford it. One of the five pillars of the faith."

"Very good. Define *Kaaba*."

"The four-story-high central shrine in the Great Mosque at Mecca. Also called the House of God, the Bayt Allah. Where the Black Stone is housed. The location toward which Muslims face when at prayer and around which they circle in *tawaf* during pilgrimage."

"Good. *Haram*."

"Sacred limit, sacred precinct, sanctuary with special laws of asylum. In Mecca it generally refers to the walled court of the Great Mosque or al-Haram al-Sharif. It can also mean the whole of Mecca and its surroundings within the boundaries of certain stone pillars."

"Very good," Martin said as Avram led the way toward where his rental car was parked. *"Ihram."*

"Purification rites the Hajj or Umra pilgrim must complete before entering the sacred territory of Mecca. It also refers to the ritual clothing designating this purified status—the apparel of submission, the garments of the next life. For men it consists of two lengths of unstitched cotton cloth."

"Umra."

"The lesser pilgrimage to Mecca. It includes the circling of *tawaf* and the 'racecourse' of the *sa'y*, but not the sites on the Plain of Arafat. It doesn't have to be done during Hajj season, either."

"Kiswa."

"Black ceremonial cloth trimmed in gold. An echo of the tent or sacred canopy under which the Black Stone was once carried. It covers the Kaaba and is replaced annually during Hajj."

"Mudayyina."

"Literally means 'Those Devoted to Religion.' The preferred name for the followers of Shaykh Muhammad ibn al-Wahabi, thus 'Wahabis,' the Western name for them. The Wahabite reinterpretation of the Hanbali teachings provided the theological underpinnings for the conquest and unification of the Arabian peninsula under the Sa'ud family. After whose patriarchate this university is named."

Avram rediscovered where his car was parked and turned down that aisle.

"This game of twenty questions has been interesting, Luis, but we're almost to my rental car, now."

"Twenty? I only count seven, so far. Just one more. *Mutawwif.*"

"Someone who guides and advises pilgrims on how to properly perform the rites of Hajj. In a broader sense, someone who helps the would-be hajji navigate the labyrinth of the pilgrimage. I could use one, I think."

"Oh? Don't you already have Professor Ankawi?"

"Book learning is one thing," Avram said. They both set down their briefcases beside the car. "I don't think that's going to get me through the checkpoints to Mecca during the Hajj, though, if that's still my destination."

"It is," Luis said coolly, leaning back against the car.

"Then your question game is less and less a game for me. Every morning I feel like Sisyphus, only the rock's getting heavier, or the hill's getting steeper, or I'm getting more and more tired. I don't know if I can push this rock where you want it to go."

"Then let me serve as a sort of *mutawwif*, if you like. First, I'm glad to see how well you've progressed under Ankawi. I'm also impressed that you appreciate the size of the task that's facing you."

"Size? I think the term is 'enormity.' "

Luis Martin smiled but continued, undaunted.

"You're right that it will take more than all Ankawi can teach you. Time is short and things are heating up. You will need to be in the Great Mosque in Mecca on the day of 9 Dhul Hijja 1437. An important anniversary. Maybe I can be of some help with that."

Luis put his case into the trunk with Avram's, glanced around, then opened it. Avram saw official-looking documents, money, and numerous travel items inside.

"For Hajj you will cease to be Avram Zaragosa. You will be Ibrahim Fayez. Mister Fayez's passport, valid for at least six months beyond the Hajj, has already been given to the Saudi authorities at the Jedda airport in preparation for your exit from the country, at which time they will return that passport to you. You and Mister Fayez bear a striking resemblance to each other and have the same up-to-date vaccinations. And here's Mister Fayez's return ticket to Buenos Aires, too."

Avram nodded, not knowing what to say as he stared at Luis's caseful of magic in the trunk.

"While a hajji," Luis continued, "the most important papers you carry will be these, Mister Fayez. This is a certificate, in compliance with Saudi embassy guidelines, issued by the imam of your local mosque in Buenos Aires. Here is an additional ID card, issued by your muallim. We've had extra photos of you made up, in case you should need them for other Saudi documents, or if you lose your visa, or what have you. These should get you past the checkpoints."

Surprise, relief, and caution tugged Avram in different directions even as he stood perfectly still.

"And then?"

"Then pray that your studies with Professor Ankawi serve you well. Non-Muslims, discovered to be such while in Mecca, have been ripped to pieces by the Hajj crowds."

"That will certainly motivate me to learn all my Hajj prayers."

"As it should. You are a devout pilgrim, Mister Fayez, so thoroughly learn the traditions and history of Hajj. Don't just memorize the prayers, understand their meaning."

"I'll do that. Saudi riyals and American dollars, too, I see. And one credit card?"

"Only one. In your name, Mister Fayez. Here's your *ihram* cloth and instructions for it, along with a variety of Argentinian travel sundries. Also a full travel itinerary, shuttle buses and cabs, with stops outlined for Mina, Muzdalifah, the Plain of Arafat, and Mount of Mercy. You probably won't get to visit all those sites, but handy for your cover story."

"I'm impressed, Luis. Very impressed."

"*De nada.* You should also pick out the traditional men's gown, the *thawb* or dishdasha. You can buy one like any tourist, almost anywhere—and without arousing undue suspicion. You might want to do it before leaving Riyadh."

"I will."

"One more thing," Martin said. He took something that looked and buzzed like an electric razor and placed it against the back of Avram's neck, near the hairline, for just a moment.

"What was that all about?" Avram asked as they closed the trunk of the car.

"I just put your implant into a more active mode. My friends under the domes in Tri-Border tell me that it will automatically ramp up four days prior to your target date, by which time you should be on the outskirts of Mecca. When the lowest circular error probability we can achieve indicates you are within ten meters of your target, it will become fully homing-activated."

"My target?"

"Let's just say I have it on good authority that the men responsible—

at the highest levels—for the death of your daughter will be on Hajj this year. In Mecca, when you are in Mecca. You might want to keep that in mind."

Before Avram had time to really take that in, Luis was passing on to other subjects.

"If at any time the implant reads your physical condition as approaching the last extremity, it will step up its activity and go to final phase on its own. A fail-safe mechanism."

"Wait! You're way ahead of me, Luis. How will I even know when it's time for me to leave Wabar for Mecca?"

"Professor Ankawi will let you know—and show you the way."

"Ankawi?"

"Don't worry. You'll see. Farewell, Avram. We'll be in touch."

Only after Luis Martin walked away and Avram was alone in the car did he begin to suspect that there might have been more motives involved in sending him to Riyadh than just his serving as convenient delivery boy for Victor and Yuri. He pondered that possibility on the drive back to the airport to return the car, and while buying a *thawb* at a tourist shop there.

He had been thinking about it now for a good part of the return flight too, in Victor's chartered and expensively modified helicopter, as it headed home to Wabar.

Out the window, as the helicopter descended in the twilight, Avram at first didn't recognize the pattern of lights from the yomes and the modular at their Wabar camp. He admonished himself for having been unobservant on previous approaches, but then he saw the rims of the ancient craters and knew that he was right: this was the right place, but the outline of the camp had changed during his absence.

Another modular building—what he and his colleagues had taken to calling a "modulab"—had been helicoptered onto the site. Getting to be quite a little settlement, way out here. He wondered vaguely if the camp might be visible to satellites from space, should anyone happen to be looking for them.

As the helicopter settled toward the earth, Avram decided to let other heads worry about that. He wondered who or what the new building might be for, and grew even more curious as he made the short rappel out of the helicopter. As he did the bent-over scurry away from the helo, under its blades, he saw half a dozen men standing at what looked suspiciously like guard positions, around the new modulab.

Things must indeed be "heating up," as Luis had put it.

SIX

FORCES CONVERGING

>>>>>>

They'd returned to Paul's compound in Tahoe to find it ablaze with color. The flowers of the late mountain spring—brodiaea, western azalea, monkey flower, fivespot, columbine, Indian pink, phlox, and lupine—bloomed everywhere about the grounds, all bending very quickly toward early summer.

Michael and Susan were buzzing with what had happened in Montana. The raid on the lab and how Darla Pittman had been caught up in it. The surprising outline Pittman had given them, especially on their second rock-climbing trip, about her own research, with its restriction fragment length-data and crystallographic images of what looked like hyperstable genetic material of otherworldly complexity.

"She suggested she might be able to learn more about the attack on the tepui," Susan told Paul almost as soon as they'd dumped their luggage in the entryway, "and pass it on to us."

"The prospect of her becoming a real ally, despite all past differences—that might be worth a lot," Michael said.

"I'm sure we can trust her," Susan said. "Otherwise I wouldn't have broadly hinted to her that some of the Mawari might still be alive somewhere."

"I think we should consider inviting her out here to Tahoe—"

"Whoa, whoa. Wait a minute, both of you," Paul balked. "I'd love to say 'Sure, if you think she's trustworthy, then I raise no objection.' I can't do that."

"Why not, Uncle Paul? We think she's on the up and up."

"Because no matter how eager I might be to broaden the circle of the trusted, I frankly don't see what would make Pittman burn her bridges so completely. It's not like she'd be going into hiding here, now would it? She'd still have her old connections. She might be the perfect plant for people wanting to get in close to the children—for their own reasons. We can't risk that. Not yet. Invite her for a visit, certainly, but don't mention the children."

Before the day was at an end they had done so, and Darla had agreed, promising to arrive in three days. The situation was changing so fast. Michael was surprised by the speed at which things were moving, despite Paul's caution. Had something happened to make the old guy so circumspect, something he hadn't told them about?

Over cocktails that evening, Michael and Susan discovered some of the reason for that change in Paul, at least in regard to what he had learned about Alii, Aubrey, Ebu, and Ka-dalun.

"Remember what I told you about what Jacinta said? That among the Mawari, language was for children, for only children have need of it?"

Susan and Michael nodded.

"They were certainly friendly and talkative enough when we got here this afternoon," Michael said.

"In the presence of ordinary adults like us, yes, they communicate on a relatively ordinary level—pretty much what you'd expect for kids their age."

"Why shouldn't they?" Susan asked. "Ordinary, twenty-first-century adults have been their surrogate parents for months now. All creatures react to that sort of nurturing."

"That's not what I meant. Among themselves these kids seem to be talking less and less, and their normal body language has almost disappeared. Not like they don't still communicate with one another—they do, and plenty—but that they're doing it through some other channel."

"I know that, after seeing that little levitation trick last time we were here," Susan said, "I should probably take your word for it. But still, what's your proof?"

Paul stared into his martini and sighed.

"Sometimes of late I've felt very strongly that the kids have been 'beaming' me—not in dreams, but while we're all wide-awake. As a playful test of their 'emergency broadcast system,' almost."

"What'd it feel like?" Michael asked.

"Nothing very clear, but I got the impression of someone else thinking or dreaming inside my head. Just the way Jacinta said, but not so sharply or distinctly as she experienced it. Afterward I got the sense that the kids were a bit frustrated with me. 'Poor stupid adults, they just don't seem to get it.'"

Paul smiled sheepishly. Michael and Susan laughed.

"I think that's generally termed *adolescence*," Michael said.

"Oh, no! It's more than that. Stick around and you'll feel it, too."

"Any idea what physiological basis there might be for such paranormal abilities?" Susan asked. "Assuming they're real?"

"Only what I've been able to glean from Jacinta's notes and my time with the kids. I think the myconeural complex, and the way it links activities in the raphe nuclei and the pineal gland, in new and unusual ways—that's what gives them the capability. Remember, those kids are old enough now to be entering puberty. If Jacinta's notes about the tepui people are correct, development of the myconeural complex must be getting pretty close to complete in them."

Susan still wasn't convinced, but Michael interrupted them with thoughts of his own.

"Paul, remember when we first brought the kids to you, you asked us if we'd experienced any 'odd mental phenomena' while we had the kids in our custody? We didn't mention it at the time but, before we saw you, Susan and I both talked about some mutual experiences that might fit into that category."

"Really? What?"

"Very detailed, vivid dreams of the massacre at the tepui. Susan and I both had them."

"At the time we decided it was just because of the bloody horrors we'd seen there," Susan said. "I still think that's the most logical explanation. It'll have to do, for this late hour of a long day."

Michael agreed, but on slipping into bed beside the already sleeping Susan that night, he did not drift off to sleep without a moment of apprehension as to what dreams might come.

—

"Yes, they finally fell prey to those tech-specs," Paul said, gesturing to a pair of augmented reality glasses perched on the edge of a table, the morning of their second day in Tahoe. "Inevitable, I suppose, given their fascination with all things Argus."

"Before we went to Montana I saw the kids working with something called 'Argus Point,' " Michael said. "I thought it might be some kind of interactive Web game.

"It might be," Paul agreed, "but I can't say for sure."

When Paul asked the kids to explain their fascination with Argus to their aunt Susan and uncle Michael, they at first just showed the three adults some sites that talked about how Zeus sent Hermes to free his beautiful paramour, Io. Zeus had changed her into a beautiful heifer to deceive his jealous wife, Hera, but Hera had managed to take Io captive anyway and place her under the ever-watchful guard of Argus All-Seeing, with his hundred eyes. Hermes, disguised as a simple herdsman, played his panpipes and told the story of how that instrument was created, until disguise, lullaby, and bedtime story put Argus enough at his ease that he shut all his eyes in sleep—at which point Hermes made the shut-eye permanent by killing him.

Paul asked the Mawari kids several times whether they had found anything linking Argus with meteorites or, more generally, space. The ever more reticent kids at last showed the three of them information on the Argus Radio Telescope at Ohio State University. In science fiction novels featuring endeavors called "Project Argus." On the SETI League's actual Project Argus, under which five thousand small, inexpensive, amateur radio telescopes, built and operated by SETI League members throughout the world, were deployed and coordinated to survey the entire sky, real time in all directions, for microwave signals of intelligent extraterrestrial origin.

In all those contexts the Argus connection made sense, but there was one in which it didn't seem to apply at all. Argus, the adults learned, was also the name of the only clandestine series of nuclear tests ever conducted by the United States—eighteen hundred kilometers off Cape Town, South Africa, on three different days in late August and early September of 1958. During the tests, each rocket-launched nuclear warhead was detonated at very high altitude.

Why such nuclear tests might have been named for a many-eyed being for whom sleep was death, the Mawari kids wouldn't or couldn't or, at any rate, *didn't* say.

—

Michael woke to the sound of a knocking at the bedroom door and Susan's voice calling his name, sounding hushed yet urgent.

"Wha—?" He had been redreaming the two days since they'd returned to Tahoe and was still groggy enough to be wondering if this was part of his dream, too.

"Get up, Michael! Paul says we've got a problem."

Fumbling on a pair of pants and tucking his nightshirt into it, Michael opened the door and saw Susan standing there, in moonlight. There were, in fact, no lights on anywhere except for the dim glow of what looked like airline emergency track-lighting, along the baseboards in the hallway. Michael was surprised he hadn't noticed it before.

"What's going on?"

"I'll let Paul explain. Follow me."

The open-floor plan and the numerous windows, which gave the main house such a great view of the lake during the day, meant they were able to navigate the house's layout by the moonlight alone. As he strode after Susan, Michael was surprised how much detail he could make out, even down to individual small objects, including a pair of ARGUS blinks on a table near one of the windows.

"In here," Susan said, snapping him out of his reverie. When they entered, Michael saw Paul sitting before a bank of a dozen closed-circuit TV monitors in what, he now realized, was some kind of safe room. The monitors showed infrared and night-vision images as well as standard video and motion sensor graphics, too. Michael also saw a closed-circuit feed from the kids' room in the guesthouse. Ka-dalun, Alii, Ebu, and Aubrey all appeared to be asleep.

"What's all this tech?" Michael asked.

"I told you the history," Paul said. "The first owner here was connected to the Vegas mob, later there was the *Godfather*-geek surveillance mogul, and then the Chinese diplomat with the big art collection, remember?"

"So what's going on now?"

"Someone cut power to us here," Paul said, glancing over his shoulder. "The house shifted over to backup generators immediately, thank heavens. Triggered an alarm that woke me up, so I came down here. The power outage isn't general. Very specifically targeted. Just us—no one else along the shore. Then I spotted these."

Paul gestured at a screen that refreshed itself at a rapid rate and showed two green dots approaching.

"What are they?"

"Boats, approaching at speed from the southeast. The security computer indicates they're probably Zodiac inflatables, judging from the low radar profiles. Headed toward us. Just before you stepped in, I spotted these others as well."

He pointed to a second screen, with its own constellation of dots—three of them. Then he combined the output from the two screens and their course plots. The second group appeared to be on an intercept course with the first.

"I thought you didn't have any guards," Susan said.

"None on-site tonight," Paul said, his eyes scanning the banks of monitors, "but I do have some in my employ. They're on their way; however, we seem to be under someone else's protection. If that's what it is."

Michael watched the screens.

"Looks like that first group will reach the shore, here, before the second can intercept them."

"Maybe," Paul said. "We should be able to pick them up on night-vision optics and mikes, now."

He flicked a switch. Instantly they heard the night sounds outside. Paul had activated a sensitive directional microphone and was scanning it in an arc across the lake. Over the lap of the waves on the shore and the rush of the breeze in the pines, they heard popping sounds, growing closer, punctuated by an occasional louder whump! and the sound of fountaining water. As the night-vision optics found the scene, Michael saw muzzle flashes and realized after a moment that he had been listening to the sounds of a very mobile firefight, rushing across the lake toward them.

"Any idea who they are?" he asked. "Or who might be on our side, if this place *is* the target?"

"Not a clue." Paul brought up another screen, on which a dotted line traced a square extending from his boat landing and across the small inlet that was also his property. He clicked on a screen button. Something moved on the night-vision screen. After a moment they saw chaos on the water and heard over the speakers a dull crunching sound. One of the two approaching dots flickered.

"One of the previous owners had an underwater privacy fence installed," Paul explained. "Its hydraulic stanchions can lift the steel net several feet above the water's surface—and fast."

"Apparently not fast enough," Susan said. "One of them made it through."

"Yes. It's at the far end of the boat landing." He brought up a graphical depiction of the landing and pier. "Correction. Motion sensors and pressure plates indicate several people on the landing, though I don't see them. Let's see if we can't persuade these invisible folk to stay right where they are."

They didn't need the microphones or the night-vision optics to see and hear the explosion this time. On the graphic of landing and pier, a section of the pier disappeared. The night-vision and infrared cameras trained on the same section indicated the same thing, only more spectacularly.

They watched as two of the boats that had been in pursuit stopped outside the underwater fence perimeter, while the third motored slowly to where the erstwhile peninsula of landing and pier had become island— its connection to the mainland quite severed—and upon which several figures now slowly raised their arms into the air above them.

"The kids are awake," Susan said quietly. Michael and Paul turned their gaze to the screen Susan had nodded toward. The kids had gotten out of their beds and were seated cross-legged in a rectangular pattern on the floor. They appeared to be unmoving, at the moment.

"More trouble," Paul said, swiveling in his chair and reluctantly donning a pair of blinks. "This time by land. Several figures approaching the boundary fences." He shook his head sharply. "We should have gotten an earlier warning—visible, infrared, sound, something. They must be in some kind of background-matching camo. Dammit. Like they just rose right up out of the ground."

He tossed a glance over his shoulder.

"Michael, Susan—get the kids and bring them here from the guesthouse."

Michael and Susan ran through the main house into the moonlit yard between it and the guesthouse. The place was eerily quiet at the moment, given the forces converging upon it. They pushed open the heavy oak door and proceeded toward the children's sleeping area. They found the four of them still seated cross-legged on the floor in the moon-shadowed room.

"Come on, kids," Susan said. "We've got to get up and get going."

As Michael helped her lift the children to their feet, it struck him that there was something heavy and trancelike about their responses. They seemed to go only where he and Susan forcibly steered them, which meant that it was taking them much longer to get the kids out of the guesthouse than it should have.

Too long. Gas and smoke canisters shot in through the windows. The heavy front door smashed open and troops in black exoskeletal suits swarmed inside, great dull insects in the moonlight. Michael felt himself darted—a quick jab of pain, then spreading lassitude and paralysis.

As he sank to his knees, he saw the children, snatched from his and Susan's hands, being quickly led away by the black-suited raiders. Yet the kids' heads and eyes were all turned toward where he and Susan were both now falling to the floor—and the children were speaking without talking, putting a round-robin of words directly into his head.

—*Uncle Michael—Aunt Susan—Don't worry—About us—We've seen—This path—Before—We want—To go—Where it—Goes—We'll show—The stars—Where to fall—Don't worry—Aunt Susan—Uncle Michael—*

The round of voices sounded tearful yet determined, as if they had made a difficult choice and now must live with it. Voices not his own, speaking so immediately in his head—disorienting. As if he weren't disoriented enough already.

He could not ponder the voices for long, however. Watching the children disappear out the door was the last thing Michael remembered before he heard a prodigious explosion from the far end of the house, where Paul had been. Then black and shining night overwhelmed him.

INTERLUDE: VIEW FROM A DEATH

As he lay dying from multiple gunshot and shrapnel wounds, Paul Larkin watched the children on a cracked but still functional room monitor. He saw them dragging their heels, moving only slowly to Susan and Michael's urging, and he understood.

The children must have seen something like this coming. If Susan and Michael had succeeded in bringing them here to him, they would be dead or dying alongside him now. They must have known, too, that they could not save him and still fulfill whatever destiny awaited them.

He watched as the black-suited invaders put Susan and Michael out of commission. Seeing them drag the children away, he sighed, tasting blood in his mouth. Remembering his best guesses as to what had happened during the previous attack on him and the kids, he suspected that the kids could have prevented these people from taking them. Were they allowing themselves to be taken captive? Why?

He would have to trust that the kids somehow knew what they were doing. It was too late for him.

If they lived, Michael and Susan would discover it all, now. Everything he'd been hiding from them, about that previous attack. They and Jim Brescoll—and maybe the Pittman woman, too, if she proved trustworthy—would have all the information they needed to go on with their investigations. He had seen to that.

That didn't mean everyone need find out everything, though. All the surveillance, all his other private records—everything in this most secure room in the compound, this room soon to be thoroughly breached and compromised—could all still be destroyed. And would be.

One of the previous owners, in a true nadir of paranoia, had equipped this security room and its adjoining safes with self-destruct devices. Those were code-cleared and ready to go, now. His hand was on the master switch for all of them.

As the black tide of blood and fire raced toward him out of the night, Paul Larkin flipped the switch. An instant after black-suited interlopers broke into the room, the devices detonated. In the blast's great light, Paul Larkin was granted a final revelation, a glimmer of the golden path the Mawari children had set out on, amid all the darker possible futures that might yet beset them.

HOPES, FEARS, EXPECTATIONS

To join Michael Miskulin and Susan Yamada at Paul Larkin's compound on the Tahoe lakeshore, Darla Pittman had to wade through an unexpected concentration of security. The first level was mostly the usual police-tape—local law enforcement treating what had happened as a break-in, kidnapping, and possible murder. That, at any rate, was the extent of the story they were giving to those few media people who managed to get close enough to the scene to earn an explanation.

The more she struggled to get through the security cocoon, however, the more layers Darla discovered it had: FBI counterterrorism special agents out of the Sacramento office, intelligence community operatives all the way from the East Coast. Larkin's estate was swarming with more law enforcement muscle and brain than a congressional investigation. At several points Darla wondered if it would require an *act* of Congress to get her in to see the very people who had invited her here.

The upside of all the security was that Darla was led by the head of Paul Larkin's private security team, Jarrod Takimoto, across the compound and into the private guesthouse where Michael and Susan waited. The two of them rose to shake Darla's hand before they resumed their seats, Michael gesturing for her to sit as well.

"Tell me again, Mister Takimoto," Susan Yamada said, before the security chief could duck out of the room. "You and your people weren't on-site . . . because?"

"Because we almost never were, Ms. Yamada. Mister Larkin always insisted we keep a low profile. Said he didn't like leading a guarded life. Or at least not being reminded of it."

"That sounds like my uncle," Michael said to Darla, shaking his head sadly. "He can be—he was—very stubborn and set in his ways at times. So now he's dead, because he didn't want a 'guarded life.' "

Michael turned from Darla to Takimoto.

"Jarrod, any chance we might have a little privacy with our guest?"

"I don't see why not. The investigators seem to be finished with this area, for now. I'll see to it you're not disturbed."

Takimoto hastily departed. Michael and Susan began to fill Darla in on what had happened—particularly the attack in which the four Mawari kids had been abducted, and during which Paul Larkin had died. Darla saw that Susan and Michael were taking the loss of the children and the death of Paul Larkin very hard, at least judging by the proof of the liquor they were drinking this early in the day. She politely declined Michael's suggestion that she join them in a drink.

Ever since she accepted their invitation to visit Tahoe, Darla had been thinking long and hard about her situation. As the conference receded into the past, the tensions stemming from her past relationship with Michael had also receded into the background, as more essential matters came to the fore. Listening to their story now, she hoped—and also feared—that she might be throwing in her lot with the right people now.

"I know how important your uncle was," Susan said, sounding puzzled and sad as she swirled the ice cubes in her glass. "I know how potentially important the Mawari kids are, too. But I'm having trouble understanding how they merit an investigation of this magnitude."

Darla took a deep breath.

"I think I may know something about that—at least as far as the kids are concerned," she began. "I think it has to do with what Michael said about a 'metaphage.' That turned out to be the keystone to my own hypotheses."

"What do you mean?" Susan asked.

Darla brought up displays on her laptop for them. She recapped the old idea that the majority of DNA was junk because it didn't obviously code for proteins—and then refuted that argument by showing them sites detailing how the discovery of Group II introns—and the little complex of catalytic RNAs and proteins known as the spliceosome—changed that old dogma. She then showed them Web pages on how other pieces of supposed genomic junk, transposons and other repetitive elements, had also eventually come to be considered "molecular-parasite immigrants," which in turn had provided important capabilities for RNA-mediated genomic regulation and epigenetic inheritance. She finished by showing them reports on how Alu-element "junk" was particularly important in brain activity, and in laying the foundation for memory and higher-order cognition in primates.

"But what's all that got to do with the Mawari kids and their meteorite mushroom stone?" Susan asked.

"What I found in that 'sclerotium,' as you called it, initially looked like space-junk DNA," Darla began.

"That's pretty much what it looked like to us, from the few tests we ran," Michael agreed.

"But it's not junk," she said, showing them nano- and microsection images from her own research at Rocky Mountain. "As I told you in Montana, it looks more like the product of synthetic biology, but of a much higher order than anything we've achieved. Using what I found, I succeeded in growing a rudimentary version of Jacinta Larkin's 'myco-neural complex.' When I ran genetic and other biochemical assays on that mix of mycelium and neurons, all sorts of interesting things popped out. Here: new tryptamine chemicals, hormones, odd code sequences."

She showed the images on the laptop to Susan and Michael. AR glasses would have been easier, but Michael and Susan didn't seem to have any about their persons, so she let it go.

"The relationship between fungal and neural material seems to be mutually beneficial: the fungal spawn obtains moisture, protection, and nutrients even in adverse environments, and the human hosts are assured a steady supply of what seem to be very potent informational substances."

"Maybe those are what Jacinta meant by 'adaptogens' in her notes?" Michael suggested.

Darla nodded.

"When I took 'junk' sequences from my other meteoritic samples," she continued, showing them an animation, "and allowed them to bind with the codons from the tepui stone, even more interesting things began to happen. Before my lab was raided, I think I managed to generate a more complete program than even the stone itself contained. I think I managed to get much closer to the full metaphage code, as you called it, Michael—though it's still probably not the whole thing."

"But what does it code for?" Susan asked. "And what does it have to do with the kids?"

Darla thought about that a moment, before calling up imagery from a site dealing with complexity theory and evolution, and then material from one of Michael's own sites, with its little movie of comets and meteorites.

"I think it's a molecular design and repair system," she said, "an extremely subtle regulatory architecture involved in the generation and shaping of higher levels of complexity across living systems generally. I think we've always only gotten fragments of it, despite the fact that its 'codons' were more stable and less prone to mutation than, say, ordinary DNA. Enough comes raining down from space over a billion years, though, and those fragments add up."

"With the ultimate possibility of creating something like a phoenix phenotype!" Michael said. "I've thought the same thing. Starting with hyperstable components, but also endowing them with the possibility of multiplicity reactivation. That would be a very good way to fight inevitable informational entropy."

"Can't we just give all this abstract stuff a *rest*?" Susan asked, exasperated. "The kids are gone! Paul is dead! And all you want to talk about is 'phoenix phenotypes'!"

"Paul would have wanted us to pursue this. That's the best way we can mourn him. He was *my* uncle, after all. You've seen the notes he left behind for us, in those e-mails. Jacinta's research, too. Somewhere in all that is the thread that will lead us back to the kids and their place in the big picture. I'm sure that'll prove Paul didn't die for nothing. I've contacted Brescoll already. What more do you want me to do?"

"Call in every favor we can, then call in some more," Susan said. "Frankly I don't see how dead viruses inside a single cell are in any way relevant to the 'big picture.'"

Darla felt awkward, listening to the couple argue their way through this.

"Maybe it'll help if we think 'similarities across scale,' " she said. "If we think of earth as being like a huge single-celled organism, then the atmosphere is its cell membrane—semi-permeable, to skystones at least. Most of what's outside stays outside, but what gets in can help shape things inside the 'cell' of the whole planet. Multiplicity reactivation, complementation, recombination of genetic elements—all would apply."

"The metaphage can rise again from its own meteoritic ashes," Michael said. "The cell a metaphage infects is not so much what you see under a microscope as what you look at through a telescope!"

"Even if we accept the idea that this thing 'enviruses' whole planets," Susan insisted, "what's the point?"

Darla took a deep breath again. This was at the bleeding edge of her thoughts on the matter. She had no fancy graphics or Web-based imagery to back her up.

"When life, mind, consciousness—whatever you want to call it—paints itself into a corner, the metaphage provides keys to open a door through the wall."

"Making a way out of no way," Michael said. "An ender of dead ends, through all its subtle regulating and generating and shaping. I like that."

"But how?" Susan asked. "And why?"

"I think the 'how' might be easier to answer," Darla said. "Say the physicists are right. That we live in a vast ensemble of parallel universes, alternate timelines, alternate worldlines."

"Mindtime, as the tepui people called it," Michael said. "All the 'what if' possibilities."

"Including a world where the children would still be here . . . and Paul would still be here? Or one where the tepui people were never massacred?"

Darla noted the meaningful glances that passed between Susan and Michael as Susan said this, but only nodded, not fully sure of the context for those loaded looks.

"In such an ensemble, odds are that, when mind or consciousness arises, it ends up being a dead end in most worlds, in most universes. Unless . . ."

"Unless someone or something is stacking the deck in favor of mind and consciousness," Michael said. "The Mawari myth of spore and spawn and their 'seven ages' that Paul mentioned, that he found in Jacinta's work."

"I think someone closer to home here knows something about it, too," Darla said. "That's why they began stealing and collecting meteorites to begin with."

Michael nodded.

"And why they've gone after your Mawari children, too," she said. "They're more unique than even you or Michael might have imagined, Susan."

"In what way?"

On her laptop Darla brought up images from neuroanatomy, beginning with diagrams of the hemisected human brain.

"I got the idea from what you and Michael suggested to me," she said. "About the relationship between the myconeural complex, the raphe nuclei, and the enlarged pineal gland. Usually, the pineal begins to shrink about the time of puberty. Throughout the course of adulthood it fills up with calcium deposits, or 'brain sand,' as it's called."

Susan laughed oddly at the phrase, but waved her on.

"I think one of the things their full myconeural complex enabled the people on that tepui to do," Darla continued, "was to become sexually mature—maybe just barely—yet retain the high pineal activity of childhood. It might be that the myconeural complex neotenized them."

"Neotenized?" Susan asked.

"The retention of juvenile characteristics in the adults of a species, that's one meaning of neoteny, anyway. It's part of a constellation of ideas regarding changes in the rate and duration of growth that developmental biologists refer to as 'heterochrony.' Evolutionarily, humans have long had a tendency in the neotenous direction."

"Hm!" Paul said. "My aunt's notes on the tepui people mentioned that they were very long-lived but also had a low reproductive rate."

"That would make sense," Darla agreed. "That'd be the likely trade-off. Puberty probably began later rather than earlier among them, too. I bet they were not only long-lived but also retained a childlike curiosity and openness to possibility, throughout adulthood, even into old age."

"What I've seen of Jacinta's notes might be read as indicating that, too," Susan agreed.

"Some of these effects might have been products of other things the myconeural complex produces or allows for," Darla said, bringing up more anatomy-class images, but these were of various amphibians and reptiles and birds rather than humans. "The pineal is a very ancient organ. All vertebrates have pineal structures. Sometimes they appear much more like an actual eye on the top of the head. In many organisms, the pineal is also biomagnetically sensitive, orienting the migrating bird or animal in relation to the earth's magnetic field. There might be a lot more involved than just the fact that the tepui people probably had little or no calcification of the pineal glands, even into old age."

"All well and good," Susan said, "but how is that relevant to what happened to the people on the tepui?"

"Everywhere on earth, not just at Caracamuni tepui," she said, bringing up images of chemical compounds, "the pineal produces many of the same tryptamines that are often also found in fungi, including dimethyltryptamine, or DMT—"

"Which is strongly psychoactive," Susan said. "All right. I think I see what you're suggesting. A deep connection between those fungi and the ubiquity and antiquity of pineal structures, right?"

"Exactly."

"And if that's the case, then some of what the tepui mushroom-stone gave these people, via the myconeural complex," Susan said, "includes indole molecules that look like very complex new tryptamines."

"Yes. Active in new ways and at lower concentrations. Supertryptamines, if you like."

Darla looked at them for response to that strange word, but saw nothing out of the ordinary. Then again, only she knew that she'd first encountered the term *supertryptamines* during the very strange trip of her near-death experience.

"And the raphe nuclei," Michael said, thinking aloud. "Might the myconeural complex have altered their function? To allow consistent high-level brain activity involving these supertryptamines? Without burnout or ill effects? At the same time allowing for any number of so-called psychic or paranormal mental phenomena? Including 'forays sideways' into mindtime, as my aunt put it?"

"Wait, wait," Darla began. "I'm not as good at shotgunning answers as you are at shotgunning questions, but yes, I think that's plausible—"

Susan, however, was shaking her head, vigorously negative.

"If the tepui people had all these miraculous powers," she said, "then why didn't they accomplish more? Hell, why couldn't they save themselves from the soldiers who destroyed them?"

They all grew quiet at that.

"My guess is, even on the tepui," Darla said, "the deeper potential connection, which the ancient fungal-pineal link only suggests, that potential wasn't fully realized. Even there on Caracamuni, the metaphage code was incomplete."

"If what Jacinta said about mindtime is right," Michael added, "then maybe, even though the Mawari were able to make 'forays' into worlds 'sideways' to ours, they still couldn't alter the courses of those worlds, or our own. What they saw in those universes-next-door was probably confusing even to them."

"I'm sure it was," Darla agreed.

"Wait a minute," Susan said. "How do you know? You seem to know a lot more about all this than we've told you."

Darla took a deep breath. Time to bite the bullet.

"I know," she said, closing her laptop, "because I've been working for the people who massacred the Mawari. I know, because a chunk of their sacred meteorite ended up in my lab. I know, because I've given my employers at least part of what they were after—supertryptamines, and self-healing, for supersoldiers."

"You bitch!" Susan said, leaping to her feet, her hands curling into claws. "Paul was right! We should never have trusted you. I should fucking kill you!"

Michael stood up quickly, just in case Susan decided to make good on her threat. What Darla said next, however, stopped them both.

"You'll have to take a number," she said. "Once my employers figure out I've left Rocky Mountain for good, once they learn I've brought my work to you, I have no doubt my employers' employers will make me a high-profile target for assassination."

"Why?" Susan asked, still standing. "Why would you work with us, in good faith?"

"Because those Mawari kids are important. More important even than supertryptamines and supersoldiers. Those four children are the only people on earth possessing that full myconeural complex, with all its effects on the pineal and the raphe nuclei and neurochemistry generally."

"Stories and legends suggest that other people throughout the world and throughout history have probably been able to see the universes 'next door,' " Michael suggested.

"True, but those children are part of a more select group. They may well be the only ones on the planet right now who, exposed to the entirety of the metaphage pattern, not only might *see* universes-next-door, but also change and *shape* them—and our own—as well."

"The ways out of no way," Michael said, "may just be sideways. . . ."

Susan frowned, still very much unconvinced, but slowly began sitting down at last.

"I admit Alii, Aubrey, Ebu, and Ka-dalun have unusual abilities," she said, "but how can you be so sure there *are* universes-next-door? That these sideways worlds even exist?"

Darla looked from one to the other of them.

"Because I've been to one," she said.

Darla explained what happened when the intruders at the lab shot her and she fell into the biosafety cabinet through which she'd been examining her latest work. As concisely as she could, she tried to describe the paranoid parallel earth she'd side-slipped into—what she remembered as Fogworld, with its post-ecodisaster drizzletowns and mist cities, awash in mind-killing nanotoxins and cruder poisons.

"That's a frightening description," Susan admitted when Darla had finished, "but did you ever think it might just be a very vivid hallucination? You *do* have a reputation for being fascinated with altered states of consciousness—and by your own admission, you were in the midst of a near-death experience."

Darla nodded. She might have been more offended by the comment than even by Susan's earlier threat to kill her, had she not at some level already been expecting such questions.

"I wondered about that myself, right after it happened. You're right—I do know what an altered state feels like, and this didn't feel like that. It was less an experience of 'near death' or 'out of body' than a moment living another life on another worldline. It was absolutely real."

Susan still looked skeptical.

"If it wasn't just a near-death experience, then what brought it on?"

Darla stood up, went around to the back of her chair, and leaned on it as she thought about her answer.

"I think I was only able to side-slip into another world because I'd been exposed to the myconeural material I was working with in the lab—material with as much or more of the metaphage code as that found in the tepui stone itself, when it first fused with its earthly fungal vector.

"You know what I find really amazing in what you've told me about the Mawari people? It took my almost dying, while simultaneously taking in more of the metaphage than they probably ever did, and still I only got a glimpse of the 'mindtime' they were apparently able to access at almost any moment."

Susan seemed a bit swayed by this, less skeptical and more curious.

"Can you prove that metaphage stuff actually changed you, and didn't just alter your mind?"

Known by the scars, she thought. And she had some. She'd been expecting the demand for a demonstration of not only mental but also physical tranformation, too. She'd not only been thinking a great deal, but also testing herself—lesser experiments, before now, but all offering hints and at last positive proof that her self-healing abilities were still with her.

"I'll prove it now," Darla said, standing up straight. "I think I can prove it has already given me something more than what even the Mawari already had. Michael, would you be so kind as to get me a sharp knife?"

Michael looked surprised and glanced at Susan, but then nodded and disappeared. In a moment he returned with a large kitchen blade.

"Thank you," Darla said, taking the blade into her right hand. She hoped this worked. In an instant she slashed a broad and gaping cut into her left arm, almost down to the bone.

"My God—"

"Darla!"

"What are you doing?"

The pain made her gasp—so much she had to fight passing out. She managed to stay conscious. She turned her bleeding arm toward them.

"Watch."

As they did, they saw, as she did, what she had hoped and expected would happen. The blood flow stopped and the gaping wound almost instantly began to close and heal. Within perhaps five minutes it had been reduced to nothing more than a thin scar.

"There you have it, Susan."

"But . . . but how?"

"A result of my exposure to that more complete myconeural I was trying to make in the lab—that's my guess, anyway. I've been thinking a lot about what happened to me, and how it happened. I think there may be precedents."

"For *that*?"

"Yes. Think of the Nuhus, the meteoritic Mesoamerican 'spears of god.' Or the meteoritic grail of Parzival."

"Or the Spear of Longinus," Michael said, "which both wounds *and* heals. They were *all* said to heal and nourish and enrich."

"And all of them were said to 'speak,' or 'grant visions,' " Darla continued, "like Jacob's dream-pillow stone, or the Black Stone of the Kaaba, or sacred skystones and hierophanic rocks from all over the world. Stones that transformed consciousness. That provided telepathic guidance and other psychic abilities traditionally associated with the pineal as the 'eye of the mind.' "

"The alchemical 'black stone' that transforms—transmutes—the alchemist!" Michael said. "Who knows what those kids might accomplish if exposed to the same stuff you were!"

"Precisely—"

"At least the rest of their people might not be dead, if they'd had that self-healing ability to begin with," Susan said. Michael looked up from the floor.

"Before the kids were taken away," he said awkwardly, "they left a message with us. Spoke it right inside our heads—Susan's and mine."

"What was the message?"

"They told us not to worry. They said they already knew the path they were to follow. Which sounds to me like they had already foreseen it. Like they already knew it, from being in mindtime."

"Something else, too," Susan said. "They repeated that we shouldn't worry, because they would 'show the stars where to fall.' "

"I don't know how," Michael said, "but they just might be able to do that, if all we've been saying about them is true."

Darla shook her head.

"Then we'd better be damn careful with them."

"Why?" Susan asked her. "They've been more sinned against than sinning, for heaven's sake."

"Exactly. They're endangered, but did you ever think *they're* also very dangerous, at least potentially?"

"We've been in close quarters with them, Darla," Susan said. "We know them. Only Paul knew them better."

"They seem innocent and loving enough to me," Michael agreed.

"Maybe, but they have been sinned against, as Susan said. Their entire families—everyone they'd ever known—were massacred by people from an advanced technological society. Now Paul Larkin, the person they knew best in such a society—perhaps the only one they trusted—

is dead. Their love or even respect for people from such societies might not extend much beyond the two of you."

Susan snorted indignantly but said nothing.

"I'm just saying you should consider it. With all they've seen and been through, isn't it at least possible those kids might not be above avenging what happened to them and their people? Avenging it in a big way? Especially if they have the means, and the motive, and the opportunity?"

She looked hard at Susan and Michael. Even Susan had subsided, apparently considering the implications.

"I don't want to sound alarmist, but that vengeance could be terrible. Maybe people besides ourselves have realized that, too. Maybe that's the reason for the magnitude of this investigation surrounding their disappearance, Susan."

Susan stared at Michael.

"Jim Brescoll," she said.

Darla saw Michael nod—almost reluctantly, it seemed to her.

"You mentioned that name before. Who's Jim Brescoll?"

"Mister NSA," Susan said. "He helped get us tangled up in all this. It's time he helped untangle things. We need to meet with him, ASAP. No excuses. Maybe he should attend your uncle's memorial service, Michael. There's a chance he can help us—and protect you, Darla, if you *do* become a target. Even if he couldn't help Paul and the children."

THE EGG IN THE SNAKE OF NIGHT

Joe Retticker turned off the road before Shanksville and headed toward his farm in the Pennsylvania hill country. As he drove he thought back to when he'd originally purchased this property—over a decade ago, during the mini-land-boom occasioned by the patriotism of those who remembered the most often forgotten of the 9/11/01 sites, and what had happened here.

He couldn't fault local real estate interests for cashing in, he supposed. At least such land purchases around this memorial site required a little more effort than so much of the other patriotic profit-taking of the time. He remembered the magnet-sticker "ribbons" slapped on vehicles everywhere in those days, common as Hakenkreuzes in Hitler's Deutschland.

Heretical and insubordinate to think such thoughts, no doubt, but with their public professions of faith and gaudy shows of patriotism, people like George Otis had always rather irked him. They'd used the fundamentalist religious hijackings of that long-ago September day to hijack the entire country. Otis, with the corpse of his terrorist-martyred nephew to drag (metaphorically, at least) into every political fray, had proved adept at positioning himself and his ilk as the new crew on the flight deck. They seemed always to be counseling their fellow citizen-passengers to trust them, to raise no ruckus, as they redirected the nation toward a previously unscheduled destination.

Stopping between the farmhouse and the barn, Retticker exhaled. He sometimes thought freedom from fear was the great idol to which his fellow countrymen would gladly sacrifice all other freedoms, no matter how hard-won. Maybe he would, too, if it came to that. Maybe it already had. Maybe *he* already had.

He opened the door, stepping out of the car and into the humidity, cricket noise, and frog sounds of an early summer night. He checked his watch, then walked toward the field from which, Doctor Vang's message had indicated, he would be picked up five minutes from now.

Walking through the night-damp grass, Retticker supposed he had more reason than ever to be annoyed with Otis. More personal reasons, too. The chasm between the path he was following and the course Otis was following had become too large to ignore. So large, in fact, that Vang himself had called for this summit.

Retticker had to admit he'd always been rather impressed with Doctor Vang, even though they'd never met in the flesh. That man was a true survivor. After serving as a CIA soldier and outlasting the collapse of the American-backed governments in Vietnam, Laos, and Cambodia, Vang had escaped from the Cambodian killing fields and, with other Hmong, emigrated to California. Overcoming profound culture shock, Vang had gone on to create such companies as the specialty supercomputer firm ParaLogics. With Crystal Memory Dynamics (another Vang spinoff), PL jointly developed chameleon-cloth "smartskin," among other products. Retticker knew that stuff, which—as the next level of stealth technology—had turned out to have all sorts of applications in the spy biz.

Since semi-retiring from his firms, Vang had headed up Tetragrammaton. Although he had taken a major hit in that capacity during the Kwok-Cho debacle, Vang was still very much a force to be reckoned with. Despite everything, Retticker had not for a moment counted the man out.

Hearing no sound of an approaching helicopter or ground vehicle yet, he checked his watch. He was at the right place at the right time. Where was his transport?

Scanning the heavens more carefully, he almost didn't notice the change. The distortion of the constellations in the night sky was subtle, but it was there. A piece of the sky was rippling toward him, reminding him oddly of something he'd seen as a boy: the peristaltic movement of an egg through the body of the black snake that had swallowed that egg moments earlier.

Retticker didn't hear the droning whisper of engines until the craft was directly above him. The "egg" of night sky burst in spotlight onto him, but only long enough for him to find the handrail of a gangway as it lowered toward him. Even as Retticker was still climbing into the belly of the stealth airship hovering above him, that same gangway began to close.

Fantastic! An uninformed observer, watching him climb a stairway of light into otherwise uninterrupted night, might have been excused for thinking of angelic visions or alien abductions. Retticker knew better. It was not his particular bailiwick, but he'd heard scuttlebutt, over the years, that several of Vang's companies were involved in building an invisiblimp or two. Or, more accurately, "prototype invisible dirigibles," since the things indeed had an airframe, as Retticker now saw.

From its superquiet hovering capability on approach, he suspected it was propelled by a wind-duction system. Solar electric engines, too—virtually no infrared signature. The way the craft had blended so perfectly into the night sky suggested the protective coloration and fast-reactive camouflage of smartskin—lightweight, body-armor-grade polyethylene fibers, incorporating vast numbers of computerized pixel-nodes.

Probably several thousand square meters' worth of interwoven photovoltaic film on the upper exterior, too, to power the electric chameleon skin of the camouflage system, along with the engines. True stealth would mean its structure probably both absorbed *and* bounced radar away tangentially, if the rumors he had heard about this airship were true.

His eyes still adjusting to the light, he stepped into a space of dark wood inlaid with mother-of-pearl, like the cabin of a spacious yacht.

"Joe Retticker, I presume?" asked a small Asian man in a very neat suit, coming forward to shake his hand. The man looked to be in his seventies, perhaps, but very spry.

"Doctor Vang! Nice airship you've got here."

"Thank you," the dapper old man said, steering him toward an elliptically shaped wet bar in the center of the room. "I'm quite proud of it. The only one of its kind with these particular amenities."

"Wonderfully stealthy," said a voice, "but not stealthy enough to avoid coming up on Congress's radar. I tried to save it for you, Doc, but . . ."

"Cuts to the black budget killed it before it could go into production," Vang said. "I exercised the option of purchasing the two extant prototypes. You know George Otis, I presume?"

Retticker nodded, shaking hands with Otis and Vang before taking a seat near them, facing the wet bar. The mirror-backed pedestal supporting the bar encased a saltwater aquarium. Amid a living coral reef, dotted with anemones and sea fans, he saw crabs and shrimp moving. Slow-jawed eels poked their heads from hollows in the rock matrix, while fish of piercing blues and yellows and greens and reds darted about—all going on about their lives, oblivious to the fact that their "ocean" was floating in the sky.

"This craft was based on the same technologies as those developed for stratellites," Vang said, when they were all seated. Retticker nodded. He was familiar with stratospheric satellite airships, hovering antennas for wireless communications.

"We went quite a bit beyond those in developing the military version, though. For aerodynamic flight and aerostatic float, we improved many of the features of the legendary deltoid Aereon. Inside this craft, I can still imagine a world where solar-powered airships stand at duty stations in the stratosphere, patiently waiting for the call to come in low and slow and linger over targets of interest."

"In ways true satellites, orbiting fast and high, never could," Retticker said, nodding.

Above the bar, surveillance monitors cycled slowly through views fore and aft, port and starboard, dorsal and ventral.

"Maybe in the same parallel universe where Howard Hughes built dozens of Hercules airlifters," Otis said with a wry smile, "and not just one *Spruce Goose*! Not in our world, I'm afraid, Doc. That bird has flown."

Vang smiled politely, even indulgently. They made polite small talk for a few moments more, but eventually could no longer avoid the real reason for the meeting.

"Doctor Vang, I'm concerned that we've been working at cross-purposes," Retticker began. "Darla Pittman accused me of the assault on her lab. I was able to deflect her suspicions, but the damage was done. I've lost one of my most valuable researchers. It's miracle enough that she survived the attack, but now she seems also to have vanished. We're having a hell of a time finding her."

"We *have* been working at cross-purposes, General," Otis acknowledged. "It was my people who launched that assault, but it was *you* who necessitated it. I have reason to believe you have not been entirely forthcoming with the results of the good doctor's experiments."

"I wasn't aware that I was under any obligation to share that information, given that it was 'my people,' as you say, who obtained that stuff in the first place," Retticker said, trying to keep his voice from betraying the anger he felt. "And your impatience—was it worth almost killing the chief investigator for that?"

"An unexpected complication," Otis said with a shrug.

"And what about my troops that yours wounded and killed, at Larkin's Lake Tahoe compound? And Larkin himself dead, too?"

"Not my intent. Larkin offed himself before my people could reach him. I thought what turned out to be your troops were sent by James Brescoll at NSA. We were on alert for that possibility—especially after Brescoll's CSS people got to the rest of that tepui rock before we could."

"That was an oversight indeed," Vang said, quietly, yet with all the weight breaking his silence gave to the few words he did speak. "Even worse than losing Larkin."

"Now Jeremy Michelson's disappeared from Fort Mead," Retticker said, "along with much of his telemorphy gear—"

"Of his own free will," Otis countered. "Doctor Michelson is with us, and safe. As those children also need to be. They need to be gotten out of the country, for safekeeping, before your friend Brescoll or one of his comrades gets hold of them."

"Brescoll is no friend of mine, and you know it."

"No, General? Then why haven't you taken Susan Yamada and Michael Miskulin out of the picture? And why have you not dealt with Major Vasques, that traitor in your midst? In spilling the beans to NSA and Brescoll, he's betrayed us all."

"He'll be dealt with."

"Soon, let's hope. I beg your forgiveness, General Retticker, if I have acted in ways that seemed impatient or overhasty, but God's Plan delayed is God's Plan denied. You see, I *pay* Fremdkunst for his meteorite obsession. I'm not all that interested in the things, beyond their role as holy objects to be stolen or destroyed so that the Plan's final holy war may begin. But those children—those young survivors—are part of the divine plan, I'm sure of it."

"Not all of us have as much insight into God's plans as you do, Mister Otis," Vang said pleasantly, "but I'm sure we all agree on the need for dealing with Vasques and safeguarding those children. You have indicated that Michelson is safely relocated to the Wabar digs in the Saudi Empty Quarter. Might the children be kept there, too, perhaps? Under Mister Fremdkunst's watchful eyes, and away from the prying eyes of others?"

Otis nodded slowly, but both he and Retticker looked to Vang, waiting for him to continue.

"I also gather that Doctor Michelson wishes to involve those children in his research, as well," Vang said slowly. "The survivors from Caracamuni tepui are currently in General Retticker's custody and protection. I will place this airship and its crew at General Retticker's disposal. I believe it might be to his advantage, and all of ours, that those children be moved to the desert. This craft has already been modified for desert conditions. It is only lightly armed—a few air-to-air, air-to-ground, and antiradar missiles—but that should prove sufficient so long as he doesn't try taking on anyone's air armada."

Retticker smiled, and nodded in cautious agreement.

"Airship and crew should be more than adequate for delivering those children and seeing to it that they are looked after. With the additional protection of guards—of course also appointed by General Retticker."

In response to a questioning glance from Vang, Retticker nodded for him to go on.

"I think it wise those guards not be informed of their destination," Vang continued, "and that they be thoroughly bodyscanned before departure. Perhaps one of those guards should be Major Vasques. Perhaps he should go missing in the desert."

No one debated those points. With some reluctance, Retticker and Otis agreed, Otis's plans and Retticker's own taking on the shapes suggested by Vang. By the time they had hammered out the logistics, the stealth airship was hovering over the drop-off point for Otis—above Fremdkunst's boat *Skyminer*, Retticker saw, from the forward and ventral cameras.

Bidding them farewell and wishing Joe luck in the Saudi desert, the political power-broker disappeared from Vang's ghostly airship, headed for the meteorite hunter's waiting boat. After commenting that he needed to confer with his crew, Vang himself disappeared, leaving Retticker behind to contemplate all that had transpired.

Retticker guessed they were about halfway back to his farm in the Pennsylvania hill country when Vang came back, to find him staring absently at the ice-cube dregs of the drink in his hand.

"You seem pensive, Joseph," Vang said, taking a seat. "What's on your mind?"

Retticker looked up at him.

"Doctor Vang, I thought the Instrumentality and Tetragrammaton were always about the long-term survival of the human species."

"True," Vang said with a barely perceptible nod. "Despite some of the wrong turns—the obsession with the posthuman, with creating a man-machine information density singularity, faster-than-light travel, all that. All we've ever tried to do, really, is make people *pay attention*. Not only to the danger evolution programmed us to see in the hungry polar bear, but also to the subtler danger in the glacier slowly melting behind that bear. To cure our shortsightedness, and so prevent our un-intended suicide."

"So how can you work with Otis? You don't really believe his 'apocalypse delayed is apocalypse denied' crap, do you?"

Vang looked away, seeming to find something of particular interest on the parquet floor of the invisible dirigible's mezzanine.

"No, I don't. We may, however, have some overlap in our goals. You see, in focusing only on the survival of the human species, we might all have been thinking too narrowly."

"What do you mean?"

As the surveillance monitors chronicled the rest of their journey back toward Retticker's farm, Vang explained. He had been tipped to the idea by Yuri Semenov, the agent he had keeping an eye on Fremd-kunst.

Vang told Retticker of Semenov's theories about bolides and nuclear blasts. About heat-shock proteins, Tunguska, and evolutionary capaci-tors. About the great mass extinctions caused by the impact of celestial bodies upon the earth, and of earth itself as a palimpsest planet. About the enormity of the calamity required to make the lightning "jump the gap" from evolution's capacitors. About the hubris of the human race, taking the prerogative of falling stars to itself. And about humanity's shortcomings in that starring role, in which the Great Actor, Man, had forced so many other species off life's stage.

"This death of a thousand small cuts," Vang said, "this slow frog-boil of global climate change—a few extinctions here, a few extinctions there, every day—it's a short-circuiting of what's meant to happen."

Retticker put his empty glass aside and stared at the busy silent life of the wet bar's aquarium. The extravagance of such an ostentatious display tank, aboard a stealth airship, struck him again for a moment, then was gone.

"Not much to be done about that," Retticker said. "My experts tell me that, when it comes to impactors from space, the rule is 'the bigger they are, the less often they fall.' "

"That's right. We can't look to the skies alone to salvage our situation. Things cannot go on as they have, however. Humanity in the early decades of the twenty-first century has steadily failed to come to grips with our four horsemen."

" 'Four Horsemen'? That sounds too much like George Otis talking."

"Different horsemen: oil, population, economics, and climate. Global petroleum production is past peak and spiraling ever more rapidly downward. Simultaneously, global human population, global economic scale, and global climate change are all still ramping up. Not a good synergy. George Otis's more traditional horsemen—War, Pestilence, Famine, Death—are more likely to come riding onto the scene than ever before."

"I thought human population growth was slowing."

Vang nodded, but not happily or enthusiastically.

"Our rate of increase is slowly decreasing. But the number of people on this planet is still growing in absolute terms."

Vang paused, struck by a thought.

"Hmm. What an odd idea!"

"What's that?"

"George Otis, thinking he's doing heaven's will, might inadvertently be helping evolution to proceed in the manner to which it has long been accustomed."

"How so?"

"Armageddon, apocalypse, rapture. Did you ever consider that that whole belief system, for all its obvious selfishness, is, perhaps unconsciously, an unselfish call for us to liberate the planet—by destroying ourselves?"

An extreme idea, Retticker thought. And yet Vang entertained it so serenely.

"No, I hadn't considered it, actually. I suppose a total spasm nuclear war would be a pretty good substitute for a five-mile-wide mountain falling from the sky, though."

"Yes. Such a full-bore Armageddon is, I should think, quite capable of sparking the lightning from evolution's capacitors."

Retticker looked fixedly at Vang as the implications of what the well-dressed elderly man had been saying fully dawned on him.

"We have to destroy the world in order to save it?"

"Yes," Vang said with a shy nod. "Politics, biblical prophecy, and the punctuated equilibrium theory of evolution all seem to converge on that."

Retticker shook his head.

"That's crazy. No one really wants that to happen, aside from people like Otis."

Vang gave him an enigmatic smile.

"It well *might* happen, whether you or I want it to, or not. That's why I want you to keep a very close eye on those Mawari children for me, Joseph. Where are you keeping them, if you don't mind my asking?"

"They're under guard at the farmhouse."

Vang looked up at the cycling screens.

"To which we have almost returned. Good."

"Those kids are somehow involved in all this doomsday stuff?"

"I'm not certain they are—and it's the uncertainty that bothers me. I have reason to believe those survivors possess the potential to become wild cards, human singularities. 'Transcendant persons,' for good or ill. I'd very much like to reap the many benefits from their potential capabilities, so we will let Otis's and Michelson's plans go forward, for now."

"They are just children, after all," Retticker said as he recognized his own land and farmhouse now appearing before and below them on the screens.

"Yes. And every mass murderer was a child once, too." Vang shook his head. "The Kwok-Cho affair considerably dampened my enthusiasm for singular and unpredictable people. I don't mean to be alarmist, but should there come a time when those young people seem inclined to terminate all of us, it might be wise to terminate them first, Joseph. I'm trusting you to make that admittedly tragic decision, if it needs to be made. I leave that, and this ship, in your hands."

Part of the floor forward of them began to drop down as it transformed itself into a gangway. Retticker descended the gangway and at last stood once more on the night-damp ground. Above him, the gangway became part of the stealthy airship again.

Retticker expected to see the distortion move slowly away through the sky—the invisible egg moving in subtle contraction through the belly of the blacksnake night—but it did not. He was surprised to see Vang standing on the ground beside him.

The slight, older man gave a brief wave of his hand and walked off into the night. So much still left unsaid, he thought, but Vang was obviously not interested in further discussion. Turning, Joe headed toward the house, to gather up the children and their guards, and to notify other troops of their sudden duty, before all of them boarded a mobile piece of the night and headed to a desert far away.

REMEMBERED UNIVERSES

One good thing about holding meetings in the office here at NSA headquarters, Jim Brescoll thought: passing through all the security to get here always impressed his visitors, especially new ones like Yamada, Pittman, and Miskulin. Dan Amaral, however—walking slightly ahead of them—had a talent for quickly growing jaded about almost anything.

Some of that security those visitors could not help but notice. Despite all the well-wishing from his wife and his all-too-grown kids, despite the good thoughts from his staff (including the hilarious self-penned "get well" poem from Amaral), despite even the ass-chewing DNI Watson had given him (especially when he'd insisted on traveling to California for Larkin's memorial almost as soon as he was back on the job)—despite it all, Jim was glad to be out of the hospital and back to work.

So glad that he had noticed the security precautions again himself, as if for the first time: the restricted Fort Meade exit ramp, with its heavy earthen berms and graceful tangle of security hardscape—strategically placed landscape boulders, barbed-wire perimeter fences, and cement barriers beneath the canopy of old oak trees. The personally coded magnetic passkeys, the matching fingerprint and retina scans, the new DNA and facial recognition biometrics—all of that could not help but make an impact, too, even if his guests didn't know about the strategically placed antitruck hydraulics, telephoto surveillance cameras, motion detectors, and eight hundred uniformed police of Crypto City's own law enforcement authority.

Jim thought that the sheer size of the secret city must still impress, if not intimidate, them. The supercomputer labs and living quarters, offices and anechoic chambers, factories and 10K-clean rooms. The more than three hundred acres of parking space for forty thousand employees. All those people, working in a restricted-access world with its own post office, fire department, encrypted television network, university, banks, libraries, drugstores, barbershops, fast-food joints, and waste disposal and recycling services. The mere fact of all that had to have an effect, even if not necessarily a conscious one.

No wonder then that when Miskulin, Pittman, and Yamada first entered the confines of his office, with its heavy antique furnishings, they seemed a bit overawed by it all, culture-shocked to quiet, if not silence.

That didn't last, of course. It never did. Especially after he pushed the button that made the pseudoholo console rise out of his desktop, its volumetric display-dome looking like half a crystal ball. He handed each of his visitors a piece of cutting-edge networking gear that took the form of a very specialized ring. Cameras in the room tracked each ring, allowing the wearers to select and manipulate apparently three-dimensional objects via natural hand gestures, even dragging objects by moving their fingers across the surface of the display-dome. His visitors took to the tech with alacrity.

Upon hearing and seeing Pittman and Miskulin's description of what these meteorite thefts were all apparently geared toward, and seeing the computer-generated "phoenix phenotype" reconstruction of Miskulin's "metaphage" they'd brought with them and displayed on the dome, Jim found that he was not happy.

"After all that happened during the Kwok-Cho affair," he told them, by way of explanation, "I am not fond of things that can rise from their own ashes."

The blank looks they gave him forced him to explain. Trying, with the aid of the display-dome, to provide the background as concisely as he could, he explained the convoluted history of the particular living-fossil program Kwok had discovered. The running of that living-fossil program, however, had to await Jaron Kwok's own hookup to the worldwide computershare. Simultaneous with the running of a simulated quantum-computing version of said program, Kwok unfortunately appeared to have spontaneously combusted, a holocaust that left only peculiar ashes behind.

"Out of those supposed ashes, however," Jim Brescoll said, blanking from the display-dome the graphics with which he'd underlined his tale, "a quantum binotech arose—one that became fully activated when exposed to the life's blood and genetics of Ben Cho, Kwok's phenotypically distinct but genotypically identical twin. And from that came Ben Cho's Metaquantum Apotheosis, near-armageddon between the United States and China, the force-field blisterdomes of the so-called MAXXs. That's why I'm not fond of anything playing the phoenix."

His office guests understood his aversion to phoenixes well enough, but he still had to explain to them how it was Cho had disappeared and the domes had arisen, almost simultaneously. That required another volumetric display program, one speculative enough to remind Jim of the NASA animations of his childhood, even as he showed it to his guests.

The little three-dimensional movie he played for them showed how, upon Cho's apotheosis, the Kwok-Cho binotech—the only traces remaining of its namesake originals—had apparently aerosolized into smart-dust and mote machines. Self-propelled, those smart-dust motes had converged toward the Sun Yat-sen Memorial Hall, the power station inside the California mountain, and several locations in the South American Tri-Border area.

In those places the mote-machines had created the domes of impenetrable force. In accordance with the cover story agreed to among those in the know and in power, the name of Mutual Assured Quantum Cryptologic Security Stations, or MAXXs, had been given to the enigmatic domes. No one quite knew how the dust mechanisms had built the things, or how they managed to keep those fields powered up. Explanations ranged from solar energy to reversed flux patches in the earth's magnetic field, created or exploited by the innumerable tiny machines.

"For all we really understand what's going on beneath them," Brescoll told them, "those sites might just as well be marked 'Here There Be Dragons.' That applies to my knowledge, too, not least of all, even though I have the dubious distinction of being the only person known to have come out again after going inside one of those domes."

His guests asked him, then, to tell them the story of his experiences under the dome in California. He found it awkward to do so. Not just because he had no fancy volumetric graphics to help him, or because he had some difficulty remembering all of it, though much of it *had* come back to him while he was in the hospital. Not even because he hated reliving his life in voice-over narration. No, the main reason for the awkwardness was because it was just so damned weird.

How to explain the way LeMoyne, Benson, and Markham had tranformed themselves? How to explain the way the three posthumans had literally played with his mind—even with the very Rip van Winkle bowling idea Dan Amaral had put in his head?

With all the vividness of overwhelming flashback, their mindgame hit him again.

One of them tosses a black ball toward white pins down an ordinary lane in an indoor alley, but the scene transforms, becomes a white bowling ball rolling down a desert bowling lane under blue sky toward pins like black monoliths arranged first in the World War II Memorial round but then morphing into the traditional wedge pin-set.

Time after time the ball grows to the blazing white of desert sun. Each time it hits the pins, however, the white sunbright bowling ball shatters as if made out of glass or pottery—or, as if actually made of rubber or plastic, bounces off the monolithic pins, themselves steadfast and unmovable as the pillars of eternity.

Those bizarre bowlers, laughing as they gamed him with their bowling variations, again and again. He shook his head. As he looked, LeMoyne, Benson, and Markham morphed into another group of two women and a man—Pittman, Yamada, and Miskulin, gazing at him expectantly.

How to explain the way such bowling then spun about the "bowlers" to become parallel worldlines like images on a kaleidoscopic roulette wheel? Or the fact that one after another they blasted Jim into those alternate worldlines by pointing at him, in surreal pistol fashion, what looked like a chambered nautilus, but packed a hell of a kick?

So strange was his experience with those three that he almost felt himself on surer ground telling his visitors about the alternate worldlines he had experienced, to which story he now gave his best effort.

Fortunately, he got unexpected support in that telling. Hearing Jim relate his experience of a universe in which a damaged mirror-ball ship of strange glowing angels sacrificed itself to crash meteoritically to earth, and other meteorites from it crashed in various pieces over time, again and again, Michael Miskulin, in particular, seemed quite pleased.

"Like Paul and Jacinta said! A ship whose crashed, stone-dormant remains left behind—in a few marginal, shielded places—something like the original strain of the metaphage."

"We think moderately pure strains of that might have hung on at the great parietal art caves," Susan Yamada added. "In Franco-Cantabria— the ceremonial centers of Altamira, Lascaux, Tito Bustillo, El Castillo, Cuevo del Juyo, and the rest."

"It was probably later, newer meteoritic falls," Pittman suggested, "of more or less intact material, that have been stumbled upon by others in deserts, seas, forests, and icefields throughout the world."

"But we think that material remained most fully intact, for the longest duration, inside a cave, inside a tepui, where it invaded a humble fungus and became sacred to the people who, much later, ate it and 'joined' with it. My aunt's notes on 'full myconeural symbiosis,' on 'mindtime' and 'quartz of a particular lattice configuration'—all in preparation for that time when the people of the tepui would 'sing their mountain to the stars'—it all fits."

"I don't know if 'it' all 'fits,' " Brescoll said, "but in one of the alternate timelines I experienced, the Caracamuni tepui slipped free of the earth and sidestepped through the fabric of the sky. Maybe it did go to the stars, there."

Miskulin seemed to find that strange idea profoundly vindicating.

"Something else, too," Jim said, a bit sheepish, wondering what his visitors might make of further talk of parallel universes. "One of the worldlines I encountered was warped by something extracted from the spore print Paul Larkin leaked to that world. Something called a supertryptamine. In one line, at least, it seemed to be involved in a madness pandemic that came close to wiping out all humanity."

"I've been someplace very much like there!" Pittman said. "Or at least to 'some other there' that also had these supertryptamines. During the attack on my lab I told you about. When I almost got killed, but the metaphage intervened, I guess. Brought me back from Death's country, where I saw one of those supertryptamine worlds, too."

"Do you know how lucky you are?" Jim Brescoll asked. "Not just that you survived and returned to health so quickly—almost miraculous on the face of it—but that this thing you were exposed to saved you, rather than killed you itself? Or turned you into some kind of monster?"

"Monster?" Pittman asked, sounding nervous. "How?"

Jim sympathized. Still, Darla Pittman presumably had that metaphage stuff—if that's what it was—running around inside her even now. It didn't appear to be contagious, but it might be best to plan for as many scenarios as possible.

"Think about it, Doctor. You've been stitching together pieces of ancient dead meteoritic code material, hoping you can get it to reanimate. That sound like the work of any famous monster-maker to you?"

"Frankenstein," Pittman said levelly.

"Exactly. What's to say that this phoenix phenotype couldn't just as easily have turned into a Frankenstein phenotype? You're damned lucky."

"Maybe we ought to call the rocks from space we've been working with 'Frankenstones,' " Miskulin joked.

"Actually, that doesn't sound like a bad name for the rock we pulled off that plateau," Jim said.

"It's gone from the tepui, then?" Susan Yamada asked.

Jim nodded. Sending CSS troops to drag that rock out of its cave, then helo it to an airport and cargo-plane it out of South America—that was about the *only* thing they'd done right since he came back from his Rip van Winkle time beneath the dome.

"And I'm glad we've got it quarantined, too—just in case."

"How did you know to move on it?" Miskulin asked.

"We knew its location from a soldier who was in the task force Retticker sent against the tepui. Apparently that officer was not happy with the way things went, down there, and he came to us. The possible futures I saw while I was under the California dome convinced me we needed to control the tepui stone, the spore print for the Mawari's sacred fungus, and the surviving Mawari kids themselves."

"We're far too late, in the case of the spore print," Pittman said. "General Retticker got me a sample of it months ago—"

"Presumably from the same spore print my uncle let Vang get his hands on," Miskulin said quietly.

"And as for the kids," Yamada said, "the fact that they've already been abducted is the major reason we're here talking to you right now."

"Those futures you say you saw," Michael said, "what role did the kids have in them?"

More secret information—all that Tetragrammaton stuff, Jim thought. Reluctantly he accessed the background material and brought it up on the display-dome, going into voice-over mode for them. Only with such background would he be able to explain to them the Tetragrammaton people and their projects and programs.

He showed them the reality of exaptation and the latent talents the Tetra types thought might be hidden in childhood's imaginary friends and fairy lands. The reason for all their secret work with inducing schizoidal, schizophrenic, multiple personality, and dissociative identity disorders—in order to "force," like a hothouse bloom, the appearance of the next stage of human evolution: the exapted "split kids," able to access capabilities latent in DNA for the great leap forward—their strange powers born from the inducing of inhuman trauma and deep suffering, in hopes of unleashing something superhuman from them.

"I'm not sure how all that will fit in with Mawari, mushrooms, and meteorites," Jim said, "but from all I can remember, I'm sure it will."

He saw Pittman and Yamada glance at each other, almost as if deciding which of them should speak first.

"I think we might have an idea," Pittman said, then launched, with occasional help from Miskulin and Yamada, into a description of the myconeural complex, the raphe nuclei, and most importantly the prolonged neoteny of the Mawari's pineal glands—and the vastly reduced need for speech among that people from puberty onward, at least according to the Larkins' notes.

"If you'd wanted to traumatize those kids," Susan Yamada said, "you probably couldn't have planned it better."

"How so?" Jim asked.

"Massacring all their people. Kicking them out into a world thousands of years into their technological future."

Jim steepled his fingers, inadvertently freeze-framing the display-dome, and pondered that.

"But I don't think this possible outcome was planned," he said at last. "If you're right, and the very 'split kids' that the Tetragrammaton crew were after are even now being somehow inadvertently realized, then it could be real trouble. It could have global repercussions. We were smart to treat their abduction as a matter of grave importance."

"But how could it have 'global repercussions'?" Susan asked. "And if they're so important, why haven't you found them?"

"This agency is doing everything it can to find them, I assure you," Jim said. "Checkpoint watchlists with Customs services worldwide. Satellite tracking of ships and aircraft, monitoring of international telecommunication of every type."

"Datamining for anything in any medium that might apply to them," Amaral put in. "A general bulletin to all humint—human intelligence—resources throughout the intelligence community. Throughout the world."

"But the world is a big place to disappear into," Jim said.

"We've been using the same methods," Amaral added, "to try to

pin down the location of someone you may have encountered, a meteoriticist named Avram Zaragosa. We know he popped up for the big
conference in Dubai, and then later in Riyadh. We presume he's somewhere in the Middle East even now. We just haven't pinned down the
exact location."

"But we will," Jim said. "For him, and the children both."

"And the global repercussions you mentioned?" Miskulin asked.

"I don't know exactly how those repercussions might be felt," Jim
admitted. "We suspect George Otis might be involved with what has
happened to the Mawari kids. Perhaps even more than Doctor Vang.
And Otis is a global player with some rather idiosyncratic beliefs."

"Otis?" Susan Yamada said, revulsion in her voice.

"Sanctimonious hypocrite and phony patriot," Amaral said, a bit
too fervently. "Doesn't deny God or Country when it pays, but an undeniable dog to both when it suits."

"I don't know about that," Jim said, smiling awkwardly despite
himself. "From our investigation, however, we're fairly certain that at
least some of the people who attacked Larkin's compound were connected to Otis's Military Executive Resource Corp."

"Why them?" Darla asked.

"Paul Larkin's security chief, Jarrod Takimoto, confirms that some
of the attackers and their modus operandi echoed an earlier attempt on
Larkin and the kids. Came in sterile, same body armor and gear, generally."

"Then why hasn't someone been arrested for orchestrating the
whole thing?" Susan asked.

"Not enough solid evidence for arrests or indictments yet. The
wheels of justice grind slowly, as always, but I'm sure the situation will
reach that point. Part of the problem is that the previous attack was
hushed up, on Larkin's own orders. The first time it was foiled in an
unknown fashion, but not this time. We don't know why."

"More unknowns," Miskulin said, shaking his head. "What do we
know about the global picture, if there is one?"

"What I think I know, from my time under the California dome, is
that somehow religious sites throughout the world are involved in all
of this, including the Black Stone of the Kaaba in Mecca."

"Paul showed us a video record of what the kids had been researching in the infosphere," Susan said. "Sacred sites with archaeoastro-
nomical alignments and 'holy stones' came up there, too."

Jim nodded.

"Holy rocks from space, yes. When I manage to recall what happened under the dome, I seem to remember stars shooting across the sky, streaking toward what looked rather like, well, missile launches."

" 'Don't worry,' " Michael Miskulin said, " 'we'll show the stars where to fall.' "

"What?"

"That's what the kids said, to me and to Susan. Said it right inside our heads."

"And?"

"And, in a recording Paul showed us, the kids were looking at star charts and astrogation data for the Apollos and the Atens. Those asteroids move in earth-crossing orbits. . . ."

Amaral looked from one to another of them, skepticism on his face.

"Oh, come on now, you don't really think—" he began, but Jim waved him to silence. Seeing where this might be headed, he placed a conference call to Wang and Lingenfelter.

"Bree? Steve? Good to have you both on the line. I have a favor to ask. I'd like you to get in touch with our W Group people. Have them contact their NASA counterparts to check on current positions for earth-crossing asteroids—and more generally, to get their predictions on meteor shower activity over, say, the next six months."

"That's more than one favor," Bree Lingenfelter said with a laugh.

"More like four or five," Wang confirmed. Nonetheless they quickly agreed and got off the line.

"W Group?" Susan asked.

"Specialists in Global Issues and Weapons Systems. My biggest brain trust."

"How about yourself?" Michael asked. "Anything along those lines in what you saw under the dome—meteors, I mean?"

"Not really," Jim said, then thought again. "Wait . . . yes, there was something. The sound of thunder, followed by stones falling out of the sky."

"Didn't meteorites used to be called 'thunderstones'?" Susan asked.

"Thunder can arise from a meteor's explosive braking in the atmosphere, particularly at the extinction point," Michael said.

"Then the shattered remnants of the stone fall to earth at gravitational-field speed, rather than cosmic velocities," Darla said, nodding.

"But some of what I saw looked like big bolts of lightning," Jim said, "and there were these light-show effects, like a big thunderstorm viewed from space."

" 'Elves' and 'sprites' would be my guess," Miskulin said.

"And mushroom clouds?" Jim asked. "When is a shooting star like a thunderstone and a mushroom cloud?"

That riddle seemed to stymie his visitors for a while, although "stymied" for them took the form of Miskulin and Pittman arguing about bolides and "Peter Pan pineal glands"—Miskulin's phrase—while Yamada and Jim looked on. Brescoll called a halt to it at last.

"We're not going to solve it all today. I don't know how these kids and their pineal glands will fit in with what might happen, but we'll keep looking for them. In the meantime, we've already got more than enough going on with these damned 'holy rocks.' "

He saw the others looking at him questioningly, even if they said nothing.

"We've got one full-blown world crisis going on because of what happened at the Dome of the Rock, remember? We certainly don't want anything similar to the Dome of the Rock incident playing out in Mecca during the Hajj. That could spiral completely out of control. It hasn't escaped our notice that there's a strong possible meteorite connection to the Great Mosque and the Kaaba. You're my best experts on that, too. I need to have all of you available at a moment's notice."

His visitors agreed, leaving with him their contact info as they took their leave of his office. As she was leaving, Darla Pittman turned to Brescoll.

"Thanks for the protection, Director," she said. "It's been hard, being AWOL from the lab, but I still have some connections there. Seems that my postdoc, Barry Levitch, has taken a sudden leave from the Rocky Mountain Labs. He's spirited away a good deal of my research material in the process. I may have trusted him too much. He's privy to the whole metaphage concept, I'm afraid."

"We'll look into his disappearance then, too," he assured her. "And I wouldn't worry so much about retaliation from Retticker. He's a good deal smoother than you might guess. Nothing too obvious or high profile."

After Dan Amaral ushered the last of the visitors out, Jim absently pushed the button that caused the volumetric display-dome to descend into his desktop and disappear. As he watched it go, Jim Brescoll wished he could make other domes, and their associated problems, disappear as easily, especially after he began scanning private and public information sources on his computer.

"Much of the Muslim world is in 'military exercises' mode," one of Amaral's field people said in a video report. "Syria's war-gaming the Dome crisis for 'geopolitical counterbalance to Israeli hegemony,' as the analysts put it."

"Iran has found the current situation to be well suited for playing along the older Sunni-Shia divide," said one of his own field observers, in a recorded picturephone message. "Behind the scenes the Iranian government is leading the chorus of doubters questioning Saudi competence in providing security for the Kaaba and the Great Mosque. The Shia are calling for a pan-Islamic multinational force to take over security duties in Mecca for the upcoming Hajj—something the Saudis have rejected, rightly viewing it as a threat to their sovereignty."

The datamining digest he'd had his techs set up—to search for anything involving thefts and meteorites—flagged his e-mail with a notice about thefts of relic spearheads from a museum in Austria and a church in Rome. Failing to see the relevance, Jim rolled his eyes and shut off the system.

"Well, Mister Fahrney," Jim said, addressing the air, "what do you think?"

An apple-cheeked, gray-haired, bouncily energetic little man emerged from a door leading into the hallway beyond Brescoll's office suite. From the cherubic smile on the billionaire's face, it was clear that he'd relished eavesdropping on the meeting. The man with the clout, his ace in the hole. Jim had called him in again, into his role as secret adviser.

"Well done, Director Brescoll. I think those three are going to prove extremely important in this matter. I also think they as yet have very little idea how important they are. Make straight the way for them, by all means!"

COVER STORIES

"You've got to answer us this time, Victor," Vida said, confronting the meteorite hunter in the original Wabar modulab. Avram and Yuri were in tow, albeit somewhat reluctantly. "You can't just put us off with a whiff of weird stuff from the Temple Mount and a lot of speculating about alchemists and Kabbalists and Templar knights. Not this time."

"Put you off about what, Vida?"

"These modulabs, and what the new people are doing here. The troops standing guard. That telepresence researcher, Michelson. And some guy who looked doped up. And now those four kids. I saw them come in—even if they did show up in the middle of the night, smuggled in aboard some kind of stealth UFO."

" 'Smuggled'?"

"And what's this thing you've got under wraps right here? What're you working on?"

Victor Fremdkunst gave her a quizzical look. On a workbench, surrounded by stone-cutting and polishing equipment, stood a curtain-draped object propped atop a pedestal.

"I'll be happy to show you," he said, walking toward the work-bench. "It's not quite finished, but I certainly wouldn't want you to think I'm 'putting you off.' "

With a flourish, Victor flipped back the draperies. What Avram, Yuri, and Vida saw there made them catch their breath.

It was beautiful. A piece of very mixed skystone, roughly the ellip-tical shape and size of an American football but sliced to incredible thinness. Incandescently shining Neumann lines and Widmanstätten structures—both, in one stone—were cut so as to perfectly highlight their patterns. Beautifully sectioned chondrule spheres shone in it, too: silicated material containing what looked like pyroxenes and olivines, glowing translucently in a rainbow of colors like stained glass from an alien cathedral. All in the same stone.

To Avram it looked as if Piet Mondrian and Jackson Pollock had collaborated on a stone canvas—by way of outer space.

"It's gorgeous," Vida breathed. "I've never seen anything like it."

"Nor had I," Victor said. "Sorry to have been so secretive about it, but I really think this will be my masterpiece. I guess it's time you found out about this tepui stone and its provenance, hmm? That history should answer most of your other questions, too, Vida. If you'll follow me to the most recently arrived of the modulabs, please. . . ."

They followed Victor to the door. Bracing themselves against the oven-blast of desert heat, they made the short but brutal walk to the newest modulab, without environment suits, through an afternoon breeze tasting of dusty iron, blowing out of the Empty Quarter.

Once indoors again, Avram, Vida, and Yuri caught their breath in the relative coolness of the new lab. Victor Fremdkunst introduced them to Joseph Retticker, Doctor Jeremy Michelson, and Doctor Barry Levitch.

His handshake as hard and firm as his gaze, his white hair and mustache trimmed to within a fraction of an inch of nonexistence, Retticker seemed always to be standing at attention. Michelson, however, shook their hands perfunctorily—a tall beak-nosed man with faraway eyes behind owlish ARGUS blinks, his face framed by unkempt, thinning red hair above shoulders hunched and stooped, as if he were embarrassed at his own height. Levitch, intermediate in height between the other two men, wore a heavy mountain-man beard, perhaps in hopes of distracting attention from his prematurely shiny-bald pate.

"Joseph," Victor said after everyone had been introduced all around, "our senior researchers here want to know about the history of the tepui stone and the young people you brought in. Think you might be able to bring them up to speed on all that?"

"With a little help from my friends here, I think we can do that," Retticker said, launching into a history that Avram found surprisingly detailed.

"Jacinta Larkin's discovery of the 'ghost people' of Caracamuni tepui, the mushroom-totemist Mawari," Retticker said, "was suppressed for many years by her brother, Paul Larkin. The sadly botched efforts of an expeditionary force dispatched to Caracamuni tepui at first appeared to have resulted in the death of all members of the small Mawari tribe. All were thought to have died during a confused skirmish in the caverns where they lived.

"During that expedition, it was found that the tribe worshipped a unique meteorite that contained extensive nonterrestrial nucleic acid materials. I'll turn things over to Barry Levitch, now. He knows more about the scientific particulars than I do."

"What Darla Pittman and I first thought might be 'space-junk DNA' proved to be anything but junk," Levitch said, before going on to lay out for them the concepts of "phoenix phenotypes" and "metaphage."

"As a result of its interaction with fungi already endemic to the tepui," Levitch explained, "the tepui stone functioned as a sort of sclerotium or mushroom stone—the ultimate source of the totemic mushroom of the Mawari. By piecing together replicating components from the tepui stone with 'space junk' from other meteoritic sources, we think Doctor Pittman managed to produce a more complete version of the metaphage than existed even in the tepui stone itself."

"Unfortunately," Retticker said, jumping in, "the Rocky Mountain Labs, where Doctors Levitch and Pittman worked, were attacked by armed gunmen. Remarkably, Doctor Pittman survived being shot to pieces—a miraculous self-healing, apparently the result of her having been exposed to the metaphage material with which she was working. The experience was nonetheless traumatic, and as a result she is now on extended leave."

"Darla Pittman was trying to grow that material out on media that mixed cerebrospinal fluid, serum, and neuronal tissue," Levitch explained, "in imitation of the myconeural complex the tepui people reportedly developed as a result of ingesting their totemic mushroom."

"Nothing 'reportedly' about it, anymore," Retticker asserted. "From medical professionals who objected to the way their patients were being treated by their 'guardian,' Paul Larkin, we learned that there were in fact four surviving 'ghost people.' In order to protect the children from Larkin's exploitation of them—and from an attack of the sort Darla Pittman had suffered—we sent in a team to remove the children from Larkin's custody. I've brought these same surviving Mawari children here, to work with Doctors Levitch and Michelson."

Levitch and Michelson eagerly described their understanding of the slowly growing myconeural complex, and its effects on the children's raphe nuclei and pineal glands.

"The so-called paranormal or parapsychological abilities attributed to the Mawari, in the legends of their South American neighbors," Michelson said, "are in fact quantum telemorphic effects. What I'm learning from the children is proving to be a breakthrough in neurophysics more important than I ever dreamed."

To underline his point, Michelson led all of them to an observation room at the other end of the modulab, where four undeniably engrossed and preoccupied youngsters, wearing what looked like exotic telepresence gear, appeared to be levitating and manipulating a variety of objects—no hands involved, and no strings attached.

Victor, Avram, Vida, and Yuri at last left Retticker and his colleagues behind, in Michelson's so-called telemorphy lab, observing the children.

"So you see," Victor said, when he and his senior researchers were again alone, "I wasn't just putting you off with that talk of knights and alchemists and Kabbalists, the lapis and the Grail and the Spear."

"Oh?" Vida asked.

"Think how what those gentlemen have described to us—the self-healing in Pittman's case, the paranormal communication and manipulation of matter with the Mawari and these kids—think how much those sound like the powers associated with the Grail and the Spear, or those 'Nuhus' you talked about, Vida. Really think about it, and you'll begin to understand why the temples and sacred cities of a dozen religions grew up around holy skystones."

"I think I see the way this 'metaphage' might have affected human history," Avram said, "and human evolution before that. Even in fragmentary and corrupted form."

"That's why Levitch is here," Victor told them. "To use our collection of sacred stones, of celestial talismans and power objects from around the world. His goal is to make an even more complete version of what Darla Pittman was working on, before she was attacked. To piece together the complete mosaic."

"And Michelson?" Yuri asked.

"He's here because those kids are here. And safe, given all this private security. Obviously, Michelson thinks he can learn a great deal from them, for his research."

"Or exploit them," Vida muttered. Victor pretended not to have heard, and instead took his leave of them, returning to the observation room to confer with Retticker and company. Yuri, Avram, and Vida headed back to their own lab space.

"A plausible cover story," Vida said as they walked through the desert evening. "I don't think it's anywhere near the whole story, though."

"No one ever gets whole story," Yuri said. Avram said nothing. He agreed with both of them.

Later that evening, the cover stories and the stories behind that cover only got more complex. Avram was alone in the yome—Yuri was out drinking with some of the newer arrivals—when a knock sounded at his door. He expected Yuri or perhaps Vida, but when he opened the door, he saw Mahmoud Ankawi standing there, a young man looking serious but content behind his beard and glasses.

Avram invited him in, but they made small talk for only a short while.

"In two days we leave," Ankawi said. "On Hajj."

"But it's still weeks away," Avram said, puzzled. "As I'm sure you know."

"This is the plan, nonetheless. I will serve as your *mutawwif*."

"All the way to Mecca?"

"All the way to Makkah, yes."

Avram gave him a hard look.

"You've been on Hajj before, right?"

"Yes," said Ankawi. "Five years ago I traveled in the sacred districts."

"You know I'm not a Muslim. So why are you helping me?"

"You forget that I am a meteorite hunter, too, Doctor. Amateur, yes, but very enthusiastic. More enthusiastic there, perhaps, than in my religious life. Think what you like."

"The Black Stone . . . you've seen it?"

"Yes. I've heard the stories, too. Ever since childhood. About how the angel Gabriel brought the stone from heaven and gave it to Father Abraham. Or how it was once white, until it turned black from the sins of the world. Some say it was light enough to float on water, others that it was inordinately heavy."

"Or maybe it can alter the gravitational field of the planet . . ." Avram said with a smirk.

"Exactly! I want to know the *scientific* truth about al Hajar al-Aswad—not just rumors and legends. That is what is most important to me."

So that was how Luis Martin and his backers had sold Ankawi on helping him in this adventure, Avram thought. Ankawi's curiosity was so strong that the man was *sure* Avram must share that obsession. It had blinded Ankawi to any other possible reason for Avram's journey. Pathetic, really.

"Not afraid that what I might discover might also damage your faith?"

"If letting you examine the Black Stone *in situ*," Ankawi said thoughtfully, "if that examination, however you're going to do it, uncovers the truth, then I'll be happy, as I said. Other non-Muslims have seen the Black Stone before, after all. Radical Muslims took the Black Stone and the Kaaba itself hostage, too, when they occupied the Great Mosque of Makkah by force—before the Saudi army drove them out by more force. Despite it all, the Black Stone has always survived."

Ankawi gave him a list of the preparations he would need to make for departure, a plausible cover story for his leaving, and a rendezvous point. Soon thereafter the bearded scholar—and betrayer of his faith?—said good-bye and departed, betraying no sense whatsoever that he was doing anything wrong.

THROWING STONES

>>>>>>>

Michael Miskulin was surprised at how quickly NSA director James Brescoll had put them up in D.C.—and even more surprised when he called them to another meeting in his offices, just two days after their first briefing. They met in a conference room off his office suite at NSA headquarters, and this time Brescoll had more of his "brain trust" with him.

Michael, Susan, and Darla were introduced to three of Brescoll's top advisers. They had met one of them—Dan Amaral—before, but not the other two. Tall, redheaded Bree Lingenfelter headed NSA's Communications Research Division and its Laboratory for Physical Sciences, both at the University of Maryland. Steve Wang, a wiry man in ARGUS blinks, was introduced to them as a researcher with Princeton's Institute for Defense Analysis. He also held positions as chief cryptologic linguist and cryptologic computer scientist with NSA's Communications and Computing Center.

"First off," Brescoll began, glancing from time to time at his notes, "let me say that I've tried to get everyone onto the same page on all this. Steve and Bree know nearly as much as I do concerning the Tetragrammaton and Kwok-Cho history, about which Dan here is also now aware. You also have Dan's report on the pattern of telecommunication connections and intercepts that suggests, despite the extensive use of anonymous remailers and throwaway cell phones, that Avigdor Fox and Ismail Hijazi were at least in occasional communication with Victor Fremdkunst and possibly George Otis as well. I've brought Dan, Bree, and Steve up to speed on what you four have told me about the Mawari, mushroom stones, meteorites, metaphages, myconeural complexes, phoenix phenotypes—"

Smiling at the alliteration, he looked up from his list.

"—pineal glands, all that. I'd also like to thank Doctor Pittman for informing us of the disappearance of her postdoctoral researcher, Barry Levitch. An NSA team has been able to reconstruct what he was last working on, from computer records he thought he had destroyed but which we were able to resurrect."

Darla Pittman nodded.

"From examining those reconstructed computer records," she said, "I think it's safe to assume that Barry is planning on extending the metaphage reconstruction work I had already done."

Brescoll nodded, then turned their attention to a related matter.

"Dan here followed up on Levitch's sudden leave-taking."

"Turns out he mentioned—to a young female colleague of his—that he might be going to the Middle East," Amaral said. "Travel and flight information suggests the same general destination for both Levitch and Doctor Jeremy Michelson."

"Who's this Michelson person?" Susan asked. "How does he fit in with what's going on?"

"We're not absolutely sure that he does," Brescoll said. "Steve and Bree here, they think he may have reason to want to work with those Mawari children. I'll let them explain."

Using the volumetric display dome on the conference desk, Wang and Lingenfelter did their show-and-tell. Michelson, they explained, had been peripherally involved in the Kwok-Cho matter as a result of his work in quantum computing and quantum cryptology. His particular work with W Group, before he went out on loan to the Telemorphy Lab at Fort Mead, had involved biological approaches to those same crypto issues, particularly quantum computational properties inherent in DNA.

Like Levitch at Rocky Mountain, Michelson also had tried to destroy the records of his work at Fort Mead by blanking his computers' memories. NSA teams had been able to reconstruct Michelson's data and notes there, too—although with much more difficulty than in Levitch's case.

Lingenfelter and Wang explained to them what "telemorphy" and "neuronal space" and "conjoint consciousness" meant in the context of Michelson's work. The recovered notes and data also suggested why certain nanotrode arrays, computer wave analysis programs, and other pattern-recognition hardware and software went missing with Michelson at his disappearance.

From a search of Michelson's reconstituted records, Wang and Lingenfelter gathered that he had been working on "quantum neuro-cryptography," unbreakable mind-to-mind and mind-to-machine communication, involving quantum teleportation of neuronal space-state configurations—something the bleeding-edge of military experimentation had also been exploring (under a slightly different name) for potential battlefield use. Michelson had also begun work on what he called "quantum telemorphic effects" involving neuronal space-states and manipulation of the fabric of spacetime at the quantum level.

"How would those work?" Susan asked. "What would be the mechanism?"

On the table's volumetric display dome, Wang called up pseudo-holographics illustrating the quantum foam and holographic field distributions, then nodded to Lingenfelter.

"Theoretically," Lingenfelter said, "our brains' cerebral hemispheres are capable of acting as interferometers responding to the presence of scalar waves. The chaotic attractors in the human brain function as a holographic field. The quantum foam, the tiniest possible scale of physical reality, also functions as a holographic field. From that fundamental similarity, Michelson was attempting to exploit a possible deep link between physical states and mental states."

"Not only the quantum foam's scalar topology affecting neural-net action potentials," Wang said, "but neural-net action potentials affecting the scalar topology of the quantum foam, too. From his understanding of that link, he was working toward what his notes call 'a technorationalized telepathic and psychokinetic capacity.' "

"But what does that have to do with the Mawari children?" Susan asked at last, sounding frustrated.

"Michelson's notes indicate that to achieve what he was after," Lingenfelter said, "he would need 'to be able to make the brain function like a room-temperature quantum computer'—"

" 'Enhanced neural sensitivity throughout the cerebral cortex' is how his notes put it," Wang interjected. " 'Chaotic, spontaneous neural activity, hypersensitive to quantum effects.' "

"Heightened or paranormal abilities, then," Michael said flatly, "connected to the consistent, sustainable, high-percentage brain activity made possible by the full myconeural complex."

Lingenfelter and Wang nodded.

"But would that be enough to 'show the stars where to fall'?" Susan asked.

Lingenfelter and Wang glanced at each other.

"Director Brescoll has informed us about his experiences under the dome," Lingenfelter said, "and about what Doctor Miskulin remembered concerning the children's interest in earth-crossers, the Apollo and Aten asteroids."

"Those earth-crossers could be used as brilliant pebbles to destroy missiles as they approach suborbit," Dan Amaral said. "When it first came up in our discussions, I didn't think it was possible. Then I remembered that there *is* a precedent."

" 'Brilliant pebbles' was a concept developed during the cold war," Brescoll said. "It didn't involve asteroids or meteors. It was about small, smart kinetic-kill vehicles in space, as part of a defense shield against missile attack."

"You could conceivably achieve the same effect," Wang said, "if you could move around rocks in space, at will. Even small ones."

"How could you move them around, though?" Darla asked. "Dragging them around with your mind, or strapping the equivalent of a 'mental rocket' to them—that seems like an awful lot of work."

Lingenfelter nodded.

"It's a big hypothetical, I know. Still, if those kids, through these 'quantum telemorphic effects' might someday be able to 'manipulate the fabric of spacetime,' as Michelson puts it, then they wouldn't need to drag asteroids around or strap a mental rocket to them."

"Gravity is the only machine you'd need in such circumstances," Wang said, "and gravity is the product of the curvature of spacetime. If those kids could shape the curvature of spacetime around those rocks, they could speed them up, slow them down, alter their orbits, do just about anything with them."

"The precedent for it is what astrophysicists call a gravitational keyhole," Michael said with a nod. "A smallish patch of space where orbital resonance effects bend the trajectory of an object passing through that space."

Darla looked worried, but Brescoll still had questions.

"But those small stones wouldn't be big enough to account for the nuclear-blast scale of the effects I saw, in one of the possibilities under the dome," Brescoll said.

The mention of that particular N-word—nuclear—jogged something in Michael's mind.

"Do any of you know anything about something called Argus?" he asked. "Or Project Argus? Or something involving Argus points? The Mawari kids were really interested in something with that name."

Brescoll and his people began calling up classified information at lightning speed, then scanning through it almost as fast.

"We know it was a series of clandestine nuclear tests back in the late 1950s," Michael said into the professionals' sudden silence, "and that it took place off South Africa, but that's about all."

The preoccupied Brescoll and his colleagues all seemed to come to similar conclusions at about the same time, at least judging by the way they glanced at one another.

"Do you know what those Argus tests were about?" Dan Amaral asked.

The three non-NSAers in the room shook their heads.

"Three rockets were launched from the USS *Norton Sound*," Brescoll said. "Each with a one-point-seven-kiloton nuclear warhead— rather small, actually. Each nuclear warhead was detonated at very high altitude, in the region known as the South Atlantic Anomaly."

"What's that?" Susan asked.

"The area where the Van Allen Radiation belts are closest to the earth," Wang said.

"The purpose of the test series," Brescoll said, "was to determine the effects of high-altitude nuclear explosions on the earth's magnetic field and the impact to military radar, communications, satellites, and ballistic missiles electronics."

"Why the South Atlantic?" Michael asked.

"The South Atlantic Anomaly was chosen because it's a potential doomsday point," Lingenfelter said. "Generate an electromagnetic pulse of sufficient magnitude there and you get global spread. World-wide EMP propagation. It would kill all unshielded electronics over the entire surface of the planet, as well as in near-earth orbit."

"Dropkick us back to the technological level that prevailed in Thomas Jefferson's lifetime, is what it would do," Amaral said. "Shut that eye of Argus, and everything else goes dead."

"But that's crazy," Darla said. "Who would want to take out everyone's electronics, including his own?"

"Someone in need of a doomsday defense," Brescoll said. "That's what caused initial interest in it, nearly sixty years ago."

" 'Doomsday defense'?" Susan asked.

"Say your opponent got off some of his retaliatory missiles and aircraft just before the missiles of your preemptive attack destroyed his civilization," Brescoll explained. "He's utterly in ruins, but his retaliatory strike is now rising toward you. If you could use the Argus Point to kill his attack before his weapons could get to your country, would you do it? Being kicked back to the eighteenth century is better than being kicked back to the Stone Age, or destroyed utterly."

"I don't see how a killer EMP is related to meteors, though . . ." Amaral began.

"I do!" Michael and Darla both said simultaneously.

The others looked at them blankly.

"Meteoroid EMP," Darla said.

"Explosive disruption of a large meteoroid generates EMP," Michael said, nodding in strong agreement.

"The shock wave of a meteor or meteoroid's explosive braking," Darla said, "propagates in the plasma around the skystone as it shatters."

"You get lots of ionizing radiation—lightning, thunder, elves, sprites, the works," Michael said. "Very low frequency and extremely low frequency electromagnetic transients of many kinds."

"Those sorts of effects were seen with atmospheric nuclear detonations of a given size, too," Jim Brescoll said, clearly pondering it. "So shooting stars, thunderstones, and mushroom clouds *can* all be one and the same, after all. Nothing nuclear required. Just a big enough rock, moving fast enough."

Darla and Michael agreed that that was essentially the case.

"How big a rock?"

Michael and Darla made some quick calculations.

"A stony or stony-iron meteoroid about a football field across should do it," Darla said.

"That would yield something in the thirty-to-fifty-megaton range," Michael said, nodding.

"How common are stones of that size?" Wang asked.

"There are plenty that size in the Apollos and Atens," Michael said.

"Even without human meddling, rocks in the ten- to one-hundred-meter-size range come shooting into earth's atmosphere a few times a century."

"And with human meddling?" Amaral asked.

Michael glanced at Darla.

"If those kids can create *targeted* gravitational keyholes, then we're a bull's-eye in a shooting gallery. You could probably fire one of the right speed and size into the right part of that South Atlantic Anomaly with very little advance notice required. I'd say we're far higher on the Torino impact-hazard scale than we've ever been before."

"Would you give me some numbers, please?" Wang asked. "Besides the skymaps, NASA also sent us a program they did in conjunction with the National Reconnaissance Office. It plots satellite reentry burn-up, but we can tweak it for our purposes. I'll need size, mass, velocity, angle of entry, altitude."

"I've got a simulation of global EMP effects running on one of the big parallel machines," Lingenfelter said. "If you can give me those same numbers, we can narrow down the megatonnage and get a better handle on the effects."

"Here," said Wang, "I'll replace the satellite graphical object with one that looks like a space rock, and give it the parameters you give me."

"Since they're compatible programs, I think we can combine the reentry and EMP graphics to give us an overall view," Lingenfelter said.

Michael and Darla began suggesting numbers. In surprisingly little time, Wang and Lingenfelter, wirelessly routing information back and forth, had put together their little simulation. It was quite the horror show.

Inside the display dome on the desk, a rock from space nearly a hundred yards across came hurtling in at more than ten miles per second, on a relatively shallow angle of entry. Some tens of miles above Earth, where the lower Van Allen Belt dipped closest to the planet's surface at the South Atlantic Anomaly, the rock underwent explosive braking and catastrophic breakup in a blast of light, heat, lightning—and a spectrum of other electromagnetic radiations far less visible.

A wave of graphical lightning spread across the globe from the South Atlantic Anomaly. This EMP lightning wave left in its immediate wake a flood of darkness, as all the lights of all the cities on the nightside Earth went out.

"Presumably the same global blackout passes over the dayside, just not so obviously," Lingenfelter said, as the scenario stopped and restarted, playing itself over again in an endless loop.

"Takes out all satellites in low Earth orbit as well," Wang commented, watching the replay.

"Of course, it would probably be more complicated than that," Lingenfelter said, gesturing at the dome display. "Especially since the South Atlantic Anomaly in the upper atmosphere currently coincides with an RFP."

" 'Request for proposals'?" Susan asked, puzzled. Bree laughed.

"Sorry. RFP stands for 'reversed flux patch' in this context. RFPs are spots in the earth's magnetic field where the field, instead of flowing outward from the Southern Hemisphere and inward at the Northern Hemisphere, as it usually does, flows in just the opposite direction, despite what prevails in each hemisphere overall. RFPs are looped holes in the geomagnetic field. They originate in the core-mantle boundary."

Wang glanced at parameters on his blinks, shaking his head at the thought of such complexity.

"But to model the interaction, if any, between the Anomaly and the reversed flux patch," he said, "we'd need to incorporate observations from the Magsat, Oersted, and CHAMP satellites, supercomputer simulations of the Earth's geodynamo, laboratory fluid-dynamo experiments, the whole works. I think we've shown you the basic gist without all that."

Darla glanced at Paul, Michael, and Susan.

"Those kids are potentially dangerous, just as I told you," she said. "Especially if they hold us responsible for the murder of all their friends and families—their entire people. What better way to punish the technologically advanced than a global EMP that knocks us all back down to their tribe's level?"

"Dammit, I wish my uncle Paul were still with us," Michael said. "He knew more about those children than anybody alive. His read on Jacinta's notes was that the Mawari might have stayed childlike longer than the rest of us, but what does that really *mean*? Does it imply they're even less emotionally mature than most kids their age?"

"A global EMP would be one helluva temper tantrum," Darla said, shaking her head. "It might result in the deaths of tens of millions of people."

"I remind you again: they're just kids," Susan said. "And these are all huge hypotheticals, as Bree herself called them."

Jim Brescoll cleared his throat, looking away from the private data streams clearly scrolling across his ARGUS blinks.

"I would agree, Ms. Yamada. Then again, Goliath probably thought David was 'just a kid,' too. He didn't see his 'hypothetical' coming."

"Judging from intelligence community threat evaluations," Amaral said, scanning the data, "no one's been paying all that much attention to old EMP test data lately."

"Why not?" Darla asked.

"No matter how much we try to be like all-seeing Argus," Brescoll said, "we still have our blind spots. The thinking has been that it'd be unlikely that terrorists could loft a multimegaton nuclear warhead on a rocket into the Van Allens."

"You'd need a nation-state to do that," Amaral said. "With ships, and missiles, and probably hydrogen bomb capability. Not too many organizations have all that. When it comes to terror and vengeance, nation-states are still the best in the business."

Michael noticed that Brescoll, though he said nothing, frowned deeply at Amaral for that comment.

"But if those kids are after some sort of vengeance," Darla said, "and if they potentially have these sorts of powers—"

"Then they could pose the ultimate asymmetric terror threat," Brescoll said.

"Hijacking asteroids," Amaral said, shaking his head. "They'd just be throwing rocks, but those rocks could bring down twenty-first-century civilization."

"But we don't even know where they *are*," Susan said. "Or even if they're still alive."

"Our best guesses are that they *are* still alive, and they're in South Asia, or the Middle East," Brescoll said.

"Where people had a tradition of throwing stones long before anyone coined the phrase *asymmetric conflict*," Amaral added. "And where things are already strained to the breaking point by the Temple Mount mess. Just from *that* the Syrians and Iranians are already saying they'll view any large-scale Israeli attack on the Palestinians as an attack on all followers of Islam, including their own peoples."

"We'd best crank up the pressure on the Saudis to implement maximum security measures for the Hajj," Brescoll reminded himself, "and accept our support in that effort, no matter how reluctant they might be to do that."

"If you're going to attribute all these potential powers to the kids,"

Susan said, sounding annoyed, "then maybe you ought to consider this, too. Maybe they aren't being used by terrorists. Maybe they aren't little terrorists themselves. Maybe they'll surprise all of us with what they might do. Even if they *are* still just children, why not assume they might change the world for the better?"

"I hope you're right, Susan," Brescoll said, "but that's still no excuse for sitting on our hands. I think several of us are going to be headed toward that same region of the world, and soon."

"One of your 'underdome' dreams, Director?" Susan asked.

"Call it that, if you like. And I'll hope your children's crusade, if that's what it is, turns out better than the previous ones did. In the meantime, I think I'll have to inform the director of national intelligence about our discussions. I've been trying to avoid it, but Watson will want to know. Issues of global EMP blackout are a bigger matter than this agency alone was ever intended to handle."

NONRANDOM DISAPPEARANCES

Joe Retticker had much to reflect on as he traveled through the starry desert night in the stealth airship Vang had loaned him.

The craft had proven surprisingly appropriate to his mission. Flying at nearly twelve miles high for most of their journey, they'd come clear across the Atlantic, through the Mediterranean, over the Negev and the Hijaz, deep into the Empty Quarter—all without arousing any real interest from the air forces of any of the countries whose airspace they had passed through. The fact that the airship never had to actually land on the soft dunes, but could float endlessly above them, made it better adapted to this desert terrain than fixed-wing planes and helicopters would be.

He supposed Vang already knew all that before sending them here, which intrigued Retticker all the more.

A plump delta-wing lifting body, the stealth airship had stood for many days moored just far enough from the Wabar digs so that distance and its smartskin camouflage prevented it from being visible to those in the camp. Now it whispered along, low and slow and under radar, a silent hearse carrying the body of Major Marc Vasques to its final disposal in the desert.

Vasques wasn't dead yet, but Retticker was sure the major would soon be—and he regretted it. Vasques had been drugged soon after coming aboard the airship, and had been kept in that state ever since, at the suggestion of both Vang and Otis. Retticker's resistance to dumping a good soldier in the desert to die, however, had only succeeded in prolonging the man's drugged half-life.

By allowing Levitch to use Vasques as an experimental subject, Retticker thought he had at last proved his loyalty to Otis and The Cause beyond all doubt. In truth, he had allowed it only because he thought that the major would at least be allowed to come out of his sedated state while undergoing that experiment.

He had proven wrong on both counts. Otis always wanted more. The particular myconeural variant Vasques was injected with only existed because Otis was impatient with how long it took for the tepuians' full myconeural complex to develop. The zealous Rapture-hastener didn't want to wait twelve months, much less twelve years. He had set Levitch to work creating a version that would grow and mature much faster.

The results had not been pleasant for Vasques, or for the general watching those results unfold. The variant Levitch had tweaked into being did grow faster, all right—cancerously fast. The turbocharged fungus quickly became a tumorous thing spreading first in Vasques's brain, then throughout his spine and nervous system. The maddening pain the major suffered was apparently not dulled at all by the madness-inducing chemicals the hyped-up fungus pumped out. The pain and fungal chemistry worked in brutal combination, if anything. Nominally to protect those around him and himself, the techs had to sedate Vasques again and again—more heavily than ever.

Retticker's best efforts seemed only to have made things worse. Looking down at Vasques's quiescent form now, Retticker was astonished that the man still lived. His body was horribly changed. A brecciated epidermis, rather like an elephantiasis of puffy broken cobblestones, covered perhaps eighty percent of his body surface. He didn't look human anymore, yet somehow his vital signs persisted, albeit weakly.

By transporting Vasques's body into the desert, Retticker was obeying Vang's earlier suggestion and Otis's demand that he get rid of Vasques in the desert. Of course, obedience is time-dependent. He chose to carry out such earlier orders *now* to secretly spite Otis's scientists and techs at the Wabar digs.

They'd have biopsied Vasques to death and then, after he finally gave up the ghost, sliced and diced him to pieces in an overthorough autopsy, if Retticker had let them. Which he had not. Vasques deserved a better end than that. If all they'd wanted to do was kill him, it would have been more humane to just take him out and shoot him.

Retticker supposed his belated obedience might queer things with Otis's people, Levitch in particular. Fortunately, Levitch was busy with the Mawari kids. He had not injected them with the accelerated fungus, but he'd been zealous enough to expose one of them—the boy, Alii—to his "more complete" metaphage.

Levitch couldn't be bothered to spearhead a formal complaint against Retticker's plans. So, under the strained pretense of "following orders," Retticker managed to get Vasques out of there before Vang or Otis or anyone else could countermand. They might never fully trust him again, but so be it. At least, here in the desert night, Retticker felt he could offer a once-loyal soldier a more dignified ending than would have awaited him at the hands of obsessed researchers.

The pilot of the stealth airship notified him that they were over the rock-strewn desert plain Retticker had chosen as the final resting place of Major Marc Vasques. From satellite and aerial imagery and from the stony appearance of the major's condition, Retticker had determined that this site would be best. If it were noted at all, in the far vaster sand-sea of the Rub' al-Khali, the major's body seen from the air would at most look like a mere optical illusion, a curiously human-shaped stone shadow, a cluster of rocks in a larger field of the same.

While Retticker directed them, two of the troops wheeled Vasques on a gurney down the invisible dirigible's gangway. Once on the ground, they quickly realized that the fist- to head-sized rocks punctuating the desert sand presented an unpassable obstacle course to the wheeled gurney. Detaching drip lines, breathing tube, monitors, and catheter, they moved the comatose Vasques from the gurney and carried him via backboard over the rough footing.

Setting the backboard down on the rocky substrate, they tossed the larger stones out of the way until they'd cleared a space on a patch of desert pavement where they could lay Vasques out at full length. Under the stars of a night still awaiting moonrise, Retticker and the men rose to stand at attention.

"For what they most deeply believe," Retticker said, "all give some, some give all. Marc Vasques has given all."

With no more ceremony than that, the three men saluted, then turned on their heels. As they walked back toward the ship, Retticker saw a meteor flash overhead, then another. Golden swords, quickly drawn from the starred black scabbard of the night, then just as swiftly sheathed again in that same scabbard. He wondered if these fiery streaks were part of the Perseid meteor shower he'd heard Fremdkunst mention.

As the airship traveled the hundred plus miles back to the Wabar digs, Retticker sat thinking about what he'd just done. True, there was no doubt now that Vasques had betrayed the secret of the tepui operation—and much else as well—to the NSA. Nonetheless, Retticker understood his reasons for doing so. He'd felt such stirrings in his own conscience, and could respect them in others.

He exhaled tiredly, puffing out his cheeks. Lines he'd encountered in a background report on Brescoll's friend Dan Amaral rose into his mind. Lines from somewhere in Shakespeare, about being so far stepped in blood that going back would be as tedious as going forward.

Too true. No going back for him now, as much as he sometimes wished he might.

What he saw as they came in low toward the Wabar digs broke his reverie. Lights, moving on the desert—from vehicles bouncing over the uneven terrain. He had his pilot break radio silence so he could contact the camp.

After being referred from one soldier and tech to another, Levitch and Michelson themselves finally came on line.

"They're gone!" Levitch said. "The Mawari kids! It's like they just stepped through the wall of the observation room when no one was looking!"

"Calm yourself, Doctor. If they haven't taken a vehicle, we'll follow their footprints across the desert."

"But that's just the problem, General," Michelson said. "You have to be here to see this—and you have to see this before you can even *begin* to believe it."

"We'll home in on your signal, and we'll be there shortly."

In a few moments the gangway folded down onto the desert where Levitch and Michelson waited. After Retticker descended from the hovering airship, the two researchers led him around to the back side of one of the modulabs, then out into the desert, flashing their headlamps on the sand before them as they went.

"It looks like they were just walking, at first," Levitch said, pointing out their steps. "But then it changes, see?"

"It's as if they suddenly became denser," Michelson said. "Like they began to wade down into the sand. Like it was quicksand, or water."

Retticker nodded. He could see the traces of the children's progress preserved in the sand, far more than it would have been in quicksand *or* water: a labyrinth of ripples, persisting long after the stones that made them had vanished.

"And this area right here," Levitch said, "this seems to be where they went underground."

"If they did," Retticker corrected. "Quite a puzzle, gentlemen, I must admit. But let's not jump to hasty conclusions. They might have escaped by more normal means than this suggests."

"Such as?" Levitch asked.

"Such as spirited away by collaborators, or cloaked against our detection in other ways. This could all be an elaborate ruse meant to confuse us."

"And if not?" Michelson asked.

"Then if they've got bodies, we can still track them, even under the sand."

"How?"

"Netsonde, Doctor Levitch. Side-scanning sonar. Ground-penetrating radar. Hell, even magnetometers might help, for all I know. Let's talk with Fremdkunst. He's been looking for rocks under the sand, right? He might well have what we need."

"There may be another wrinkle, General," Michelson said. "They didn't take any of the quantum telemorphic gear with them."

"I'd think that would be a *good* thing."

"Not necessarily. The fact that those kids have done all this without the QT gear suggests they don't need such gear anymore."

"What do you mean?"

Michelson and Levitch glanced at each other.

"Doctor Levitch and I have been trying to puzzle this out since the kids' disappearance. Our combined work may have resulted in an unexpected synergy in those kids."

"Taken together with their full myconeural complex, and the potential effects on it of the expanded metaphage I exposed them to," Levitch said, "we think they may be able to alter the shape of the spacetime fabric at will."

Retticker wondered about the word *exposed*. A fine euphemism. Never mention experimental injections, by air-hypo, of an untested substance. No, never.

"How?"

"I think they've learned to use the telemorphic tools so well that they've fully incorporated the properties of those tools into their neuronal spaces," Michelson said. "That would give them transparent access to pretty much the whole infosphere. More important, if they did in fact walk through the wall of the lab, and if they did in fact disappear into the sand, it's possible they're projecting or teleporting quantum information densities into that spacetime fabric around them, as a means of shaping it."

"Which means they'd be . . . doing what? Manipulating the sand psychokinetically?"

"Telemorphically."

"Without the need of any mechanical assistance," Levitch added.

"Wonderful," Retticker said. "I thought you injected only one of them."

"I did. Maybe Alii is doing this for the rest of them. Or maybe he has somehow infected them with the expanded metaphage. I'm not sure."

Retticker suddenly felt very tired.

"I'm going to find Fremdkunst. The sooner we get those kids back under our control, the better."

As he walked away, he could not help thinking again of that pattern in the sand under the headlamps, and the image in his head of those kids wading into the desert there. As Vasques literally, and he himself indirectly, had waded into blood during that tepui massacre. And afterward.

Blood and sand. Those children—if they remained like other children at all—still had bodies. Even if they had somehow managed the trick of flowing like water underground, through the sands of the Empty Quarter. If they were still flesh and blood, he would find them.

INTERLUDE: MISTER SANDMAN, DREAM ME A DREAM

Leaving Brescoll's offices, walking with Brescoll, Miskulin, and Yamada, Darla Pittman passed out and collapsed to the floor in the corridor.

She is leaving a laboratory, walking through a wall. She knows that, somewhere behind her, are the Wabar craters. She is sinking into the sand. She is moving through the desert, half walking, half swimming. Beneath the sand . . .

—*Hello, Doctor Pittman.*

—*Isn't this fun?*

—*You worry about what we'll do.*

—Don't worry.

She is sharing their experience, their point of view. Everything they are feeling, she is feeling. What the children mostly feel is exhilaration, as sand flows around body and body flows through sand, neither quite touching the other. Like astronauts in outerspace, like skydivers in airspace, they move through sandspace.

Later, they come up out of the sand, rising like divers from water. They stand on the surface and walk across it, through a stony patch. They come to an odd-looking pile of rocks—long and low, with scraps of cloth on it. A man of sand and stone lies there, wearing the remains of a uniform, but he is mostly naked and still as a corpse.

His skin a camouflage of landscape grown from his body, he doesn't really look human anymore.

—He has what we have, Doctor Darla.

—Only different.

—What you have.

—Only different.

—In him they made it faster.

—Out of control.

—He is dying.

—We don't want him to die.

—Let's try to stop it.

THE DREAM-TELLING

At Darla Pittman's bedside in Crypto City's main infirmary, James Brescoll was beginning to drift off to sleep himself when he felt his arm suddenly grabbed. Darla Pittman was wide-awake and bolt upright in bed.

"Director, I know where the children are!" she said.

Jim Brescoll stared at her. In earlier times he might have asked her how she knew this, but having himself undergone, under the dome, a strange unconsciousness or alternative consciousness, he was inclined to believe her. Especially since she had been exposed to the new and improved version of the metaphage, and had spent the last ten hours in unusually prolonged dream sleep, her lidded eyes REMming madly.

"Where?"

His latest reports from the field had narrowed down the most likely locations of the Mawari children to three places in the Middle East and south Asia: at the Big and Little Craters, south of Jerusalem and the

Dead Sea in Israel, at the Wabar craters complex on the Arabian Peninsula, and the Chintamani stone in India. He was very curious to see if her pronouncement on their whereabouts matched his other sources, of which she could not yet be aware.

"The Wabar craters," Darla said. "Or they were, until a while ago. I was with them when they escaped the research camp there. They showed me what they were seeing."

"Wait, wait," Brescoll said. "Let me bring your friends in on this."

Jim stepped into the hall outside Darla's room. In the waiting area nearby he found Yamada and Miskulin, curled up or sprawled on the furniture, in various stages of sleep. He woke them, told them Darla was awake, explained to them what she was claiming.

They followed him back into her room. When they got there, they found Darla had already gotten out of bed and was seated in the chair Jim had vacated moments earlier. She finished adjusting her hospital gown and told them what'd she'd experienced, as briefly as she could.

"Do you know where they're going? What direction they're heading?" Jim asked.

"I'm not exactly sure. Before I woke up, I remember they'd come out of the sand. Judging by where the sun was, I'd say they were headed west, maybe a little northwest."

She told them about the strange stone-encrusted man the kids were so concerned about, and the suggestion that, like her and like the kids, he, too, had been somehow touched by the metaphage.

"Do you know who he might be?" Brescoll asked. "We need to find him."

"We've got to find those kids," Susan said. "They might starve or die of thirst."

"They grew up on a tepui—a desert of too much rain," Michael said, shaking his head. "Now they're in a desert of too little."

"I wouldn't want to bet on how well—or poorly—they might adapt," Darla said. "If I saw what I think I saw, all bets are off."

Jim nodded, preoccupied. He agreed that the Mawari children had to be found, though for some reason he didn't think they were in extremis just yet. He thought they just might know more about what they were doing than worried adults were willing to give them credit for.

"You said they were headed west, or maybe slightly north of west," he said. "Did you get any sense of their ultimate destination?"

"I'm not sure. What lies in that direction if you keep going that way?"

Brescoll exhaled, puffing out his cheeks.

"Mecca."

That was not what he'd particularly wanted to say or hear, but there it was. The child survivors of a terrible massacre, children possibly possessed of unknowable powers, maybe bent on revenge—and headed toward the very place on earth most sacred to over a billion of the world's people, with the season of the Hajj at hand.

Time and past time to really push on his friends in the State Department, even to the secretary herself. Time to get the whole departmental apparatus impressing upon the Saudis the desperate need for heightened security precautions—and at least covert Western aid—during this year's Hajj.

A dangerous gambit, of course. If the world learned that the Saudis had accepted an offer of covert security assistance from the West after publicly rejecting the offer of a pan-Islamic security force, it would not look good.

"Ever worn smart armor before?" Brescoll asked them, getting only questioning looks in return. "Where you're going, you're probably going to need it."

"Where are we going?" Darla asked.

"The Wabar craters research encampment," he said. "Or its environs in the Empty Quarter. As scientific participant-observers, *not* soldiers."

"You won't be joining us, Director?" Susan asked.

"No, I'm afraid not," he said unhappily. "Since the episode at the MAXX in California, our director of national intelligence has restricted me from any further, um, fieldwork. Don't worry, though. I still have a few tricks up my sleeve that might be helpful to you, even from here."

As they filed out, he stopped Amaral.

"Dan, you've been working on the whereabouts of that meteorite scientist, Zaragosa . . ."

"Avram Zaragosa, yes. What about it?"

"Get a description of him to the CSS troops before they go into Wabar, would you?"

"A hunch, Jim?"

"Let's just say I hate loose ends—and this particular one's been running around loose for too long."

DESERT HISTORY LESSON

Avram Zaragosa thanked heaven that he and Mahmoud Ankawi were not traveling by camel. The all-terrain quad-cycles on which they rode were not the most comfortable transport in the world, but he was certain they were better than camels.

He did wonder, however, if he would ever again experience a time of day both calm *and* cool. During the blinding heat of the day, while the quad ATVs charged up their solar power units, he and Mahmoud tried to sleep, despite the lack of any coolness to be found when the sun beat the landscape to brass. The chameleon-fabric tent was of little help. Although the material was fine camouflage and provided adequate shade, it didn't breathe well enough to keep the enclosure from quickly becoming stifling. What little sleep Avram managed to get was haunted by dreams of the world breaking apart under his feet as he walked, with magma hot as molten iron showing through the cracks as he leapt from dark stone to dark stone.

Through the evening, through the night, and into the dawn of each day following, he and Mahmoud could not escape the tense alertness required for picking their slow, careful way through the desert. Goggled for night vision, they stayed vigilant for any onset of blowing sand. So far, however, the weather had held for them—monotonously clear and hot.

Even without sandstorms, the going was not easy. The traffic arteries he and Mahmoud traveled, such as they were, lay between what the Bedu called *uruqin,* or "veins"—orderly and persistent formations of dunes and sand mountains. Yet even in such vein-valleys they could not avoid encountering the occasional *sebkhas,* salt-encrusted silt plains that were firm driving surfaces one moment and sinking sands the next.

When they hit the soft spots they had to adjust speed and steer their way out of them, knowing that to stop would be to get stuck, and *that* would mean the backbreaking and time-consuming task of digging out. The small supply trailer each quad ATV towed along behind it also didn't make this speeding up, and slowing down, and steering out any easier.

Through predawn twilight after their fourth night of travel, they moved across a wadi under a sky of lambent Bunsen-burner blue. Still several days between the all-too-infrequent (and too frequently undrinkable) water holes, Avram asked his traveling companion the question that had been bothering him for the last several nights.

"Mahmoud, has anyone tried this before?"

"Tried what?"

"Traveling the seven hundred miles from Wabar to Mecca, in summer and by night, on all-terrain vehicles."

Mahmoud said nothing, apparently pondering his answer.

"I don't believe so. When you consider that our route has inevitable detours, it's more like a thousand miles, actually. But then again, no one has had ATV quads like these before, either. Don't worry, my friend. We have plenty of time, plenty of water, plenty of food, and plenty of spare parts. GPS, too—no navigating by the position of Jupiter, like in the old days!"

Remembering how Yuri Semenov had also so proudly relied on GPS, Avram groaned inwardly.

"Enjoy the night stars of God's heaven!" Mahmoud continued. "By the time we hit the checkpoints for Makkah, you'll be able to pass for a surly old man of the desert! All we have to do in our travels is avoid human company, and human detection, as much as possible."

"Why's that?"

"Because the only people who are likely to be out here are smugglers or the Saudi army. The former have too little respect for law, and the latter too much."

Avram nodded. Avoid human company and detection. Not so very different, really, from the cover story Avram left behind him at Wabar—that his ex-wife had died, and that he was returning home to Argentina to mourn her passing and go into seclusion, at least for a time. Ankawi, much more simply, only claimed he was going on Hajj.

As their night journeys continued, Mahmoud seemed to feel compelled to talk over the quiet low hum of their ATVs. Maybe he was trying to keep Avram's mind off the difficulties of their travels across this greatest of sand seas. Maybe he talked to keep them both awake. Or maybe because they spent too much time awake already—too many hours wired on too much coffee—and loquacity was how he responded to their being always sleep-deprived, overtired, and overwrought by this endless nightly sojourning.

Avram was willing enough to listen. Anything he learned about Islam and its history helped soothe his "Fraud Complex," the continuing sense that he was not only an imposter but an impersonator playing an imposter. In brief, practical conversation, Mahmoud spoke Arabic with him, but was kind enough, when he launched into longer topics, to speak the second language they both shared—English.

From Mahmoud's night-visioned travel lectures, too, Avram learned much about his guide's deeper reasons for assisting him in what he understood to be Avram's "enterprise."

"I think the Black Stone is at the heart of a greater mystery,"

Ankawi told him as they made their way through desert night. "Not just whether it's a meteorite or not. A man clothed in white is said to have removed a black stone from the Prophet's body when he was a child, and the Prophet had an interesting relationship to the Black Stone all his life."

"So it was already part of the Kaaba, even then?"

Mahmoud nodded.

"As tent people," he said, "the Bedu did not go in for elaborate architecture, in the early days. When they built, they built simply. *Kaaba* just means 'cube,' right? There were many Kaabas, many cubic houses or temples of god, in pre-Islamic times."

Avram nodded, which he supposed was visible enough to prompt Mahmoud to continue.

"During the first several decades of the Prophet Muhammad's life, Makkah was a remarkably tolerant and ecumenical place. The city was a trading center on the caravan route, with ready access to the camel herds of the nearby Bedu. Its Kaaba was surrounded by three hundred and sixty gods of various religions, including images of Jesus and Mary.

"Each Arab tribe already had their protecting star from among the Houses of the Moon. They also revered the subtle beings known as djinn, so having a sort of pantheon of the Arabian Peninsula in their city . . . this wasn't a big stretch for the local people. The sacred rule of the city was that the faithful of all religions should have access to the sanctuary without discrimination and there should be no conflict within ten miles of it, which made for a more peaceful place overall.

"Basically, that was good for business. The chief citizens of Makkah could say to foreign traders, 'Look, you're going to be here for three months, but feel free to worship your homeland's gods while in Makkah. We have them already set up in our Kaaba, see?' "

"Were there any 'main gods' worshipped there?" Avram asked, suspecting that not all gods would have been created equal.

"Before the Prophet's eventual capture of the city, the most important divinities worshipped in Makkah's Kaaba were the male god al-Lah and his daughters or sisters, the goddesses al-Lat, al-Uzzah, and Manat. Al-Lat was worshipped in the shape of a square stone. Al-Uzzah was identified with the morning star and worshipped as a thigh-bone-shaped slab in the desert between al Talf and Makkah. Manat was worshipped as a black stone on the road between Makkah and Medina—"

"And that was the source of the Black Stone of the Kaaba?" Avram asked.

"That's not certain. The Black Stone revered today is one of those worshipped long before Prophet Muhammad's time. As to which deity was worshipped in the Black Stone of the Kaaba, that's another question. Some say the Black Stone was originally al-Lah in the form of the moon god, Hubal. Others say it was dedicated to one or the other of the goddesses, usually al-Uzzah or Manat. The Hulama, the rationalist school of Islam, recognizes that the Black Stone was identified with both the Great Goddess in her triple form, and with the moon god. In all cases, the stones associated with Hubal, with Manat, with Uzzah, and with Lat—each was said to have fallen from the sky."

"So the whole place was dedicated to meteorite worship?"

"More than that. The entire structure of worship in Makkah is related to the skies. The Kaaba itself is aligned for lunar and stellar observation. The seven circumambulations, performed in a sort of labyrinth walk around the Kaaba, were originally associated with the worship of the seven planets of the Babylonian system and their orbits."

"Seems like a long stretch from being that sort of astronomical temple to being the center of Islam," Avram said. They were passing over a long stretch of largely featureless silt plain, flanked by high sand hills on either side.

"A long stretch indeed," Mahmoud agreed. "Only much later did the spiritual tolerance found at Makkah come to be damned as 'blasphemous polytheism' and 'the worshipping of idols.' The Prophet Muhammad's overriding goal, you see, was to unite all the Arabian tribes into a single political force held together by a common religious faith. Yet even when the Prophet abolished the idols of the old religion at Makkah, he still could not bring himself to destroy that old religion's holiest object, namely the Black Stone in the Kaaba itself."

"Why not?"

"Ah, that's a difficult one. That's where the whole ancient controversy of the satanic verses comes into play."

"I thought that was only a story."

"No, no. It's a fact or at least historical. According to the historian Tabari, the Prophet was meditating near the Black Stone in the Kaaba one day. He had a revelation that allowed the Triple Goddesses of Makkah, the three female aspects of the divine, to have a place in his theology . . . without compromising his monotheism. In the Koran, Sura fifty-three nineteen says, 'Have you then considered al-Lat and al-Uzza, / And Manat, the third, the last? / These are the exalted birds / whose intercession is approved.'

"The Quraysh—the tribe that ruled Makkah, Muhammad's own people—thought the Prophet's new revelation was wonderful. It echoed the invocation the Quraysh themselves chanted to the goddesses as they circumambulated the Kaaba and its Black Stone. The exalted birds, or *gharaniq,* were like the angels and djinn that many Arab people had long believed in. In the eyes of the Quraysh, by referring to the triple goddesses as 'the exalted birds whose intercession is approved,' the Prophet had given his stamp of approval to them and to their worship."

"So what happened, then?"

"During the great Night Journey, the angel Gabriel told the Prophet that those verses were inspired by Satan, so Muhammad removed them."

Avram nodded. He knew about the Prophet's journey, which took him by winged creature along the axis mundi as far as Jerusalem and back in a single night—supposedly under the influence of a sacred plant, according to some scientists, though they could never quite agree *which* sacred plant.

"The Prophet's latter rejection of the goddesses—and also his rejecting the possibility of female angels—led to his conflict with the Quraysh," Mahmoud continued. "Their persecution of the Prophet and his followers eventually resulted in his flight to Medina. Yet despite its being identified to some degree with the discredited goddesses, the Prophet never rejected the Black Stone. If anything, he showed exceeding fondness for it."

"How so?"

"Under the treaty at Hudaybiyah, the Prophet was permitted to return to the Kaaba during his Lesser Pilgrimage. The histories say that the Prophet, riding his steed Qaswa, led a great crowd of white-garbed pilgrims into the holy city, all of them crying out, 'Here I am at your service, O God!' When he reached the Kaaba, Muhammad dismounted and kissed the Black Stone, embraced it and stroked it, before making the circumambulations followed by the entire crowd of pilgrims."

"Is that the journey where he smashed all the idols?"

"No. That was during his triumphal return to Makkah, at the head of ten thousand soldiers. While the Quraysh watched, he called out

'The truth has come, and falsehood has vanished!' as he smashed each idol. He ordered all pictures of the pagan deities obliterated except, according to tradition, for some frescoes of Jesus and Mary. And, of course, the Black Stone was not to be harmed.

"It was strange, really. Initially, the Prophet called for 'No compulsion of religion.' There was no ban on human symbols of the divine, as happened later. A great part of the holiness of Makkah was originally its religious tolerance, but that all changed.

"Later, even the Black Stone the Prophet himself so honored became suspect. Pilgrims began to recite Caliph Omar's warning about it: 'I know well you are a stone that can neither do good nor evil, and I would not kiss you had I not seen the Prophet kiss you, on whom be prayer and the blessings of God.' "

Avram shook his head.

"Wouldn't knowing that history tend to weaken one's faith?"

He saw Mahmoud smile into the darkness.

"Does knowing that Jacob's dream-pillow stone, or that the Ark of the Covenant, too, might well have been meteoritic . . . does that weaken the faith of Jews? Does knowing that the Star of Bethlehem might have been a double meteor, or Jesus' 'stone rejected by the builders which has become the cornerstone,' or even the darkening of the sky and shaking of the earth at his death . . . does knowing that those may trace back to meteors and meteorites weaken the faith of Christians?"

"Probably not," Avram agreed. "I suppose you're familiar with the work of researchers like Darla Pittman and Michael Miskulin?"

"Of course," Mahmoud said. "Very interesting ideas, though I think the former is too focused on the biochemical, the latter too much on the extraterrestrial. For all that their ideas may enrage some people, does it really shake the faith of those same people?"

"I suppose not, if they're still enraged."

"Well then, the same is always true when it comes to what people believe versus how they act. Don't assume that Arabs or Muslims are any more fully explained by Islam than the Irish are by Catholicism. Not all the Irish are Catholic, nor all the Arabs Muslim, nor all the Muslims Arabs. Islam itself is not monolithic, nor is it hermetically sealed off from the rest of world culture. The Muslim world and the West have been in a strong feedback relationship with each other for well over a thousand years. Politics and religion have long since gotten all mixed together on both sides of the spyglass."

"What do you mean?"

"Salvation politics and liberation theology. Wahab and Saud and Reagan. The cold war and the Afghanistan jihad. Neoconservatives and radical Islamists. Muslim Brotherhood and quietist Salafism and the Internet. Governmental and nongovernmental terrorisms. The state under socialism, the corporation under capitalism, the *umma* under Islam. Distributing the wealth or, more accurately, apportioning the scarcity. All are flip sides of the same coin. Objects in the mirror, or through the wrong end of the telescope, are closer than they appear."

Mahmoud broke off as they steered out of a patch of soft sand on the *sebkha,* moving on to the minutely higher ground closer to the right-hand sand hill.

"Every way we know the world—but especially religious faith—is like a camera obscura," Mahmoud continued. "A chamber of secret darkness, a black box, with a lens or peephole to let the light of a greater world shine an image into the dark chamber. I saw a wonderful one at the Greenwich Observatory, in England, where I went to university. I told you I went to school there, didn't I?"

Avram nodded, and refrained from saying "About half a dozen times," although he did think it.

"The sciences, arts, humanities—they're black boxes with peepholes, too. Philosophy, say, or comparative religion—my discipline—is a box whose peephole looks out at other boxes."

Avram laughed. Then, with an abrupt pang, he remembered Vida talking about continents of knowledge, shorelines of mystery, oceans of ignorance. When he took his too-sudden leave of her, she had hinted that she might decide to go to Mecca on Hajj after all, since she was already in Arabia—that is, if she could find a male family member to accompany her. That aspect of Islamic law irked her, but she was not (and probably could not pass for) a woman over forty-five years of age who, according to those same laws, could be sponsored in travel by others than the males in her family.

If she did manage to go, he knew that among the thousands upon thousands of hajjis, odds were that he would not encounter her. Even if by some inscrutable fortune their paths did cross, she likely would not recognize him.

What if she did, though? What would his options be? He tried not to think about that, hoping only that he would be able to always keep before him, with aching clarity, the image of his daughter's remains— and the imperative of revenge for that terrible crime.

"What do you see out the 'comparative religion' peephole?" Avram asked.

"Judaism, tracing its origins back to Moses, and Christianity back to Christ, and, through the Prophet, Islam tracing its origin back to Abraham. Sadly, in every one of those faiths, the original revelation has been corrupted by later political accretions. In each it is harder and harder to see the truth that came into the darkness through that particular peephole. That's why I'm a fundamental secularist, or a secular fundamentalist, if you prefer."

An odd thing to say, Avram thought. Recalling Vida's comment about Mahmoud's unexpected fluency in Farsi, and Vida's own diasporan family history, he wondered if Mahmoud might be a son of an old-line Baathist or something.

"Okay, but how do meteorites tie into that?"

"Ah, that's where I'm more fundamentalist than anyone! I want to tear away the corruptions that have accreted and get back to the cornerstone of all these faiths—the sacred skystone, which, in every case, provided the lens or peephole through which the initial revelation came! The Black Stone the angel Gabriel brought down from the sky and gave to Abraham. The pillow-stone that gave Jacob his dream-vision. The grail-cup and the bleeding head of the spear that pierced Jesus' side. All the aniconic deity-stones Pittman writes about. They all stood by sacred springs throughout the Mediterranean, just as the Black Stone still stands near Zamzam, the sacred spring once holy to al-Uzzah, goddess of springs.

"The Great Mosque at Makkah is probably the last place where that ancient complex of meteoritic stone and sacred spring can still be found—preserved by the very same accretions that have obscured its meaning. The presence of that Black Stone once made the Kaaba and the area around it a place of peace and religious tolerance. I think the power is still there to spread that peace throughout the world, if we can just recover it. I think that's what you and everyone back at the Wabar camp are actually all about, whether you know it or not."

"What do you mean?" Avram asked, trying to keep any note of suspicion out of his voice.

"Oh, come now, Doctor Zaragosa! I saw what was going on at Wabar. I saw the many meteorite samples Victor Fremdkunst shipped there, and the extraction work your fellow scientists were doing on them. I saw those children they brought in, too."

"And that's connected to the Black Stone . . . how?"

"In Makkah, you'll see that the Black Stone is worshipped in a patched-together form, its fragments sealed in pitch and bound together with silver wire. What is happening at Wabar is also a 'patching together.' From a mosaic of skystones brought from all over the world, you too were trying to extract and splice together the pure form of whatever material power once made those stones holy objects of veneration, bringers of peace. Those innocent children are part of that work, too, whether you believe it or not."

Avram said nothing, he just stared at Mahmoud as they rode through the night. Mahmoud smiled broadly, taking Avram's silence as proof of the rightness of his speculation. In fact, Avram was silent not from being stunned at the rightness of Mahmoud's speculation, but rather at the man's stupendous wrongness about Avram's own role.

What would the man think if it turned out that Avram was not traveling to Mecca to patch things together but rather to blow things apart? To kill or destroy the men responsible for his daughter's death? To steal or destroy the Black Stone itself, even as his daughter, Enide, had been stolen from him, destroyed, blown to pieces?

The longer he traveled, the more certain he became that the goal of his journey was not just to steal the "bringer of peace" at Mecca, but to break that peace, smash it to dust. If that brought a war to shake the round world right down to its imagined cornerstones, so be it.

Mahmoud was so caught up in his own myth of corruptions and accretions—call it "The Fall That Befell the Fallen Stars"—that he'd completely missed what Avram might be about. For all his talk of mirrors and peepholes, Mahmoud had failed to see what Avram, given his secret perspective, now clearly saw: the mirror opposite of nongovernmental religious terrorists attacking secular financial and military centers would be government-backed political terrorists attacking holy sites.

Avram shook his head—and only from doing so did he see a light far off to the northeast.

"Mahmoud!" he said, pointing. "Looks like we've got company coming!"

They both brought their quad ATVs to a halt. A distant searchlight seemed to be scanning the desert and moving in their general direction.

"A helicopter, judging from the altitude and speed."

Avram nodded.

"Let's get these quads parked close together. We can toss the chameleon tent over us and them."

"Like a camouflage tarp—good idea."

Working quickly, they did so. Now they could only watch and wait to see what happened.

The helicopter came on, its searchlight stalking like a great single bright-footed leg before it. They could hear the machine coming now, its sound and its light growing closer. They gasped a sigh of relief as the light passed near and then flashed beyond their position—at a goodly slant, given that the helicopter was perhaps half a kilometer to the south and east of them. The two did not truly begin to relax, however, until the sound and light had faded far enough away that they were sure it wasn't going to be swinging in a wide circle back toward them.

"That was pretty close," Mahmoud said as they came out from under the tarp.

Avram shrugged.

"Do you think they were looking for us?" he asked his *mutawwif*.

"I'm not sure. The army is always on alert for smugglers out here."

"Maybe we should be more watchful during our night rides in the future," Avram suggested. "More careful where we make camp during the day, too."

Mahmoud nodded. They folded up the tent and packed away gear before remounting their ATVs and taking up their course again. As they rolled onward over the Arabian sand sea, they had little more to say. They stayed that way, silent in the desert silence, under the stars and the moon, until the sun came up out of the earth.

TARGET ZONE INTERLUDE

Dammit! Vida thought, awakened from a sound sleep. What now?

She heard the whump! of explosion followed by the nattering, drumming sound of automatic weapons fire, punctuated by the occasional louder, single shot. Looking—cautiously—out the triangular yome windows, she saw tracer bullets arcing into the sky, and heard the hollow whoosh of rocket-propelled grenades. At about that same instant she heard the sound of helicopters coming in low and fast, then circling and returning fire.

Stay? Run? Into the desert? Into the night? She looked out the windows again, to see the edge of the nearest Wabar crater glittering in the fire from what, a moment before, had been the camp's "security barrack." It was a far sturdier building than her yome, and it was nothing but a broken column of fire, now.

To hell with this. She charged out the back door of the yome. Almost immediately she collided with someone—one of the binotechnicians. Several other techs were with him. As she picked herself off the ground, she saw by the light of the growing conflagration that the helicopters were hovering very near the ground, troops sliding like spidery offspring to earth on lines from the helos' bellies.

"Don't shoot! We're unarmed!" She shouted it in both English and Arabic, and the group of techs began doing the same. Although she was only trying to get herself out of the chaos and confusion of a night battle, she now found she was leading the group.

She should have *known* this was going to happen. First Avram and Ankawi left, supposedly separately. Then, only hours ago, Fremdkunst and Michelson and Levitch had been seen loading up the old Zahid Humvees and heading into the desert. Desert rats, forsaking the Wabar camp as its fortune sank. They must have known this was coming— and left everybody else to twist in the wind. She could have kicked herself for not paying better attention to the signs.

They had not walked far when a line of tracered gunfire sprayed up sand before them.

"We're civilians! Noncombatants!" she shouted. "We're unarmed, damn you!"

The only answer she received was laughter. Derisive male laughter.

After a moment, a squad of men approached them. Their leader, a young man with a razor-thin mustache and a smirking, haughty manner, demanded in Arabic if any of them knew a man named Zaragosa.

"Even if I did, I wouldn't tell you, you idiot dog!" Vida said. She regretted it even before the butt of his gun impacted the side of her head.

When she came to, she found herself propped up against the wall of one of the modulabs with the rest of the techs. There were more of them now—and more guards, too. Several of them spoke English— American English. Two of them grabbed her by the arms, hauled her up, and dragged her out of the group.

This is going to be some night, she thought.

A BRIEF SOJOURN IN WABAR

Michael glanced out the window of the helicopter as the helo droned on through the desert night, playing its spotlight before it. That had been Darla's idea—scanning the desert for the Mawari kids. An off chance, but worth taking.

Around him the raiding party of Central Security Service soldiers sat in the same stealthy smart armor he, Darla, and Susan also wore, and in whose operation they had been given a crash course. Amaral had opted out when it came to such smart-armored adventuring, deciding instead to remain with Brescoll at NSA headquarters.

Not that Director Brescoll would be out of the loop. Before they had left the States, the director had walked them through old OPS 1 and the revamped National Security Operations Center—across the "NSOC" acronym initials inlaid in the floor, through automatic glass doors, under the seals of the three armed-service organizations that made up NSA's military forces, the Central Security Services.

"This place always makes me think of a combination White House situation room and NASA-JPL deep-space monitoring facility," Brescoll said as he led them through the labyrinth of low-walled cubicles and workstations that mazed the floor, each section separated by target-category.

Michael found himself agreeing with the director's description. The place indeed looked to be the love child of political and technological imperatives—a hive of telepresent command, control, communications, and intelligence activities. Computer monitors glowed atop the tables and desks. Large, flat-panel video display screens covered the walls, mapping time and space in sometimes inscrutable fashion.

Several of the younger techs wore augmented reality glasses, heads-up displays for everyday life, including the new ARGUS blinks. Others had eyetracking pseudoholo display screens on their desk-tops. A goodly number of interactive display domes—shiny and new, by the looks of them—seemed to occupy most of the niche between the numerous "flashbar" pseudoholos and the much less common "air-benders," the more impressive (and expensive) holographic projector units, suspending their fully dimensional data-ghosts over a very few workstations.

They passed through the buzz of Room 3E099 to a much more private room just beyond it.

"The Executive Command Suite," Brescoll told them as they entered. "If it smells new and improved in here, that's because it is. Setting this up was one of the first orders of business after I succeeded to the directorship."

Brescoll demonstrated the way in which the ECS functioned as a sort of meta-NSOC, possessing many of the capabilities of the entire Center but operable by a single person, if need be.

"We can't get you behind the eyeballs of distant people the way the Mawari kids apparently did with you, Doctor Pittman," Brescoll told them, "but we've got the next best thing. Our friends in the National Reconnaisance Office are moving one of their sky-eye satellites into geosynch orbit over the Arabian Peninsula between Wabar and Mecca. Optical and auditory feeds from your smart-armor, along with many other inputs, will be channeled real-time to the equipment here. What you see and hear there, Dan and I will see and hear here."

Although at most times he had a healthy paranoia about anything having to do with reconnaisance and surveillance, Michael found Brescoll's statement oddly reassuring, especially after Brescoll carefully laid out for them how wrought-up things had become, since the Temple Mount incident in the entire region from the eastern Med to the Himalayas.

"We had a helluva time getting Saudi clearance for this operation," Brescoll told them before they left the ECS. "They only agreed to allow it if their own forces also participated. Of course, if anything goes wrong, they'll disavow any knowledge of the plan and claim they had to destroy the invaders—that's you, people—on grounds of protecting their borders and national sovereignty."

Such revelations didn't exactly encourage faith, hope, and charity, Michael thought. Or peace, love, and understanding, either. Right now, all he was really trying to do was encourage himself to stay awake—no easy task, given the hours they'd spent on flights getting here, the monotony of the desert over which they flew, and the relentless rhythmic thudding of the military helicopter's props. Susan and Darla, he saw, were already dozing, though the CSS troops still remained resolutely awake and alert.

His payoff for staying awake was witnessing the terrible beauty of the firefight already under way as they approached the Wabar research camp. Tracer bullets lit up the night sky before them. Defenders on the ground were firing upon Saudi helicopters coming around from the east and the south as they themselves approached from the north.

They hovered only long enough for the CSS troops to pile out of the helo, then they were rising and circling again. By this time Darla and Susan were awake, too. With their young CSS liaison officer they watched spellbound from above as the firefight and its shifting visual Morse code of tracer rounds, punctuated by occasional mortar and grenade bursts—or lit longer by falling starshell flares—eventually spelled out victory for the combined Saudi and CSS forces.

Their liaison officer took a radio call. He then informed them that the camp had been secured, and the helicopter dropped more slowly toward earth. They leapt the short distance to the sand and ran out from beneath the prop wash—amid the stink of cordite and burning human flesh. One of the other CSS soldiers saluted their liaison. As the helicopter lifted into a holding pattern, both the CSS soldiers led Michael, Susan, and Darla toward first one modular building, then another.

In the first, CSS guards stood around a small group of frightened men and women, civilians who, under questioning, identified themselves variously as molecular geneticists, biochemists, and bino- or nanotechnicians. All except for one—a defiant woman whom the CSS troops had cut away from the others and were questioning concerning the whereabouts of someone named Avram Zaragosa. Michael thought he recognized the name, and the woman, too. From the ECOL conference. Vida something. A meteoriticist.

They proceeded into another section of the lab. From some remaining scattered examples still in the lab, Michael, Darla, and Susan confirmed the nature of their work.

"Were they working with extractions from meteorites?"

They were startled to hear Dan Amaral say it into the speakers mounted in their helmets. It was the first they had heard from either Amaral or Brescoll since they had left Brescoll's ECS lair, from which Amaral's voice was presumably now coming.

Once past that startlement, Michael and Darla agreed that was indeed what the scientists and techs here were working on. When Michael asked the clustered scientists under guard where the meteorite samples themselves were, the experts were even more guarded in their responses.

It took a while, but Michael, Susan, and Darla eventually got them to admit that Victor Fremdkunst—hours earlier—had most of what he'd initially brought to the camp gathered together in front of the lab. Then, at the head of a small caravan of Humvees and ATVs, he and a Russian national, a meteoriticist by the name of Yuri Semenov, had driven off with what appeared to be crates of meteorite specimens, into the desert. Whether his goal was disposal or departure, the scientists and technicians under guard could not, or would not, say.

Even while gathering that information, they received word that one of the reconnoitering helicopter crews had come across a tarped pile of crates. From the description of the contents, it seemed Fremdkunst and Semenov had left behind a goodly portion of those same meteoritic samples.

"I'm amazed Fremdkunst would abandon any part of his precious collections," Michael said.

"He must have been in a hell of a hurry," Darla agreed. "Semenov, too."

"Either that," Brescoll informed them from the ECS, far away, "or the craft in which they departed in didn't have the room, or the lift capacity."

"Let's not make the same mistake ourselves," Michael said. "We need to get those crates winched up into the helicopter we came in, and pronto."

Michael overheard Brescoll and the CSS liaison giving orders to that effect, even as he, Susan, and Darla walked to the next modular laboratory building. Once they entered, Darla immediately recognized a lab setup resembling her own at Rocky Mountain—or the remnant of such a set up, at any rate. She presumed it was Barry Levitch's lab space, though Barry himself seemed to have departed. Susan and Michael, meanwhile, examined another section of the building, where rather unusual telepresence equipment seemed to have been left behind.

"Our people here say what you're looking at resembles the gear Michelson was working with in the Telemorphy Lab at Fort Mead," Brescoll said. "They say he absconded from there with more of that gear than you're seeing, though."

The same realization was rising into Michael's thoughts—and probably Susan's and Darla's, too—when Brescoll gave voice to it from afar.

"Fremdkunst, Michelson, and Levitch seem to have flown the coop," the director said. "Our sources indicate Retticker might well have been at Wabar also. If he *was* there, and he's gone now too, I think it's safe to assume they were tipped off to the impending raid."

"By whom?" Michael asked.

"We can't say with certainty," Brescoll said into their helmet speakers. "Dan says Fremdkunst has connections in the Saudi government, so maybe it was from their end. General Retticker has connections with people on our end who might have been loose-lipped, too. The important thing now is to find out where they've gone—and if they're pursuing the kids, or already have them."

"I suggest we head west," Darla said suddenly. "Mecca is almost due west of Wabar, after all."

"Informed intuition, Doctor Pittman?" Brescoll asked.

"Maybe. But perhaps no more untrustworthy than your remembrance of things under the dome, eh, Director?"

"Perhaps not."

"It makes sense," Susan said. "We came in from the north, and Michael says the Saudis came in from the south and east."

"Westward ho, then," the director said. "We'll divert as many of our radar and satellite sources to your search area as we can spare. Lieutenant Carling, your liaison, will set your transport in motion as soon as the crew has returned with your meteorite crates. The majority of the CSS and Saudi forces will finish mop-up operations and secure the Wabar area while you reconnoiter."

They left the already hastily abandoned labs. Waiting for their crate-laden helicopter to return, they walked toward the sand-sunken Wabar craters themselves.

"Even by night vision you can see at least three crater rims," Michael said. "Or parts thereof."

"One's eleven meters across, one's sixty-four meters, and the biggest is one hundred sixteen meters in diameter," Darla said wistfully. "Sorry . . . long but distant familiarity."

"I've always wanted to explore this place, too," Michael said, sympathizing.

"No time," Susan said as a helicopter came in low and fast over the horizon. Soon it was hovering impatiently overhead.

"No, not this time," Darla agreed.

Their helo dropped winch lines with attached harnesses toward them. Michael hoped things were moving westward, and not worst-ward. At least they'd recovered a goodly percentage of Fremdkunst's meteorites. He'd bet that, in the materials recovered here at Wabar, they'd just *happen* to find slices from a lot of the skystones stolen from around the world.

Around him, the predawn light lay like a diaphanous veil upon the still-shining stars.

MORNING FLIGHT

This invisible dirigible both did and didn't make a good getaway vehicle, Retticker thought. They were at most a ghost on any number of detection systems—radar, infrared, visible optical. Yet the craft was most efficient cruising high in the stratosphere, where its tens of thousands of cubic meters of helium expanded twentyfold more than at sea level, and its solar-powered engines and high-altitude propellers were most efficient. Limping along on reduced solar, through denser air, and with only the slight help of hydro fuel-cell backups and low-altitude props, they were not exactly burning through the morning sky. Especially now, while dune-hopping to decrease the chance of anyone getting a radar fix on them.

Given the resources Vang and Otis commanded—and at least the possibility that international law enforcement agencies might come hunting them—he'd have thought they'd have a faster getaway vehicle in reserve. Even as he thought it, however, Retticker realized that ground vehicles wouldn't fit the bill—too slow and easily targetable. The highly modified helicopters and fixed-wing aircraft that could land on or take off from the sand sea surrounding Wabar were few and far between, too. No choice but to make do with what they had.

He debated with himself about whether to land and sit tight or stay airborne. The chameleon-cloth camouflage might prove more effective on the ground, especially combined with the immensity of the potential search area of the entire Empty Quarter. Anyone looking for them would inevitably have to cover a good chunk of this France-size dune ocean. Even the heat of the day, when it came into its own, would be his ally against anyone trying to locate them by plane or helo.

Yet landing and sitting tight also might make them sitting ducks. Maybe better to stay on the move, and go to ground only when a threat was imminent—counting only then on the brute vastness of the desert to hide them. Flying by night, and holing up in the heat of the day.

As presumably the Mawari kids were doing. And maybe Zaragosa and Ankawi, too, already a week and a half into their crazy jaunt across the desert, if what he'd gathered from Fremdkunst's speculations about their activities proved to be true.

Assuming, of course, that any of those people had managed to stay alive in the deadly drought, dust, and heat of this sun-hammered place.

As he pondered it, the stealth airship flew on, an inversion of the world: all the shades of sand and earth on top, the brass-and-blue of the sky on the bottom. Many fish used the same upside-down logic in their protective coloration schemes. Retticker knew, however, that that didn't necessarily protect those fish from being seen and picked off by birds from above, or other predators from below. He'd feel a lot more comfortable if this aircraft could somehow pass to stratospheric altitude without being detected—and the sooner the better.

Although Fremdkunst, Michelson, Levitch, and Semenov were in the crowded lounge with him, Retticker said nothing of this to them. Michelson and Levitch were asleep, or nearly so, after sampling the well-stocked bar. Semenov seemed to be in a drunken stupor. Fremd-kunst was still managing to stay awake, probably out of anger at being forced to leave so many of his beloved meteorites behind. The "tepui art piece" itself was aboard, however, for all that it was very much un-needed ballast.

Retticker sighed inwardly. He'd had no choice. Fremdkunst and Se-menov had wanted to load them up with too damned much stuff, and he had to make a command decision that made no one happy. So there Fremdkunst now sat, furiously accessing via blinks the readouts from the ground-scanning and earth-penetrating detection systems they had rigged up on board, before their hurried departure from Wabar.

So far the search had not produced evidence of the Mawari kids—or anyone else in this wasteland. Retticker wondered how much Fremd-kunst's nonstealthed detection gear raised their radar cross-section. Probably best to let that go, though. At least for the time being.

"I'm going to join the crew up forward and see if they have any news," Retticker said, to no one in particular, as he stood up. Fremd-kunst gave him a belated nod, too caught up in his searching to do much of anything else.

"Good to see you, General," said the pilot, a square-jawed black man named McGuire. Ex-military, like everyone else Vang crewed this ship with. "We were just getting ready to send someone to find you."

"Oh? Trouble?"

"We don't know yet," said the crew's communications and counter-measures officer. "Two blips have been executing a pretty standard search pattern out of Wabar. The one farther east apparently just got into the air a few minutes ago and doesn't seem to have tagged us at all yet. But the closer one appears to be roughly paralleling our course now—almost as if they're losing us and finding us again."

Good God, Retticker thought. How are they managing that? This same crew on this same craft had slipped through the airspace of nearly a dozen nations during the middle of an international crisis, over At-lantic Ocean and Mediterranean, above mountain ranges and deep into this ocean of sand, without their once being effectively detected. How could someone have picked up their location so fast?

"Better begin evasive maneuvers, Mister McGuire," Retticker sug-gested.

"Yes sir."

"You might want to reconsider that, General."

Looking over his shoulder, Retticker saw it was Fremdkunst who had spoken, about the same instant Retticker recognized the man's voice. There was something of the loaded gun in Fremdkunst's tone, which gave him pause.

"Why 'might' I want to do that?"

"Because I think I've located those kids," Fremdkunst said, taking off his blinks and handing them to Retticker, who put them on.

"What am I looking at?"

"A gravimetric display. I took a chance and thought I'd try it. I didn't really expect to find anything, but it seems I'm wrong. See that dashed line, following the dot? Slightly to the north and west of our position?"

"Yes."

"I ran an analysis. It's a gravitational anomaly, and it's moving."

"So?"

"Gravitational anomalies of that strength don't ordinarily move. It would be like the mountain coming to Muhammad."

"What makes you think it's the Mawari kids?"

"If our sleeping geniuses in the lounge are right, and these kids can telekinetically alter the shape of the spacetime fabric, the way that alteration would most likely manifest itself is gravitationally. Gravity is the curvature of spacetime, the shape of that fabric. Like Einstein said."

"Supposing you're right, what do you suggest we do?"

"Given that those kids are our top priority, I suggest we make a beeline to intersect that mobile anomaly."

Retticker considered it.

"No, not a beeline. Even if those are the Mawari kids, it'll do us no good if we gather them up and then somebody else gathers us up." He handed over the blinks to the airship captain, then continued. "If you'd be so kind, Mister McGuire, pull down the course from Victor's gravimetrics and plot us a diminishing zigzag trajectory—one that intersects this gravitational anomaly our friend here finds so interesting."

Fremdkunst shrugged, at least partially appeased, and disappeared below again. Retticker gazed at the screens showing the morning desert, still trying to figure out how they'd been detected.

Staring at an image from one of the portside cameras, he saw it: something moving where nothing should be moving. Like Fremdkunst's gravitational anomaly. He cursed fiercely under his breath as he tumbled to the explanation.

EVIDENCE FROM ABSENCE

From the Executive Command Suite at NSA, Jim Brescoll and Dan Amaral watched a myriad of display screens and domes. On them, events in the desert unfolded as the helicopter that had earlier left Wabar—the only one spared for the search, initially—continued its pursuit. The second helo, loaded with soldiers, was now airborne, too.

"We've got an increasingly solid fix on that ghost ship out of Wabar," Brescoll explained over throat mike to the CSS crew and its passengers aboard the search helo—Pittman, Yamada, and Miskulin among them. "We've found something that supplements what the spotty radar feeds hint at. Satellite optical scans show no object, but they do show a moving shadow. I'm sending you course coordinates now."

"Any idea what kind of aircraft we're looking for?" the CSS helicopter pilot asked.

"Our best evidence is from absence," Brescoll said. "Lack of infrared signature. Virtually invisible radar or light-spectrum profile. Low air speed. The one thing we *do* have is anamorphic analysis of the shape of its shadow."

"Which suggests what, sir?"

"Best guess is that what you're looking for is a stealth airship. It's from a black budget program that ran way over budget, until Congress found out and killed it. You won't be able to see the thing until you're practically on top of it, I'm afraid—though you might be able to see its shadow."

"If it's from a program Congress killed," Susan asked over the helo noise, "what's it doing flying around out here?"

"A Doctor Vang bought back the only two prototypes built. For 'continuing research.' Turns out his companies were primary contractors on the craft."

From the corner of his eye, Jim saw Dan Amaral nodding vigorously and smugly at the mention of Vang's name.

"Is it armed?" asked the pilot.

Jim looked through the spec sheet his analysts had given him.

"This particular prototype wasn't, but it could have undergone a postproduction retrofit in that direction. A missile coming at you out of what looks like empty air is not beyond the realm of the possible."

"Rules of engagement, Director?"

"Track and observe, but do not engage. The Saudi troop helo is diverting to your coordinates as we speak. Hold back safely and let them take point on this."

"And if our bogey fires on us, Director?"

"Then return fire. We'll give you the best real-time we can on any missile's point of origin, should it come to that."

FLIGHT AND FIGHT

"General," McGuire told Retticker, "we have a problem."

"Say it."

"Radar indicates that our pursuer has a better fix on our position now, but also appears to have slowed. A second pursuer has altered course and is headed in our direction."

"I think they're following the motion of our shadow over the desert," Retticker said. "We're not transparent."

"No sir. This airship was developed for close-in night work, but day work was to be stand-off and high-altitude. We could pop up to elevation and disperse the shadow cone."

"That would make us more vulnerable to radar detection, wouldn't it?" Retticker asked.

"Yes sir. Potentially. Especially since our first pursuer, at least, appears to have a closer fix on our present location."

"What's their time to intercept us, versus our time to intercepting Victor's gravitational anomaly?"

"The first pursuer slowed, as I said. Apparently waiting to be joined by the second, which is just about to happen. If we assume both continue at the speed of that second pursuer . . ." McGuire gave him the figures for both sets of intercepts—their own and their pursuers'. They were virtually identical.

"And the time to execute the pop-up, versus coming into missile range—them of us, us of them?"

McGuire and his crew gave him more figures.

"And there are only those two craft pursuing us?"

"Yes sir. Unless they have something stealthed like ours."

"We'll have to take that chance. What little surprise we have left is our best bet, wouldn't you agree?"

"Yes sir. We'll start the pop-up now. As soon as they are within range, we will commence firing."

DOWNINGS

"We have radar confirmation of incoming missile attack," the CSS helo pilot said, sounding surreally calm over Brescoll's speakers in the ECS. "Taking evasive action. We have visual confirmation. Do you have origin coordinates?"

"Sending," Brescoll said. During a pause of almost unendurable length, he watched the reads on his screens, the Saudi helo slightly ahead and to the west, now, of the CSS flier.

"Received. Trajectory match confirmed. We are returning fire."

Over myriad displays he and Amaral, telepresent witnesses, watched the air battle unfold. The helos, having loosed four birds between them, were making a run for lower air, trying to put a sand mountain—several hundred feet in height—between themselves and the stealther's missile flight. Brescoll said a quick prayer they'd make that cover.

They almost did.

"—hit. Saudi ship hit," said the pilot. "Two impacts. We're hit. Tail rotor spiked. We're going in."

Brescoll and Amaral watched helplessly as altitude readouts for both craft dwindled. The video feed from the CSS helo showed a sand mountain growing until it filled the screen. A sound like an eighteen-wheeler plowing into a runaway-truck catchramp filled the speakers. That sound had barely shrieked its way through the ECS before all their screens and all their displays from the helo went dead.

Brescoll puffed out his cheeks, hoping and praying no one had died in those downings. Nothing to do now but keep going until he had more info. Operate from knowledge, not from fear.

"The airship . . . did they manage to hit it?"

CALCULATED RISK

Retticker and the crew had no time to celebrate the downing of their pursuers before their own craft was viciously shaken.

"What the hell was that? Were we hit?"

McGuire and his crew quickly scanned sensors from throughout the ship. On one of the portside cameras they saw a fireball erupt some distance ahead of them. As Retticker watched and waited, Fremdkunst, Levitch, Semenov, and Michelson piled in behind him.

"Yes, and no, sir."

"Explain."

"One of the helos' air-to-air missiles appears to have torn completely through the smartskin on one of our portside control surfaces. Without exploding."

"And what we're seeing now—?" Fremdkunst asked.

"—is its belated detonation," Retticker said.

"Yes sir. My guess is it passed through without encountering any of the structural members. Or we'd probably be too busy to watch this. Just dumb luck."

"Better lucky than smart," Retticker said. "And we're still airworthy?"

"She's steering a bit more like a tank than usual," McGuire said, "but she'll keep flying. The problem is, that big hole in the smartskin makes us a lot easier to detect. Sir, I recommend we put down and effect repairs as quickly as possible."

"Good. We can kill a couple of birds with one stone here. It's coming onto the blaze of noon, so our shadow as we settle toward ground again will be minimized. Assuming we have no other immediate pursuers, we'll wait out the day and make the repairs, then continue the flight tonight."

"May I suggest an alternative, General?" Victor Fremdkunst said.

"Go ahead."

"Since we're going to be mooring anyway, why don't we put down where that anomaly is tracking?"

"Good idea. Where is it now?"

"It's altered course. I'll patch it through to Captain McGuire."

McGuire gave a startled look.

"Problems, McGuire?"

"That 'anomaly' seems to be headed toward the area where the pursuit helicopters went down."

"Hmm!" Retticker said. "Maybe not such a good idea, Victor."

"A calculated risk, General, but I think one worth taking. I've already contacted George Otis's people for backup support, should we need it."

Retticker pondered it. He'd be damned if he'd let Otis get his fingers into all this before he had a chance to thoroughly investigate it. Still, Fremdkunst had a point. He supposed he owed Victor something, for forcing him to leave a big clutch of his beloved sky rocks behind.

"I agree. Mister McGuire, put us down near where those pursuit helos went down. A good deal more gently than they landed, if you don't mind. Take it nice and slow on the way there, too."

TORTURED MUSIC

Ankawi had said not to worry, Avram thought. That they had plenty of time, plenty of water, plenty of food, plenty of spare parts, and plenty of GPS. That, by the time they finished this mad trip, Avram would be able to easily pass for a surly old man of the desert.

At least Mahmoud was right about the last part. This trip had aged them both. No denying that.

Water holes in the deep desert had turned out to be polluted oil wastes, or dotted with camel dung, or tasting of Epsom salts. Sandstorms blew grit and dust into eyes, nose, mouth, ears—every unprotected orifice or uncovered cranny—at seventy miles an hour, until he felt as if they were living inside a wind tunnel chaffed with sandpaper. Increasing frequency of breakdowns of the ATVs followed each sandblast battering, made worse by the slow learning curves of himself and Mahmoud as mechanics.

Their food supply was running low, except for the endless dried dates. Sleep deprivation that not even the nocturnal regimen of coffee could quite overcome brought on the yawning jitters night after night as they drove on, increasingly hungry and thirsty. Their eyes had grown weary from seeing too much sand and too many stars, above a desert not cut by so much as an empty road since they crossed the highway running between As Sulaymaniyah and As Sulayyil, south of the town of Layla.

Even the GPS was functioning more sporadically, as it and its solar battery had more and more trouble talking to each other. Which meant they had to spend more time course-correcting, which meant they fell further behind schedule each night.

All of it wore on him. He barely noticed anymore the spectacular beauty of the infrequent rock outcroppings in dawn light—the pink and purple sandstones, the bloodred ironstone, the black basalts. Even Mahmoud was not as talkative as before.

They'd camped this dawn by a briny water hole at the bottom of an amphitheater of high dunes with steep slipfaces. They were just waking from their sporadic morning naps in the chameleon tent when two helicopters battered the air overhead—barely clearing the high dunes in their frenzied push eastward, and leaving Avram ready to lose his grip on sanity altogether.

"They ought to rename this place the Not-So-Empty Quarter," he muttered, as what sounded like the drone of a turboprop plane continued to fill the horseshoe of dunes where they were encamped. "Sounds like that guy in the plane is circling right in on us!"

"Those were helicopters that went over," Mahmoud said suddenly, putting on his boots. "Not a plane. That's not a plane we're hearing."

He got up, opened the tent flap, and stepped outside.

"Mahmoud, what are you doing? It's broad day! Do you want them to spot us?"

"There's no one out here. That drone is from the *dunes*! These are singing sands! I've been fascinated with them since I was little!"

Convinced that Mahmoud had finally cracked, Avram put on his boots and stepped out into the heat of the climbing sun. Scanning the sky, he saw it was true. Despite the deep rhythmic droning all around them, there were in fact no aircraft to be seen.

"The Bedu once believed the singing, booming, or barking of the sands was caused by djinns," Mahmoud said, walking toward the nearest dune and beginning to climb it. "Actually, it's sand slides. On high dunes with steep, metastable or quasi-stable slipfaces—like these around us."

Avram walked toward Mahmoud, noticing that his partner's trek up the nearest dune had begun to add new pitches and tones to the droning sound. He saw Mahmoud bend down and take up a handful of the sand.

"Well-sorted, medium-size grains," Mahmoud said, examining the stuff in his hand. "Highly polished, too. Blown a good distance by the wind, probably season after season, for generations."

He stood up, letting the sand gradually drizzle out between his fingers.

"Take a big enough mound of this kind of sand, with a steep enough slipface for sand slides to really get moving down it. Then, when you disturb it, it can emit a lot of acoustical energy. Those helicopters going over, loud and low like that, triggered the sand slides— and this sound."

As Avram climbed up the dune toward him, he stopped. Beneath his feet he felt an unmistakable throbbing and pulsing below the sand's surface, as if the dead desert were alive in a way he had never imagined.

"Feels like a weak earthquake," he called to Mahmoud, who nodded.

"Seismic signals, probably broadband output up to twenty hertz, maybe other tones in the fifty-to-eighty range. Those are the most common. It can make other sounds, too, I'll bet."

With that, Mahmoud began to leap and run about like a madman in the blistering sun, up and down and across the dune face, stopping and kicking the sand vigorously at various points. Soon Avram heard an entire orchestra of sounds: roars and booms and squeaks, sirens and zithers, kettledrums and harpsichords.

Avram ran in the opposite direction and, from a distance, joined Mahmoud in playing the landscape, running and kicking and laughing and rolling down the dunes, like men driven insane by the heat.

A sweet madness, he thought as he tired. Much sweeter than the madness of their night-journeying, toward the greater madness of a greater world. Toward a madness, perhaps, that would torment a worldscape, torture from it a terrible music of vengeance beyond imagining.

Finally, too hot and dirty and tired to continue, he plunked himself down beside Mahmoud atop the tallest dune and watched the sun scream toward noon.

"What do you think those helicopters were about?"

"As long as they're not about us," Mahmoud said, "they're not our concern. What's behind us is not what we need to worry about."

The sun was too close to zenith for them to endure any more. Only mad dogs and Englishmen, as the old saying went. They turned without a word and walked back down to their camp, the sand booming softly beneath their boots.

NINE

MIRACLES AND WONDERS

>>>>>>>

When Michael Miskulin regained consciousness, he knew from the pain that he was in a bad way. Opening his eyes and gingerly turning his head, he saw, scattered on the burning sands before his face, thin slices of shining metal like coins of an alien treasury. It took him a moment to realize what they were.

Meteorite samples.

The fury of the crash came back to him vaguely. He realized now that the impact had been severe enough that it had ripped open the helicopter. Amazing the thing hadn't burst into flame, given that smash-up—though he did smell what he presumed was aviation fuel.

This wasn't supposed to happen. The good guys weren't supposed to make these kinds of mistakes. He was probably only still alive because he'd been wearing smart armor. Despite that protection, he wasn't doing well, crushed and three quarters buried by . . .

Dislodged crates of meteoritic samples. Saved by his smart armor from the disaster that had spewed him out into the desert, only to die beneath broken crates of meteorite samples the crash had slammed atop him at the same time. Good Doctor Meteor felled at last by his long, incurable obsession with falling stars.

The irony of it was not only annoying but embarrassing. Their pursuit of those fleeing Wabar was not supposed to put all their precious lives at risk—or risk all these precious samples, either. Mistakes or no, he decided he'd rather not be slowly crushed to death this way, or incinerated when that av-gas went up.

"Susan!" he rasped out. "Darla!"

No voices came in answer, but another answer came, nonetheless.

The tonnage of broken material heaped above him began to shift off from above, to lift off, carefully, in sections. He wondered if he had gone deaf, for he heard no machinery—but no, he wasn't deaf. He could hear the scrape and grind of the broken packaging and the clatter of the falling skystones themselves.

When the last of the heap had been removed, he found he was being carefully rolled onto his back. He stared up at the dirty faces of two children who, despite their ragamuffin looks and clothes, were still recognizably their Mawari kids—the youngest one, Ka-dalun, and the boy, Alii.

He felt searing pain as they straightened out his arms and legs. Flashing for a moment on Darla's old worry that the kids might be after some sort of elaborate revenge for what had happened to their people, he cried out as loud as he could. They ignored him, focusing instead on cleaning his wounds with water from his canteen, removing clothing and doing general debridement on his bloody lacerations with a soldier's field knife. They examined the deep, confused tattooing of his contusions, as well as the simple or compound fractures on his limbs and torso.

As the pain began to decrease with surprising rapidity, however, other questions sprang to his mind. How did they learn this stuff? They probably used a much higher percentage of their brains than non-myconeuralized human beings did, granted. They'd accessed the entire infosphere at Larkin's place in Tahoe, he knew that. Hell, maybe they were still doing that somehow, even now. But all the knowledge in the world didn't account for the fact that they seemed to be able to move aside huge piles of debris or untwist and unbend metal by simply willing it so.

Nor did knowledge alone explain how their touch was healing him, bringing him back from death's door with a rapidity he knew was quite beyond the capacity of medical science to explain, much less achieve.

They raised him to a sitting position and brought the canteen to his lips.

"Here, Uncle Michael," Ka-dalun said, in a voice that sounded like it hadn't been used much lately. Alii had gone to help the other two girls with Susan and Darla, he now saw. "You should feel better now."

Michael nodded and watched as the four children ministered to all the injured and dying. He saw the burning ruin of the Saudi troop helo and realized it had taken the brunt of the attack. How many died? And why?

When all who could be mended were mending and had been provided with shade, the children moved on to another, and stranger, task.

He could only watch as they walked among the meteoritic fragments scattered on the sand, their hands held palms down, faraway looks in their eyes. On the sand below their hands, the fragments flipped and twisted, despite the fact that he could see nothing physically touching them. From a relative few of those bewitched stones, little fountains of what looked like strings of light or threads of sparks bent and leapt toward the palms of the children.

The children then approached the few boxes that were still more or less intact. These, too, were filled with stacked meteoritic samples—mostly carbonaceous chondrites, Michael saw from the labeling. What came out of the boxes toward the children standing before them was like a daylight fireworks display—cloud chamber traceries of particle/antiparticle collision tracks—but one in which the whoosh, whistle, and bang were replaced by loud rustling, clinking, and rattling of what could only have been the skystones in their boxes, writhing as if possessed.

A triangular cloud-shadow, passing over a dune in the middle distance, caught the kids' attention. Michael saw it, too. Looking up, he thought it odd, for he saw no cloud that could make such a very regular shadow—no clouds at all, as a matter of fact.

Focusing on where he thought the shadow might be coming from, he saw a slippage in the sky, of which he became more and more certain as the shadow grew closer. After a moment he realized that it must be the shadow of the stealth craft they'd been chasing, and which had shot them down. He spotted a thin crescent line, too, like a meniscus of surface tension separating oil and water, where the desert tan of the airship's top side was not quite completely hidden by its sky-blue underside.

The children, he saw, had gotten that faraway look in their eyes again. With a start he realized they were indeed looking far away—farther indeed than eyes *could* look.

Out of the sand, like a scuba diver breaking the surface of a calm sea, came a thing of sand and stone in the roughed-in shape of a man. The brecciated man rose completely out of the sand sea and strode upon its surface, a sphinx out for a stroll in the desert. This sphinx, however, picked up a rocket-propelled grenade launcher one of the troops had been carrying.

Glancing at the children, the stoneman nodded and took aim at a particular location on the stealth airship, now quite close. Down from the airship flew a brace of missiles, exploding to either side of the stoneman. He ignored them and fired at the slowly turning craft. A small mushroom of orange fire mottled with black smoke burst on the sky-blue underside of the airship. Almost immediately the airship began to roll, and pitch up, and yaw away from them.

Michael wondered if he were really seeing all this, or if it might just be some strange sort of near-death experience, with other people's lives passing before his eyes.

SWIMRUN, CLIMBFLY

After the airship spun away, the Mawari girls Aubrey and Ebu took Darla by the hands and led her toward where the stoneman stood.

We have to leave now, the girls thought into her head. *Immediately.*

"But what about about Susan and Michael?" Darla asked aloud, uncomfortable with the idea of beaming thoughts into someone else's brain. "What about Ka-dalun and Alii?"

Their way lies along a different path from ours. From yours and Major Vasques's, too.

Darla felt the sand softening below her as they sank into it.

"But why?"

Because you and the major are most like us. In all the world. Relax now. We'll teach you how to move.

Fighting off the sensation of drowning as the sand closed over her head, Darla found she could still breathe—once she forced herself to do so. The sensation was both profoundly strange and oddly familiar.

Like when she'd learned to scuba dive in Hawaii, years before. Her diving instructor had his students remove their masks and put their faces in the water, while at the same time continuing to breathe through regulators from their air tanks. It took awhile, but Darla and nearly all her fellow students at last learned to keep breathing, despite their bodies' reflexive resistance to breathing while their faces were unmasked and underwater.

Beneath the sand, of course, the visibility was worse—far more limited—and the experience more claustrophobic than even her worst day of scuba diving during an algal bloom off southern California. Moving through the sand (which was cooler with depth) felt odd, too. Soon, however, she felt the girls' hands helping her, guiding her, teaching her how to fall and catch herself from falling as she strode forward.

It was like learning how to walk all over again. It was also, she imagined, rather like being a satellite in orbit, forever falling toward its planet but never reaching it, falling and being caught from falling, until "toward" transformed to "around."

As she moved with the girls and the stone major, she realized that she could swimrun and climbfly remarkably fast this way—far faster than she had ever run on earth, or swum underwater, or rappelled down a rock face. The strangeness of it gave way to pure exhilaration. Darla felt her face breaking into the kind of smile she hadn't felt since the second time she rode a roller coaster.

A PARTING OF WAYS

The stealth airship's crash into a *sebkha* silt-flat was not nearly as catastrophic as what the downed helicopter had suffered, but it was bad enough. As Joe Retticker and his crew got out and surveyed the damage, it soon became clear that the airship was going to be grounded for a while.

The sound and then sight of not one but two helicopters, coming in low over the dunes, set the crew and his fellow passengers to jumping up and down or at least waving with considerable enthusiasm. As the helicopters turned and then began to settle toward the ground, he saw the tires swivel downward and inflate into doughnut-shaped pontoons, so that they settled onto, rather than into, the *sebkha*.

He was wondering at the expense of such a cutting-edge modification when doors in both helicopters slid forward and Military Executive Resource Corp troops stormed out. In their wake their commander came striding toward him. Despite the man's smart armor, Retticker quickly recognized him as George Otis himself.

"Hello, Joe," Otis said, smiling. "Looks like you've run into a little trouble."

"A bit."

"Your GPS locator beacon must have gotten damaged in the crash," Otis said. "Lucky thing we were tracking you when you went down. We're here to help."

McGuire gave Retticker a sidewise glance at the mention of the GPS being out, then shrugged. Otis, meanwhile, signaled to two squads of his troops. The first MERC unit cut Fremdkunst, Michelson, and Levitch away from them, leaving Joe Retticker standing beside Yuri Semenov and the crew of the airship. The second squad ran inside the airship. A moment later they returned, their commander reporting to Otis on the damages the craft had sustained.

McGuire's sidewise glance at him lengthened.

"General," Otis said, tonguing a toothpick in his mouth, "you and your folks sit tight while we go see what happened to the people in that helicopter that was following you. Victor here says those poor escaped children might be over there where that helo went down, too. We've only got so much room, I'm afraid, but don't worry. We'll send someone after you. In the meantime, I suggest you take cover in that invisiblimp of yours."

With that, George Otis turned on his heel and headed toward the helicopter from which he'd so recently emerged, taking Michelson, Levitch, and Fremdkunst with him. The MERC troops covered their retreat.

As the helicopter lifted off, Retticker glanced at McGuire and Semenov, to his left and right respectively. He made no move to follow Otis's suggestion, however.

"Looks like there's been a parting of the ways."

"How do you mean?" Semenov asked.

"If I'm not mistaken, Yuri, all of us who've been left behind worked for Doctor Vang. Including you."

Realization began to dawn on Semenov's face, as he figured out what Retticker had already surmised. The allegiances of Fremdkunst, Levitch, and Michelson had been to Otis all along.

"I think I'd better go see what the hell they were talking about with the GPS," McGuire said, turning toward the downed airship. His two fellow crew members turned with him and began to trudge through the sand, back toward the downed stealthship.

"Slow up a bit on that, Mister McGuire."

"General?"

"Not so fast. Just wait a bit. If I'm right, we'll soon see."

Moments later, a flashbomb went off in the vicinity of the airship.

"What the hell was that?"

"A focused electromagnetic pulse bomb, I believe," Retticker said, after another long moment. "Saw one demonstrated at Camp Pendleton, once upon a time. I'd be willing to wager most of our electronics are as good as scrap right about now. All GPS locators, all avionic sys—"

A second, much louder blast sent them all diving for the ground. When they looked up again from embracing the desert, they saw that the downed airship had been reduced to burning rubble.

Retticker stood with the others. Slowly. In the shadeless desert.

"Gentlemen," he said at last, "from his 'suggestion,' I believe that was the end George Otis intended for us. We're on our own from here on out."

Retticker and the men decided to trek over the desert, toward what remained of the downed helicopters. Given how thoroughly their stealth ship had been destroyed, they figured they'd have better luck being spotted by search-and-rescue teams at that location. Their pursuers, after all, had not been hiding from the world. They must have been in contact with someone beyond the great sand sea.

BROAD WINK OF THE MIND

Michael and Susan sat on the sand, not far from the wreckage of the helo they'd once flown aboard. Both of them were still trying to wrap their minds around what the children had done, when the brecciated man came and did what *he* did. They had by no means yet managed to make full sense of any of that before Darla, Ebu, Aubrey, and the breccia-skinned man, with only the most perfunctory of farewells, waded into the sand and vanished beneath the desert.

Alii and Ka-dalun had been left behind with them, but the kids hadn't been inclined to explain very much. The adults' confusion only intensified when a brace of helicopters came gyring in out of the late afternoon light. Landing on tires that swiveled and ballooned into sand pontoons, the two helos disgorged troops who, guns drawn, quickly surrounded them.

From their uniforms and insignia, Michael recognized them as private security troops of something called Military Executive Resource Corporation. Once the surviving CSS helo crew members had been bound and gagged by the MERC troops as part of their securing the landing zone, a silver-haired man strode confidently toward them.

"Uncle George! Uncle George!" shouted Ka-dalun and Alii, breaking away from Susan and Michael and running toward the silver-haired man. Just as the man, with an immense smile, gathered the two youngsters into his arms and stared over their shoulders at Michael and Susan, Michael recognized him.

George Otis. Michael and Susan stood some distance away, but they could not help overhearing what the kids were saying—and they could scarcely believe what they were hearing.

"Thanks for sending us information on shooting stars, Uncle George!" Ka-dalun said happily. "And the End Times, too!" Alii added. As the two children turned with "Uncle George" and headed back toward the helo from which he'd come, their "Uncle" regaled them with the news that he'd brought with him spears from Vienna and Rome, Armenia and Antarctica.

Michael glanced at Susan, who looked as stunned as he felt. Prodded by their guards, they followed in the direction in which the children and Otis were walking.

That was what puzzled Michael most. He knew something of the abilities the Mawari kids possessed. He had seen them himself. Surely they could have disappeared into the sand like their fellows, or evaded capture in some other way? But they had done nothing. Instead, they had run shouting and laughing into the arms of George Otis.

"Maybe Darla Pittman was right," Michael muttered to Susan. "Maybe the kids are out for revenge." No sooner had Susan shaken her head no, and nodded toward the kids, than it was as if someone had flashed a broad wink into his mind.

The children weren't even looking at him, yet he felt this odd reassurance could only have come from them. If so, what *was* their game plan? What were they trying to do? As he and Susan were taken as prisoners for transport aboard one of Otis's helicopters, Michael found it more than a little difficult to predict how the future might unfold.

CEREMONY OF INNOCENCE

Darla Pittman, Marc Vasques, Aubrey, and Ebu came up out of the sand at civil twilight, the twilight of color. Civil twilight was turning into nautical twilight, the twilight of shadows, when the two girls, each carrying a knife taken from the crash site, approached Darla and Marc with them.

"Give me your right hand, please," Aubrey said to Marc. Ebu said the same to Darla. Both adults did as asked. Simultaneously the girls slashed open the palm of each adult's right hand—deeply, until the blood flowed. Almost before the pain of what had just happened could fully register with the adults, the girls placed Darla's and Marc's bloody palms together, pressing them surprisingly hard palm to palm, mingling their blood as if in some ceremony of bonding or kinship.

"What was that all about?" Vasques asked, staring at the spot of coagulating blood, where Aubrey had somehow managed to find a chink in his stony armor.

"Your guess is as good as mine," Darla answered—and it was true, for the children had already walked away, and were not telling.

PRETERITION

Retticker, Semenov, and the stealthship crew slogged and paused and slogged again, over dune and flat, through evening into night into morning. Through it all, Retticker's mind pinballed repeatedly over the same table, bouncing against the bumpers of betrayal, the flippers of Otis's active malevolence and Vang's not-so-benign neglect. The lowest basin of attraction that his mind always returned to, however, and which always rocketed his thoughts back up to the top of the table, for yet another go-round, was the image of the sand-and-stone man taking aim and firing at their stealth craft.

Was it him? Had Vasques somehow survived? Had the man he had left to die in the desert come back to haunt him? That pebbled sphinx on the target monitors, who seemed afraid of nothing, was he the final preterit product—grown from tepui meteorite mushroom-stone and years of supersoldier research?

Did Otis know? Everyone presumed Vasques was dead. Michelson and Levitch might have recognized the brecciated man, and Otis had taken the two scientists with him. Those two, however, had not been with Retticker on the flight deck of the stealth ship when the sphinx came awalking and ashooting. So it was quite possible that only Retticker knew the true identity of the "desert camouflaged" soldier who had shot down their airship.

In the midst of such thoughts, they came in sight of the helicopter crash zones. No sooner had the small band of heat-exhausted men reached the area of the downed birds, however, than they spotted a heavy-lift helicopter coming their way.

Those aboard the helo must have spotted them, too, for it began to gyre in on their position. Soon it was hovering before them, disgorging troops from its belly who leapt and lined down to the sand.

The troops shouted to one another, and he recognized phrases in Arabic. So did McGuire, who drew his fifty-caliber handgun from its holster and held it, in casual but ready fashion, beside his leg. As the troops approached, Retticker recognized CSS insignia. The helo was jointly crewed by CSS and Saudi personnel.

"Put away that elephant gun, Mac," Retticker said. "It's over. For us, anyway."

Retticker slowly raised his hands above his head.

TWO OLD FIGHTERS

Jim Brescoll sat alone behind his desk at NSA. The day shift at Crypto City had long ago left for the evening. He rubbed his eyes and soldiered on, as this day joined the several others that had passed, all too eventfully, since he'd last gotten a decent night's sleep.

Not only were the exact locations of the Mawari kids and Avram Zaragosa still unknown, but Pittman, Yamada, and Miskulin had gone missing, too. About the only good breaks he'd gotten were the recovery of the surviving members of the CSS helo crew—bound and gagged, it was true—and the rescue and capture of Retticker, Semenov, and the airship crew.

Sleep-deprived he was, and sleep-deprived he would likely continue to be. His CSS people were still in Saudi, hospitalized for observation. Taken into custody, Retticker, Semenov, and the airship crew had been transported to the United States as expeditiously as possible.

It was a somewhat bedraggled and jet-lagged Joe Retticker who had finally been brought before him for "debriefing." There they had sat, two old fighters, alternately coworkers and opponents, both punch-drunk with exhaustion.

If Jim was to believe Retticker's story, he and Semenov and the crew had been betrayed by George Otis to suffer a fiery fate in the desert. As to why that had happened, Retticker would only suggest that those who had been left to die had been Vang's people, while those who had been rescued—Fremdkunst, Levitch, and Michelson, in particular—had been Otis's creatures. No honor among thieves, Jim thought, even as he kept that thought to himself.

Retticker's own situation—as "material witness" if not prisoner—had at first made the man rather terse and taciturn in his responses to Jim's further queries. Initially, the general couldn't or wouldn't speculate exactly how Zaragosa fit in, or where he or the Mawari kids might be right now, or what their roles might turn out to be in the developing situation. His persistent caginess won Jim's grudging admiration. Even tethered to the stake, Retticker was one old bear who was not going down without a fight.

Gradually, though, the depths of Retticker's anger at being betrayed— at Otis, and even at Vang—provided Jim an opening. Slowly they hammered out a deal, in which Retticker would tell what he knew in exchange for Brescoll's guarantee of protection.

Before long, Retticker had confirmed what Brescoll had already expected: that the Mawari children seemed to have developed extremely unusual powers before their escape. Retticker also volunteered the idea that NSA might want to try tracking at least the kids via gravimetric analysis.

Jim knew well that to get information, one sometimes also had to give information. He revealed to the general the potential uses the Mawari kids might make of their powers. He also told the general of Zaragosa's daughter, Enide, who had been killed by a suicide bomber while father and daughter had been touring Israel with a meteorite exhibition. He confided to Retticker, too, the possibility that Zaragosa might be motivated by the desire to avenge his daughter's death— perhaps in a spectacular manner.

Retticker nodded thoughtfully at that, before responding.

"All I knew was that he's a meteoriticist," he said. "No one told me all this other history, but it makes sense in the context of the larger picture."

"What picture is that?" Jim asked.

"Revenge. I did some focused thinking as we were making our way through the desert. The prospect of dying concentrates your thoughts, that way."

"And?"

"And I remember some things Fremdkunst in particular said. I think I can tell you the date, time, and location toward which all the covert work at Wabar was tending, if not the nature of the mission itself."

Jim sat up straighter in his chair at that.

"So when and where, then?"

"Mecca is where. The Kaaba in the Great Mosque. 'When' is nine Dhul Hijja. Check it on your computer to see what date it corresponds to this year on the Western calendar."

Jim did so. The date was only days away.

"September eleven."

"Precisely, Director. How better to let everyone know the patience of your long, slow revenge, than to coldly accomplish it on the date of that particular anniversary, a decade and a half after the original event?"

"But who? Whose revenge?"

"Many people might be candidates. Personally, I suspect George Otis most of all." He heard the anger kindling in Retticker's voice, which the general quickly managed to rein in. "Then again, I may just be biased."

This time it was the director's turn to nod thoughtfully, as he considered the implications. The death of Otis's nephew—the young man many had considered to be his heir apparent—on September 11, 2001, was an association between the man and date well known even to the most casual observers of American political culture.

"Otis's revenge, Zaragosa's revenge," Brescoll said. "Perhaps the Mawari kids' revenge, too. For what happened to their people."

"Maybe," Retticker said with a slow nod. "But what happened to their tribe had no initial connection to the Middle East. Believe me, I know. Otis told me he thought those kids were part of God's Plan, but it was Doctor Vang who was always more interested in them. For Otis, I think the kids were mainly part of God's Plan B, at most."

"God's Plan B?"

"Maybe provide a cover story for what is really going on. Or, you mentioned scenarios for the possible applications of their capabilities. Perhaps Otis might still want to use them to drop a big rock onto a city, in such a way as to make it look like a nuclear attack. If they could do that, and if that were needed."

"Needed? For what?"

"Armageddon. Rapture. Apocalypse. The final nuclear showdown, where everybody gets to use all the nukes we've been sitting on for so long."

Brescoll remembered verses in Revelation he hadn't thought of in years.

"Stars falling to earth like late fruit from a fig tree shaken by the wind," he said. "The great star Wormwood blazing like a torch as it falls from the sky. The much anticipated fulfillment of prophecy, by making the prophecy self-fulfilling."

"Yes. The fallen star given the key to the shaft of the abyss. George

Otis knows those Scripture passages quite well, I'm sure. But I got the sense, at first, that Otis was just humoring Victor Fremdkunst when it came to some of the meteorite stuff—just stringing Victor along, in case some of the falling-star stuff did prove to be important. To get and keep Vang's money and Tri-Border connections on board, too."

"I thought you said he took Fremdkunst along with him, when he left you behind."

"He did. MERC is one of his companies, and it's been involved in supersoldier R and D almost as long as I have. Maybe he thinks what Victor has discovered will be valuable to him and MERC, after all." Retticker paused, as if he might say more on that, only to change the subject instead. "But I don't think falling stars are how The End will begin."

"Something in Mecca?" Jim suggested.

"That scenario was war-gamed long before Otis ever considered it," Retticker said. "But yes. Mecca. Either before, or after, or simultaneously with something going down on the Palestinians. In Gaza would be my guess."

"What kind of something?"

"Fuel-air bombing. Some type of aerosolized fuel-cloud with secondary detonations. Blast and shock-wave overpressures like a nuke, but with less fire and no radioactivity."

Jim whistled softly through his teeth. He tried to get Retticker to say more on that—his own connections in the Israeli Defense Forces? Otis's connections there?—but Retticker would contribute nothing further. The interview was at an end.

"General, for your protection, I'm assigning you to our Crypto City town jail," he told Retticker. "Our Special Operations Unit oversees it. I once spent some time there myself, during the Kwok-Cho affair. It's not so bad."

Retticker nodded. They both stood.

"I'll have to be content with that, then. I'll be more content, though, if you nail that bastard Otis."

"We'll do our best."

Then Retticker was gone, without saying any more. What he'd already said had been enough, at any rate. Enough to make the director send out a flurry of messages to the Pentagon, to State, to the Israeli embassy and the IDF liaison. He gave all of them the heads-up on a fuel-air bomb scenario and suggested heightened security around all fuel-air munitions. He particularly warned the IDF liaison to have the Israel Defense Forces keep an eye out for rogue elements in its own ranks—Kahanists, or other extremists who might have Christian Zionist or Dominionist connections.

With a sigh he realized that such messages were all he could do in that theater for now. He hoped even that much didn't sound so paranoid that it would be ignored.

Beyond all that, however, what Retticker had said was enough to keep Jim soldiering on. He knew he'd be awake with these matters all night. He examined the high-security measures the Saudis had put in place at the Great Mosque. He researched the history of that place, and the warnings that history gave of other "rogue elements." Of the several hundred Sunni radicals—many of them connected with the Saudi national guard—who, under Najdi family scion Juhaiman ibn Muhammad ibn Saif al Utaiba, had captured the Great Mosque complex on November 20, 1979. Of their taking hundreds of pilgrims hostage and so thoroughly stymieing the Saudi security forces that French paratroopers were called in to help recover the complex—after a two-week siege in which 250 people died, including 127 Saudi troops.

The Saudis had eventually beheaded sixty-seven captured militants for participating in the uprising. Ever since, as the divinely designated "Defenders of the Two Holy Mosques," the Saudis had been very sensitive to security issues in Mecca and Medina. They were especially so now, what with the Shia in Iran and around the Gulf once again questioning their competence.

The sort of frontal assault Juhaiman al Utaiba had made nearly forty years ago could stand little chance of succeeding against current security. What might, though? Missiles? Suicide bombers?

No nation-state he could think of would purposely launch a missile attack on the holiest shrine of Islam, unless the world situation had already gone completely over the brink, into the sort of apocalyptic endgame Otis apparently envisioned. Thankfully, despite all that had happened on the Temple Mount, despite the fever-pitched tensions between Israel and Syria and Iran, no one seemed to be that crazy. Not even in an Arab world balkanized and gamed by Great Power players for more than two centuries.

Might it go that crazy? The history of Arab and Muslim states in regard to the Palestinians had always been complicated. Their refugee status, all that. And no one ever did much to prevent or avenge the massacres at Sabra and Shatila—where the Christians were involved, too—all those years ago.

You never knew, though. It might come down to who were the greatest pariahs: the Israelis, the Palestinians, or the Americans. Syria and Iran, maybe other Muslim states—they all might now have reached put-up-or-shut-up time. He just hoped what they "put up" didn't turn out to be nuclear-tipped missiles, because then the Israelis would put 'em up, too.

Looking for any kind of silver lining to such lowering clouds, he consoled himself that, at the Great Mosque, the Saudis already had up and running the best explosives and biowar detection equipment in the world. No appreciable quantity of any known explosive or even highly flammable substance could pass through the Saudi safeguards unnoticed, not even if it were hidden inside the body of a human bomber. The same was true for all known biowar agents. Even should someone manage to suborn the security personnel, the simple ritual clothing the Hajj pilgrims wore would work against the likelihood of a successful suicide bombing, too, since no really threatening amount of explosive material could be concealed beneath it.

Even if someone—Zaragosa, say?—were bent on revenge through some sort of spectacular symbolic violence—like blowing up the Kaaba?—even if someone could get through, what could he really do, with no weapons and no explosives? Set himself on fire? How, with no fuel?

Spontaneous human combustion, Jim joked wryly to himself. The more he thought about it, however, the less a joke it became. During the Kwok-Cho affair, Jaron Kwok had managed to vanish in something more than "a puff of smoke"—something that looked rather like spontaneous combustion.

Despite the lateness of the hour, he phoned Wang, Lingenfelter, and Amaral. He was unable to reach Dan, but he got hold of Steve and Bree. Within an hour they had joined him in his office. After making the appropriate apologies for such midnight-oil madness, he began to lay out his concerns to them.

"I wouldn't have bothered you to come down here at this hour if I hadn't recalled receiving information, some time back, that Doctor Vang and George Otis were funding research into the debunking of spontaneous human combustion. What I want to know is: Would it be possible to turn the 'anomalous ignition' Jaron Kwok suffered into a weapon?"

Lingenfelter and Wang glanced in perplexity at each other.

"We're not even sure it *was* an ignition," Steve said. "Most of our colleagues favor the idea that Kwok was, in essence, turned into a human palimpsest, written over by information from a parallel universe. I don't see what you're getting at."

"I mean, would it be possible to turn someone into a human bomb? Not by taking an explosive device and strapping it onto him or stuffing it into him, but by creating something that would completely bypass all bomb-detection equipment . . . by turning the body itself into an explosive device. Is that possible?"

Wang and Lingenfelter glanced at each other again.

"Explosion is just fast combustion," Bree said with a shrug. "I suppose if you could accomplish the slow version you could also achieve the fast one."

Wang nodded.

"If you could instantaneously convert a human body entirely to energy, the result would probably have a yield in at least the high-kiloton range. But the idea that you could make someone into a 'meat bomb' or a 'body bomb' . . . just the thought of it makes my head explode, so to speak."

"Very funny," Jim said. "But I do recall that some in my predecessor's Instrumentality cabal were very big on what they called 'controlled cryptastrophes' and 'virtualization bombs.' "

Wang and Lingenfelter squirmed uncomfortably in their chairs, at the same time, as if struck by the same thought.

"Well?"

"There *is* a way your human bomb might happen," Steve Wang said. Bree Lingenfelter nodded in agreement.

"How?"

"The plenum physicists believe the total number of universes is essentially infinite," Bree said, "but with the peculiarity that, from within any given universe, only that particular universe may be considered 'real.' All of the others are at best only 'virtual.' For a variety of reasons stemming from quantum entanglement and teleportation effects, displacement from real to virtual would most likely result in annihilation of the quantum cryptographic device and an area of some specifically calculable size around it."

Jim nodded slowly.

"Might that displacement area be about the size of a human body?"

"It might," Steve said. "Though for entanglement and teleportation to cause such a displacement or parallel-universe overwrite, and the corresponding annihilation, it would require all the DNA in the 'bomber's' body to function as a quantum computational system."

" 'A universe-bandwidth quantum Turing machine based on the interaction of binotech and DNA,' " Brescoll said, quoting his predecessor, " 'and capable of handling unprecedented densities of information.' "

Wang and Lingenfelter nodded.

"In a weird way it would be the mirror opposite of the telemorphy work Michelson was doing with the Mawari children," Wang said, newly struck by the idea, and seemingly still in the process of working it out in his own mind.

"Mirror opposite? How so?"

"The quantum telemorphy state-sharing that Michelson was working on, according to his notes, was like the kind of nonlinear memory that appears when two standing waves merge, travel as one for a time, and then separate into their two former selves again. In the *annihilation* case, though, what would ordinarily be a wave of translation instantaneously interacts with its self-generated mirror opposite, as it were. The state-sharing results in destructive self-interference."

"Wouldn't conservation of energy, or information, or something like that prevent such a thing from happening?" Jim asked.

"Normally, yes," Steve said. "Quantum teleportation doesn't transport a whole particle from one place to another but rather teleports the quantum state of a particle at one location to a particle at a different location. The quantum state of the original particle is destroyed, but that same quantum state is reincarnated on another particle at the destination, without the original having to cross any intervening distance. But in the annihilation case, it's as if the original particle is destroyed, without its quantum state being able to find anywhere else to be reincarnated. A ghost, permanently virtual, never incarnating in any universe, passed over by an infinitude of universes."

Lingenfelter nodded with considerable enthusiasm, given the hour of night.

"What Steve's suggesting resembles matter-antimatter annihilation, in a way," Bree said. "Particles, waves—the effect would be much the same. Even such quantum-state oblivion would leave a trace, though. Your human bomb's explosion would be that trace, as the quantum device inside him oblivioned itself."

"This quantum device . . . could it be small enough to be implanted in a human body? Obscure enough to escape detection in a quick security X-ray?"

Lingenfelter and Wang glanced at each other, then nodded, almost reluctantly.

Jim whistled softly as the shadow of what he feared began to take on substance.

"Can you think of any way to detect such an implant, chemically?"

Wang looked at Lingenfelter.

"That's a tough one," Bree said. "Most of the components could be made of silicon, silica, or silicate. Silicon is the most common element in the earth's crust. Silica occurs naturally as quartz, sand, flint, agate, lots of others—and artificially in everything from glass to concrete. If the quantum DNA effect is triggered by a nonimmunogenic binotech implant—silica nanoparticles doped with organics, say—that would *still* make it difficult to distinguish them from any of a large number of abundant natural silicates that contain organic radicals."

Jim nodded. It would be like looking for a few particular grains of sand in the desert vastness of the Empty Quarter.

"Have your people narrow it down for me on the organics, if they can. How about blocking the signal that triggers the implant?"

"Doable," Wang said, "if you know the nature of the signal. If you don't know where it's coming from, where it's going to, when it's going to be sent, or what its frequency is—at the very least—then we'll have a heck of a time picking it out of the background noise."

"Do we know any of that information?" Bree asked.

Jim pondered that a moment before answering.

"Only when it's going to be sent, and where it's most likely to be originating from."

His two best scientific advisers looked expectantly at him. He exhaled slowly, before he spoke.

"Most likely it'll be sent from the vicinity of the Kaaba in the Great Mosque at Mecca. On September eleven."

He didn't need to say any more. Steve and Bree nodded, fully aware of the gravity of the situation. They made no complaints as their discussion ended and they excused themselves in order to get to work. As his advisers were going out the door of his office, however, Jim overheard Bree mutter about how there just wasn't enough time, not with the countdown to zero soon to be measurable not in days but in hours.

Yes, he thought as he stared at his desktop. Not enough time.

He was just about to call it a night—or an early morning—when he looked up at a noise to see Dan Amaral stumble in, hollow-eyed and clutching a cup of coffee. Jim frowned.

"I know, I know," Dan said. "Day late and a dollar short. I was reviewing interrogation vids of all the people taken into custody at Wabar—for ten hours straight, yesterday. I turned off all my contact machines so I could get some sleep. Sorry. What's going on? I thought I saw Bree and Steve leaving the building. Mind bringing me up to speed?"

Grudgingly, Jim recapped his discussions with Retticker, and Wang, and Lingenfelter. As he was finishing up the review, however, a couple of thoughts occurred to him.

"Dan, that woman CSS took into custody at Wabar, the meteoriticist—"

"Vida Nasr?"

"Yes, that's the one. She can identify Zaragosa?"

"So she claims."

"Think she might be willing to go to Mecca to ID him?"

"Hmm! That's odd. She's already suggested as much herself. You gotten psychic in your old age, or what?"

"Not that I know of. We need to talk with her, though."

"We've got her in Riyadh, at the moment. She's got family in the Gulf. She could travel with her brother to Mecca, if it came to that."

"We may need her to do more than just serve as our eyes and ears in the Holy City, too."

"If she'll do it," Amaral said. "Anything else?"

"Yes. Victor Fremdkunst seems to have been one of the people Otis rescued. Back around the time I brought you into this whole meteorite mess, I seem to recall you saying something about Fremdkunst having a research camp in Israel, some Sodom and Gomorrah–linked thing . . ."

"Near the Big and Little Craters, yes. What about it?"

"I'm thinking some of our people who are missing in action might have ended up there."

Amaral nodded.

"Might be worth hooking up with the Israelis and checking that place out, too," he agreed. "But there's not a lot of time before the drop-dead date."

"I'm well aware of that. It'll just have to be *enough* time, for all our sakes."

PURER VENGEANCE

After the gravel plain of Abu Bahr, flat and featureless, after the dead bushes in the wind-bent sands, after passing beneath the shadow of Saudi Arabia's second-highest mountain, Ibrahim Jebel, along the dry riverbed of the Wadi Turabah, after all that, coming into Taif was a blessing beyond measure.

Or so Avram felt, anyway, as he and Mahmoud rode out of the desert of the Najd. Their battered bodies on their battered ATVs were welcomed at last by cool breezes as they climbed the Taif-Jeddah Escarpment Road, to the city nestled between granite hills on the eastern slope of the Hijaz, a mile and more above sea level.

They were welcomed, too, by the guards who checked their papers. "Checked" was the word, for the officers gave those documents only the most cursory of glances, especially after Mahmoud began regaling them with the story of how he and his comrade from South America, Ibrahim Fayez, rejoiced to have now come to Taif—the traditional gateway for pilgrims headed east on Hajj to Mecca—after traveling by night, for weeks, on ATVs, from deep in the sands of the Rub' al-Khali.

The chief of the men who stopped them was a fellow sporting an extravagant black mustache, and whose uniform stopped where it gave way to the traditional red-and-white kaffiyeh head cloth. He proudly informed them that he was of the Banu Thaqif people. Although he and his people had long since settled into a life of industrious farming, herding, and trade, they still had a broad and deep reverence for the desert and the ancient ways. To him, what Avram and Mahmoud had done was equal parts heroic, spiritual, and spit-in-the-eye-of-fate crazy.

So it was that—no matter how much Avram might have wanted to stay out of the spotlight—the two travelers entered the city of Taif, official summer seat of the Saudi government, under escort of local representatives of that same government.

Despite the fact that Taif was a city of some 350,000 souls now swollen to nearly double that by bureaucrats, summer tourists, and hajjis, the story of two men who had accomplished the Empty Quarter crossing to Mecca, at night and on ATVs—that was worthy of at least local press attention. Or so the extravagantly mustached officer believed, as he happily cell-phoned contacts in the local media to inform them that he and his "special friends" were coming into town.

Providing Mahmoud and Avram with hands-free two-way radio headsets so that he might serve as their guide, the mustached officer drove his government-issue car behind them as they proceeded, at his direction, on their sandstorm-blasted ATVs. Navigating streets lined with palms and oleanders, they passed through a city of modern government offices of marble and glass—the King's Office, the Council of Ministers, Ministries too numerous to mention. Buildings where, according to Mahmoud, the Taif accords ending the war in Lebanon had been negotiated, and where the Kuwaiti government in exile had been housed during the Gulf War of 1990–91—all cheek by jowl with old mud edifices fronted with carved wooden doors and wooden louvre windows.

They passed the rambling Great Mosque on King Faisal Street before coming into the center of the city. There, amid the most traditional buildings, they passed the markets with their Bedouin Taif *souqs,* where shopkeepers bargained with customers over the prices of Bedu carpets and jewelry, souvenirs, gold, silver, spices—and very non-Bedu electronics and French perfumes.

The sight of the *souqs* led the officer to tell them about the most celebrated of all the annual market fairs of ancient Arabia, the Suq Okaz, to which by camel and donkey had come spices, perfumes, produce, rugs, camel-hair tents, sheepskins, jewelry, and pottery. Where, two thousand years before poetry-slams and battles-of-the-bands, poets and singers boasted their talents in combats lyrical rather than bloody.

As the officer guided them on a circuitous route through the city—pointing out to them particularly the white Shubra Palace, summer residence of King Abdul Aziz, the founder of the modern Arabian Kingdom, who had died in Taif in 1953—it became clear to Avram how proud the man was of this town, whose name (as he told them) meant "encompassing" in Arabic.

Certainly his knowledge of the place seemed so, as he exclaimed on the dammed wadis and terraced fields that had made possible the area's many crops, among them the pomegranates, roses, grapes, and light golden honey it had produced seemingly forever. He dwelt particularly on the sweet red roses and the rose farmers, human bees who from ancient times had gathered petals and sent them by camel caravan to Mecca, where they were pressed into attar for perfumes famous throughout the Islamic world.

Leading them through a city that seemed all roses and gardens and parks breeding exotic wildlife—gazelles and Arabian oryx and the houbara bustard Avram had already hunted through falcon's eyes—the officer at last brought them to King Fahd Park, with its lake, playgrounds, gazebos, walking paths, and mosque.

And a small clutch of local media awaiting their arrival, and their words.

Mahmoud gave interview after interview, and Avram grew more nervous with each one.

"What are you doing?" Avram asked, pulling him aside in a break between two such question sessions.

"I'm hiding us in plain sight, my friend," he said. "You'll see."

And he did see. By evening they were in the papers and on local TV—and hotel managers were offering them lodging free of charge.

From the newspapers, Mahmoud cut out clippings about their journey. He left Avram, in his stumbling Arabic, to graciously turn down such manager's offers. Avram/Ibrahim tried to explain that they had grown used to camping under the stars—attempting to live up to some obscure expectation of desert explorers, even as he desperately longed for a hot shower and a night between clean sheets white and cool as folded snow, in a well-made bed, in a high-rise hotel with elevators and room service and maids and bellmen.

"I hope you know what you're doing," Avram said to Mahmoud as they remounted their ATVs in preparation for heading down the Taif-Jeddah Road.

"Don't worry!" Mahmoud said, flashing at him a handful of newspaper clippings about their journey. "These are almost better than any passport or certificate between here and the Great Mosque in Makkah."

The locals they spoke with grew expansive at the mention of the Taif-Jeddah Road. They claimed it was a breathtaking marvel of engineering, passing through rugged mountains, past spectacular vistas—and they also did not neglect to mention that it wound its way around ninety-three hairpin turns, and was especially dangerous to travel after sunset. Which just happened to be precisely the time they left King Fahd Park.

The ride along the escarpment toward Jeddah out of Taif was indeed spectacular, and spectacularly dangerous in the long shadows of twilight. The only stretch of road Avram had ever seen that remotely compared to it was the Palm to Pines Highway in southern California, which he had driven with a fellow meteoriticist some years back, between a conference at Palomar Observatory and a flight out of the Palm Springs airport. On that trip his American colleague had told him stories of crotch-rocket motorcyclists who had plastered themselves at high speeds onto the trunks of great pine trees along that highway.

The memory did not instill confidence in him now, for Palm to Pines was a walk in King Fahd Park compared to this escarpment highway. The road under them now seemed to writhe like a head-smashed snake in the falling dark—until Avram was at last able, via shouting and hand gestures, to convince Mahmoud to stop for the night.

No more than ten minutes after they'd pulled off the road and pitched camp, Mahmoud was sound asleep in his sleeping bag. Avram envied his fellow traveler such dead slumber. After all that had happened that day and all that would likely happen tomorrow, he could use the rest.

Still, he could not sleep. Taking a seat on a wind-sculpted rock, he looked up and watched the night sky deepen to astronomical twilight, as dark as the heavens ever get. The glowing sandstorm of the Milky Way hovered above him at the horizon of infinity. From time to time, a grain from that sandstorm, a shooting star, would cut a golden slash across that sky—a rip in the unbounded darkness that healed instantly, leaving no scar behind.

He thought of his destination and the culmination of his mission. He rubbed the space above the implant at the back of his neck, and wondered at the purpose for which it had actually been put there. He doubted it was as Mahmoud believed: to locate him for rescue, after he somehow managed to snatch the Black Stone of the Kaaba, or at least a piece of it—for truth, science, and the future peace of all humanity. Yet he could bring into the Greatest Mosque no tools or gear for doing that, not even so much as a hammer and chisel, nor a sample bag in which to stow any specimen.

Avram did not doubt that Luis and his collaborators might have already arranged for delivery of such items, perhaps to be handed over in the very heart of the Great Mosque of Mecca itself. Perhaps that was what the implant was for: for them to find him, to whatever purpose.

Somehow, though, he doubted it was for that. True, Luis had been keeping him informed on a slim need-to-know basis, but his "control" clearly also did not expect Avram to be stupidly passive, either. Luis had dropped enough hints to suggest that his stealing the Black Stone, or a piece of it, was only a feint. Why else bring in someone who had the motive for revenge that Avram had?

But if the implant was not for them to find him, then what was it for? Some kind of mind-control thing, to goad him on his mission? If so, it wasn't necessary.

The fire of revenge had not been burned out of him by his time in the desert. The hot hate of all Muslims that had filled him after Enide's killing had, however, been tempered by time into a weapon more pure and precise. Having now met and spent time with so many people raised in that faith, he did not see Islam as any more likely to spawn a culture of violence than Judaism, or Christianity, or any other religion—or scientific secularism, for that matter—given the same historical circumstances.

No, what mattered was that those responsible for his daughter's death would be on Hajj in Mecca at the same time as himself.

His purer vengeance had become stronger and more focused the closer to Mecca they got, but he suspected *that* was his own doing, not the implant's. Since he'd passed inside the four-day time window and the implant had gone active (if Luis's timetable was to be credited), he hadn't noticed any major changes in his thoughts, or his ideas, or his affect. Then again, if the implant was somehow subtly controlling his mind—the very thing he would be using to detect that control—could he ever really know?

Might the implant be intended to guide him to the person or persons who might facilitate his revenge for what had been done to Enide? Or, conversely, might it guide him to those responsible for his daughter's death, so that he might personally avenge himself on them?

The date when he would tick to zero, however, was just too meaningful to that larger world of revenge for it to be coincidental. He had seen the news headlines in the papers from which Mahmoud had clipped the small articles about their exploit. One paper was in English for the tourists, but even his Arabic wasn't so bad that he couldn't figure out, from the Arab-language papers, how excruciatingly tense were the relations between Israel and the Islamic world at this juncture. Particularly those with Syria and Iran.

He had dipped back into the contemporary world long enough today to realize that. Long enough to realize the myriad ways an attack on the Black Stone of the Kaaba, by an Argentinian Jew, could trigger the final conflict too many in the region so devoutly desired.

Maybe his implant was some sort of ground targeting for a missile strike on the Kaaba itself? Or something even more immediately fatal?

He smiled sadly at the thought that his Jewishness might be part of that apocalypse-triggering event. He had never been religious, nor had his parents before him. He was no more devoutly Jewish than Vida Nasr was devoutly Muslim, or Victor Fremdkunst devoutly Christian. Nor was he so devoutly secularist as Mahmoud claimed to be.

He thought of who and what he had seen that day. The city of Taif had been so beautiful after the long desert that he thought Vida must have been wrong, that cities must be more than just the desert domesticated. Their escort, too, so proud of that same city.

A pity that it might all be destroyed and returned wild desert once again.

Looking up at the stars, he thought of all the wars waged in the name of various gods. He thought of how infinitely inventive were the sciences in creating new means of destruction. The fault lies not in our stars, but in ourselves. That was what Victor had said in another context.

To impose our designs upon heaven, but make heaven responsible for imposing those designs upon us—*that* was all too human a thing to do. The problem lay not so much in what people believed as in the fact that it was people—flawed, imperfect, metaphysically malcoded—doing the believing.

It took all the houses of humanity, all the constellations and consternations of its sciences and religions and cultures and politics, to turn a young girl, along with herself, into a suicide bomber. To have that suicide bomber turn another young girl into blasted fragments of mere meat. To reduce his daughter to that phantom limb that still pressed against his chest with a weight far greater than flesh.

Avram looked up at the glowing sands of the endless desert hanging above his head. Maybe only a newer and bigger holocaust can teach us to behave better, he thought.

Let the storm of the stars we have made come down on all of us, in a great shattering blast. I will play my part. I will have my revenge, consequences and collateral damage be damned. Maybe *this* time we will learn our lesson so well that we will never have to learn anything more, ever again.

SILVER LINING

>>>>>>>

Michael woke to the sound of gunfire and explosions. Glancing toward Susan's cot, he saw in the dim light that she was also awake.

"What now?" she asked.

What indeed. So much had happened. The downing of their CSS-crewed helicopter while pursuing the stealth airship. The damaging of that same airship by the sand-and-stone man. The disappearance of him, Darla, Aubrey, and Ebu into the sands. The arrival, soon thereafter, of MERC troops and Otis, who had left the bound-and-gagged helo crew survivors behind and taken aboard their helicopters Michael and Susan as prisoners, and Ka-dalun and Alii as . . . something else.

The helicopters that transported them apparently never left Saudi airspace as near as Michael could tell. They were transferred then to trucks, and it was not until they at last came to a stop that Michael had any good idea where they were.

He and Susan were marched out of the trucks toward one temporary building, while Ka-dalun and Alii were marched in a different direction, toward another. The crater-rimmed terrain, the similarity of the temporary structures here to what they'd seen at Wabar, what he knew of Victor Fremdkunst's work in trying to connect meteoritic impacts to stories of ancient destruction—from all these Michael guessed they were most likely at a work site beside the Little Crater, south of Jerusalem and the Dead Sea.

And so they had been for nearly two days, worrying about the Mawari kids, wondering what might become of all of them. The only silver lining to the thunderhead above them was the fact that he and Susan, in the midst of the extremity of their situation, had begun to realize again how much they needed each other and genuinely cared for each other—something the whirl of events had prevented for too long.

The gunfire and percussive whump of small explosions grew closer now. The door of their building smashed open hard enough on its hinges to strike and rebound off the wall to which it was attached. Men in black combat fatigues and night-vision gear entered crouching, guns drawn, taking up positions along the walls. He and Susan stood shocked, but not so shocked that they didn't raise their hands above their heads.

The strike team shouted to each other in a language Michael didn't really understand but guessed might be Hebrew. Apparently they were declaring the place clear and secured. An instant later a man came in without crouching and strode toward Susan and himself.

"Michael Miskulin? Susan Yamada?" the man asked, mispronouncing both their names, although not so unrecognizably that he and Susan didn't know he meant them. "Follow me, please."

The man who had accosted them by name led them out onto a sandy and rocky flat space where sights of fire and smells of smoke and detonated explosives filled the air. He saw places where others—civilians and military prisoners—were being herded into separate groups. Passing some of the other civilians standing or walking under guard, he thought he recognized one of them as Jeremy Michelson, the telepresence scientist Brescoll had showed them in photos.

Beyond the man he saw other troops, and beyond all of them he could see where rocks like snarled teeth jutted into the star-filled sky, the broken rim of what might or might not have been a meteor crater— the jury was still out, he knew, despite all of Fremdkunst's work.

Michael guessed the soldiers were Mossad or Israel Defense Forces, but a moment later he realized not all of them fit that category. Ahead he saw a CSS officer he recognized, who approached them.

"Doctor Yamada, Doctor Miskulin," the officer said, holding a connection helmet for each of them. "The director would like a word with you."

Somewhat reluctantly, he and Susan put on the helmets and were immediately linked to Director Brescoll, in his Executive Command Suite, far off in Crypto City.

"Susan. Michael. Glad to have you back among us. Looks like our guess as to your location proved right after all."

"What about Ka-dalun and Alii?" Susan asked. "They were brought in with us."

"No, we haven't recovered them as of yet. Imagery from satellites and reconnaissance drones indicates two vehicles departed your location something less than an hour ago. One was headed north, the other south."

"Which one do we follow," Michael asked, "to find the kids?"

"Good to hear you're interested in taking on that job. Saves me the trouble of asking you to consider suiting up in smart armor again. We're sending you north. To Jerusalem."

"Why there?"

"Partly because of things two of the people from Wabar—Vida Nasr and Yuri Semenov—have told us about the Temple Mount. Also because we think we may be picking up an interesting gravimetric signature, moving north. It may be from the two Mawari children who were being held in that same camp with you."

THE HEART'S TURBULENCE

It was along the Taif-Jeddah Escarpment Road that Avram had begun to notice the road signs with the title "al-Mukarramah"—"the Ennobled"—attached to the name of Mecca. Not too far along the ring road to Mecca he noticed other signs, most prominently those reading "Stop for Inspections—Entry Prohibited to Non-Muslims." At the first of these checkpoints, the soldiers who stepped from their kiosk beside the road diligently checked their papers. Out of curiosity the soldiers had also looked over their sandblasted and battered ATVs. That was just the opening Mahmoud had needed to tell them the story of their desert crossing and show them the newsclippings from the Taif papers covering their exploit, as proof.

It seemed one of the soldiers must have radioed to the checkpoints ahead, along the rest of their roundabout route, for from then on their papers were barely looked at. They were either waved through, saluted, given the thumbs-up sign, or at most asked to tell the tale of their journey again. By the time they left their ATVs in the proud keeping of the soldiers at a final checkpoint (to await their return) Avram had almost expected to be carried on the shoulders of pilgrims to the Great Mosque itself.

They had, instead, joined pilgrims in a van that shot along through sun-baked and treeless ridges of the Hijaz. His fears that coverage in the Taif press might give them away now seemed unfounded. Passing under a giant concrete Koran the size of a freeway overpass, he and Mahmoud chanted with their fellow pilgrims the Talbiyya, which Avram thought of as the Prayer of Readiness: "I am here to serve you, Allah! Here I am! I am here because you are incomparable. Here I am! Praise, blessings, and the kingdom belong only to you. Nothing compares to you."

In the van they at last came into the high valley amid the mountains where the lights of Mecca shown before them in the twilight. A constellation of earthbound stars sloshed up toward one rim of the granite bowl in which the city nestled. Amid a great throng of fellow pilgrims, he and Mahmoud made their long way on foot up Umm al-Qura Road, past the point where motor vehicles were banned, to look down at last on the enormous key-shaped Great Mosque glowing under floodlights, the crowds turning their labyrinthine circuits in the head of that key. Climbing stairs, they entered the Haram via the Bab al Salaam, the Gate of Peace. Leaving their sandals at the threshold and stepping right-foot-first across it, they chanted with their fellow pilgrims the ritual greeting: "This is your sanctuary, this your city, this your servant. Peace is yours, you are salvation. Grant us salvation and guide us through the gates of Paradise."

They passed through the pillared halls, long galleries and arcades filled with acres of pilgrim prayer-groups and families from all over the planet, sitting on carpets reading the Koran, or praying, or conversing. The air that had been still and stifling was now moved by a swift breeze. As they rested, Avram felt the marble pillar beneath his hand grow cooler to his touch.

The winds were changing, but in what direction? He only hoped no one could see the turbulence in his heart—and that, to everyone around him, his mounting anxiety and apprehension would be indistinguishable from religious intensity.

ALL HORROR'S EVE

Sitting atop a ridge in the Hijaz as the sun went down, Darla watched as the lights of Mecca and the Mina Valley began to rise into the sky. Each glow from below was a star in the constellation of the Hajj. The floodlights of the Great Mosque, there to the west. The shrine at Mina, nearly due north. Muzdalifah, to the northeast. Across the Plain of Arafat, to the tent city near the Mount of Mercy—and the Mosque of Nimira, closer to the foot of this southern range.

She was so caught up in contemplating the stars as they came out in the sky and on the earth that she almost didn't notice Marc Vasques approaching her in the twilight, dressed in the *thawb* he had pilfered from the camp of a sleeping Bedouin. He was coming from the direction where Aubrey and Ebu sat, dressed already in what they called their *ihram* attire, or "the clothing of the next life"—however it was they knew *that*. They sat facing each other, communing, Darla knew, with their now distant age-mates, Ka-dalun and Alii.

"Good to be up from under the ground," the major said, sitting down on a rock facing her, shedding and setting aside the belt with its two knives, and the assault rifle too, all of which Marc had taken from the fallen troops at the helicopter crash site. "Good to be out under the stars again."

Darla nodded.

"I'm happy to have another day of that subterranean travel behind me, too."

"It's a strange method of transport, I'll grant you that," Vasques said. "Not without its appeal, though, if you feel the need for speed."

Darla smiled into the falling darkness.

"Even the exhilaration of acceleration begins to fade eventually. Have to get off the roller coaster sometime."

"Maybe this is the last day, if the kids are right. They were right enough about that blood-sharing thing, weird as it seemed at the time."

Darla nodded.

"Yes," she said, walking over and sitting down beside him, touching his face in a way that was both clinical and very friendly, at the same time. "I have noticed that you don't look so much like a walking section of cobblestone street anymore."

As she drew her hand away, Marc laughed.

"Not unless I want to. That's the strange part. Here. Shine your headlamp on my hand."

She did so. As she watched, the skin on the back of Marc's hand visibly swelled, hardened, and took on that brecciated, stony cast again. Just as quickly the swollen and hardened condition smoothed and faded away.

"You made it do that?" Darla asked.

"Yep," he said, then laughed again. "Weird, huh? For years I wore and tested smart armor. Now I've *become* smart armor."

"That's a weird superpower to have," she said with a chuckle.

"You're telling me?" he said, but then grew more serious. "Maybe the 'super' part is right, though. Darla, I don't pretend to know from 'gravitational anomalies' or 'metaphage mosaics' or 'metadiamonds' or 'silica nanoparticles,' but I do know those kids have turned into something a helluva lot different from what even we are."

Darla nodded.

"Yet when they took me away from the crash site, they said that you and I were the most like them in all the world."

"Which just shows you how different from *everyone* they really are," he said. "I was part of the raid that killed off most of their tribe. They know that. They could have left me for dead when they found me in the desert. They could have killed me in revenge for what I did to their people. They could have done it anytime. Maybe they still will, but somehow I doubt it."

"I know," Darla said, glancing toward where Aubrey and Ebu sat. "I used to think they might be bent on revenge, because of their history, and because what I'd heard and seen of them made them seem cold and superficial. Miskulin said they resembled children with autism or Asperger's, that they were superfocused. That's really it."

"Superheroes seem superficial," Marc said, "because they're superfocused. Only we don't know what it is they're focusing on."

"Exactly. I think now that, if these kids are bent on revenge, it's not any kind of revenge I can understand by that name."

Marc looked away, into his own memories.

"They're different not only from us, but even from what their own people were. These kids . . . they can reach far deeper inside our heads than their people could. Especially when they try to show us how the threads or spawn or strings, whatever they are, are weaving together. The whole mindtime thing."

Darla nodded. The girls had taught them both their "Cave of Night, Seed of Light" nursery rhyme cosmogony. She understood now that the apparent verb tense simplicity of that poem—and of the entire Mawari language—had everything to do with mindtime. That vast system of branching universes in some sense *spatialized* time, rendering past, present, and future *one* in a higher dimension. Everything is *present* in mindtime, because everything is present in mindtime.

She had to agreed too with Susan Yamada's suggestion that that rhyme had deeper allusions to spores and spawn, and threads or strings. She understood what "A day is a mushroom on the spawn bed of time" might mean. And yes, all of that was (as Susan had also suggested) quite appropriate to a people who'd had a sacral relationship with a metaphage-inflected fungus, so far as that went. Yet that didn't go far enough.

"Their connection with the other two, with Ka-dalun and Alii, doesn't seem to be limited by space and time," she said, still watching the girls. "I think they can probably reach into anybody's head who will give them an opening, now."

"And that infosphere stuff they can pull straight out of the air!" Marc said. "I keep trying not to think of them with little dish antennas growing out of their heads. It's like they've got the eavesdropping and code-crunching capabilities of the whole damn NSA inside each of their skulls."

"I don't know what Director Brescoll would think of your analogy," she said with a smirk, "but that *could* be a consequence of Michelson's work with them. After Barry hit them with the rest of the metaphage material he'd extracted."

He leaned forward, closer to her.

"I suppose these kids have to face the same problem any intelligence agency faces, in the end," Marc said. "Too much information. Too many sources. Like trying to drink from a firehose."

"The more they know, the more they must realize they don't know," she said, looking long and sidewise at them. "They can't know everything. They're no longer children, but they aren't yet gods."

Reflexively, she shivered, although the September night was still quite warm. Just as reflexively, Marc put his arm around her shoulder. Aware something had changed between them, they turned toward each other, looked in each other's eyes, and kissed. She touched his face lightly again.

"I know what superpower I gave you," she said, her attempted Mae West flippancy faltering on the huskiness of her voice, "but what superpower do you have for me?"

Glancing quickly toward Aubrey and Ebu and seeing the two of them still preoccupied in their usual superfocused fashion, Darla and Marc slipped down behind the rocks and out of sight. The superpower Marc had for her was a much more enjoyable way of mingling bloodlines than that involving knives and slashed palms.

No sooner had they finished, however, than a deluge of thoughts not their own cascaded into their heads.

The overwhelming complexity of mindtime, of thread and strings and spawn of universes weaving and being woven. Two men they knew—Vang and Otis—arguing about spears and grails, about heresies and faiths, about power and compassion, while being watched by Alii and Ka-dalun. Cargo planes with great cylindrical canisters aboard. Heavy-lift helicopters carrying similar devices. Radar imagery. Tracking data . . .

Marc! Darla! It's happening! Darla! Marc! The clock has ticked—over for the world—to celebrate—with a day of horror—the anniversary— of a day of horror—

Darla wanted to tell them to slow down, to wait a minute, to explain, but at that instant both she and Marc heard the scrape of booted feet in sand, no matter how stealthily the wearers of those boots might be trying to move. Darla broke into a run in the direction of the children. Marc gathered up rifle and knife belt and covered her retreat.

"Hello, Major Vasques, Doctor Pittman!" a voice from the darkness called to them. "Before you do anything rash, consider this: you have what amounts to a cliff at your backs. We have all your escape routes blocked and our numbers are significantly stronger than yours. Best for you and the children to come along with us as quietly as possible."

"Who's 'we'?" Marc shouted into the night. He handed the assault rifle to Darla.

"The people wearing the night-vision goggles—bimodal binoculars, actually—and pointing their guns at you. Victor Fremdkunst here. Greetings!"

"Barry Levitch here. Hi, Darla!"

"Barry, you thieving sonuvabitch!" Darla yelled at her erstwhile postdoc. "You stole my work—and betrayed its intent!"

"We did nothing of the kind. We merely carried it to its logical conclusion."

"This from the man who talked about a world with no religious relics and monuments to worship or destroy, and look who you and Fremdkunst are working for!"

"Give it up, Darla. Otis can chase his 'Spear of Destiny' to his heart's content. I just followed the money. You and those kids can't just slip off underground this time, so you come on, now. We can follow you gravimetrically if we have to. That's how we found you. The children might get hurt, too. Let's not make this any harder than it has to be."

Marc! Darla! Come with us!

"Can't risk it," Darla said, both thinking the words and subvocalizing them. "No time. We have to stop them from tracking you."

"We'll cover your escape," Marc said. "Go. Do it!"

Uncertainty, confusion, and distraction flooded Darla's mind from a source outside herself.

"Go! Now!"

Reluctantly she felt as much as saw the children disappearing into the earth. Then she was too busy feeling and seeing many other things—as she started shooting.

APPROVED SIGNS

The balloon has gone up, Joe Retticker thought. That much was obvious from the frenetic, if not frantic, activity around him as he was escorted under CSS guard into the National Security Operations Center, Room 3E099. Aswarm with technicians in augmented reality glasses or seated before computer monitors and various three-dimensional display tech—volumetric domes, pseudoholo flashbar eyetrackers, air-bending holographic projectors—the situation-room maze of workstations and cubicles was clearly processing one hell of a lot of telepresent information.

Retticker had been to Strategic Air Command's Cheyenne Mountain Complex and NASA's Mission Control facilities in Houston during the heydays of both. With its large flat-panel video display screens covering the walls, NSOC 3E099 was much like those, only faster. The imagery on its various display tech flash-cut from scene to scene almost more quickly than he could follow.

What he saw flashing across the hanging flat-panels, however, gave him pause even as the imagery itself moved and shifted without pause. He saw map and time graphics, mainly focused on the Middle East. On several screens he saw air-traffic-control radar information, triangular red icons moving through Israeli airspace. Another screen showed the Great Mosque in Mecca from above, roughly key-shaped, with the *ihram*-clad Hajj pilgrims walking the rounds of their seven-circuit labyrinth, spiraling in toward the black monolith of the Kaaba and back out again.

Before he was ushered into the considerably greater privacy of the Executive Command Suite, just beyond the buzzing hive of Room 3E099, he thought he also saw sky-eye satellite visuals of the Arabian peninsula. Real-time optical feeds from several other locations too, including the force-field blisterdomes of the American and Chinese MAXX facilities and the smaller Labyrinth Key sites, mainly in the South American Tri-Border.

The gravity of the situation was fully brought home to him, however, by the fact that, seated next to Director Brescoll, was the director of national intelligence himself, Ethan Watson, running his hand nervously through his sandy hair and looking very uncomfortable.

"General Retticker, sit down please," Brescoll said peremptorily, preoccupied with something on his ARGUS blinks. "We seem to have located Avram Zaragosa. Traveling under the name of 'Ibrahim Fayez,' photographed and interviewed in a local paper in Taif, not far from Mecca, a day and a half ago." He turned back to the long-distance phone call he'd been on. "This 'Mister Fayez' is at the top of our watch list, and very dangerous. Take him into custody at your earliest opportunity."

Inundated by this flood of information, Retticker sat down slowly. He watched as Brescoll began rapidly blinking up on the ECS's main flat panels a burst of American satellite and AWACS data, split-screened, beside Israel Defense Force air-traffic-control radar tracking.

"It now seems your fuel-air bombing scenario may be under way, as well, Joe," Brescoll continued. "As a result of your debriefing, we flagged the Israelis to intensify security around their MAD FAE munitions and keep an eye out for an attack by elements from within their own ranks. That attack has happened within the last hour."

Through Retticker's mind shot images of missiles or bomb canisters, bursting open precisely, instantaneously spreading mushroom-cap or umbrella-shaped clouds of fuel—then those clouds just as instantly being set ablaze by secondary detonations, flashing from white to black-orange in an eyeblink.

"Any idea who's behind it?"

"Early reports indicate radical Kahanist nationalists, some of them within IDF, attempted to take over MAD FAE support and delivery systems at three bases. Heightened security stopped them at one. From two other bases, however, we now have confirmation that a total of four aircraft with fuel-air munitions aboard have just left the ground—

two fixed-wing cargo aircraft and two helicopters. We have fighters waiting on the deck of the *Lincoln* in the eastern Med. The Israelis have just put fighters in the air and are awaiting anything else we can give them. You said you thought the targets would be in Gaza, didn't you?"

"That's right."

"Why Gaza?" DNI Watson asked.

"That's where George Otis believed such an attack would be most effective."

"I've known George Otis for years," Watson said dismissively. "I can't believe he's behind this."

"You'd best tell Mister Watson what you know about this, General," Brescoll said.

Retticker told him. About the trip to Temple Mount and the Dome of the Rock. About Otis's general elation that his "friends" in the Knesset, decrying the failure of the two-state solution, had called for the annihilation of the "House of Esau" and the "Amalekites."

"That's the Palestinians, according to the Kahanists and Christian Zionists," Brescoll said. Retticker nodded.

"Otis knew—and apparently those Knesset members knew, too—how effective surgical fuel-air bombing strikes would be for such a close-quarters civilian genocide," Retticker said.

"But why do such a thing?" Watson asked.

"Otis read such an event as the fulfillment of a scripture passage in the Book of Obadiah. He thought the outbreak of such calamities and catastrophes would be approved signs of the end-times—and would lead the unchurched to turn, in unprecedented numbers, to Jesus Christ for salvation."

Watson drummed his fingers nervously on the table as Retticker finished up. Odd, Retticker thought. Watson had a reputation for being a cool political operator. Perhaps he already suspected more of what George Otis had been up to than he was letting on.

"What course of action would you recommend to the Israelis?" Watson asked at last.

"Immediate shootdown of the aircraft carrying the MAD FAE devices."

Watson looked from him to Brescoll.

"Do it," he said. "Put out the word via DoD command chain. I'll inform the president."

"And if the Israelis can't or won't take them out?" Retticker asked.

"Then let's pray it's not too late to do it ourselves."

"Hell," he heard Brescoll mutter, "we should be praying already anyway."

The next instant Watson was so busy on the phone it was as if Retticker and Brescoll had ceased to exist. Retticker, however, had little time to note that, for a moment later Doctor Jeremy Michelson, looking hollow-eyed with fatigue, was escorted into the ECS under guard, just as Retticker himself had been, not too many minutes earlier.

SPIRITUAL TOKAMAK

After perhaps half an hour resting, Avram and Mahmoud made their way through enough of the colonnaded immensity to stand, here and now, looking out onto the great courtyard and the long porticoes at its edges. All of this vast architecture framed and surrounded—but somehow did not fully contain—the Kaaba at its center and the crowds around it, endlessly turning and being turned, beneath the pavilion of floodlights, beneath the greater canopy of the night sky.

At long last, Avram was looking upon his goal with his own eyes. Before him stood the 160,000-square-yard parallelogram of the floodlit courtyard of Haram al-Sharif, the Noble Sanctuary of the Great Mosque at Mecca. The edifice was capable of containing nearly one and a quarter million people on a crowded Hajj day. To Avram's secret relief, not nearly that many were here on this night.

Across a broad, roofless forum, he saw where the stone floor gave way to a marble ellipse as smooth and white as a skating rink. At the center of that lake of frozen whiteness, reflected in its surface, stood the Kaaba, still point of the turning world, a building turned four-story-tall black monolith by its own *ihram* attire, the drape of the *kiswa*.

He had seen film and video of this scene, shots from above in which the pilgrims, shrunken by distance, were obliviously walking their seven-circuit labyrinth. To him, they had looked like the wheels-within-wheels or fields-within-fields of a toroidal machine—a crowd-rotor turning around a tall black bar-magnet stator in an enormous dynamo.

From ground level, however, the effect was different—different even from what he and Mahmoud had seen from the Umm al-Qura Road at their arrival. The sense of spiraling toward a core or singularity, and then spiraling back out again—an attraction seemingly magnetic, electric, gravitic, and far more—was still there. What was rotor and what stator was less clear here, however. The crowds hid the Kaaba's base with the density of their own bodies and, watching them, Avram had the odd relativistic sensation that it was not the crowds that were turning but the Kaaba, the black-draped edifice rotating and somehow levitating above the masses of pilgrims.

The night breeze ruffling its cover made the building seem all the more tenuously held by gravity, ready to float off into the sky despite its undeniable massiveness. If the ritual energy of what he looked on now could make even the Kaaba seem so weightless, how much more insubstantial did it make Avram himself feel as he looked toward the eastern corner of that same *kiswa*-draped edifice!

There stood al Hajar al-Aswad itself. The Black Stone. The Right Hand of God. The Navel of the World, in its shining bezel mount. Obscured by crowds turning around it, he could only from moment to moment catch a glimpse of it: pupil at the center of a vertical silver eye, suspended in the midst of a ceremonial hurricane. Silver-horizoned black hole, at the center of a spiral-armed galaxy of human bodies turning.

Avram felt as if he were weightless in deep space, staring edge-on at a glowing sandstorm of stars, everything turning around that obscured singularity, every grain of sand a star and every star a human soul. The vertiginous fear of what he was at last about to undertake shook him so hard he did not know whether to fall up or to fall down.

Around him, men and women wept and prayed, prayed and wept, stunned and overcome by the majesty of the sight before them. Avram looked away, rubbing his eyes, trying to steady and calm himself with reassuring memories of what he'd already accomplished. Dimly he saw Mahmoud moving down from the tiered arcade, toward the floor of the great courtyard and its turning mass of humanity.

When he looked back again, men and women continued to weep and pray, but Avram breathed no easier. The dizzying fear that had gripped him on looking at the Kaaba and its turning crowds was almost overpowering now. He steeled himself against it.

If I could walk through the Gate of Peace, so far from peaceful in my mind, and still not be struck down, Avram thought, then I will *not* be struck down.

He stepped down into the courtyard itself. Looking toward the stone, he said, "Allah, I intend to circle your sacred house. Make the way easy for me and accept my seven circuits in your name." On the edge of the doughnut-ring of turning pilgrims, he straightened his *ihram* and raised his hand in saluting the stone. Joining the crowds in their coun-

terclockwise circling, he was surprised how vigorous these first circuits of the *tawaf* were, even though he knew the Arabic word for the
strong pace they set was *ramal,* which meant "moving the shoulders as
if walking in sand."

Each time a jostling human circuit completed itself by coming in
line with the Stone again, he called out "Allahu akbar!"—"God is
great!"—with all the rest. It was not until he had completed the third
such circuit, however, that he noticed he was being paced by a modestly
dressed woman who, with unexpected assertiveness, grasped him by
the shoulder. The mode of her dress was so unfamiliar that he almost
didn't recognize Vida when she spoke to him.

"Avram, listen to me!" Vida called aloud in English, near his ear,
while everyone around them endlessly prayed or exclaimed on the
greatness of God in Arabic and myriad other languages. "The NSA—
they told me you've got an implant in your head. They say it could turn
you into a human bomb! Please, stop! They don't know when it'll happen, or even *if* it will happen, but for everyone's sake, don't go through
with this! You don't know what you're doing!"

As the motion of the crowd swept him toward the quicker circuits
ringing around the Kaaba—on toward the inner field-lines of plasma-
tized humanity swirling in this vast spiritual-energy tokamak—the madness crashed in upon him. Friends don't let friends blow up the Kaaba!
he thought hysterically—and it was all he could do to keep the laughter from popping the top of his head back like the lid of a foot-pedal
trash can. He saw Mahmoud, an eddy in the flux, stopped and glancing over his shoulder, waiting as the flow brought Avram and Vida up
beside him.

"Thanks for giving me the final piece, Vida," Avram said, as coldly
controlled as he could manage. "I *do* know what I'm doing, now."

Moving onward, he saw two very short women—he would have almost said girls—sweep past him, unaccompanied, swift as ice-skaters
over the floodlit white marble beneath their feet. Something familiar
about them, though he could not put his finger on it, and did not have
time to, in any case.

UNLIKE IN THE MOVIES

Darla had fired in the direction of Fremdkunst's and Levitch's voices,
before tucking and rolling as Brescoll's smart-armor trainers had shown
her. Slamming up painfully behind a rock, she cursed quietly at herself.

They made it look so damn easy in their brief training—and even easier in the movies!

She would've felt a good deal more confident if she were in fact wearing such armor now. Or if she had "become" smart armor, as Marc had. She squeezed off three more rounds, hoping she had distracted their opponents long enough for Marc to get to work.

Flashes of automatic weapons fire erupted in the night, followed by the occasional scream or horrible strangulated gurgling sound. Gradually the weapons fire began to subside. After several moments of aching silence, Victor Fremdkunst and Barry Levitch fell at her feet, cast down. Darla switched on her LED headlamp. Behind the two men, a bloody, stone-skinned Marc Vasques stood. He was wearing night-vision infrared goggles.

"Here, you might need these, now that the kids are gone," he said, flipping up the bimod binoc goggles and tossing her a pair, too. She nodded. With the kids to guide them, they'd had no problem with the subterranean dark, but with them gone, she and Marc were almost as blind as anyone else in the night.

"I suspect they thought I'd be easier to kill," Vasques said quietly. "Bit of a surprise, for them. Once I managed to borrow this night-sight gear, things began to turn our way. Thought you might find these two gents useful. Oh, and one of them had this, too."

Into the light shining from her headlamp, a rectangular box about the size of a woman's handbag came flying. Darla caught it and saw that it was a combination GPS/gravimeter—an expensive handheld model. She placed the unit on the rock and unceremoniously smashed it with the rifle butt until it was quite thoroughly broken.

"What are you doing?" Fremdkunst asked, unable to contain himself any longer.

"We know where the kids are," Darla said, nodding her head in the direction of the Mina Valley, beyond the ridge, toward Mecca. "We don't need to track them."

Vasques pulled Levitch and Fremdkunst to their feet.

"What I want to know," he said to them, "is why you were so intent on capturing those kids."

Neither Levitch nor Fremdkunst volunteered any information. That didn't much bother Darla, however. She figured they'd probably grow more talkative on the long walk to police custody.

OVERPRESSURE

Jim Brescoll was so busy with everything happening over Gaza that he barely noticed when Bree Lingenfelter and Steve Wang joined them, moments after Michelson, under guard, had been brought in. Had he the time to think about it, he probably would have thought the place was getting quite crowded, since DNI Watson was still in ECS with them too, watching events unfold.

On his blinks and on the big flatscreens before him, the imagery pumped to Director Brescoll from his analysts in NSOC 3E099 showed Gaza, Israel, and the eastern Med—bird's-eye and star's-eye views from NRO surveillance satellites and Aurora overflight aircraft.

A more topographically stripped-down screen showed radar-tracked air-traffic icons in motion, vectors of aircraft whose simple geometric representations belied the complexities of the situation. This loftier and more abstract data flooding the director's way was augmented with human-scale sights and sounds, including real-time pilot chatter from Israeli and American aircraft—even pilot camera shots, though patchy and time-delayed.

Nor were they eyeless in Gaza itself. Through his IDF connections, Dan Amaral, out on the floor of NSOC 3E099, patched them into helmet-cam hookups with Israeli units bordering all the target zones.

Jim thanked all and whatever gods there might be that none of the aircraft commandeered by the Kahanists had reached any of their targets . . . so far. Of the two Kahanist-controlled helicopters headed toward Rafah, one had been shot down by Israeli jets. The crew of the other, apparently deciding that they weren't quite ready to make the ultimate sacrifice, had turned and been forced down in Israeli territory. The commandeered fixed-wing aircraft headed toward al-Bureij had likewise been destroyed, though by whom was as yet unclear, since it had been struck simultaneously by machine-cannon fire from an Israeli fighter and an air-to-air missile loosed from a navy-version Joint Tactical Fighter from the *Lincoln*.

That left only the last commandeered plane, now nearly over An-Nuseirat. Missed entirely by air-to-airs from two Israeli strike fighters, it had, perversely, been hit by an Israeli antiaircraft missile launched from a ground battery. The lumbering plane was undoubtedly damaged and losing altitude. Hit and going down, yes, but that descent was too controlled for Jim's liking—and still tracking to target. Must have a hell of a pilot on board, Jim thought grudgingly.

One of the satellites picked it up first: an abrupt bright flash. Even through the sound-damping walls separating the Executive Command Suite from NSOC 3E099, Jim heard a sound much closer than and almost as telling as the flash: the involuntary groan of the personnel in the big room next door.

For all the powers of command, control, communication, and intelligence of which they were masters, they still had not been able to prevent the strike.

Amaral came over the line. Brescoll put the call on conference for all in ECS to hear.

"We have visual confirmation, Jim. It's An-Nuseirat. Looks like we've got a fuel-air detonation at low predetermined altitude. Dead center on the community."

Jim took off his blinks and rubbed his eyes. Scenes continued to play over the screens in ECS, all of them confirming the bad news.

"What was the population density at ground zero?" he asked at last.

"High," Amaral said. "It was a refugee camp for years and years. Figure about four thousand people per square kilometer."

"Right," Brescoll said, forcing himself to consider the ramifications. He looked toward Retticker, whose guards (along with Michelson's) still waited outside the door. Both men were still here because they remained valuable information sources. Might as well use them. "General, any idea on worst-case scenario for damage?"

Retticker pondered it a moment before speaking.

"A thousand-pound-per-square-inch overpressure, out to a thousand yards from detonation point."

Jim nodded slowly.

"So, within roughly a square kilometer, no one outside a hardened bunker could have survived. Four thousand dead, as a first estimate."

Retticker nodded. Ethan Watson leaned forward.

"Mister Amaral, you have considerable expertise in the region. What do you believe the Arab and Muslim response will be?"

"Sir, in the wake of the Temple Mount events, the Iranians and Syrians were already on record saying they would view any mass-destructive Israeli attack on the Palestinians as an attack on all followers of Islam, including the peoples of their own nations."

"But the Israeli government forces were clearly trying to stop the attacks!"

" 'Trying' is the operative word, sir. The Israeli efforts, and their failure, will likely *both* be read as a ploy. The fact of thousands dead is going to make it difficult for governments in the region to show restraint, even if they were inclined to do so. The rarer action lies in virtue than in vengeance, but that's probably too rare to be expected here. Too much history already. I think we may be looking at the beginning of a theater nuclear war."

Jim turned to Watson.

"We'll put our early-warning satellite systems on high alert for flare-ups of missiles leaving silos, or going into suborbital boost phase," he said. "Heightened surveillance from Syria to Pakistan. Reconnaissance systems tracking the movement of tanks and armored columns through the desert, and planes through the air. South to Arabia and Sudan, west to Morocco."

Watson nodded, not happily.

"Director Brescoll, Mister Amaral—how do you expect the launches themselves to play out, if they do?"

"Decapitation strikes," Jim said. Retticker concurred.

"Launches against Tel Aviv and Jerusalem," Amaral suggested. "Response against Damascus, Tehran, possibly Karachi. We don't know exactly how the Arabian peninsula will go. There are added wrinkles if Jerusalem gets hit, too."

"Oh?"

"A strike against the heartland of Western faith . . ." Amaral said, trailing off. Jim knew what Dan was thinking: the worst kind of synergy between and among Islamofascist, Judeofascist, and Christofascist groups.

"The Israelis have over two hundred nuclear devices," Jim admitted. "There are some groups, both there and here, who might view any attack on the historic heart of Judaism and Christianity as sufficient grounds for the destruction of the historic heart of Islam. Turning Riyadh, Jedda, even Mecca, into glass—that might not be beyond the realm of the possible."

"If anything happens in Mecca now," Amaral said, "all bets are off. There are millions of pilgrims from all over the world in Mecca at the moment. A nuclear strike there could quickly escalate to global war."

Watson looked up at the imagery still playing over the screens.

"I'll confer with the Pentagon. We'll urge the president to go to highest defense condition. We have no choice in the matter."

SORROW, AND HOPE

Darla and Marc had not marched Victor Fremdkunst and Barry Levitch long or far when Darla was almost bent double by a sudden pang.
Marc called them to a halt.

"You felt it, too?" Marc asked, keeping an eye on both their captives and Darla as she slowly straightened up, then nodded.

"From the kids," she said, looking off to the north. "Something
very bad has happened. Something that reminds them of what happened to their own people."

Marc nodded slowly.

"Like getting sucker punched by a fist full of deep sadness. Sorrow.
I felt it on the tepui, but this was far more powerful."

"Regret, too, for not being able to stop it in time."

" 'Too late.' That's what I felt."

"Something else beyond that, though," Darla said. "Too late for
some things, but maybe not too late for everything."

Fremdkunst and Levitch looked at them as if they were speaking
gibberish, then glanced at each other as if they doubted the sanity of
their captors. Marc and Darla prodded them to move on.

UNCHARACTERISTIC BEHAVIOR

For Michael and Susan, the wave of sorrow, regret, and pain that
seized them coincided with a bright flash like lightning toward the
west. George Otis, being marched from a villa south of Jerusalem,
burst into praise and laughter at the sight of it.

"Thank you, Jesus! Praise the Lord! Nothing can stop The Plan
now! From its scattered fragments I have reforged the Spear of Destiny
in a form more powerful than any yet wielded by human hands!"

Michael saw Susan eye the man narrowly, anger in her face, and
moved to stop her before she did something she might regret later.

Their own sphere of operations had been going well, up to now.
Brescoll and his people at NSA, suspecting that the gravimetric signature they'd discovered might be linked to the Mawari kids, had traced
that signal here, to this very location, before it stopped, just over forty-
five minutes earlier. Joining the CSS and Mossad troops on this raid,
they'd taken little fire before Otis's MERC bodyguard stood down and
surrendered, apparently on Otis's orders. Now the man himself was in

custody, though none of the Mawari kids had been found on the premises.

Susan was madder—and moving faster—than Michael realized. By the time he caught up to her and, with the help of two soldiers, restrained her, she had already smashed Otis across the face. The blow, from a fist gauntleted in smart armor and augmented by exoskeletal servomotors, would have knocked Otis to the ground had he not been held up by his captors. It was still powerful enough to muss the man's perfectly coiffed helmet of silver hair more than a little, and leave him bleeding from nose and lip.

"You pietistic bastard!" Susan shrieked, despite the restraining hands on her. "What in the name of hell have you done? Where are the kids?"

Her vehemence caught Michael by surprise. This wasn't like her. Why was she doing this?

With a handkerchief Otis, undaunted, mopped lightly at the blood coming from his nose and upper lip.

"In the name of hell, nothing," he said, with a somewhat pained smile. "In the name of heaven, everything."

"Let it go, Susan," Michael said. "Don't let it make you like him." She ignored him, still straining against the arms of those who restrained her.

"No need to worry about that, son," Otis said. "You people will never understand. God doesn't rule by 'consensus.' God doesn't believe in 'democracy' or 'diplomatic solutions.' His Word is law. No Congress of Angels overrides his veto—and He doesn't negotiate with Satan! The final destruction of the Amalekite House of Esau has begun. Before very much longer the Kaaba and its idolatrous Black Stone will be blasted into dust, one way or another. The Lord has given us the strength to do impossible things! We have claimed the spear and solved its secrets! We hold the destiny of the world in our hands! I shall rule this world as its Governor, for God and under God, whose Plan now reveals itself in all its majesty!"

"The children!" Susan shouted. "What have you done with them?"

"I gave them to Vang," he said with a shrug. "I had no need of them anymore. You may look for Ka-dalun and Alii, as they call themselves, with Vang."

"Why? Why him?"

"Not that I need to explain myself to the likes of you," Otis said, dabbing at his blood as it coagulated and seeming to become belatedly disoriented from the blow he'd suffered, "but I suppose I owed him for some of the operatives he lost. The general and that Russian fellow. Oh, and the crew of that airship, too—the one that got destroyed. And, farther back, for putting me in touch with the strange folks beneath the Tri-Border domes."

He paused to straighten up, but his disorientation only grew.

"In exchange for the children, you know, he also promised to fly me out of here in that remaining ghost taxi of his. Either I misplaced it somehow, or the children tricked me and took the artifact—but only a temporary setback, I assure you. After this tribulation time, I will rule in God's name. I've been betrayed, but no matter. 'For all flesh is as grass,' Scripture says, 'and all the glory of man as the flower of grass. The grass withereth, and the flower thereof falleth away.' "

No sooner had Otis finished speaking than Michael felt Susan abruptly relaxing against his arms.

"Thank you, Mister Otis," she said. "I've helmet-recorded your every word. I think I'll forward it on to Director Brescoll at NSA. Maybe, if the Divine Plan doesn't work out quite as you've predicted, the courts might be interested, too. I hope you enjoy withering and falling away—in prison."

Michael thought he saw a flash of doubt flicker across Otis's face, but he couldn't be sure.

EYES AND MIRRORS

"Avram, don't make me do this!" Vida said when they had just about completed another circuit of the Kaaba.

Mahmoud beside him, Avram stared at her even as the pressure of circling humanity called them onward.

"Do what?"

"This."

Vida began screaming and pointing at Avram. A circle opened around them.

"Infidel! An unbeliever—come to desecrate the Holy Shrine!"

Avram listened, stunned, as she screamed variants of those words—in Arabic, Farsi, Urdu, French, English. Men in the crowd began turning toward them.

Mahmoud stepped around him and toward Vida. In his upraised

hand flashed a knife of ceramic, white as the floodlit marble floor. Ankawi slashed down with the blade to silence Vida, striking her upraised arm and then her upper left chest, outward from the collarbone.

As Vida fell backward, Avram put out his hands, gripping and stopping Mahmoud from striking again.

"Mahmoud! Stop! What are you doing?"

"Your mission must be accomplished," Ankawi said, a wild look in his eyes. Avram wanted to say something, to explain, but in the next instant Ankawi turned to Vida and spoke to her in Farsi.

"Woman, cease! Allah wills that this shall happen! Only fire and the sword can cleanse the world of the abomination that names itself Israel! The will of Allah must be fulfilled!"

Avram felt turned to stone. Had he heard right? Could he trust his understanding of Farsi? Was Mahmoud only acting a role *now*? What role? For whom? For Vida? For the crowds surrounding them? Had he been acting all along? Avram had pitied Mahmoud as a fool taken in by his own scientific enthusiasms, his own fundamental secularism—a dupe unable to see the potential danger of Avram's mission. But who might really have been played for a fool? And who would pity him?

As men tackled and bowled both him and Mahmoud to the ground, away from the Kaaba, Avram was thinking, in a strangely detached way, of mirrors and telescopes. He had believed that nongovernmental religious terrorists who attacked centers of secular power would stay on one side of the mirror, and government-backed political terrorists who attacked holy sites would stay on the other side. So wrong. So very wrong.

Had Mahmoud, playing knave to Avram's fool . . . had even he, in some unconscious way, actually revealed the truth of his own mission when he said politics and religion were all mixed together on both sides of the equation? Despite the pain of being kicked and struck by innumerable fists and feet now, Avram most feared that, in this war of mirrors in which he'd become lost, the boundary between salvation politics and liberation theology, the separation between government-backed political terror and nongovernmental religious terror—all such distinctions vanished at infinity.

Looking inward toward the Kaaba, he realized he was still too far away for his implant to trigger. He doubted he would ever get close enough now. But did it matter? Luis had said that if Avram's implant ever read his physical condition as approaching the last extremity, it would go to final activation on its own. A fail-safe mechanism, he'd called it.

Under the repeated blows and strikes, Avram's pain had become so excruciating he was surprised he could still think at all—and yet he could, with aching clarity. Even as his body continued to struggle with his attackers, his mind calmly informed him that he was dying as fast as could be reasonably expected. Nothing to do now but wait.

Intermittently, through the movement of the intervening bodies of the crowd, he could see the Black Stone in its silvery mount. The vertical eye, watching him, like the eyes of so many others distracted by the spectacle of transgression and punishment.

Or *was* that eye distracted? While many nearby stood preoccupied with his situation, he saw those two short, girlish women again, beside the Black Stone itself, their hands raised to it, touching it, just above their heads. He thought he saw light pouring from the pupil of that eye—fountaining sparks, bright strings and threads and cords of cloud-chamber traceries bending and leaping and rope-dancing into the girls' palms. One of the women turned to face him, and he knew where he had seen the girl before.

At the camp, by the craters at Wabar. In Michelson's lab.

A SONG TO SHAPE THE TIME

Although they were separated by hundreds of miles, it was in the same instant that Darla and Marc, most powerfully, and Michael and Susan, only slightly less so, heard inside their minds the full grandeur of the song that the Mawari would have used to sing their mountain to the stars, if the threads of this world's timelines had allowed.

It was the same cryptic, cosmogonic nursery rhyme—of "cave of night" and "seed of light," a toy for the minds of alien children—unfolding into the Mawaris' full tale of spore and spawn and seven ages. Now, hearing the fully realized opus in their own minds, they recognized this was not just a chant to tell a story: it was a hymn for weaving the very fabric of space and time—and embedded within it, as in a hologram, resided all the structures of all possible spaces and times.

Much of what it sang into their minds was beyond their minds' ability to comprehend, but some of it they already knew or were capable of knowing.

The history of the Mawari, of their sacred stone and totemic mushroom, of their search for quartz stones of a particular lattice configuration as parts for the building of a shamanic machine with which to defy space and time and gravity.

Of the role of sacred stones in tents and temples and holy cities throughout the world. Of the presence and powers of all the spears of God, the meteoritic Nuhus, the starborn Excalibur of Arthur, Odin's Gungnir, the diamond thunderbolt Vajra thrown by and returning to the hand of a Hindu deity. Of Parzival's stone exiled from the stars. Of the lapis, the philosopher's stone. Of the spear head supposedly forged by Tubal-Cain, of meteoritic iron during the Bronze Age. Of the spear of Longinus, sought for its powers by Mauritius, Constantine the Great, Charles Martel, Charlemagne, a thousand years of Holy Roman Emporers, and Hitler. Of the Templars, assassins, Kabbalists, alchemists, and Grail knights who all sought transforming power and the power to transform.

Of tupilak and fairy folk. Of phoenix phenotypes and metaphages, metadiamond cages and silica nanoparticles. Of the meteorite in Mecca as open-ended superstring spawnthread weaving to the plenum of all possible universes. Of cosmic ancestors from the end of time and back again—of that, too, it sang.

All only pieces of truth. All liquidly sparking shards fallen from the infinite, destined to return to the infinite, paradoxically never having left the infinite. Hearing that song of songs, Michael and Susan, Darla and Marc, for all they did not understand, still understood that the children yet had their piece to say.

BRILLIANT PEBBLES

Few human beings on earth were more aware than Jim Brescoll of just how much piece needed saying at that moment. In the crowded Executive Command Suite at NSA, he'd at last gotten Wang and Lingenfelter blinked up and connected into the system.

"We have ground confirmation of satellite intelligence," one of his National Reconnaissance Office analysts said over the ECS speakers. "Missile launch flares in southern and western Asia. Syria, Iran, and Pakistan confirmed. Wait. We have indication of launch—eastern Mediterranean. Israel. Negev desert."

So it had finally come to this. Although it was only the madness the world had been preparing for, all his life, one scenario after another, he could still hardly believe it.

Director Brescoll wished this, too, were only a drill, some apocalyptic war-gaming scenario to be contemplated and evaluated at leisure afterward. In any truly apocalyptic situation, there might well be no *afterward*—or at least no one to recollect in tranquillity what happened in the thermonuclear heat of a totally destructive passion.

He blinked up maps plotting satellite and telescopic scans of the rising missiles, as well as ground-based and airborne radar tracking. In a moment, after the satellite shots and plotting graphics had settled down, everyone in the room could see what was happening. The situation was growing grimmer by the minute.

Then, in no particular order, missile trajectories began to disappear.

"NRO, do we have malfunction?" Jim asked.

"I don't know, sir. One minute we're tracking ballistics, and the next minute there's nothing there. Like each track just vanished."

"Or something destroyed them," Wang said abruptly, following the readout on his blinks and on the imagery on the big screens. "Director, I thought I saw meteor traces on that satellite shot. Can we get the NRO astronomers in on this? I think that 'brilliant pebbles' scenario may actually be under way!"

Brescoll put out the call. During the moments it took for the analysts to come on line with their data, more missile trajectories disappeared. Once the spy-satellite and ground telemetry data was checked and posted to the flatscreens and display domes in ECS, it was clear that a very strange sort of meteor storm was indeed taking place.

"Look!" Wang said. "It's like shooting stars are being targeted on the rising missiles—to knock them down!"

THE PLAY BETWEEN MARVELS

The hundreds of miles separating Ka-dalun and Alii from Ebu and Aubrey were no separation to them, playing together a common game on uncommon ground, in a sky of mind.

The uncommon ground was woven of a song, the song of their people, of cave of night and seed of light. Of how, in the void of endings, the spore of beginnings bursts into spawn. Of how the threads of spawn, absorbing the stuff of the void, knit it into stars. Whose spores, bursting into spawn, absorb the stuff of stars and knit it into worlds. Whose spores, bursting into spawn, absorb the stuff of worlds and knit it into life. Whose spores, bursting into spawn, absorb the stuff of life and knit it into mind. Whose spores, bursting into spawn, absorb the stuff of mind and knit it into worldminds. Whose spores, bursting into spawn, absorb the stuff of worldminds and knit it into starminds. Whose spores, bursting into spawn, absorb the stuff of starminds and knit it into universal mind, the void of endings, the void that has taken all things into itself, whose spore is the spore of beginnings, the fullness that pours all things out of itself.

On that uncommon ground even the common game of marbles the children played was played in the most complex way. The marbles were all always in motion, falling through space like bullets toward a blue bull's-eye of a world. The children shifted the shape of the ground under those marbles, too, so that the speed of the marbles also shifted.

The power to shift the shape of space came from a song they had found, which fell now from the sky their minds made:

> *When the stars—*
> *Threw down their spears—*
> *And water'd heaven—*
> *With their tears—*
> *Did he smile—*
> *His work to see—*
> *Did he—*
> *Who made—*
> *The Lamb—*
> *Make thee?*

And they sang it in joy and laughter, despite all darkness and all pain, for they knew that the weapon of heaven powerful enough to overcome all one's enemies must first pass through one's own heart.

CHANCE AND NECESSITY

As more of the astronomical data came in, Jim saw it was true. Stars falling to earth, he thought. Like late figs from a fig tree shaken by the wind. Only not nearly so randomly. Were the Mawari children indeed "showing the stars where to fall," as they'd promised Michael and Susan?

Soon all the trajectories of the initial missile flights were gone from everyone's view. They were no longer being tracked.

"No one has a missile defense shield anywhere near that good," Retticker said. "At least none I ever heard tell of."

"Look at the trajectories of the meteors," Lingenfelter suggested. "All earth-crossers—Apollo and Aten asteroids. Being used as gravity-powered kinetic-kill vehicles."

As they watched, the strange storm continued.

"Those Mawari kids—they could do this," Michelson said. Everyone in the ECS stared at him. "All the properties of the quantum telemorphic tools we trained them on, they fully incorporated that into their neuronal space-states. If they can teleport quantum information densities into the spacetime fabric, they can reshape the curvature of spacetime to control the orbits of those rocks."

"They're taking out those missiles by throwing spacetime curve-balls at them," Wang said, a gleeful awe in his voice.

"Just as we predicted!" Lingenfelter said.

Brescoll flicked his blinks up onto his forehead and gave her a side-long glance.

"I thought you said all this was a 'big hypothetical—' "

"Well, yes, but now we can *see* it!"

Jim shook his head and put the blinks back down over his eyes. They could predict it in their own minds, but they wouldn't believe it until they'd seen it with their own eyes. He continued observing what was happening with any missile flight launching from anywhere in the region. In a moment the pattern was clear.

"Looks like the stars are coming down on anything rising with hostile intent," Brescoll said. "How the stars would know 'intent,' though, I have no idea."

"I don't think the star throwers need to know intent, exactly," Michelson said. "The telemorphic properties those kids incorporated give them transparent access to everything in the infosphere."

"I thought the MAXX domes were supposed to prevent that kind of access," Lingenfelter said.

"Maybe the folks under the domes are allowing this to happen," Brescoll said, sounding more authoritative than he felt, given that the thought had only that moment occurred to him. "Maybe they're some-how working in tandem with what the kids are doing."

"All SCADA—supervisory control and data acquisition—systems worldwide would be absolutely transparent to them, as well," Michelson said. "They know everything that can be known about where those missiles are launching from, what their targets are, under what orders—"

"If Michelson here is right," Retticker put in, "they'd probably know all that for aircraft- and artillery-delivered munitions, too. Director, if this is about hitting things with space rocks, I'd suggest you get Yuri Semenov out of your happy holding tank and bring him up here, ASAP."

Jim nodded and sent out that order, even as the people in the room around him broke into excited chatter. Jim refrained from joining in, still contemplating what had apparently happened. He saw, on the screen, that the terminator line of dawn had just risen over Pakistan.

Small fiery stones burning out of the sky, streaking toward other streaks rising on columns of cloud by day, pillars of fire by night. He remembered seeing those images under the dome of the MAXX in California. Seemingly, it had come true. He had seen other things as well, though. Great bursts of forking lightning. Vast thunderclaps. Mushroom clouds rising. Those had not come true—not yet, thank God.

And who *was* to be thanked? Those around him seemed content with their explanations. Watson was calling it a miracle, while Michelson dismissed the miraculous as merely the simultaneous action of chance and necessity.

Maybe. Yet whether what had happened was the result of divine intervention, or the intervention of mortals wielding a technology so advanced as to be indistinguishable from divinity, he could not say. Absently he called up images of the MAXXs in California and China, and the blister domes in Tri-Border. Looking at them reminded him of another vision he'd dreamed under the dome, one involving the Black Stone of the Kaaba in Mecca.

He searched the infosphere for live imagery of the Great Mosque, and there it was. Nothing involving spy satellites or overflights was needed, as it turned out. Al-Jazeera 4 was showing all Hajj, all the time. On the screen there did seem to be some sort of snarl in the lines of flow around the Kaaba, though he couldn't be sure as to its cause. He began to quiet down the others in the ECS.

"Wait a minute, people. Wait a minute. Don't break out the champagne quite yet. We still haven't accounted for Avram Zaragosa. No final location on him—and the Saudis confirm that his alter ego, Ibrahim Fayez, entered Mecca late yesterday their time. We're not home free yet."

RISING BEFORE THE SUN

As the crowd about him broke his bones and began to tear Avram apart, his mind still wanted to make sense of the chaos around him, even as his body struggled wildly for life.

The people in the crowd thought they were serving God by tearing him limb from limb, but whose God? Which God? What God?

Especially if what he suspected would soon happen to him *did* soon happen.

Somehow Vida managed to stop their brutalizing of him and clear a space around him. A miracle. As her face hovered above his, however, Avram realized her miracle was too late. He felt only the lassitude of a man approaching death, with no illusions about his end. He was entering his last extremity, with all that might entail.

Suddenly he felt himself floating weightlessly upward. Rather like the sensation of drifting up from bed, relaxed and rising in relaxation, shortly after he had just begun to nod off in the sleep of ordinary days and nights. Unlike the waves that had at times lifted him from gravity at the edge of sleep, however, this time the floating upward didn't stop, the wave didn't break. No crash or undertow pulled him down, only a feeling like a great wave lifting and lifting him.

His body canted slightly and he found himself looking toward the Kaaba. He saw beside it the two girls seemingly ablaze with light, each holding one fiery palm toward him. As he rose and rose, he sailed far above the Kaaba, out of the floodlit confines of the Great Mosque entirely. Soaring into the starry sky, he wondered distantly if this might be some near-death, out-of-body manifestation he was experiencing.

He felt his breathing growing labored, as if with an altitude far higher even than that to which this weightless flight had lifted him. He gasped for breath, fighting to keep his exhale from becoming a death rattle.

He did not succeed. The implant monitoring his vital signs determined he had reached last extremity. It uploaded its location and diagnostics to a Saudi military communications satellite built jointly by, and leased from, Otis Diversified and ParaLogics.

Receipt of that information on Avram's location and condition caused the satellite to download the implant's triggering instructions.

Receiving those, the implant sent a shiver through Avram's flesh as it transformed the entirety of his body's DNA into a computational system focused like an informational lens on the implant itself.

Pumped to supercritical information density, the implant imploded, displacing from real to virtual.

The explosive combustion of Avram Zaragosa's body was the single most important trace the device left of that virtualization.

The lifting wave broke. For a moment, a stillborn shooting star, achingly bright, flashed in the firmament, a fiery apotheosis high above predawn Mecca.

HYPERVELOCITY OBJECT

In the ECS, Jim Brescoll watched in amazement the Meccan scene transpiring on Al-Jazeera 4—as did the rest of the impromptu think tank surrounding him, including its latest captive addition, Yuri Semenov. The network had only three cameras in play, so the view kept switching from a long shot of the Kaaba, to the two figures standing beside it blazing with light, to the human figure rising above the crowd, finally shrinking to a glowing dot before disappearing from view.

The Jazeera cameras didn't capture the moment of ignition when that rising human form exploded into a very short-lived nova. Several of the satellites looking for missile launch flares and nuclear detonations, however, *did* record the scene.

"Any estimate on altitude and location of that burst?" Jim asked.

"Thirty thousand feet," Bree Lingenfelter said, surveying the data funneled to them from the big room next door. "About three miles due east of the Great Mosque."

"Estimated yield?"

"Nothing exact," Wang said, surveying the data on his blinks. "A good deal less than complete conversion of a body to energy. Three to five kilotons, best guess. Half a Hiroshima at worst, but maybe a good deal less. Might raise some dust on the ground, but nothing too dangerous."

"Fallout? EMP?"

"No nuclear debris indicated," Bree said. "Readings are still hovering around background level. Should be some ground-effect EMP, but no reports of it. Odd."

"How 'odd'?"

"I've cross-referenced Oersted and Magsat data. For a blast that size the signature is surprisingly contained, electromagnetically speaking."

"Leave it for now. Let's see if our image analysts can use the Jazeera footage to build us a picture of that person who got lofted out of the crowd."

In moments the Jazeera pixels had been computer-massaged enough to yield a bloodied face. A bit more pixel-massaging removed the blood.

"All right, let's compare that to the most recent shots we have for Avram Zaragosa."

The two most recent images—of Ibrahim Fayez on a local news show out of Taif, and from a Saudi checkpoint near Mecca, respectively—matched the face of the man lofted from the Great Mosque.

Compared to Avram Zaragosa's actual passport picture, the man called Ibrahim Fayez and the man lofted from the Mosque looked very much like Zaragosa might have looked had he lost considerable weight, gotten sun-bronzed, and started growing a beard during a journey through the Empty Quarter.

Avram Zaragosa seemed a very plausible candidate for the unidentified flying man who exploded.

"Time to break out the champagne yet?" Amaral asked.

"Not quite," Brescoll said. "Someone at NASA just sent this on several priority channels. For me."

He blinked the message to the tabletop display dome. One section was grainy, stuttering footage of an unfamiliar rock from space, with a numerical readout beside it. The little movie that accompanied the grainy telescopic footage, however, was disturbingly familiar: graphics of a large skystone coming in at a relatively shallow angle of attack, braking and breaking up explosively in light, heat, and lightning some distance above the earth, sending an EMP lightning wave racing around the planet, putting out on the nightside earth all the lights of civilization.

"Oh, hell," Bree said. Brescoll nodded glumly. Now he wished he hadn't sent Miskulin and Yamada into the field. Meteoriticists were in short supply. He glanced at Yuri Semenov expectantly. You'll have to do, he thought.

"Jittery numbers, on frames of filmed rock?" Semenov asked. "May be coordinates on celestial sphere? Swing some radio, some optical telescopes onto them, for confirmation, can you?"

Out in the big room, teams went to work. In moments they had a fix on the object.

"What did they find?" Jim asked impatiently. "Is it actually out there?"

"We'll patch it through to the flatscreens and blinks," Steve said. Same rock, less grainy.

"How big?" Semenov asked.

"Roughly ninety meters in diameter," Bree said.

"How fast?"

"Approaching at approximately twelve miles per second," Wang said.

"Hypervelocity object, then. How close?"

Wang read him the figure in miles and kilometers.

"That will put it well inside moon orbit—very soon," Semenov said. "Point of extinction?"

Lingenfelter gave him the figures, in miles and kilometers above the earth. Then she gave him latitude and longitude. Semenov whistled softly.

"Let me guess," Jim said. "It will burst at the lowest spot in the lower Van Allen Belt. Smack dab in the South Atlantic Anomaly."

Semenov nodded, much impressed by the director's "guess."

"This just doesn't make sense," Jim said. "Why save the world from nuclear missile exchange, only to bring on a global blackout that'll kill millions?"

Semenov looked ready to say something, but at that moment the jittery-rock and EMP-roll imagery was replaced by the face of an elderly Asian man, looking nervous. Jim had once met the man, in the flesh, but he doubted anyone had ever seen Doctor Vang looking nervous.

"Hello, Director Brescoll. My children are misbehaving, I'm afraid."

MENTAL FIGHT

Michael thought the Temple Mount looked surprisingly peaceful in the dawn, all its trees and stones clear and calm in the sunrise. If, however, what Director Brescoll said was true—when he commanded them here posthaste to debrief Doctor Vang—then it seemed all too likely to prove the false calm of a false dawn, the last day of the old world, the first day of a new dark age.

Brescoll had told him and Susan of the great stone the children had apparently set on a course to blind Argus. "The mountain from the stars that they are singing *to* earth," Michael told his audience in the distant ECS. "Just the inverse of 'singing their mountain to the stars,' the way Jacinta always said the Mawari planned."

Yet Michael found hope in that very idea of singing. The kids had sung much into his head that he did not understand, but he could not help trusting them, even in the midst of the baleful news of a great star falling.

Even as the gangway unfolded from the last stealth airship on earth, as if the heavens were opening.

Even as Doctor Vang and the crew of his craft walked down that gangway.

Even as those who had just stepped down from that stairway to heaven walked with the glum determination of the living dead, approaching Michael and Susan and the waiting peacekeepers, across the plaza in front of the scorched Dome of the Rock.

"Doctor Vang?" Michael asked as the blue-helmeted soldiers brought the weary-looking old man in their direction. "I'm Michael Miskulin, and this—"

"—is Susan Yamada," Vang said as he sat down on a bench, facing the Dome. "I know who you are. My children are quite fond of you."

" 'Your' children?" Susan asked. She and Michael turned their backs on the plaza and the Dome to address the man seated and slumped before them.

"Mine . . . though not mine alone. The Instrumentality's. Your uncle's and your aunt's, too, Michael. Yours as well—both of you. I presume Director Brescoll told you of our plans to precipitate the next stage of human evolution?"

Michael and Susan nodded.

"The Instrumentality's 'split kids,' right?" Michael asked. "Tetra-grammaton's 'tesseractors'?"

"The ones who can hack their own DNA to become human starships, or whatever they were supposed to become," Susan said sourly. "The ones who had to be tormented, in the name of the great leap forward."

"I would prefer to think of them not as tormented," Vang said, "but as those whom the 'curse' *cures*. They are all that and more, the Mawari children. Ka-dalun and Alii. Aubrey and Ebu. They named themselves that—and it should have been a warning to us all. I believed they would not disobey their parent. I thought I could use them. I thought I could control them. I was the one who drummed to them across the Web, with word of Project Argus and its implications."

"Why on earth do that?"

"To wake people up," he said tiredly. "To restore the glory of Tetra-grammaton and the Instrumentality. To make all humanity see the need to plan for the long-term survival of our species. To rouse us from our lemminglike drive to self-destruction. Surely you can understand that, Michael."

Michael pondered it. The apocalyptic progress of humanity via overpopulation, environmental destruction, aggressive territorial expansion, and all the rest were perhaps clearer to him than to most people, but the way things had turned out didn't make sense, even to him.

"How would steering the children toward Project Argus help that?"

"It would have allowed us to take the whole world hostage for its own good. The threat of closing all the eyes of Argus, of shutting down the entire global system, in order to hard-reboot it, if necessary. And it *is* necessary, for in the great endgame, both science and religion have failed.

"Those who see the world through stained-glass windows view science as a joke without a punch line, claiming to provisionally explain what it cannot ultimately understand. Those who view the world through telescope and microscope see religion as a punch line without a joke, claiming to ultimately understand what it cannot even provisionally explain. Yet any understanding that is significantly incomplete cannot accurately determine which of its data are or are not completely insignificant. The scientists believed too strongly in the reality of *things,* the religionists too strongly in the literality of *words.* A third way was needed. A way in which explanation and understanding, journey and goal, the maze of science and the labyrinth of religion would become one."

"And if the world would not listen to the new way?" Michael asked.

"The slate would be wiped clean again, by a much bigger rock even than that now headed toward Argus. Shut down the planetary ecosystem and force it to restart in a new form."

"And the children?" Susan asked, coaxing, but not so impatiently as she might once have.

"From all those meteorite fragments, from what they contained, we hoped those children would fashion themselves into the stained-glass telescope—would *become* that new way. They would have, too, if I just could have controlled them. If I just could have used them. But they used me, you see? To contact the worlds under the domes, and beyond.

To reach inside my head, to prevent me from destroying them. What I could not destroy I could not control. They've turned everything I planned into a mad kaleidoscope of their own making. I have been trying to fight them with my mind, and I am so tired. I have lost that mental fight."

"Where are they?" Michael asked. By way of answer, Vang pointed. Susan and Michael turned in time to see, descending the stairway that vanished into the stealth-crafted sky, two beings with light flowing up like sensitive flame from their heads and shoulders. They seemed no longer children now. Perhaps they were no longer human.

PILLAR OF FIRE

The dawn terminator moved west past Jerusalem, past the smoldering ruins of An-Nuseirat in Gaza, then over the calm blue of the Mediterranean Sea. Jim Brescoll and all with him in the Executive Command Suite at NSA could only watch, with equal powerlessness, as another terminator, poised to kick humanity back to before the dawn of the Electronic Age, plummeted in from space toward the still-dark sky above the south Atlantic.

The stone to blind Argus was only moments away from extinction point. Radar and infrared astronomical satellites had long since picked up its progress. Bree and Steve monitored the data from the Magsat, Magstar, Oersted II, and Gauss satellites for any signs of EMP, any changes in the earth's electromagnetism. Real-time imagery of the Temple Mount in Jerusalem, the Great Mosque in Mecca, and the force-field blisterdomes in China and North and South America played on in the ECS, ignored for the moment in the face of more immediate calamity.

Now the meteoroid began to show up optically as a meteor on every telescope turned in its direction. A British cruiser, some miles to the west of where the star was falling, caught its progress on camera, without magnification. At every wavelength and apparent distance, however, the image was the same: a head growing brighter and more pronounced, a tail lengthening in light. As Jim watched, the meteoroid's approach to Earth from space reminded him, perversely, of sperm and egg coming together in vast anticonception, a consummation devoutly to be unwished.

The incandescently burning, stadium-size skystone explosively braked and shattered at the Argus point. At that instant, the South Atlantic Anomaly became far more anomalous. It took the human watchers a moment to determine the specifics of that strangeness, however.

"This can't be right," Bree said.

"What can't?"

"None of the satellites are showing any significant electromagnetic propagation outward from the extinction point," Steve Wang said. "The only EM signature out there is something about a mile across at most. It appears to be behaving like a confined plasma."

The camera view from the British cruiser to the west was even more startling. From a stillborn star at the extinction point, what looked like millions of confined lightnings speared down in a coherent column toward the ocean's surface—and, glowing through the water, disappeared beneath it. As the pillar of fire disappeared beneath the waves, a sound like thunder came to them over that distant camera's attached microphone.

Wang and Lingenfelter simultaneously blinked up a contour map of the planet showing global readouts of reversed flux patch positions.

"Two new reversed flux patches have just appeared," Wang said, "in—"

"Mecca and Jerusalem," Jim Brescoll said.

He didn't need to see their contour maps. An unseen bubble of force, growing at Temple Mount, was already pushing blue-helmeted soldiers before it as it expanded. A similar phenomenon, surrounding the Kaaba in the Great Mosque, was at the same time, gently but persistently, sweeping clear of worshippers the space around the monolithic black cube.

SELECTIVELY PERMEABLE MEMBRANE

In the plaza fronting the Dome of the Rock, Michael and Susan were more than willing to move quickly out of the way of the transparent circle of force as it spread, invisibly but tangibly, in every direction about the children's location.

Even as the earth beneath their feet was shaken by what felt like persistent small earthquakes, Michael found himself looking over his shoulder again and again, fascinated by the nature of that bubble of force even as he ran from it. The only sign of the otherwise invisible membrane's movement was a slight shimmer as it passed fluidly over the buildings, walls, courtyards, trees, and shrubs of the Temple Mount, without harming them—while it yet remained steadfastly impermeable to human bodies.

The transparent bubble of force continued to spread. Michael thought it wouldn't be long before the thing covered the entirety of the Temple Mount—and, with it, sites sacred to all Judaism, Christianity, and Islam.

RIGHT ASCENSION

Brescoll blink-shifted the feeds from Mecca and Jerusalem to the main screens. Through his myriad Argus eyes he had access to what was going on there, from all levels of data penetration, all manner of perspectives.

"The expansion of the fields seems to have stopped," Bree Lingenfelter said.

"About thirty-five acres are under the bubble at the Temple Mount," Steve Wang said. "Dome of the Rock, al Aqsa, the Western Wall—the whole of the Mount, it looks like. The force-field footprint in the Great Mosque is smaller, perhaps only a tenth the size of that in Jerusalem. Seismic activity around both seems to be increasing."

Jim nodded. From distant microphones he heard the sound of a vast, incredible music. Dust began to well up around the edges of the shimmering bubbles of force in Mecca and Jerusalem. Then, as he watched, the Kaaba in its rippling black *kiswa* seemed to slowly grow taller. With a strange feeling of déjà vu, he realized that the Kaaba was not growing but separating, detaching itself from the earth at a ring of thinning dust.

He remembered where he had seen something like this before. Under the dome in California, when the posthuman creatures which LeMoyne, Benson, and Markham had become had shown him other worldlines. Including one in which the flat-topped mountain of Caracamuni tepui had sundered itself from the earth and, smoothly as a mushroom in the night, ascended in a bubble of force invisible but for the way the light bent around it, like the heat-wave shimmer from desert and mirage.

That same great feat of levitation was now accelerating in both Mecca and Jerusalem. The ensphered Kaaba and the ensphered Temple Mount were both lifting into the air on a wave of angelic song almost unbearable in its beauty. As he watched, he saw that the orb of force lifting its acres of sacred sites from each location left behind a void, a crater conforming to the pattern of flaws inherent in the underlying rock.

The orbs of force, absconding with their enclosed sacred sites, were rising into the heavens—where he thought he saw, in dim outline, vast creatures pale as the moon in midmorning, come out of the sky, to stand there, winged and glowing and waiting.

STRANGE ANGELS

After seeing (via bimodal binoculars) what looked like a human form rising into the sky and exploding, Darla and Marc had slowed the pace of the march with their captives. They finally decided not to descend at all from the ridgetop overlooking the Mina Valley. Even if the song the children had sung into their heads had not compelled them to remain nearby—in witness and farewell, if nothing else—there was just too much going on at the Great Mosque in the valley below, for them to break away just yet.

They too saw the moon-pale creatures waiting. Viewing the scene from the top of the ridge, they in fact saw those entities before they noticed the Kaaba rising toward them.

"Good God!" Fremdkunst said. "They look almost like angels!"

In Jerusalem, where Susan and Michael saw them, too, there were many who would have agreed with that assessment. Marc and Darla and Susan and Michael, however, knew they were strange angels indeed.

CRESCENDO

Jim Brescoll immediately suspected that, in the days to come, there'd be many disagreements over the nature of this music he thought he was hearing and the pale figures he thought he was seeing. He had no more time to wonder at that, however. At just that moment he thought he caught glimpses of human figures, small but glowing, inside the bubbles of force rising above the cities of Jerusalem and Mecca.

"Can we zoom in on the corner of the Kaaba there?" Jim said to the techs in the big room. "The eastern one, I think it is? And into the courtyard in front of the Dome of the Rock?"

What Jim saw as the images zoomed was also what Susan and

Michael saw through binoculars from Jerusalem, what Marc and Darla saw through their bimod binocs on the ridgetop above Mecca and the Mina Valley—and what eventually billions of people throughout the world would see, playing again and again on their screens. In each ensphered sacred site, two figures still barely recognizable as human children were dissolving into bright strings and threads and traceries of light, viscous like thin oil or honey, flowing and unraveling and fountaining against gravity into the ensphered space all about them, pooling and spreading out at that boundary invisible but for refractive shimmer.

Out of all those billions who would eventually view such scenes and hear their music, however, perhaps only Jim Brescoll had seen before something like what that flowing pale fire was doing now to the orbs of force ensphering those glowing figures, and the sacred sites drifting upward with them. Jim remembered that *other* world he had been shown, in which the tepui that had been home to these strange children and their people had also risen into the sky in a bubble of force and begun to shine, with a light like inverted alpenglow.

As he watched the children fountaining away in honeyed light, the husks of their mortal forms vanishing into golden vortices and glowing helices, he saw again that glow at the bounds of each sphere. It increased in intensity until, in a brilliant burst of white-gold light, the ensphered Kaaba and Temple Mount both simultaneously disappeared, just as an ensphered tepui, in another world and time, had also done.

The song that had lifted the orbs built to a crescendo of terrible beauty, until the instant the orbs and all they contained vanished. Silently and completely as a soap bubble bursting in a sky of late summer, the orbs were gone, leaving behind only wispy fading vortices of helical laddered light, twisting stardust stairways dispersing in morning breezes through skies from which strange angels had also vanished—all disappearing as completely as the night-glowing sandstorm of the galaxy, always impending, disappeared before the early-morning light of a nearer star.

Skies from which, without other lightning before or falling stones after, there now issued a clap of thunder heard around the globe, via myriad media, to become part of innumerable memories.

⬎⬎⬎⬎⬎⬎⬎

Waiting for Vida Nasr amid the parklike grounds of Castel Gandolfo, Jim Brescoll was struck again by a peculiar sense of déjà vu. He glanced at the Castel and the old observatory domes of the Specola Vaticana, but no, it wasn't that. He'd never been to this scientific installation on a hilltop southeast of Rome, any more than he'd ever previously been to the annual ECOL, the Exobiology Conference on the Origins of Life, now under way in this place.

His gaze lingered on the tall green columns of the Italian cypress trees—towers to the ramparts of the Castel's high, square-topped hedges. They were casting long shadows as the sun declined toward evening, but that wasn't quite the source of his sense of "already seen," either. Likewise, none of what he was looking at had come up in anything he could remember from his time under the dome in California, or in dreams since.

Looking across the large courtyard, Jim was still puzzling over the feeling when he saw Brother Guy LeConte, the conference organizer and head of the observatory. The monk nodded to him as LeConte, along with Vida Nasr, hurried along one of the stone paths that radiated, sundial-fashion, across the Vatican Observatory's lawns. As Brother Guy parted from Vida, she headed toward Jim. He stood up and introduced himself formally to Doctor Nasr.

"Brother Guy seems to have hit pay dirt with the theme of this year's ECOL," Nasr said as they watched LeConte, surrounded by a pilot-fish cloud of reporters, go on about his business. "What's usually a small-ish gathering of specialists in some fairly arcane fields has come up on everybody's radar, it seems."

"Not so very surprising," Jim said as they sat down together on the bench, "given the interest first generated by the meteorite thefts, and then all the more so from those strange events the tepui children pre-cipitated in the Middle East." He looked at his conference brochure and its title. "Still, calling it 'The Stained-Glass Telescope: Astrobiol-ogy and the Sacred' does seem to have been inspired."

Even if he knew who had inspired it, and how Brother Guy had got-ten that inspiration.

"Quite the high profile with media and governments everywhere," Vida agreed. "Including your own."

"You saw that we put the tepui stone on display here, I presume?"

"I did," Vida said. "And the guards around it, too."

"Yes. We're making a much more coordinated effort to keep track of star stones, worldwide."

"I just hope the new interest in protecting the stones, on the part of nations and scientific organizations, doesn't make it more difficult to share information about them."

"Honestly, I don't think it will," Jim said as he turned to his rather dog-eared hard-copy conference program and the notes he had scrib-bled there. "A successful conference for all involved—perhaps Brother Guy not least of all. Right man at the right time."

"How so?"

"He's ordained religious. What happened in the Middle East has created a huge hubbub among religious organizations."

"Oh, yes. That's right. All of the debate, all of the attempts to understand the theological implications of what happened."

"Exactly. Those implications are already having a tremendous im-pact on the fundamentals of belief. Despite its rather ecclesiastical-sounding title, I found LeConte's address of welcome, 'Sanctus Situs Absconditus,' fascinating."

"Yes," Nasr said. "Historically solid, on the traditional importance of the Temple Mount and Mecca sites to Christians, Jews, and Mus-lims. Interesting speculation, too, about how the Peoples of the Book are responding to the 'absconding' of those sites and the craters left be-hind in their places."

"You agree with LeConte's conclusions, then?"

"Overall, yes. He largely left out the fact that the Church also lost relics outside the Middle East—Spear of Longinus material mostly—but the craters themselves are already being viewed, by many of the faithful, as signs that the holy sites themselves will return. Until those sites do in fact return, the craters are themselves to be considered holy."

"Even as teams of scientific investigators work side by side with the worshippers," Jim said, shaking his head in some disbelief, "to try to unravel their mysteries. That's a big change."

"Maybe," Vida said. "But still controversial. Only Muslim scientists are allowed at the crater in Mecca—and only those who disavow any possibility that the Mawari children might have been any satanic-verse embodiment of Allah and his three sister-goddesses. I'm still the only woman allowed there, too—and me only because of my 'special circumstances.' "

Jim moved uncomfortably on the bench.

"Yes. About those special circumstances. I want to personally apologize on behalf of my agency and my government for putting you in harm's way in the Avram Zaragosa matter."

"No need," Vida said, but Jim noticed that her hand went unconsciously to where she had been stabbed, then just as quickly vanished. "I hoped there might be something I could do to stop Avram, to help him. I hoped I could get to the good man I thought I knew."

Jim nodded.

"His desire to avenge his daughter was just too strong. They played upon that—Luis Martin, the old spy who puppetmastered him. Whose strings, in their turn, were pulled by rogue elements of CIA and Mossad, with money and connections in Tri-Border. All part of a powerful cell of Christian Zionist and Kahanist extremists, working ultimately for George Otis. At least that's the latest and best intelligence, on a *very* complicated web of relationships."

"And Mahmoud Ankawi?" Vida asked.

"The strangest of them all. Passing for secular, but in fact a deep-cover Mudayyin jihadist with renegade security connections of his own in the Arab world. Quite from the other side in all this, yet finally after the same thing Otis and his agreeable puppets were also after: the final confrontation demanded by God—or so their respective religious sects claim. And in Otis's case, personal power as part of the Elect, afterward."

"Peoples of the Book who'd turned bibliolaters, in every case," Vida said. "What happened at the holy sites has not been good for their particular point of view. But Avram didn't seem particularly religious . . ."

"No, just a man terribly wounded by the death of his daughter. Everything we've been able to learn about him suggests he wasn't an end-timer of any sort, just someone whose pain could be exploited by others. From what I've read of the Saudis' interrogation of Mahmoud Ankawi, I can't help thinking Avram Zaragosa was more sinned against than sinning, in many ways."

Vida stiffened visibly.

"And the thousands of Palestinians who were incinerated, who died in the holocaust at An-Nuseirat . . . they *weren't* more sinned against?"

Jim looked into his hands in his lap, but found no answer there.

"Clearly they were, too."

"When are 'rogue elements' really just foreign policy by other means, Director? That's what I want to know. Despite all the apologies, all the trials of the perpetrators, all the firings, all the theological debates and negotiations that have been going on ever since that day, I still don't know what to believe."

"That I can't tell you. What I *can* say is that it could have been far worse. It could have escalated to global nuclear holocaust, if the Mawari kids hadn't knocked down our spears and given us some breathing space. A breathing space that still prevails, for now."

"But for how long?"

"Who knows? Free will means the right to be wrong. We've exercised that right a lot, as a species. Nobody intervened like this before. Not during Hitler's holocaust of the Jews. Or the Ottoman genocide of the Armenians. Or the African diaspora during slavery. Or the genocide of the native peoples of the New World by European conquerors. Still, the fact that we haven't yet destroyed ourselves as a species, even though we've had the means to do so for decades—that gives me hope."

Vida gave him a long look.

"I hope you're right."

"I think I am. You know about the kerogen-rich meteorites that crashed in deserts and forests throughout the world that day?"

"The 'oil of heaven' asteroids. I've heard rumors."

"A great windfall—maybe enough to smooth the transition from fossil fuels to a low-carbon economy."

"But even such starfall windfalls won't last forever, Director. I've already heard rumblings, here, that those meteoritic oil tankers will upset the world economy. Even something *good* we manage to turn *bad*."

"Too often, yes. But not always. That binotech they left behind— the stuff sequestering carbon from the atmosphere—it appears to be slowly moderating greenhouse-gas effects. Damping down the human-induced global climate changes, preventing the whole system from spiraling out of control. And no one has yet figured out a way to make that good wind blow anybody ill."

"Give us time, Director, and someone will."

"Nonetheless, there's still what happened with those kids— especially the way they disappeared. Serious, yet playful. A solemn celebration of their farewell, ending in self-consuming transcendent *fireworks*. That suggests to me that maybe, just maybe, we're making progress in our evolution."

"It would probably have to be our cultural evolution, then. Biological evolution isn't progressive."

"Hard to say. When I debriefed Miskulin and Yamada—as I'm also debriefing you now, Doctor Nasr—they told me about a 'third way' Doctor Vang and his people were after, in their entanglement with these kids."

"I didn't know that in agreeing to talk with you, Director, I'd also consented to being 'debriefed.' But go on—what third way?"

"In leaving the way they left, and in leaving behind what they left behind, maybe the Mawari children pointed the way to the new synthesis Doctor Vang hoped for. A synthesis to reconcile the 'endless time' promulgated by evolutionary science with the 'timeless end' prophesied by eschatological religion. Or so my experts suggest."

"But not Doctor Vang himself?"

"No," Jim said with a slight smile. "Though I've been very much in touch with him, he remains reticent on the subject, especially since the court cases involving him have not yet come to trial."

"Though not so reticent as George Otis?"

Jim's smile turned to a wince. That had been mishandled. The man's obsession with the kids' absconding with his reconstructed "Spear of Destiny" was perhaps understandable—if they had in fact done so. Stranger was his repeated consternation over whether Christ's blood had given the spear its supposed healing power and paranormal capabilities, or vice versa—and whether or not that latter possibility was heretical in light of the timing of the Resurrection. During interrogation, he only answered questions to the extent that he might turn them into esoteric discussions about such matters, and whether or not "destiny" was only about "power" or might also involve some balance with "compassion." Otis had not been under suicide watch, as he should have been. He managed to hang himself in his cell, and the story had broken in the media.

"No, not so reticent as Otis. But Fremdkunst, Levitch, and Michelson—even Yuri Semenov and Joe Retticker—they have all proven quite talkative."

"No doubt."

"You know," he said, "one of the few things Vang has said to me about all this has to do with what he thinks those kids might have left behind, besides oil from heaven and binotech carbon sequestration."

"What's that?"

" 'Every generation's children are aliens in the world of their parents, but the children growing up in the world after the Mawari will be more alien than any preceding generation. Watch out for the next generation!' "

"That's an odd warning."

"I thought so, too. I mean, not enough time has yet passed to get a good gauge on any particular change, if one has happened. So far there's no indication of any general myconeural infection. Of course, it's always possible the Mawari children got beyond the need for such grosser expedients."

"Are you suggesting," Vida asked, incredulous, "that those children left behind some as-yet-undetected infection of *all* the planet's children?"

"Not my suggestion, Vang's. But if Alii, Aubrey, Ka-dalun, and Ebu did leave some novel infection or even 'inflection' of chemistry or biology—one that might make their particular pineal effect permanent, say—then how might they have done it? Direct manipulation of the genome? Some sort of myconeural binotech?"

"If Vang's right," Vida said, looking out across the courtyard as twilight began to settle over it, "there's a question much deeper even than those: What might the alien children of such a next generation be like?"

"Yes. Would they have more persistently childlike minds, in longer-lived bodies? Or would they be somehow permanently stunted? Would they be more imaginative and creative, or merely more frivolous? Less libidinal or inclined to reproduce, like the tepuians . . . or more reckless?"

"Or, if they barely ever attain to sexual maturity," Vida said, nodding, "perhaps even less capable of reproducing at all. A generation beyond generation. In a way, it's a logical extension of humanity's long evolutionary trend toward the retention of juvenile characteristics into adulthood."

"The very meaning of neoteny, or so I'm told."

"No, not *the* meaning," Vida said. "A meaning. There's another meaning of neoteny, a more disturbing one: the attainment of sexual maturity by an organism still in its larval stage."

"Why should that be more disturbing?"

Vida looked away, across the darkening hilltop grounds.

"What if the latter definition is the one that has actually applied to all humanity, throughout all its history? What if we, *Homo sapiens sapiens,* have not been so wise or thoughtful as we have always thought ourselves to be? What if we have instead been, all along, a species of creature able to sexually reproduce without actually becoming truly adult, truly mature?"

Reminded of the odd cocooned transformation Ben Cho had undergone at the end of his mortal days, Jim shivered. Had Miskulin and even the Instrumentality been right, in some sense? Had some piece of genetic programming essential for humanity's true maturity been lost out there among the stars? Were the darknesses of human history, all the wrongness in the human species, indeed the proof that the human creature lacked an all-important puzzle piece? The piece that might allow human beings to at last become truly adult creatures, mature and wise?

Was it that missing puzzle piece that had been restored to Ebu and Ka-dalun, to Aubrey and Alii—and to Jaron Kwok and Ben Cho—in different ways?

"Attaining maturity—that *would* be progress in our evolution," Jim said quietly.

"Call it that, but it might be very painful for those of us who are already supposedly mature," Vida said. "What if the next generation with their Peter Pan pineals—Miskulin called them that, in his presentation— what if they exhibit not just the usual alienness of adolescence but something far different?"

"Like what?"

"Like what if their relationship to the preceding generation is less like children to parents, and more like birds to dinosaurs?"

The sight of Wang and Lingenfelter waving to him from the nearest entrance to Castel Gandolfo distracted Jim. He waved back to them absently. Judging by the crowd streaming out at that door, the day's last session had just ended, but Jim had been almost too preoccupied with Vida to notice.

He was surprised to see Vida waving more vigorously to them now than he had himself, but then he saw that Michael Miskulin, Susan Yamada, Darla Pittman, and Dan Amaral had spotted him and Vida, too. They looked like they might make their leisurely way over to them, once they'd extricated themselves from the exiting crowd.

"Yes," Jim said absently. "Birds. With their biomagnetically sensitive pineals orienting them to the earth's magnetic field."

"I caught Steve Wang and Bree Lingenfelter's presentation, too," she said with a smile and a nod. "About how the Mawari kids managed to navigate underground, and all that."

"Also how they managed to use the looped-hole of that reversed flux patch," Jim said, "to lasso the EMP of that meteoroid—the one that should have shut down the world when it crashed into the South Atlantic Anomaly."

"And instead 'channeled that pulse into and through the earth for their own uses,' " Vida said with a quizzical smile, " 'levitating the Kaaba and Temple Mount into the sky!' I don't think that's the whole story. That's what my presentation is going to be about."

"Oh?"

"I was originally thinking of presenting on the particular oil-of-heaven I was exposed to, but I think Darla would do a better job with that. I was so impressed with her presentation I passed my notes on to her today. Wang and Lingenfelter's explanation, though, doesn't take the gravitics sufficiently into account."

"Why do you think that?"

"We already know those kids, once they'd been exposed to the full metaphage, were manipulating spacetime curvature, right? What Miskulin and Yamada were saying today about the myth system of the Mawari plugs right into what I'm going to be talking about. Spawn, threads, strings—it's just what I saw when those two kids were standing beside the Hajar al-Aswad, at the corner of the Kaaba."

"And that ties into 'spacetime curvature' somehow?"

"All superstrings are open-ended and trapped in a given dimension, except the graviton. As a closed loop, it passes unhindered across the membranes separating each dimension. I think what they tapped into in the Black Stone was gravitonically linked to higher dimensions, across the plenum of all possible universes. And back. Which is why the graviton loop *appears* closed, and why the Black Stone appealed to those kids so much. If you want to know more, stick around for my presentation."

Hearing Vida beginning to make connections between the Mawari kids and parallel universes, Jim's heart skipped a beat. He thought of strange angels, and wondered about Markham, Benson, and LeMoyne. Kwok and Cho, too. And perhaps all the other bodhisattvas and strange guardian angels out there at the end of all time.

Darla, Susan, Michael, and Dan joined them. They were getting to be quite a little mob. Jim listened as Vida talked with them about what she and Jim had been discussing earlier. About Aubrey, Ebu, Ka-dalun, and Alii, about parents and children, about descendants far different from their forebears. He noticed that, in the conversation, the child Darla did *not* speak about was the one she was carrying—the one fathered by Marc Vasques, to whom she was now engaged to be married. Jim had a particular interest in that child, given his mother's and father's backgrounds. Perhaps that was something else the Mawari children had left behind.

"Kids are always aliens," Michael said. "But then, so is everybody."

"How's that?" Jim asked.

"We've always been at least part alien, because part of what we are comes from the stars. Homegrown life from nonlife, sure, but also life from elsewhere—back to the very beginning."

"Maybe so," Susan said, squeezing Michael's hand, "but at least the Mawari kids didn't forget their adoptive parents!"

True, Jim thought. When the shooting stars fell like ripe figs from a tree shaken by high wind, it wasn't only stars shown where to fall in order to take out missiles. Or even just kerogen meteors and carbon-sequestering dust motes.

Miskulin and Yamada, traveling to the site of an abandoned benitoite mine Larkin had owned, found that a particular type of meteorite had cratered there—a pallasite made up almost entirely of peridot. And even Jim himself had received a gift from the children, if he could call it that.

In a strange dream, they told him not to forget that, if you bang your heart against the mountain long and hard enough, sometimes it's the mountain that breaks.

He thought of a burning mountain, older than earth, falling across the sky.

It had happened before.

Suddenly he realized why he'd felt that sense of déjà vu.

Yes, Jim thought. Back to the very beginning. Back to the primordial earth, born out of gravitationally fused skystones. If the cornerstone of here came from elsewhere, then native to the sky is not alien to the earth.

Back to Eden. Back to a humanity sufficient to have stood but free to fall. Like the stars now coming out above him, as night also fell. Like the universe in which those stars were embedded. All the stars, in all the universes.

In a plenum of infinite possible worlds, every day is doomsday somewhere, but no day is doomsday everywhere. Timeless ends in endless times.

He felt a hand on his arm.

"You look preoccupied, Jim," Darla said. "Everything all right?"

"Everything's fine. Just thinking."

"About what?"

"About how the stone the builders reject sometimes becomes the cornerstone," he said, craning his neck to look into the deepening twilight as it filled slowly with stars. "About how the data thought to be insignificant sometimes turns out to be pivotal. About science and religion, and the wonder that's cornerstone to both."

A shooting star slashed overhead. He and his friends pointed.

"Make a wish!" Darla said, but Jim did not ask for anything. He was just thankful that showing the stars where to fall was not *his* responsibility.

ACKNOWLEDGMENTS

>>>>>>>

My thanks to agent Chris Lotts of Ralph M. Vicinanza Ltd., and editor Steve Saffel, then at Del Rey Books, for giving me the green light, in 2003, to write a book about meteorites, mushroom stones, Mawari, and Mecca. My thanks to Steve for his extensive notes on the manuscript, to editor Jim Minz for shepherding the book to publication, and to everyone at Del Rey for their patience with my long research and writing process.

Thanks are also due to electrician Roger Coates, who in September of 2005 unwittingly gave me the worst kind of shock a writer can experience, and to Horton Newsom, museum curator at the Institute of Meteoritics at the University of New Mexico, for alleviating that shock by roundly refuting the shibboleth of "highly radioactive meteorites." Thanks, too, to Dr. Lisa Weston for pointing out Martin Frobisher's connection to John Dee, and suggesting that at least the initial "black stone" discovered by Frobisher's 1576 expedition to Meta Incognita might be meteoritic. And thanks again to Michael Lepper, for showing me his specimens of benitoite.

>>>>>>>

Howard V. Hendrix has held a variety of jobs ranging from hospital phlebotomist to fish hatchery manager to university professor and administrator. His current university teaching is bolstered by an academic pedigree that includes a B.S. in biology from Xavier University (1980) and an M.A. and Ph.D. in English literature, both earned from the University of California, Riverside, in 1982 and 1987, respectively. Hendrix is the author of several novels and shorter science fiction and experimental pieces. His repertoire also includes numerous political essays and works of literary criticism in addition to a book on landscape irrigation, *Reliable Rain,* which he coauthored with Stuart Straw. Mr. Hendrix is an avid gardener. He and his wife, Laurel, live near Shaver Lake, California, where they are members of the Pine Ridge Volunteer Fire Department. They enjoy backpacking and snowshoeing in the Sierras, and training in Brazilian jujitsu.